Halcyon

A.C. Miller

For everyone who told me to hurry up and get my second book finished, I hope you enjoy this one.

2 May 2192

Sam

It's been three months.

I can still see the blood on MacMillan. I can see the rage in my eyes. I can feel the pain in my heart. Almost as if I was removed from myself while dislodging and jamming the arrows into his torso, I can see every second of what took place—and I hate it. I hate remembering what he did to her. It kills me to think of it, but I can't stop.

Every time I look around this field, I can see what I did. . .what he did.

My feet hang off the edge of the stage—the same stage MacMillan plodded across while our loved ones died behind him; the same stage all of us were too afraid to jump onto; the same nightmare I can't erase.

My heels bounce off the wood; the gentle tapping of my shoes echoes in the wind. I fiddle with a dandelion between my forefingers while slowly pulling off its petals. One by one they fall, aimlessly drifting toward the creaking wrought-iron gates at the end of the field.

He killed her. He deserved to die.

I scratch my chin and turn around. No longer present are those bodies that swayed with each gust a few months ago; there's no more MacMillan, Abby, Mom, Dad, Arthur. They're gone. That world no longer exists. Even though the rest of us are still here, we're not trapped. We're not stuck in the fear that tried to drown us. We're finally free, in a sense, just not free of the pain. I don't know if we ever will be.

I turn back toward the empty field in front of me. The patch where MacMillan laid is bare; the spot where Abby passed is covered in flowers. I hop off the stage and wander toward *her* before dropping the stem into the pile.

"You're still here?" comes a voice.

"Yea," I mutter, the wind muting my reply.

Taking a few steps, Elise stops beside me and puts her hand on my shoulder.

Neither of us speaks. The quieted howl of the wind gliding through the gates rings around the field. *I can still hear the rope. I can feel the anxiety, the panic, the pain coursing through my arms and into my legs.* The agony never recedes. No matter what we do to move on, we struggle. Maybe I'm worse than others. Maybe I can't let go of what happened and they can; maybe something's wrong with me. Time can keep moving forward, but it can't heal this. Nothing can get rid of that memory—nothing can stop the rope from swaying. I'll always feel that moment. Always.

"Are you going to be okay?" she asks. "You've come here a lot."

"Every day," I mumble under my breath.

Elise lightly nods. "We don't have to leave. You know that, right?"

"I know."

But we do.

"We can stay here as long as you need. It may not feel like home, but it's better than what it was."

"I don't think it can ever be better," I say. "It doesn't feel like home."

She looks away.

"Maybe we should just leave today. Maybe we should just go back out those gates right now."

"I don't think that will help. It was almost worse for you out there." She slides her hand off my shoulder.

I look down. "How can we move forward if we're afraid of what's out there? How do we survive and search for a new world? How the hell do we do what we promised we would do when it's painful to even think of the outside?" I ask.

Elise keeps her stare in the distance.

I hate this. I feel trapped, afraid of what I want. I want to run, but I don't. I want to flee and never come back, but I don't. Elise is right. The outside nearly killed me; it ate away at who I was.

"You have to channel what's killing you," she says turning her head back to face me.

"How do I do that? If I think about it too much I become worthless."

"You have to acknowledge the pain and use it as fuel to keep you moving forward, to keep you from ending up in the same spot," she says, her eyes glancing toward the roses.

"It's easier said than done," I reply as I itch my eyes.

"For starters, you can stop coming here every day."

"I have to."

"Why?"

"Because we're going back out there. There's pain there. There's pain here. There's pain at 'home.' I have to get used to this."

"Nobody should get used to pain," she retorts. Stepping in front of me, Elise places both her hands on my shoulders. I can feel her callused palms. "Look at me, Sam."

I look up. My eyes start to water.

"Pain is temporary. Fear is forever. If you lead yourself to believe something bad is going to happen, something bad will always happen. If you move forward thinking nothing can break you, nothing will. You have to be stronger than what's eating you."

"I can't," I cry, wrapping my arms around her waist. "I can't do this."

She squeezes tightly. Her hands rub against my shoulder blades. "Yes, you can, Sam. You've overcome everything and you're still standing."

I wish I could stop the emotions. I wish I could become robotic and just go through the motions, but then nothing would matter. Everything I would do would be for nothing, for no one. As much as I hate these feelings, they're important. They keep my feet on the ground. *I just don't like crying.*

"You're strongest when faced with the end," mutters Elise. With her head on mine, she continues, "I heard you punched Arthur when you were chained up."

A slight smirk crosses my lips. "Who told you that?"

"Who do you think?"

"Sean."

"Yep. He also told me how much stronger than him you were when he was shot. He felt the pain and the fear, but you kept him here. You were stronger than him."

I don't reply. I sniffle into Elise's chest.

I can still see the blood seeping through Sean's shirt; I can hear the knives clinking together as Marcus pries at the bullet. I can feel it all. I can't stop these memories and that's just something I need to accept. They'll always be there.

"No matter what you're feeling, we're all going through it with you, Sam," whispers Elise. "We're all lost in the chaos, too."

I tighten my grip around Elise's waist. "At least Arthur's not out there," I say. "At least no one will be trying to get into my head."

"Without the chips, nobody can get into our heads. We'll be freer than ever. We can finally see what the 'pop point' is all about—minus the popping," laughs Elise.

I smile. "And we won't have to survive on berries and gross water every day."

"See, there are better things for us. We'll have rations, more people, more clothes, fresh water, everything. The journey will be well worth it."

I pull away from Elise and look into her eyes. I half-smile and wipe my face. "There won't be any Lurkers."

"There won't be any Lurkers," she slowly repeats. A smile growing across her reddened cheeks, she tucks her dark brown hair behind her ears and turns her head to the side.

I can see movement in the distance.

"Over here," shouts Elise—the wind quickly un-tucking her hair.

I look over.

"I figured you guys would be here," grins my brother, Sean. Behind him are Rosie and Miles. Mitch is still back by the gates, but he's heading this way, too.

Elise reaches for Sean's hand. "Sam and I were just talking about when to head out. We're getting eager," she says.

"We'd like to spend a couple more days volunteering at the infirmary," says Mitch, itching his cheek—the scars on his left hand becoming apparent. Bloodshot and purple, Mitch's hand hasn't recovered since being shut in the gates a few months back. From what I've learned, he helped Sean get inside, but couldn't get himself back in. As he pushed Sean in, his hand became trapped. He eventually got it out and disappeared into the forest, only to come back once he heard the cheers when Marcus, Kyle, and I found those who were kicked out by MacMillan, but he hasn't been the same. Like my mind, Mitch's is caught up in the past, afraid of the damage an unknowable future could cause.

"Yea, we told Dr. Tierney we'd help out for a few more days. She's teaching us plenty, so we're ready for almost anything once we're back out there," says Sean.

I clench my hand into a fist; the nub of my injured pinky digs into my palm. "So, I won't lose any more fingers?" I laugh, my faux smile hiding the fact that the wound that still bothers me.

"That's the plan," smiles Rosie as her light green eyes quickly glance toward my hand. "We don't want anyone to lose anything."

"Good thing we shouldn't have to worry about any of that," says Sean. "The outside has been pretty clear for the past month." He half-smiles and turns back toward the front gates. "Marcus, Kyle, and Ella should be back from their excursion outside the wall by tonight, so we'll know what it's like. If they didn't find anything, our journey back out there will be a lot more enjoyable than my previous two times."

"We can only hope," I say.

Sean smiles. "Third time's the charm, right?"

I know it will be better, but every moment I spend thinking about what's out there or what could still be out there, I ache. Just because MacMillan's dead doesn't mean the outside is safe. For all we know, shutting down the grid opened up this world to outsiders, and I don't know if we're ready for that.

We still haven't seen any others. Marcus, Kyle, and Ella have gone outside the wall at least five times since March and everyone they've brought back has had the same tracking chip the rest of us were sent out with. The kids are starved and scared, but they're glad to be home regardless of how distraught they all are.

There's one girl in particular who Marcus found barely breathing, unconscious, and facedown in a pit of mud a month ago. Her name is Melanie Stanton, and she hasn't spoken since she came back. I wish I knew why, too; Melanie's someone I know. . .she's someone I had a crush on before I was sent out last year. And now, she's back here with unexplainable cuts and bruises. With lacerations across the entirety of her back, she spent two weeks in the infirmary recuperating before she was sent home.

I stopped by to visit her last week, but she remained silent. She's in shock and I don't blame her. I just wish she would speak. I want to know if she saw something different than the Lurkers— something that would give us a clue about what's still out there. But, at the same time, I don't want to put her through any more trauma.

I just hope she knows that I'll always listen; after all, crushes don't just disappear overnight. I still remember the time she caught me staring in Separation class and she laughed. My cheeks were never redder. Not even the physical act of Separation caught me as off guard as a girl catching me looking at her. I can feel my cheeks growing red just thinking about it. *I need to think about something else.*

"Hey, Sean," I say.

"Yea?"

"Do you know how many others are going to go with us when we head back out there? Is it just our group or have you talked to anyone else?"

"So far, I know four others plan to come with."

"Who?" asks Elise.

"A few men who were in the Elite Guard, but were kicked out when they disobeyed MacMillan, and a nurse by the name of Marisa." Sean smiles and looks over at Elise. "Oh, and Camden thinks he's coming, but I'm not letting him go out there."

Elise grins.

"Who's that?" asks Miles.

"He was in the first group Marcus brought back. He was separated about a week before we got to Nimbus. He busted his leg up pretty bad out there and I saw him a lot when I had to see Dr. Tierney for checkups on my chest. We became friends pretty quickly. He was quiet at first, but once he started talking," Sean laughs, "he started to act like the strongest kid ever."

"How's his leg, by the way?" asks Elise.

"Better, but he still can't put any pressure on it."

I step away from the conversation and head back toward the stage; Sean and Elise continue to chatter behind me. I can hear Rosie clear her throat and ask, "Do you think any others will decide to join before we leave?"

Before anyone can answer, I'm out of earshot.

I hop onto the stage. The wood creaks beneath my shoes; the wind rustles against the rotting floorboards. With each gust, the ghosts of that fateful day reappear on stage. One by one they line up. I can see the marks on their necks, the sadness in their eyes, and I can feel the pain in their hearts. I can feel it all. And no matter what I do to move on, no matter what I do to try and forget, that pain won't leave. I'll never stop seeing them. I'll never forget the looks on Mom and Dad's faces.

I turn back toward the flowers behind me. All I see is *her.* All I see is the blood on her chest as the slight glint in her eye disappears. No matter where I look, I see what I don't want to see; I feel what I don't want to feel. *Maybe I should stop coming here. Maybe I should just stay home.* The reality of it is, there's nowhere I can go that will make me forget.

Nimbus, the city, the outside, and everything in between have played a role in my suffering, but maybe this time is different. Maybe out there, I'll be able to move on. Maybe the outside will finally help me forget.

Elise

Nimbus has changed a lot since my fourteenth birthday, and even more since February. After the gates were re-opened, the streets flooded with euphoric citizens happy to be given a second chance; they sang, they danced, they ate, they enjoyed every second of Nimbus without MacMillan, but eventually the joy stopped—and it only took a couple of weeks.

Ultimately, parents realized they would now have those eleven years with their children, so rather than focusing on keeping Nimbus afloat, everyone sort of just disappeared indoors. No one took over for MacMillan. No one changed anything about how Nimbus was run. The only thing that was unanimously agreed upon was the outlawing of Separation.

I rub the back of my neck and step beside Sean. He waves his hand into the air; the gates begin to open.

Since MacMillan was a tyrant, there was no succession of power. The founding families would be next in line, but none of them dared to step in since we learned what Sam discovered: that none of them were ever separated. Since then, they've remained out of sight, hidden away like the eleven years they each spent pretending to be outside.

Besides them, there aren't any other options. There isn't a special council or anything that decides how to handle this sort of thing. MacMillan did everything. And since we took him out of power, power has no one to switch hands to. Sean has the most experience to take over, but he's going back out with us. Marcus and Kyle are both smart enough to fix this place, but they've also decided to go back out there. Nobody wants to be a part of Nimbus anymore; we all just want to find something new, something better.

Even with the ability to mold Nimbus from scratch, the desire isn't there. I don't want to grow old behind these walls. I don't even want to spend another week here. Nimbus kicked us out.

Nothing can change that. No amount of words or actions can wipe away the anger and the pain associated with this place. We just need to get out.

"What time did they say they would be back?" asks Sam as he rubs the scar on the end of his pinky.

"He said by sunset," responds Sean.

"And when is that?" I ask.

"Sometime after eight," answers Marisa as she steps in from our left, her dark hazel eyes locking onto mine. Just like she did now, Marisa sort of came out of nowhere to begin with. She was the doctor Marcus and Sam found once the gates re-opened in February. She's the one who treated Sean's bullet wound when Dr. Tierney was busy with other patients. And really, since then, she's sort of worked her way into our tight-knit group. She's outgoing and resourceful, plus she's a nurse, so we could really use her help once we get moving.

"What time is it now?" asks Sam, his hand moving up to his head before going back and forth over his fresh buzz cut.

I look toward Sean.

"About eight," he answers.

"So they should be here," I say.

"They'll be here," he replies, as he steps toward me.

I shoot a glance his way. He's stretching out his left shoulder just as Dr. Tierney recommended. After being shot just beside his heart, he lost quite a bit of strength and flexibility in his left arm while it was in a sling. Now, it seems just about every time I see Sean, he's doing shoulder circles or something similar. *I'm just glad he's okay. I'm glad the bullet didn't kill him.*

He smiles. I move toward him and brush my hand through his auburn hair; he wraps his arm around my waist.

I grin. Yet, as we stand here and wait for Marcus, Kyle, and Ella, a part of me wants to run. I don't know why and I don't want to know, but some part of me is telling me to go beyond the gates. My stomach twists.

I take a step forward; Sean's hand falls off my waist.

It's a different feeling than I had in the past. It's not like my headaches or my nightmares; it's more like someone or something is pulling me out.

I stand still. My hands slip into the pockets of my jeans. I take another step.

With each passing second, the outside remains just as empty as the moment before it. Marcus's face doesn't appear in the shadowed moonlight; a glint of light on Kyle's glasses doesn't exist; Ella's golden brown hair doesn't flash ahead. They're nowhere in sight and yet here we stand, hoping they'll just waltz right back in like they never left.

But that never happens. Each time they come back, they're more scarred than the last. Even if no one will admit it, I can see it in their eyes; I can feel it in their actions, their words. No one is the same after going outside no matter the reason. Yet, they keep going back out there. They keep hoping that one of these times they'll stumble across something different, but it hasn't happened. That won't happen until we go out beyond the barrier.

I take two steps forward.

"Anyone see them yet?" hollers Sean.

"Nope," answers Sam.

I lean forward. I glide my fingers up and down the cold steel of the wall.

"Elise, do you see them?" asks Sean.

I shake my head and take another step. I can feel the wind glide up my arms and across my chest. The hairs on my forearms stand up; my calves stiffen. The wind takes hold of me. I arch my back and take a deep breath.

I feel free. My hand slips off the steel. I take another step— the darkness of the wavering trees shadows me. I take another step. And another. And another. I can hear a voice shout behind me, but I don't care to discern its message. I just want to keep moving. I want to get away from Nimbus.

No longer can I stay behind those walls and just hope for change. Nothing's going to happen. Nothing will ever change behind that steel. Absolutely nothing. At least out here, I don't know what to expect. At least out here, I'm free.

With my head up, I keep moving forward.

"Elise, what are you doing?" comes a voice from ahead of me.

"Yea, why are you so far out?" questions another.

I tilt my head down. Marcus and Ella stand ahead of me. Kyle breathes heavily behind them.

"Elise?" says Marcus again. "What are you doing?"

"I-I don't know," I stutter.

"We said we'd be back after eight," smirks Ella. Pushing her bangs from her eyes, she itches the ridge of her nose. "Were you just eager?"

"I guess so," I softly reply.

I didn't realize how far I'd gone. I could feel myself moving forward. The air was changing and the light was fading, but I didn't think I was beyond the wall. I turn around. I can barely see Sean. *Why didn't anyone stop me?*

"Well, let's get back behind the gates. I never like being out here at night," says Kyle hoarsely before letting out a slight cough.

"Did you find anything or anyone?" I ask.

Marcus shakes his head. "Nothing."

"Do you think everyone who's still alive has come back?"

"No. I think too many people remember the number one rule of Separation: don't come back toward the wall." Stretching his back, Marcus strides toward the open gates. Under his breath, he mutters, "No matter where we go or who we see, we can't make them all believe us anyways."

"Why's that?" I ask.

"Haven't you noticed?" grumbles Ella. "Since March, we've only brought back a handful of kids. Our past two trips, we haven't seen anyone alive."

"So why do you keep going out?"

Marcus turns around. "Hope," he mutters.

"You're almost asking too much," I smile.

"That's what I keep telling him," says Kyle as he pushes up his glasses.

"If you don't hold out hope, then what are you doing?" says Marcus with a hint of disdain in his voice as if my asking agitates him.

I don't bother to respond—even though my mind is begging to ask what happened. Marcus isn't one to be over-emotional, especially if that emotion is anger. These excursions are killing him.

I turn to my side. Kyle looks at me with weary eyes before moving up closer to Marcus whereupon he drapes his arm around Marcus's shoulders.

They remain ahead of us. Marcus waves his arm at the group gathered just inside Nimbus.

Sean yells an inaudible phrase as we near the open gates. Marcus speed walks past everyone—including Kyle—as he heads farther into Nimbus.

What happened? I think again.

When we first met Marcus at the library, he was kind, resourceful, happy; he was everything we weren't. Nothing was able to bend his spirit no matter what happened. Yet, something in the past few months has changed just about every aspect of who he is. It feels like he's about to snap. We're all fragile in some way. I just hope this isn't what breaks him. We need Marcus.

I turn to face Sean.

"Why did he just walk on by?" asks Sean.

"I don't know," I reply.

Ella takes a step beside me. "We saw something out there."

Kyle gently places his hand on Ella's shoulder before chasing Marcus down. Watching as he moves out of sight, Ella turns back toward Sean and I.

"What did you see?" I ask.

"Collin."

"From the library?" quickly replies Sean.

"Yes," answers Ella.

"What about him?"

"H-his. . ." she trails off.

"His what?"

"His body," sobs Ella. Wiping her face, she looks down. "It wasn't burnt. He didn't die in the fire. He. . .he was still breathing."

"Where? What?" My mind can't gather the words to form a coherent sentence.

Sean's voice quiets as he looks warily at her. "Ella," he says somberly. "What did you see?"

"He had a mark on his neck," she whispers.

"The mark of the Lurkers?"

"No."

"What was it?" I ask.

"He was one of Marcus's best friends at the library. He didn't deserve to die this way!" she shouts.

I wrap my arm around her and pull her closer to me. I don't say anything nor does Sean.

Ella leans her head into my shoulder.

"Take your time," I mutter.

"Thanks," she sniffles before continuing again. "There was an 'X' in the middle of three circles. One circle was in the bottom half of the 'X,' then one on the left, and one on the right. The whole thing was sort of smashed together." She takes a slight breath and pulls her wavy hair back behind her ears. "He-he just kept covering it up."

"Did he say anything?"

"He couldn't."

Sean takes a step back, bites his lip, and looks away. "Someone put him there," he mutters. "If he didn't die at the library. . ." he mumbles.

"Then what?" chimes in Sam, as he steps beside Sean. "What the heck happened?"

"We don't know," says Ella. "We couldn't get anything out of him." She wipes her forehead. "All I know is that mark isn't one I've ever seen. It was carved into him."

Carved? The Lurkers were maniacal, but even they didn't do that.

"How deep?" asks Marisa—her eyebrows rising as she leans forward.

"I don't know. The blood looked dry."

Marisa strokes her neck. "I guess it doesn't really matter. Just a few cuts to that region won't allow the victim much time to survive."

"How much time would you guess?" asks Ella.

"Really depends on how deep, but I would say with the shapes you listed, less than an hour. He probably couldn't speak because he feared opening the wounds and spilling any more blood."

"So, whoever hurt him was probably close by. I wonder why they didn't go after you," adds Miles as he steps closer to the misshapen circle we've formed.

"We didn't see anyone else," replies Ella. "It was quiet."

"Who would leave someone to die like that? If it wasn't the Lurkers, then who was it?" I ask.

"I don't know," mutters Ella. "Someone else is out there. Someone we never saw."

"And you haven't seen anything like this before?" asks Sean.

"Never."

Nobody speaks. We all quietly drift our focus to the ground. I start to pick at my fingernails; I chip the edge off one and flick it into the dirt.

Whatever happened out there was new. In my ten years outside Nimbus, I never saw a mark like that. The burnt 'S' and 'L' on the cheeks of the Shadow Lurkers was the only symbol outside those walls, and we all knew what that meant. We all knew if we saw that, the end was near. But, this is different. This feels worse.

Three circles.

Whoever did that to him found a way into our world—unless they've been here the whole time, watching us, studying us. Thinking about it makes my skin crawl. My anxious picking speeds up. I drop another nail into the dirt.

When MacMillan was in charge, nothing changed. We never saw anyone new and it felt like no one could cross into our world. We don't know if the grid prevented others from entering, we just know outsiders were never seen—or felt, for that matter. Now, whatever happened to Collin feels like our fault.

But he disappeared when the grid was still running.

I thrust my hands into my pockets and look up. "Did anyone ever see Collin after the fire?"

Everyone stares into each other's eyes. Then, they all slowly shake their heads in unison.

I speak again. "If nobody saw him, how did he get out without a scratch?"

"Was there a back door?" asks Sean.

"Yea," nods Miles. "But it was barricaded so the Lurkers couldn't come in overnight without making noise."

"Was there any reason that barricade could have been broken down before the fire?"

"No. The door was checked every day. Nothing ever moved."

"Then how did any of this happen?" angrily questions Sam. "If there was no other way out, Collin would have been on the street with us when we killed Arthur. Since he wasn't, someone else had to have taken him. Someone even the Lurkers might not have known about."

"Hold your horses, Sam," quips Sean. "We don't know that. We don't know if Collin found another way out and kept running. We can't just assume someone captured him while we were all around him."

"But what if someone did? That mark isn't one I've ever seen."

"I've never seen it either," adds Marisa. "I've worked in the infirmary for three years since I got back from my Separation and I've never seen it on anyone. Even on the deceased brought back for an autopsy."

Ella digs her incisors into her bottom lip. "If no one has ever seen this symbol, what can we make of it? Should we even go out there now? Should we just stay here forever?"

Rosie steps close to Ella. With tears in her eyes, she wipes her cheeks. "We can't stay. Collin wouldn't want that."

"She's right. We have to go," I say. "Whoever did that to him might come here. At least us going out might be able to prevent anyone who stays here from the same fate."

"Elise is right," mutters Sean. "We have to go. And we should go soon."

"Why soon?"

"They found Collin on this excursion for a reason. He could have been out there in March or April, but he wasn't. Whatever happened to him, we may never know, but it seems three months is all we get." He pauses and takes a deep breath. "We have to go back out tomorrow."

"Tomorrow?" moans Miles. He arches his neck; his wandering eyes look around the empty sky. He bites at his cracked lips. "We're not ready to go tomorrow," he says, his voice quieting with each word.

"We have to be."

"And what if we're not?" asks Mitch.

"Then stay behind."

Mitch's eyes wander around the walls before quickly glancing outside the still-open gates. He doesn't speak. He focuses on the opening—the moonlight cascading on the dirt path with its luminance. He lightly shakes his head and walks away.

"Does that mean you're staying?" shouts Sean.

"It doesn't mean anything," responds Mitch before disappearing down the street.

Sean runs after him.

I turn to Sam. "Will you be ready to go tomorrow?"

His wide, unblinking eyes gaze around at Ella, Miles, Marisa, Rosie, and me. "I will."

"What about everyone else?" I ask, as a slight twinge starts to pulse along my scalp.

"I'll be ready," smiles Marisa.

"Same here," answers Miles.

"I'm ready," replies Rosie.

"What about you, Ella?" I ask.

"I'll be ready, but I don't know about Marcus." Ella rubs the back of her neck. "Seeing Collin like that really hurt him—even more so than when the library burnt down and when we lost Malcolm."

"Do you think you can talk to him?"

"I can try."

"I'll help," adds Rosie, and the two of them walk away.

"The rest of you should probably make sure you're fully packed and rested for tomorrow," I say. "I need to go talk to my brother."

Miles and Marisa walk separate directions. Sam stays beside me.

"Why don't you go get ready, Sam?"

He fidgets with his pinky. "I don't know if I want to go now."

"Why's that?"

Sam's voice cracks. "What if that mark means something?" His lips shake. "What if whoever gave that to Collin will come after me?"

"Whoever gave that to him might come after all of us, but we'll be in a group. They won't be able to hurt us."

"The outside will always hurt us," he softly says. "Especially when we don't think it will." Then, without giving me a chance to say anything, Sam turns toward the cobblestone street behind him and heads home.

The outside will always hurt us, I think.

I turn around and head right. Moving past the infirmary, I manage a light grin at Marisa as she steps inside. Camden waves from the door—his leg wrapped in an off-white cast full of signatures—as he leans forward on his crutches. I flash a half smile; his wave becomes more enthusiastic.

The outside will always hurt us, I think again.

Sam has a point. Even when we feel like we're in the clear, something happens. It's been months since my last headache, since my last feeling of guilt, or even fear. Now, my head is throbbing. With each step, the ache pushes itself further into my skull.

I thrust my hands into the sides of my head. The aching persists. I fall to my knees just as everything around me starts to spin. I close my eyes and fall onto my back. I can't feel anything.

***

The world around me is pitch black. I can't see. I can't hear. I can't breathe. Nothing I do to try and move my fingers, my toes, my lips, anything, works. I'm stuck.

A light flickers above me. In and out, in and out, in and out, the light bounces around the atmosphere before it shines heavily into my eyes. Now, I can blink, but I still can't move. I close my eyes as traces of the light flutter behind my eyelids. Inaudible voices start to echo around me. The murmurs grow louder before they turn into applause and I'm thrust toward the light above me.

Suddenly, I can move my extremities. I can see everything, but I still feel nothing. The murmurs have turned to cheers as the crowd around me roars in awe. I grab onto the light; it becomes a rope. I pull myself upward as a man extends his arm from a plank above. Helping me up onto the platform, he points forward before aiming his index finger downward. As I follow his finger, it disappears.

The room goes black again. The once-raucous cheers have dissolved. A light flickers on beneath me. I watch as it grows brighter and brighter and brighter.

***

"Elise, are you okay?" asks a familiar voice.

I look up. My brother, Zeke, hovers above me.

He kneels down beside me and places a callused hand against the back of my head. He helps me sit up.

"Yea, yea, I think so," I softly reply.

"What happened?"

"I had some sort of dream. It felt like the ones I had outside Nimbus."

I thought those were gone. I thought I was free from the circus.

Zeke moves his hand onto my shoulder. "When was the last time you had one of those?" he asks, his eyes widening as he helps me to my feet.

"Months," I mutter. "I haven't had one since Arthur was alive."

"Do you think that means. . ." he trails off. "It can't be."

"I shot him between the eyes. He's dead," I smirk. "It can't be that. It has to be something else." *Hell, I hope it's something else.*

"Hopefully it's nothing. Maybe just the thought of going back out there has your mind in knots."

"Maybe. . ."

He wraps his arm around my back; we start to walk back home.

I try not to dwell on what just happened. I want to forget what I saw. I want to forget everything about those horrible nightmares—even if that one meant something. I don't want to go back there, and I'll do whatever it takes to avoid falling back into that mess.

"Speaking of the outside, I've been meaning to talk to you about that," I say, softly, almost hushed.

"Yea? What about it?" he asks.

We arrive home. The front porch swing lightly glides back and forth in the wind. The brightly colored, flower-patterned pillow cushions start to slip underneath the arm rests. I step onto the porch and grab one. Placing it against the back of the swing, I take a seat. Zeke sits beside me.

"Have you decided if you're going back out there with us?"

"Yea, I have," he quietly answers.

"And?"

"Do you remember my 'pop point' experience?"

"Yea, what about it?"

Zeke takes a deep breath. He closes his eyes and rests his head against the back of the swing. He bites his bottom lip and exhales. With his focus on the back of his eyelids, he starts to speak. "When I was out there, I felt something, something I've never felt." He leans forward and opens his eyes. Dropping his elbows to his knees, he clasps his hands together and looks around. "It wasn't just the aching in my head. My whole body started to tense up."

I try to interject, but he waves me off.

With his eyes aimlessly wandering around the empty street in front of us, he starts to speak again. "It felt like someone was trying to pull me down. I get the anxiety and the fear associated with the outside, but I never felt that. It was more than just the ache; something didn't want me out there. Something wanted me to stay put. Like, if I had made it beyond the pop point, maybe I was going to see something I shouldn't have."

"Like what?" I ask.

"That's just it. I don't know and I don't want to know."

"Does that mean you're not coming with us?"

He nods his head and doesn't speak. He curls his bottom lip beneath his teeth. He turns toward me. "I don't want you to go out there, Elise. I don't want to lose you, too."

My mind spits out the first thing it grabs onto. I mutter, "I have to."

"Nobody has to," he replies.

"I can't stay here anymore. I can't be in Nimbus anymore."

"But why? It's safe here now."

"But, it's not. This place is falling apart just like the city. This whole world, this whole idea, this, everything," I stammer, pointing around Nimbus. "It's all falling apart. No one wants to lead. No one cares. I can't live and die here knowing I could have done something to change my fate."

He stands up. "But it's safe!" he loudly shouts, as he steps off the porch. "Nimbus is safe now. Nobody can get in and nobody has a reason to go out. I don't see why you don't get that. You can die within a day outside these walls. At least, in here, you're guaranteed life."

"But I don't want that life, Zeke!" I cry back. "I don't want to live here knowing nothing's going to happen. I can't live a life without reason. I can't spend my days fading into obscurity. I have to go out there. . ." I trail off. ". . .I have to do this."

Zeke starts to anxiously rub the back of his neck. "Okay," he says. "If that's what you want, you can go. You can do whatever you want. Just know, I'm not going. I can't go out there again. Even without the chip in my head, I can't experience what's out there. I'm sorry, Elise. I just can't."

My cheeks start to tremble. I can feel a warmth coursing through them and into my eyes. I start to cry. Zeke wraps his arms around me and drops his head onto my shoulder.

We don't need to speak. Everything's been said. All I can do is let him know I'll be okay, that I won't die out there like so many kids before us—and I don't need words for that.

I squeeze Zeke tighter. My eyes continue to leak. This could be the last time I see my brother; this could be the last moment we get to be there for each other; this could be the end of his world. Heck, the end of mine. But when you're separated from family for eleven years and then you have maybe a year to catch up, nothing matters, because after you've become acquainted again, you get kicked out.

There's a reason parents in Nimbus wait eleven years between kids: nobody wants to send two out at the same time. That's why twins are a parent's worst nightmare. But, at the same time, that's twenty-two potential years without a sibling. I was around Zeke for the first two years of my life, but I was young, so I knew nothing about him. I only had a year before I turned fourteen to catch up on eleven lost years. It was like meeting a stranger.

And when we finally got close again, it was my turn to be separated.

Then, war happened.

I'm twenty-four and my brother is thirty-five. I've known him for three years. That's why I hate it here. If Separation didn't exist, I'd have known him for twenty-four years, not three, not ten, twenty-freaking-four. But, that's not how Nimbus works. *So, why bother? Why try to create new memories when the world around us is dying?*

I love my brother, but I don't know him.

I guess we'll always practically be strangers. Three years isn't enough time. Apparently, we need eleven to learn anything.

Sean

Mitch leans against a lamppost. The light flickers above him. He looks up.

"So what is it, Mitch? Are you staying or are you coming with us?"

We've been discussing his plans for what feels like an hour. He hasn't given an answer. All we've done is wander down the streets far enough to the point that we're at the back end of Nimbus. There's a lamppost ten feet from the wall and a bench resting against the steel. I head toward the bench as Mitch remains beneath the light.

"I don't know!" he shouts.

There's no one around us. There's nothing but a vegetable garden with un-watered, wilting stems, and a few rundown houses.

I scratch the scar on my chest while my eyes divert down the broken cobblestone. There are only a few houses this deep into Nimbus and those that are this far back are abandoned.

I turn my gaze to Mitch; his hand catches my glance—similar to Sam's, it's discolored. Most of the broken bones from being shut in the gate haven't healed, and Marisa claims they probably won't due to the severity of the injury. He's had four surgeries, but nothing's fixed it. It's gotten to the point that the wound has become his sole focus—his reason for avoiding anything that could end the same way.

"I don't think I can. I'm useless," whispers Mitch.

I lean forward. "Nobody's useless."

"What can I do? I can basically only use one arm. I have no purpose."

"Yes you do," I retort. "You have heart. Without you, I might not be here. Without you pushing me through that gate, everything that happened in February might not have happened. You're a hero, Mitch, and we need you out there."

"Heroes don't live forever," he gibes. "I had my moment and now I have to live with it every day."

"But you get to live. You're alive. You're still here."

"That's right. I am, so I should keep living. Out there," he points, "I could be dead in an instant."

The light stops flickering. It shines brightly, illuminating the worn-down neighborhood.

"We all could," I quietly reply.

"What was that?"

"Nothing."

"Whatever you said, you said it quietly for a reason." Mitch steps away from the post. Walking across the path, he kicks a loose piece of rock toward the broken steps of house 2107—also known as the first home created here. Since Nimbus was founded in 2107, they started house numbers at that. Not one, but 2107. The houses go past 2192, though. It's an odd set-up, considering each year, more houses toward the bottom of the list get left behind. When someone dies, someone else who's just come back from the outside typically occupies his or her home, but those at the back never get new tenants because more of us die out there than in here. And new houses aren't built because there isn't enough room. It seems everyone is slowly working toward the exit, like time has pushed this world toward its end.

"I'm just saying, you belong with us, Mitch. We're all fighting for the same purpose."

"A purpose that could kill you. That's what I don't get," he stammers. "We've all already been out there. We know what it's like. We're finally safe and now some of you want to go back out there like nothing happened. It doesn't make sense to me."

I take a breath and sit down. I don't know what to say. My mind's running back and forth, trying to grab onto words it can't find. Mitch has a point—one I don't know if I can refute. We're all allowed our reasons.

"I can't stop you," I sigh.

"And you can't help me," he mutters. "That game. . ." he cuts off. "That . . .world, it tried to kill me. I fought to get back here. I did what I could to not be out there." He strokes his mustache before sliding his hand down his face. "So. . .I can't justify going back out. I just have to do what I can to survive."

I stand up and start walking down the path.

"You're okay with that, Sean?" asks Mitch, his voice fearful and full of uncertainty.

I don't turn around. With my gaze focused on the road ahead, I say, "It's your life, Mitch. I'm not in charge of what you do with it. We don't live in that world anymore," before continuing down the path.

He doesn't follow.

3 May 2192

Sam

We're about to leave, but not by force, by choice. And as much as I want to get away from Nimbus, today feels more painful than the last time I left. Mom and Dad aren't here to say goodbye; Abby's not waiting outside for me; Sean's not standing atop the wall watching my every move. Everything about this exit feels off, yet it's still happening.

I can't stop this because I want this.

I need this.

No matter what happens outside these walls, it's better than what would happen inside. Everyone who still resides here doesn't want to; they're either here to experience those eleven potentially missed years with their child, or they're staving off an inevitable demise. Or both.

There's no future in Nimbus without a leader. Even with MacMillan, Nimbus had a future. It was horrible, but it was something. Now that nobody's in charge, there's no future here. The only thing left behind the steel is death. Even if those who aren't leaving don't see that, they have to feel it.

I step out the front door of my parents' home and take a seat on the steps. Setting my backpack beside me, I pull my cargo shorts toward my knees. A light breeze brushes past as birds chirp overhead. No one steps out of his or her home next door; no one waltzes down the street to say hello; everything is quiet.

I could shout and no one would respond. I open my mouth to test my theory, but quickly close it just as one of the passing birds drops its breakfast on a nearby lamppost. I smirk, my stare focused on the black and white bird as it flies over the wall and away from Nimbus.

Like the bird, I wish I could fly away from here. I wish I could aimlessly flutter into the distance, forgetting everything about the world behind me. Casually flapping my wings as I dance into the grey sky, oblivious to nature's predators desiring my flesh. *If only*, I think. If only being unaware meant you were safe; if only it meant you'd never have to worry.

I stand up.

Elise and Sean are probably already at the gate. Marcus and Kyle probably are, too. And as much as I'm ready to leave, I don't want to be the first one there. After all, that was my last night on a real mattress. That was the last night of any semblance of peace—the last chance to have a moment that supersedes all the negativity and suffering I associate with this place. I laugh to myself. *Even sleep can't rid the nightmares.*

I pick up my bag and head down the steps. I look left. *She's* not there. My stomach tenses; my fingers tingle as my wrists start to feel disconnected from my arms. I shake my head and turn back to face my home. The feelings fade. The longing doesn't.

The scratched dark blue shutters of the front window sit still against the darkened white frame of the house. They don't rattle in the wind. The peeling silver of the door handle protruding from the bulky wood doesn't jiggle with each gust. Nothing moves. House 2156 is rotting, but not enough to announce it. I place my foot on the front step and manage a half-smile before turning down the street and heading toward the gates.

I don't look back. I don't want to think of that place anymore.

As I walk down the cobblestone path, the eerie stillness of nature bothers me. Unlike the gusts that pushed through the broken windows of the shack, or the farmhouse, catching on the fractured glass, the wind in Nimbus is quiet. I can feel it, but I can't hear it. The wind chimes beside me move, but don't emit sound. It's as if the world behind this wall isn't real, like it isn't meant to exist.

The only sound that crosses my eardrums is the birds. More start to move off rooftops, seemingly chasing the muted wind. I stop and watch—slowly spinning in a circle, as I attempt to follow each one from the beginning. Gazing in wonderment as they freely float above me, I follow their path. Some converge atop a chimney across the way; others fly beyond the wall and out into the forest. No matter where they go, they're free. I envy their flight, the ability to flee any situation by drifting into the sky. Unlike the birds, my feet are always rooted to the ground.

My laces drag against the cobblestone, unraveling themselves beneath my shoes; I trip.

Shit.

Maybe I wasn't meant to be that free. Maybe no one is. I pick myself back up and continue down the path toward the steel gates. The cobblestone turns to dirt, and I'm left with nothing but a few strides toward the front of Nimbus. The gates are already open. Sean, Elise, Marcus, Kyle, Marisa, Ella, Miles, and Rosie wait. The others Sean mentioned haven't shown up.

A kid on crutches in khaki shorts with a green graphic t-shirt is talking to Sean. Marcus, Kyle, Ella, Rosie, and Miles are standing in a small circle with their backpacks around them. Elise and Marisa are chatting while Marisa points outside the wall. I look forward. The trees lightly curl in the wind—an abrupt cracking sound in the distance penetrates my ears. I shake my head.

"I see you finally decided to show up," laughs Sean. The kid beside him chuckles, but attempts to conceal it so I don't notice.

I press my lips together, feigning a smile. "I was thinking about just skipping today," I say sarcastically.

Sean smiles. "Of course you were," he mutters before gesturing toward the boy he was talking with beforehand. "Sam, this is Camden."

"It's nice to meet you," I say.

He nods. "You, too. Sean's told me a lot about you."

"Only good things, I hope."

Camden smiles. "He made it seem like if you could survive everything you survived, I could get by with this bum leg." He looks down at the cast extending from his foot to his kneecap, and smiles. "It's just one leg. I have another."

"You need both to get by out there," playfully smiles Sean. "Plus, if you go out there, who's going to watch over Nimbus while I'm gone?"

Camden grins. "Certainly not MacMillan."

I smile and pat Camden on the shoulder before making my way toward Elise.

With her hand on the back of her neck, Elise laughs. Marisa's eyes shift to the left, acknowledging my presence. Elise turns around. "What took you so long?" she asks half-heartedly.

"I just wanted to be sure I was well-rested."

"Good thinking," says Marisa. "We can't have anyone out there with too little sleep."

"How much did you get?" I ask while slowly wedging my hands into my pockets.

Marisa laughs, "Oh, you know, a couple hours."

I chuckle. "Oh yea?"

"No, no, silly. I got enough. Certainly more than I'll get once we get out there."

"She's got a point," replies Elise. "I hope you're ready for longer nights."

I nod. *Of course I am.* I don't want to be, but that's the reality of this situation. I know what I'm up against. We all do; at least we should. I take a step toward the open gate. A bird perches itself against the top of the steel. Cawing into the wind, it hops down the wall and out of sight.

"Is this all who are coming?" asks Marisa, breaking my focus.

"I'm not sure. I thought Sean said some former Elite Guard members were coming with." I look up at Elise. She turns her stare toward Sean—he gives Camden a half hug before striding toward us.

"What's up?" he asks.

"Is this all who are coming?"

"Ralph, Derrick, and Juan should be here soon. I think they just went to the armory to grab a few guns."

"How many is a few?" asks Elise, her brows sharpening. "We're not trying to start a war out there."

"I know. Just enough for protection in case we run into any unwanted attention. You're more than welcome to use your bow, but I told Ralph to grab a better model in case you'd rather have that," answers Sean.

Turning to face me, Elise mutters, "Do you want my bow?"

The words don't find me; I spit out the first thing that comes up, "I can't."

"Why not?"

I try to think of a reason, but my train of thought is stalled, unwilling to glide forward.

"Well?" she asks again.

"You've had it for almost eleven years," I finally say. "I don't think it'd feel right for me to use it."

She smiles. "I needed it then. I think it's only right for you to use it for the next ten."

Ten years? I think. *We're going to need to fight for ten years?*

I don't respond. I don't even know what to say. I don't want the bow and I can't articulate why. I just don't.

I take a step between Elise and Marisa toward the open gate. I stare at the opening ahead of us. There's a small trail before trees overtake everything in the distance. I take another step. And another. I can hear muffled voices behind me. The trees bend into the dirt path; a rabbit scurries in the distance. The branches continue to bow toward the trail, like they're reaching for one another. I lift my left foot to take another step. My foot arcs into the sky; the trees fall into each other; the world goes black; the only light finding its way into my vision is that atop the trees. It's not the sun, nor is it fire. It's lampposts.

***

I fall forward—my incomplete step mocked by the newfound brick in front of me. *Where am I?* I think. The trees have become dark lampposts illuminated by large orbs atop each one. In between the lights sit a series of benches—each with perfectly trimmed shrubs on both sides. There's no one ahead of me and no one behind me. The lights only highlight the path; the rest of the area is pitch black.

"Where am I?" I ask aloud.

My words don't yield a response.

"Where am I?" I ask again, this time louder.

Once again, silence follows my question.

I stand up and start to move down the path. With each step, my heels echo against the walkway, making them the only sound in this place. I start to grow frightened.

"Hello?" I ask, hoping someone will respond this time. Yet, my words don't find anyone. They continue to elude anything that could give me an answer. "Is anyone there?" I say, expecting the same results as before.

I keep walking. The echoes don't fade, but the path ends. I walk back to the beginning, and back to the end once more. There's no one here. The brick extends a maximum of thirty feet, and beyond that is shadows. My mind starts to run in circles, but the pain in my pinky doesn't exist. The anxiety that has bothered me for months isn't real anymore. I can't feel anything, but I can move. *This is different.*

I take a seat at the first bench to the left. As I sit, the lights start to flicker.

"Who's doing that?" I ask, knowing my speech won't return even the slightest jest.

"Just a friend," whispers a womanly voice.

I turn left. I whip right. Nobody's here.

"If you're my friend, show yourself," I mutter. My hands start to shake upon my thighs.

"You're not ready," she softly laughs.

"Why?"

"You'll see."

***

Sean tugs at my shirt. Elise is on her knees in front of me, a look of worry spread across her face.

"What's going on?" I ask.

"Did you see something?" asks Elise, dismayed.

"Just a path, but there were lampposts and benches and a woman tried talking to me." I itch the ridge of my nose. "What happened? I thought I was done seeing things like that!" I shout.

Elise shakes her head. She leans forward and puts her hands on my shoulders. "Neither of us are done."

"What do you mean?"

"I had a headache and another circus-like nightmare last night on my way home."

"Elise, what do you mean?" I ask again, firmly.

"I-it's not over," she mumbles.

"What's not over?"

"This!" she loudly says, but doesn't yell. "These nightmares, these visions, whatever was happening to us out there is happening again. But this time, it's something new."

"What do you think that means?" asks Sean.

"That Nimbus isn't it," I reply.

"So, you're saying there's something else out there?" interjects Marisa.

I curl my knees toward my chest. Marcus, Kyle, and the others come toward us. "Yea. That dream wasn't like the ones I had out there. It was more peaceful than the fire, the shadows, and the torment of Arthur."

"How so?"

"There was a woman."

"What did she look like?" asks Marcus.

"I never saw her. She sounded older than me, older than us."

"How old?" asks Ella.

I turn to face her. Her pupils are dilated; her muddled stare makes me wish I had better answers. "I-I'm not sure. Forties or fifties. Nowhere near MacMillan's age."

"Did she want anything?" asks Marcus as he bends down to one knee, his hazelnut skin glistening in the light.

"I don't know. She said I wasn't ready."

"Ready for what?"

"I don't know!" I angrily retort. "I'm sorry, but I don't know what happened or what any of this means. I don't know why this is happening to me again. . .I don't have a chip!"

"Neither do I," adds Elise.

No one speaks. Everyone stands silently.

What am I waiting for? What will I see? Who was she? I don't know how to answer anything. I don't even know what to believe anymore. Without Separation, the grid, MacMillan, all of it, I should have nothing to fear. Yet, the moment I step outside the walls of Nimbus, I'm blindsided by some sort of daydream or vision. I don't know what it means, or why this woman chose me. I don't even know how it happened. If the chip's gone, and my mind can't be controlled anymore, *how is any of this possible?*

"Sam," comes a quiet, dispirited voice from behind me.

I turn around. There stands Melanie. She wipes her baggy, sodden eyes. Her once-perfectly straight dark brown hair sits disheveled behind her head. Clad in sweatpants and a white shirt larger than her meager frame, she takes a small step toward me.

"Melanie," I whisper.

"What are you doing here?"

She reaches for me. I extend my arm. Our fingers entwine as I stand up.

I ask again. "What are you doing here?"

She pulls my arm down, my head gets closer to hers. Placing her cold hands upon my cheeks, she leans toward my ear. "I know who she is," she whispers.

"Who?" I quietly answer.

"Don't listen to her."

"Who is she?" I ask again.

"Don't listen to anything she says," continues Melanie.

"Melanie!" comes a voice from behind us. I turn back. Melanie's parents are sprinting toward us. They shout her name once more.

"Who is she, Melanie? Please tell me," I quickly ask.

Her eyelids rise as a tear falls down her pale cheek. "Don't listen to her, Sam. Stay away from her."

"Please, Melanie."

"Don't go to her."

"Melanie!" scream her parents once more as they approach us.

"Where is she?"

Grabbing my cheeks once more, Melanie leans into my ear and whispers, "Halcyon," just as her parents grab her and take her away.

Elise

Halcyon. Who or what is that?
The word sounds familiar, but the definition eludes me.
"What was she talking about, Sam?" asks Marcus.
"I told you. She told me not to listen to the woman in my head," he quickly replies.
"I get that, but what is Halcyon?"
"I know as much as you do."
"Let's not focus on that," says Sean, as he leans against the steel. "We have bigger things to worry about than whatever Melanie saw out there."
I laugh. "Do we, though? This is the first time she's spoken since Marcus brought her back. Whatever she saw means something, Sean."
He glares at me.
"She's right," adds Marisa. "She waited until now to say something."
It's like she wants us to stay, to avoid what she's been keeping from us. But we know nothing of Halcyon. We don't know if it's a place, a person, or just something she saw in her head. Maybe, like Sam and I, Melanie was plagued by an incessant ache trying to guide her toward the end—and if that's the case, *why would we stay behind?*
"It means something," grumbles Sam. Arching his spine, he lifts his backpack, only to pull it tighter over his shoulders.
Marcus tilts his head. His eyes wander around Nimbus. "But what? She chose you, Sam. She said what she said to you for a reason."
Spellbound, Sam stares into the forest. He lets out a light cough while his eyes remain transfixed on the outside. "I don't know why she chose me. I. . .I just have a feeling that whomever I heard, Melanie met. I know that sounds crazy, but I get this feeling that she

told me because she knows this woman will try to torture me like Arthur." Sam sighs. "It's strange, but I believe it."

"Then why do you want to go out there?" asks Miles.

"Because I have to. I want to."

"Even if there's another person out there trying to get into your head?"

"Yea, even then. It all means something," mutters Sam. "Everything happens for a reason."

"And not all reasons are enjoyable," I add.

Sam nods. "If I've learned anything in the past few months, it's that anything is better than the hell behind these gates. Anything," he repeats.

Maybe not anything, I think to myself, but don't dare say aloud. I know where Sam's coming from; I know the pain he's endured, and his reasons for wanting to leave, but 'anything' is broad. Almost too broad.

I get a sense that some of the others feel the same way, but nobody speaks; nobody bothers to say anything more about the situation. It feels like everyone knows what's ahead—that they get the sense Arthur wasn't the only evil lurking in the forest, and beyond.

I look around at the others. Marcus's eyes meet mine before they shift toward Sam.

"If that woman isn't from here," he says, "how could Melanie have met her?"

"I don't know," answers Sam. "I don't know if I want to know."

Sean steps toward Sam. Placing his hand on his shoulder, he sighs. "We can't worry about what she saw, Sam. It could mean something. It could not. We have to worry about our plans—not a person we don't know to exist."

Sam angrily snaps back. "I don't get why you don't believe any of this." Quickly turning around, he stares into Sean's eyes, clearly agitated. "I heard a woman in my head then Melanie told me she knows who that woman is. That's not a coincidence, Sean. That's not just an accident. There's someone out there. She might be here. She might not be, but that doesn't matter. What matters is that we adhere to what Melanie said and we stay away from this woman." Furiously biting his bottom lip, he steps closer to his brother. "I don't get why you don't see this; it's almost as if you're trying to avoid it."

Sean cocks his head to the side. He looks at Sam steely-eyed. "Maybe I am, Sam. Maybe I don't want to believe it because I don't want you to be hurt any more. Is that so much of a problem?"

"It is."

"Why?"

"Because I'm going to get hurt. You're going to get hurt. Elise, Marcus, Miles, Rosie, all of us are going to get hurt. That's how this world works, and the sooner you get that through your head, the better." Sam storms outside the gates. Sean stays on his heels.

Grabbing onto Sam's backpack, Sean stops him in his tracks. Sam tries to move forward, but Sean keeps a firm grip on his bag. "Stop, Sam!" he shouts.

"No!" Sam retorts.

"Look at me!"

"No!"

Sean quickly jolts in front of Sam and yanks off Sam's backpack. Sam tries to run forward, but Sean pounces and grabs him by the back of the shirt. "Stop trying to run, Sam."

I don't know what to say, or what to feel. I stay back.

Sam screams, "Let go of me!"

Sean refuses. Marcus and Kyle run toward them.

What's happening? It felt like Sam had a grasp on reality, like he wasn't afraid of what was ahead, but now, now he seems just as lost as before.

I want to intervene, but there's nothing I can say. Everything I've said in the past isn't relevant. Every word I've used to calm him down before can't be justified with what's transpired over the past hour. What he saw in his head and what Melanie told him mean something. It doesn't matter if Sean sees it not; what matters is that it's real.

This world has a grip on Sam. The nails of fate keep digging into him, scratching him until he bleeds—until he's wounded. It doesn't matter what he does to stave off his demons, they keep coming, and slowly, but surely, they're tearing through him.

And if Sam falls, so do I. After all, I'm already scarred.

Sam screams into the skies. Birds flutter away. I run toward Sam and Sean.

"Sam, you need to calm down," exhales Sean. "You need to breathe."

"I can't," exclaims Sam. "I can't."

Sean lets go. Sam falls limp in the dirt.

I scream, but nothing comes out. An overwhelming darkness overcomes my vision.

***

"Sam!" I shout. The words are articulate; they're not muted. My voice bounces around the darkness. I can't see anything.

"Elise!" shouts a voice back.

"Sam?" I say to myself.

"It's me. What are you doing here?" he responds.

Here? "Where are we?"

Sam steps in front of me. His cold hand brushes mine. "I-I was just here," he mutters, his voice fluctuating in volume.

"Sam," I say again. "Where are we?"

He doesn't respond. His hands tremble as he grabs onto mine.

I take a step forward. The darkness fades—a miniscule light bursts forth. Then another. And another. Sam's no longer beside me, but at the end of the path. Sitting with his back perched against a bench, he looks across the way.

"Sam, how'd you get over there so fast?" I ask, unsure if I want an answer.

"What are you talking about? I've been over here the whole time. Couldn't you see me?"

"No, I just saw black. I took a step and this path popped into my vision."

Sam doesn't respond.

"Sam, where are we?"

He stays silent. I can't tell if he's really here, or if it's all in my head. Unlike the past, I can feel my hands, my feet, my chest. I'm breathing. I'm here. Nothing's locking me into place. This isn't like the sequences I've fallen into before. This is different. *I'm not supposed to be here.*

"That's right," comes a female voice from ahead. Sam doesn't flinch at the sound of the voice; he simply looks down.

"Who are you?" I ask.

"She won't tell you," answers Sam. "She never told me."

"What has she told you, Sam?"

He goes quiet again. As if he can hear me one moment and not the next, I stop trying to speak to him. Instead, I try to walk toward him. Yet, the moment I step forward, the benches start to dissolve. The lights start to flicker. I attempt to run toward Sam, but the more I step, the quicker everything around me fades into the ground.

"Sam!" I scream.

My cry yields silence. I stop. Everything stays in its current state. The benches sit on the black surface like flakes of ash waiting to be reignited, while incandescent bulbs sit between each pile slowly rolling back and forth as if my next step would cause them to shatter—sending the light away from the ash and into the emptiness around me.

I lift my foot, but don't step. "Sam, can you hear me?" I ask into the opaque.

"Yes," he replies.

"What's happening?"

"She says you're not supposed to be here."

"Then why am I here?"

Sam goes silent again.

"Why am I here?" I ask, this time loudly.

Sam doesn't respond, but I can see footsteps ahead of me. There's no body, no face, nothing, just prints walking toward me. The marks push the darkened path in front of me from side to side like thick, oily water, yet nothing changes. My foot is still in the air, and the space around me is still. The footsteps don't make a sound; they just vibrate in the black, puddle-like area in front of me.

"Who are you?" I ask.

The invisible being stops. A shrill cry erupts around me, forcing me to quickly plant my foot into the ground. Everything dissipates.

***

"What the hell was that?" asks Marcus. Heavily breathing as he leans over me, he wipes his forehead. "What just happened?"

I sit up and glance toward Sam. He's staring blankly into the sky. "Is he okay?" I ask.

"He's breathing, but he's not speaking," answers Sean.

I don't bother to stand; I quickly crawl a few feet toward Sam. His eyes are open, his pupils dilated enough that the black nearly hides the amber behind it. I place my hand on his chest. I can feel his heart beating slowly against my palm. "Sam," I whisper. I lean closer to his ear. "Sam, run."

His feet start to twitch.

"Where is he?" asks Sean.

"I don't know," I reply.

"Did you see him?"

"Yes, but I don't know where we were. It was some path with benches and lampposts; everything around us was pitch black. All I could see was that path."

"Did you hear anyone else?" asks Marcus.

I take a deep breath and turn to face him. He's sweating. He's engaged in what's happening almost as if it'll give him some sort of clarity about what he's seen. "I heard the voice Sam heard."

"The woman?" adds Rosie.

"Yes."

I turn back toward Sam. With his wide, unblinking eyes fixated on the passing clouds, his feet continue to twitch. I lean in once more. "Run faster."

Sam's feet start kicking against the dirt. His eyes close.

"Sam!" shouts Sean.

"Give him a second," I calmly reply.

Marisa falls to her knees opposite me. Placing her hand underneath Sam's head, she holds him away from the dirt. Sam's eyes close and start to flinch—his pupils racing behind his eyelids.

"Is he going to be okay?" asks Miles.

In one sudden breath, Sam's torso flies forward. His eyes wide open, his mouth agape as he tries to breathe. Reaching for his face, he places his hands against his cheeks, then slowly slides them across his body as if he's ensuring he's here, and not *there*.

"Sam?" I ask quietly.

Rapidly panting, his head lightly shakes as he looks at his surroundings.

"Sam," I say again.

"Wh-where?" he stutters.

"Where, what?"

"Where am I?"

"You're safe. You're with us. We're just outside Nimbus."

He turns toward me. His face is pale, his eyes are bloodshot; he's lost. *What did she say to him?*

Sean pulls Sam to his feet.

Sam starts to itch the back of his head.

Getting to my feet, I place a hand on Sam's shoulder. "Are you okay?" I ask.

"No," he mumbles. "I'm not."

"What did you see?"

He turns around and wraps his arms around me. "I saw her."

"What did she look like?" I softly reply.

"I didn't see a face."

"What are you two whispering about?" asks Sean.

"Sam saw the woman," I answer.

"Did you recognize her?" asks Kyle.

"I didn't see her face, just a cloak. She sat next to me. She said she was excited to meet me." Sam's fingers roll in and out of his palms. He lets go of me and looks at Sean. "She also said something else."

Glumly looking at his brother, Sean lowers his voice. "What did she say?"

Sam gulps. "She said, they know all about me. . .and the girl."

My stomach drops. Marisa catches me as I start to fall.

"Who are these people?" I ask, short of breath.

"I don't know," Sam mutters. "We haven't even left and something new is happening. I don't get it."

"I-I don't think we're supposed to."

"Do we even go at this point?" asks Miles. Stepping to my side, he runs his hand through his short, curly black hair while looking around before speaking again. "We're about a hundred feet outside of Nimbus and look what's happening. We don't have chips. We're free, but something is still happening. And whatever it is, it doesn't feel right."

Marcus exhales, "He's right. I hate to say it, but he's right. We never experienced anything like this on our excursions, but the moment we try to leave with you guys, this happens. It's odd."

"That doesn't mean it should stop us from going," retorts Marisa.

"Why doesn't it?" responds Miles.

"Who's to say this won't happen in Nimbus? Whoever's in their heads is going to find us regardless. I say we just keep moving."

I agree. "She's right. The only way to put an end to what's trying to stop us is to find this woman."

"Do you really want to find someone we know nothing about?" asks Miles. Agitatedly looking around, he bites his bottom lip. "This almost feels worse than the Lurkers."

I smirk. "And look what we did to them."

"But look what they did to me," Sam says, digging his thumb into the nub atop his pinky. He then points to the scar on his leg. I try to input that the scar was inadvertent and not a part of the Lurkers, but before I can open my mouth, Sam continues. "If they can do that and get into my head. . ."

This time, I interject. "MacMillan was in our heads."

Sam continues as if he didn't hear me. ". . .then who's to say this woman can't do the same? I've met her twice, in a sense. With the Lurkers, it wasn't this fast." He takes a breath. "She's clearly excited to meet me. So much so that she's almost pulling us to her."

"And you still want to go?" asks Miles, loudly. "You actually want to meet the person who could hurt you more than Arthur or MacMillan ever did, especially after you just recommended that we stay away?"

Sam nods.

"Why?" Miles asks again. "Why do you lead yourself into torment, despair, into a path of pure evil?"

"Because if I don't do it, everyone will suffer. If I don't keep moving forward, you have to live with where you are now." Sam's voice shakes. "If I stand still, I might as well be dead."

Miles doesn't provide a response. He takes a step back beside Ella.

"Let's just move," sighs Marcus. "Nothing's going to get any better the more we sit here and fight about it."

Kyle steps beside Marcus and puts his hand on his shoulder. Lightly squeezing Marcus's shoulder, Kyle shifts his attention to Miles. "You know Marcus is right."

Miles stays quiet. His cheeks quiver as he grinds his molars.

"Plus, the sooner we head out, the sooner we'll learn about this woman."

"Don't be so excited," laughs Marisa.

"Why shouldn't I be?"

"Because you just saw what she did to Sam and Elise. Imagine if that were you."

Kyle shrugs his shoulders and pushes his glasses further up his nose. Rosie shakes her head at him and steps toward me.

"Whatever you need, Elise. I got your back," she softly says. Lifting her hair above her head, Rosie ties it into a ponytail and smiles. "Just remember, you're not in this alone. We can do it."

I manage a half-smile. Unlike the others, Rosie's head is held high. Marcus, Kyle, Ella, Miles, they've all been uncharacteristic lately. Miles is afraid. He's been a little worried since *that day*, but he persists. He knows he's scared, but he keeps moving. The others, though, are starting to break. The cracks are visible. Marcus isn't himself and nobody can fix him. What he saw out there is blinding his once-enthusiastic ambition, and no matter what Kyle or Ella tells him, the words escape meaning.

Kyle, on the other hand, spent nearly eleven full years at the library when he was outside. No amount of excursions can embolden you. When you shy away from what's out there for so long, there's not much that can toughen you up. Sometimes bloodshed is the only way. And I don't think he wants to be plagued with the nightmares a wound out there can cause.

Next to Kyle, Ella at least seems a little more in touch with reality. Her focus is off, but her desire is there. Seeing Collin hurt her, but not as much as it hurt Marcus. I believe in Ella. Heck, I believe in everyone, but it gets to a point where there's only so much you can do before the cracks connect, and the pieces start to fall.

Then there's Rosie. Each day, each hour, she doesn't seem to fear anything. No matter what we're doing or where we're going, she's ready. She was even there when I fainted in the field—she helped ensure I was okay when Sam went to help Sean. Since that horrific day, she's been helpful in every aspect. No matter the task, she'll do it. No matter the difficulty, she'll insist it isn't a problem.

To me, Rosie feels like the embodiment of who I once was— who I wish I could still be. She reminds me of the old, worn-out, yellow poster I had at the foot of my bed in Nimbus; the one thing

Zeke brought home with him when he was brought back for his re-entrance exam.

It had a woman on it. A woman named Rosie. I close my eyes and smile. *You're right, Rosie, we can do it.*

"Let's just go," I mutter.

"Yea," softly replies Sam. "I'm tired of waiting."

I look over at Sean. He almost looks depressed. "Are you okay?" I ask.

He feigns a grin and looks into the forest.

This is uncharted territory for him, for us. I've always been the one who's been tormented by something beyond my control. Not Sean. He's never had anyone in his head throwing him into nightmares he couldn't imagine; he's never had to deal with complete desperation on a similar level—and I think that's what's kept him levelheaded. But now, I think his lack of control over everything is hurting him. It's hurting us. Telling him I love him or that it will be okay won't do anything, nor will the rapid succession of these nightmares improve how he feels. I can't help myself, and what happens to me, but now it seems that we're almost to the point where I can't even help him.

I ask again. "Are you okay, Sean?"

"I don't know. I figured this shit was over. I thought you guys would be in the clear once the chips were taken out."

"I guess there's more to this world than we know," I sigh.

Stepping beside me, Marisa smiles, almost maliciously. "More than you'll probably care to know."

I throw a glare her way. "What's that supposed to mean?"

"Just that we'll never understand why the world is the way it is. No matter what we discover or who we find, the pieces might never sort themselves out."

"That's because Nimbus brainwashed us from the beginning," states Sean. "They never gave us a chance to understand."

"That's true," replies Marisa. "Maybe whoever this woman in your head is," she looks at me, "maybe she'll help sort out the past."

I shrug my shoulders and bite my bottom lip. "Let's just go," I say bitterly.

Sean waves his hand into the air. Everyone steps toward us.

"It's time to move," he exclaims. "This is your last chance to stay behind."

Everyone remains still except Miles. He takes a step back.

"Does this mean you're staying behind?" asks Sean.

Miles turns around and points toward the gates. There, stand three men clad in ballistic vests with backpacks and an array of guns at their sides.

Sean smiles. "I knew they'd show up eventually."

At this point, it doesn't matter who joins this odyssey. It doesn't matter how much protection we have, or how much food and clothing we have. The only thing that holds any value is where we'll end up—and that's something we can't answer. Really, I don't know if we'll ever be able to. As long as there's someone or something else in my head—in Sam's head—the end will be invisible. The future will be hidden.

No amount of preparation can stave off what's ahead.

I force a smile at Sean, masking the emotions I don't care to emit. "Let's move," I mutter.

He grabs my hand. Yet, I feel nothing. The love, the devotion, everything we've given each other since we met, feels nonexistent. Whatever's happening this time is starting to bother me more than I thought possible. It's starting to bring back the fear I thought I was past.

I entwine my fingers in his. I try to remember why he's here, why we're all here.

Sean lifts his other hand into the sky. "Let's move," he yells.

The gates start to close. The grinding steel echoes throughout.

This is it.

This is the end of Nimbus and the beginning of the next chapter.

4 May 2192

Sean

With the path long gone, the only thing ahead of us is the unknown.

We don't know if we'll see Lurkers, vagrants, or kids unaware of what took place in Nimbus a few months ago. There are no expectations. The only thing we know is crossing the barrier won't kill us—we know our heads won't burst.

I scratch the scruff on my chin and turn toward Elise. "How long do you think it will take to get beyond the barrier?"

"A few days," she quietly responds. "It didn't take Zeke long to get there."

"It's crazy how something that used to be so dangerous isn't too far away, and I never encountered it before."

Footsteps louden behind me. Ella steps to my left. "Rosie felt it," she mutters. "Didn't you, Rosie?" she gestures backward. I turn around. Rosie bites her lip, twisting her smile.

"Yea," mumbles Rosie. "I felt it."

"The pop point?" I ask.

Rosie looks away, but keeps moving forward. "Not to that extent, but yes. . .my first week out here I felt it."

"How far did you get?" inquires Elise. "The doctors said my brother got farther than most do without his chip exploding."

"I'm not sure. I felt an ache." Rosie digs two fingers into her forehead. "It was more of a pulse. The farther I got, the quicker the beats became." She stops in her tracks.

I turn around. Elise and Ella stop beside me. "What made you decide to stop and turn around?"

"The shriek."

"What shriek?" questions Elise. Taking a step backward, she stands beside Rosie. "What happened?"

"The farther you get, the louder it becomes," replies Rosie, her fingers still digging into her skull.

"What did it sound like?"

"I can't explain it. It was horrible. A deafening cry begging you to stop. As the pulsing intensified, so did the shrill, piercing sound. I eventually stopped and so did the noise. When I turned around, it faded."

"I wonder why that happens," I say.

"It wasn't the chip that caused it," answers Rosie. "No, it was someone. I know it was."

Sam steps beside Rosie and puts his arm on her shoulder. "Did you see anyone?"

She looks down. "No. Nothing."

"Then how do you know it was someone?" I ask.

"You can tell when something's in your head and something isn't," she replies bitterly. "There was someone near me. Someone warning me."

Elise looks around the forest before speaking. "Maybe that's why Zeke never mentioned that sound. Maybe it wasn't there for him."

"I don't know. Maybe not."

"Do you think it was a Lurker?" asks Sam, a shivering ounce of despair in his voice. "Do you think one of them was trying to stop you?"

Rosie stands up. "No, it was definitely a woman. I don't think any women were Lurkers."

"I hope it wasn't the woman in my head," frowns Sam. "I don't want to think that she's been working her way into this group before I even met you guys."

"I don't know, Sam. I don't even want to know," mutters Rosie. "All I want is to keep moving. I've been trying to forget that experience for six years."

"Then let's keep moving," I state. "We have a long road ahead of us."

Slight grumbles fill the air behind me, but everyone persists. We know our path isn't pretty but every second we spend standing still, our feet stuck in the mud, is time wasted. If we keep stopping to learn about everyone's past, the future we're chasing will elude us.

Sadly, the only seconds we can afford to lose are the ones in my brother's and Elise's heads. It pains me to think it; hell, it bothers me to see anyone suffer. But, it's inevitable. Sam's right. We're all going to get hurt. I just need to get that through my head before it's too late, before I succumb to the weakness that almost killed me in Nimbus.

I rub the scar on my chest. I can still see Jaxon glaring at me. His dark grey eyes mocking my torment as I stumble into the steel, blood pouring down my chest. I can feel the icy hand of death tugging at my shirt telling me it's my time. I can feel it all, but I can't let it guide me. I'm still here.

I entwine my fingers in Elise's.

You're okay. Sam's okay. Elise is okay. We're all okay. I take a deep breath.

We may be crumbling. We may be dying, but we're going to fight until the end. Even if the direction we're going hurts, we're all here for a reason.

And whoever's communicating with Sam is leading the way. Whoever she is, she's the only connection we have to what might be out here; she's the only thing I fear whether I want to admit it to anyone or not. The Lurkers might still be wandering in the shadows, but without a leader, they're inept. They won't bother us without reason, especially knowing that we've already bested them.

I kick a broken branch to the side. One of my friends from the guard coughs.

"Are we going to the city?" asks Juan. "I haven't been there in years."

"We'll probably have to pass through," I answer.

"We can't avoid it?" asks Sam. "Can't we just go around it?"

"If it's quicker to go through, we'll go through."

Sam sighs.

I try to be tough to make everything easier for everyone else. I try to act like I'm not afraid, but deep down, I'm terrified.

Nobody's cut out to live like we have. No matter how strong someone may act on the outside, everyone's already broken. For crying out loud, this is my third time out here. No one should be separated from his or her home three damn times—even if the final one is by choice.

I'm just glad this is the last time. Now, nothing can make me go back to Nimbus; nothing can send me back to a place that was more focused on filling children's minds with worthless knowledge than preparing them for their future. It didn't matter that we had fate in front of us; it didn't matter that our future was practically already decided. None of it mattered to Nimbus as long as we played along.

I don't care if MacMillan's rules were about building an Elite society. That's bullshit. All he wanted was a world he was in charge of. He didn't care who was in it. He just cared that they listened. And if they didn't, well, Separation would handle that. Or, a gun would.

I lightly exhale and shake my head.

Elise's beautiful blue eyes glance up at me. "What was that for?"

"Nothing," I reply. "It's nothing."

"It's something. What are you thinking about?"

"I'm just glad we're not in Nimbus."

She smiles.

At least, out here, I have a purpose. I don't have to stand atop a wall watching frightened kids try to stay close to home even though they know they aren't supposed to. Too many times I watched other members of the Guard kill innocent—no, innocuous—kids. We weren't innocent in the eyes of Nimbus. We knew our place according to law.

Now, I don't have to intentionally fire my rifle in the vicinity of someone more afraid than I am. I never wanted to kill anyone to begin with. Killing isn't who I am; killing is what I did to survive, and now I won't have to do it to please the mocking grin of the devil. I'll do it to get by, just like I used to. I'll never kill in the name of Nimbus again. Never.

All I ever wanted was to survive for Elise, for Sam, for Mom, and for Dad. If I had it my way, I wouldn't have been in the Guard. Then again, if I had it my way, no one would be forced into a position upon passing his or her re-entrance exam. They'd be allowed to do whatever they desired without the possibility of being hanged for disagreeing. Or, in other situations: separated twice.

No one would ever have to go through what I went through, or what that girl many years ago went through. Being separated once is enough. I'm lucky to still be alive. Heck, I wonder if that girl who was separated for a second time before me is still alive. I glance over at Sam.

He lifts his brows, questioning my gaze. "Yea?" he asks.

"What was the name of the girl who was separated twice and what'd she do again?"

"I don't know her name. Her brother was Wesley. Wesley Pearson, I think. And she gave Wesley a map."

Footsteps, rattling bags, and the clicking of an open canteen echo around us. I scratch the back of my head and glance back at Sam. "How long ago was that again?"

Sam's eyes wander around. "I think it was when I was eleven."

If she's alive, she's three years older than I am. If she's alive, we were out here at the same time for a while. *Maybe she was the one who stole my hook.*

I turn my focus to Elise. "Do you remember the night my hook was stolen?"

"Vaguely."

Sam intervenes. "What happened to it?"

"I'm not really sure," I mutter. "One night Elise and I went to bed in the shack, and when we woke up my hook was gone. The door was still locked. The windows weren't any more broken than before, but it was gone." I bite the inside of my cheek. "But there was something in its place."

"A rabbit," Elise says quietly.

"A rabbit?" asks Sam.

"And more firewood," I add.

"Why would someone steal your hook and give you food and warmth? That doesn't sound like anything I've heard about the outside."

"It never happened again," I say.

"I don't even get why it happened to begin with," replies Elise. "Why would someone steal a hook and provide us with a means to keep going?"

"Why didn't you tell us this before?" asks Sam. "Why didn't you ever tell Abby and I that there was some decency out here?"

Elise smirks. "Because it's uncommon. I didn't want to get your hopes up for a false reality."

Sam's hand fidgets. He burrows his pinky into his palm. "I don't think anything could have gotten my hopes up. . .I still don't," he trails off.

I don't answer. I simply put my hand on Sam's shoulder and pull him into my side. He shakes it off and feigns a smile.

"Hey Sean," comes Marcus from behind.

Taken aback by the sudden utterance from Marcus, I stop. Everyone stops beside me. The trees gently sway in the wind around us, yet they emit empty sound. Canteens go from constant jingling against shifting backpacks to a halt—not even the swishing of water crosses my eardrums. Everything goes silent.

"Yea?" I reply.

Marcus looks down. "It-it was here," he mumbles.

"What was here?"

Ella tightly purses her lips and halfway nods. Rosie does the same.

Collin?

Kyle steps ahead of Marcus. Marcus remains mum on the incident. "This is where we saw him," Kyle says softly. Pushing up his glasses, his eyes dart to the right.

"How do you know it was here if he's not here?" asks Elise.

"Marcus etched a reminder into the tree."

Kyle and Marcus step toward it.

I move closer to Kyle. There, carved into the tree is the symbol they mentioned before: the 'X' with three circles. Yet, something's off.

"Kyle," I mutter.

"What?" he answers.

"Why is the bark the bottom circle sits on removed?"

Kyle takes a step closer. "I-I have no idea," he stammers.

"Huh?" questions Marcus. "How is that possible?"

"There's someone else out here," grimaces Elise.

"But where?"

"I know as much as you do, but why else would someone remove the bark like that? They're trying to make a point."

"What kind of point, Elise?" asks Sam. "I don't get why someone would do any of this."

"We're not supposed to get it," I say. "We're never supposed to."

That's how it's always been and how it will always be. This route we've chosen isn't for clarity or answers; it's just another escape, just another attempt to side-step fate. I don't think we'll ever truly understand this world. It would take coming face-to-face with true suffering, true horror, to understand why everything is the way it is. Even then, I'm not sure we'd grasp the complete depth of our reality.

This world is too broken to give us what we want directly—that's why I've almost given up on expecting answers, and instead just been focusing on finding a way out.

"Let's just keep moving," I mutter underneath my breath as my train of thought nearly mutes the volume of my voice.

My words yield an immediate response from Marcus, who's still trying to fathom this enigma. "Why? We haven't even been outside the wall for a day and now we know someone's been here since we were last here less than a week ago! Why would we move forward when there's someone telling us to stop?"

Before I can answer, Marcus cuts me off.

"There are no words for this. There's no logic behind this. The only discernible takeaway from this nightmare is that we're not alone." He pauses and takes a breath. "We all knew this in some sense with what's been happening with Sam, but I think we have reason to believe that whoever is in his head, and Elise's, isn't the only person out here. I think she's just the beginning of what we'll find. I think those three circles are our map, and the bottom one has something to do with us." He rubs the back of his neck and looks directly into my eyes. "And if it is that, I don't know if I want to follow it."

"Why do you think that's a map?" I ask.

"What do we know of Nimbus?" he responds.

"What do you mean?"

"What were we taught about the world in which Nimbus exists? What were we taught about its surroundings, its shape?" he says passionately.

"Nothing," answers Sam.

"That's right. The only thing we know is that Nimbus is encircled by a wall. We know nothing about the shape of the outside, of the barrier surrounding it. But, what if we assume it's a circle? What if we forge ahead believing everything is a circle?"

"If we do that, what does that do for our path?" I ask.

"It gives us direction."

"How?"

Pointing at the marking on the tree, Marcus plants his index finger into what's left of the bottom circle. "Imagine Nimbus is at the bottom of this circle. I mean, nobody ever really went behind Nimbus. We went out the front doors and went straight." Moving his finger upward, he continues, "If Nimbus is truly at the bottom, all this open area here would be the forest and somewhere farther along would be the city. Then, beyond that would be the barrier." Sliding his hand further up the bottom circle, he stops at the edge before the bottom right line of the 'X' between this circle and the one in the upper right. "This would be the 'pop point.' Now, we can cross that, which could lead into a different place. Which, hypothetically, could be Halcyon."

"What about the other circle?"

"That could be it," he answers. "We don't know what each circle represents, but I feel like it has to mean something."

If this is a map, why would someone give it to us? Why would they kill just to show us everything around us?

"If the circles are different places, what's the 'X' in the middle?" asks Ella.

"Maybe it's another barrier or wall between Nimbus and Halcyon," replies Marcus. "Maybe it's just empty space, or a point of reference to show no circles overlap."

Sam coughs. "Or maybe it's marking something? You know, 'X marks the spot.'"

"But what's 'the spot' in this case?" questions Miles as he throws his bag into the dirt before taking a seat on it. "Maybe that's what Melanie told you. Maybe that's this Halcyon thing."

"Any of it could be that," answers Sam. "The only way we can know is by choosing a path and sticking to it."

"If this is a map," I add, albeit unsurely, "Do you think we should go straight for the center of the 'X' or explore more?"

"I think we should explore more," quickly answers Marcus. "For all we know, the middle could be the end."

"For all we know, each of those other circles could be the end. And if the bottom one is, indeed, Nimbus, maybe this shows that it already found its end."

"Then what do you suggest we do, Sean?" asks Kyle, almost angrily.

"I'm not suggesting anything," I retort.

"Let's just keep moving," states Marcus, showing a hint of his former optimism. "If we keep doing this thing where we sit and argue, we'll never get anywhere. Let's just keep moving and we'll end up where we end up."

"We know where we're going to end up," quietly mentions Sam to the point that I'm certain I'm the only one who heard him.

I grab his forearm. "What's that supposed to mean?"

"You know what it means, Sean. We're going to end up wherever this woman wants us to. It wouldn't matter if we chose a path. I mean, it's not like we even know where we are to begin with." He shakes off my hand and moves back toward the tree.

He's right. Sooner or later we'll end up where we're supposed to—where this woman is pulling Sam and Elise. It doesn't matter what we want; it never has. Maybe there isn't a way out. Maybe our only hope is to follow her voice. Regardless of how illogical or depressing it feels to chase the sound of someone I've never heard, nor seen, it's the only guiding force we have. And, sometimes, you have to listen to your head even if it's saying the opposite of what you want, or what you think you want.

The truth is, we don't know what we want. We claim we desire a world without walls, a world where we aren't forced into a fear-based system of survival. But, that's the thing—everything we've encountered has been rooted in evil. We're outside Nimbus now. There aren't any walls, Separation isn't a part of our choice, but we're still scared. There's really nothing that can stop fear when the unknown obscures your next step.

Sam

The night sky is endless. It spans across everything we see, everything we feel; it blankets our path to the point that no amount of flashlights can illuminate clarity within it. There isn't enough light in this world to guide us in the right direction, simply because there isn't a right direction.

Elongated beams highlight scurrying critters, decrepit bark, sporadic puddles, a body or two, but they don't show life. We're yet to see someone else out here; we're yet to talk to anyone who isn't a part of this group. The woman in my head doesn't count. She's not here. I don't know if she ever will be, and I'm not sure if I want her to be.

Even if our fate is to see her, I don't think I'll be ready. I don't even know how to have a positive outlook anymore. Every time I feel ready, something happens. Every time I feel strong enough, I'm pushed down until I'm as weak as the crumbling bark surrounding my every move. No amount of words or phrases thoughtfully created to perk up my enthusiasm work for me. My mind's fallen into a place of irreparable damage, and the only way to fix it is for everything to end—for these mind games to stop.

"Hey Sam," comes a muffled voice from behind me.

I turn around.

Rosie's light briefly shines into my eyes. I squint and look away. She apologizes and aims the beam toward the trees ahead of us. "I want to talk to you about something," she says, almost anxiously.

"What about?"

"About the girl who was separated twice before Sean."

"What about her?" I quickly reply.

Aimlessly shining her flashlight from side to side, Rosie grabs onto my wrist and pulls my ear toward her mouth. "I think she's still alive."

"Why do you say that?"

With her grip growing tighter, she whispers, "She was the one who shrieked—who kept me from going too far beyond the barrier."

I loosen her grasp. "Why do you think that?" I whisper back, unsure why such a conversation needs to remain quiet.

"I saw her."

"And you didn't say this before, why?"

"I don't like talking about it. I don't like everyone prying on my past. It was painful."

I mutter, "I know the feeling." In reality, I do, but maybe not as much as Rosie does. I didn't have much time outside Nimbus, but every day I was *home,* someone I had never met would come up to me and ask about my story. It became a challenge to recall the suffering, to willingly divulge what haunted me for months—heck, what still haunts me. It eventually got to a point where I would just brush them off and walk away.

A tree comes between Rosie and I. She steps right. I step left. She quickly glides back to my side, as Sean and Elise remain ahead of us while the others move slowly behind. "I think this woman might have something to do with the one in your head."

"What do you mean?" I ask. "The woman in my head is older than the girl who was separated twice first. She's only a few years older than Sean, whereas whoever I keep hearing is at least half MacMillan's age."

Still speaking in a hushed manner, Rosie turns toward me. "I'm not saying they're the same people. I'm saying there's something that ties them together."

"And what do you think that is?"

"I think that girl, Wesley's older sister, right?"

I nod.

"Well, I think she knows the woman in your head. I think she kept me alive to ensure we'd meet, to ensure we'd venture off toward this Halcyon place."

"We don't even know if Halcyon is a place," I smirk. "None of us even know what it means."

Rosie rolls her eyes. Another tree separates our intimacy.

"Sam, I'm just saying, don't be so sure that there aren't more outside forces guiding us to where we're supposed to be. Everything out here seems to work like clockwork." Her eyes analyze everything around us almost like the slow-moving hand of a clock. "The hands never falter; they move seamlessly as if every single move is calculated and pre-determined. Don't you ever feel that there's something out here you can't control?" Before I can so much as open my mouth, she grabs back onto my arm. "You know, besides what's in your head."

"I don't think any of us can control fate."

"If you could, would you want to?"

My eyes wander away from our conversation. I bite the inside of my cheek and stare into an area of the forest void of our lights. The moonlight escapes from behind a passing cloud and shines through an opening of trees—immediately illuminating someone, or something. I'm not sure what I'm seeing; I can't tell if it's just another corpse.

Rosie mumbles something. I can't hear anything. I keep staring into the distance.

My feet stop moving forward, and instead shift to my left. I start walking away from Rosie, from the group. I can't hear if someone is trying to stop me, but the more I walk, the clearer the sight becomes. Someone is standing there. A woman cloaked in a charcoal grey robe, her light brown hair falling out the sides of a hood, stands still against a tree. Her head is cocked forward making it impossible to see her face. I keep walking.

I can feel someone's hand brush against my back, but I don't turn around.

"Hello?" I say as I get closer to the woman. She doesn't flinch at the sound of my voice, nor does she move even the slightest.

Is she dead? I think.

The closer I get, the more the moonlight fades.

"Hello?" I say again.

A light breeze blows the woman's hair to the side.

"Hell—" I say as I'm cut off by the woman's left hand swiftly rising from her side.

"You're going the wrong way," she mutters.

"Where are we supposed to be going?"

"That way," she points toward me; her soft pale skin glistens in the light.

"Why that way?"

She becomes silent as her hands glide toward her hood. She grasps onto the ends of the fabric.

"Why that way?" I ask again.

With her head down, she drops the hood behind her.

"Sam!" comes Rosie's voice from behind me. "What are you doing over here?"

I glance back at Rosie. "I'm talking to this woman," I reply before gesturing back toward the now-empty space in front of me.

"Sam. . ." Elise says exhaustedly, as she and the others catch up to Rosie and me.

"I swear someone was just here."

"No one's there, Sam," answers Rosie.

"E-Elise?" I stutter. "Did you see anyone?"

She shakes her head side to side.

This can't be real. This can't be happening. I'm used to my deepest, darkest fears becoming my reality, but I'm not used to what I see in my head jumping into the present.

If someone has the ability to remove themselves from their own reality to plunge into another's, then the forces at work in this world are more unimaginable than we've ever thought. Bone-chilling, immobilizing nightmares are one thing, but supplanting yourself into someone else's physical spectrum is another. At least in the nightmares there's an escape. In the present, there isn't one.

My skin begins to crawl. As if the verity of what just happened is now hitting me—like my body, my mind, needed time to process what I saw.

"She was there," I say feebly, my lips quivering. "She was there."

"Who?" calmly asks Elise. "Was it *her*?"

I subtly nod. Not enough to concur, but enough to show my fear, to let her know that I'm afraid.

I don't want to be afraid. I don't want to fear a woman who's seemingly trying to help me, in some sense. I just want to keep moving and keep believing my reality is what I make it, not what someone else makes it.

"Sam?" Elise mutters my name again.

"I-I don't know," I stutter. "I just saw her hand and her hair. I never saw her face."

"Did you see that marking?" asks Marcus.

"No. I couldn't see her neck."

I press my palm into my forehead and turn around. The woman's still not there, and it appears as if she never was.

My mind can't sort out if it was real or not. I didn't touch the cloak, her hair, her hand, nothing. No aspect of what I saw was tangible; I just saw it. I just felt her presence. *But that doesn't mean it was real, that doesn't mean anything.* I turn my hand into a fist and bury my knuckles into the center of my forehead. The digging ceases the headache trying to flare, but it doesn't prevent my thoughts from going left and right, up and down, forward and backward.

"I-I can't. . ." I stammer as I turn around to face the crowd.

Marisa steps past Rosie and Elise. She pulls my hand down from my forehead and places her cold fingers onto it. "You can't what, Sam?" she asks. Her other hand grazes the nape of my neck.

My fear subsides. My anxiety lessens as her relaxing touch soothes the indiscernible images sprinting through my head.

As if nothing ever happened, I close my eyes and take a deep breath.

"You can't what?" she asks again.

"I don't remember," I whisper.

Marisa releases her hands.

As if no one else heard me, Sean steps forward. "What can't you remember?"

"That's an impossible question," I smirk.

"What about: what else do you remember? Did she say anything?"

"She just said we were going the wrong way."

"Which way did she tell you to go?" asks Marisa. Pulling out her canteen, she hands it to me.

I look at the metal; a half-inch thick blue line wraps around the small bottle. I rub my thumb against the color before taking a drink. I hand it back to her. Wiping my mouth, I point ahead.

"Sounds about right," replies Marisa casually.

"What do you mean?" questions Marcus, his brows furrowing as he gazes at Marisa.

"I just find it a bit odd that we stopped right here and now we're just going to essentially go right from where we were. Almost like this was the exact turn we were always supposed to make."

"Eventually it will get to a point where everything stops being odd and it just starts being normal," grins Elise.

"How long until then?" asks Marisa.

"I'm still not there," retorts Elise, almost sarcastically and bit irritably. Tucking her bangs behind her ears, she looks at me before turning around.

I move toward her.

"Should we go this way?" I ask.

Elise looks at me unsurely. Her lips mouth "yes," but her eyes mark uncertainty. Her muted glance makes me lose any belief in an answer she could give me. I aim my flashlight ahead; Elise remains mum.

I trudge forward.

My light glazes over blossoming flowers, some as white as the stars twinkling in the sky, others as red as the crimson of the scarf Abby used to wear. The dark, textured flowers wiggle with each gust, seemingly desiring to lift from their stems—to fly farther into the forest, away from the starving blackness.

I shine the beam forward again. No darkened hues of various petals linger in the distance; nothing that could remind me of Abby jumps into my vision. Instead, she just sits casually in my thoughts. My arms warm. My breathing slows.

I miss her. We pass a bush. I tear a flower from its stem, place my flashlight in my armpit, and start to rip the petals off one by one. Each rip sees the deep red of the petals fade into the darkness below me as if they never existed, as if the only thing that kept them relevant was my flashlight, or the clammy grip of my fingertips upon the stem.

The trees grow sparse. I yank another flower from its resting place, and repeat until there's a trail behind me—one I don't care to look back at. I continue this process until the trees are few and far between, until the final plant stem falls from my hand into the dirt.

My arms become cold.

Elise shines her flashlight across my path. "Sam," she mutters; a slight cough follows.

"Yea?"

"Look to your right."

I don't refuse; I don't debate her words. I listen. With the glossy residue of the plant clinging to my fingertips, I wipe my hands

on my pants and grab my light from underneath my shoulder. Slowly
shining it to my side, I watch as the ray of yellow latches itself onto
the olive-colored skin of someone perched against a tree. I aim the
beam up from the man's hands to his chest, and toward his face. I
can't make out any wounds at this distance, but unlike past bodies,
this one's chest is moving. Not fast, not normal, but slowly, sadly.
He's alive.

"Elise," I say softly.

She leans forward. "Yes?"

I glance behind me. Everyone's stopped. "He's breathing."

"What are you looking at?" asks Marcus, his questioning gaze
heightened by his crooked head and wandering eyes.

"Shine your lights over there," I say, pointing in the direction
of mine.

Everyone obliges.

Kyle's mouth drops. The second his light catches a glimpse of
the man, he shouts, "Ted!"

Marcus, Kyle, Rosie, Ella, and Miles rush toward Ted. Their
backpacks frantically rattle from side to side as they sprint toward
him. I glance over at Elise. Her eyes widen. Sean steps between us
and starts to run toward the others. Without a word, Elise and I do
the same.

We huff and puff our way toward the suffering man, our
backpacks slowing down our attempted sprints. I keep my eyes
focused ahead; the others approach Ted.

Immediately tossing his backpack to his side, Marcus slides
onto his knees, and puts his hand against Ted's chest.

Ted's dry, crusted lips part, but nothing comes out.

Kyle falls onto his knees to the left of Ted. He leans in close.

The others surround him—each person angrily disconnecting
themselves from their backpacks only to stumble onto their knees in
front of Ted.

Marcus's hand goes back and forth against Ted's chest. With
wide, unblinking eyes, Marcus asks, "What happened?"

With his mouth still agape, Ted's cracked lips slowly purse
together. He closes his eyes and tilts his head back, revealing the
same mark we've seen in the past: the three circles with the 'X.'

The second he lifts his head back toward the crumbling bark,
the cuts open. Kyle quickly presses his hands into Ted's neck to stop

the limited blood from spilling any further. Marisa pulls gauze from her bag and hands it to Kyle.

Aghast, Marcus's words grow urgent. "Ted, what happened? Tell us anything you can. Anything. Quickly."

His face growing pale, Ted tries to speak. "They took us," he mutters weakly. He coughs.

"Who?" begs Kyle, the blood soaking through the rags and onto his hands.

Ted doesn't answer. He coughs again.

"He's dying," exclaims Marisa. "We'd be lucky to get even a few more words out of him."

Losing color, Ted closes his eyes. "Dark room," he says quietly. "Three."

"Three what?" Marcus cries. "Three what?"

"Circles," Ted answers breathlessly. "Bottom. . .go-gone," he stutters.

Marcus sobs. "Please, Ted, don't die. Don't die like Collin."

Suddenly, Marcus's hand stops moving.

The forest goes silent. Not so much as the buzzing of insects exists, or even the muffled dragging of leaves against the dirt. The air around us feels dead; even the moonlight shies away from us. Flashlights roll back and forth in the dirt. No one speaks.

He's dead. There's nothing we can do. The only hope we have is to piece together the few things he was able to say.

I grab Elise's hand and pull her away from the others. "Do you think the dark room was the dungeon?" I quietly ask.

She shakes her head. "It can't be. He mentioned there were three circles in that room. There wasn't any mention of those in the city."

"Then where do you think he was?"

She shrugs her shoulders. "I know as much as you do, Sam. I'm more curious about the bottom circle being gone just like it was on the tree."

I look over at Ted. His dry eyes stare into the sky while the marking on his neck continues to bleed. Kyle's hand no longer covers the wound, so the blood seeps into Ted's shirt. The others look away, but I can't. With my focus still on Ted, I speak, "If the circles are a map, it could mean Nimbus is dead." The blood from the 'X' in Ted's neck spills over the bottom circle—nearly covering up its entirety. Still looking away from Elise, I say, "Marcus mentioned that if the marking was a map, Nimbus could be at the bottom. MacMillan is dead, so maybe it was etched off on the tree, and was blacked out on what Ted saw, to indicate that it no longer exists."

Elise glances at Marcus—he catches her stare and moves toward us.

Slowly dragging the tip of his index finger against his lips, Marcus asks, "Do you two know what Ted meant by 'they?'"

I release a slight exhale and shake my head. "It could mean anything."

"What about you, Elise?"

"Unfortunately not. I doubt it's the Lurkers."

His eyes full of uncertainty, Marcus looks back at Ted. "Who would do this? Who would kill our friends and then place their dying bodies on our path? It doesn't make any sense!"

"Do you think it's a warning?" adds Sean, as he steps into our small, misshapen circle.

"Warning us about what?"

"About what lies ahead."

A light pulse trickles across my forehead. I thrust my knuckles into it. "Why would they use people from our past to show us what lies ahead? Wouldn't this be the opposite of that?" I close my eyes and look down as the pulsing intensifies. "It more so feels like they're trying to help us."

"How is this helping us?" exclaims Kyle. "If anything, it's killing us quicker."

The pulsing beats faster and faster. It feels like my heart is in my head, like every word I say isn't supposed to be said. *I think someone's trying to show me something.* I fall to my knees. My eyes remain closed.

***

"You're the only one who understands, Sam."

I keep my eyes closed. I don't want to see this dream. I don't want to see this woman; all I want is to be guided.

"Open your eyes, Sam. I'm right here. I just want to help," says the woman again. I can feel a chill of air against the nape of my neck.

I don't speak.

The space around me tightens. "Those who hide away in darkness can't grasp the reality of this world. You saw what happened to those loonies MacMillan called his 'Lurkers.'"

I take a breath. My eyes remain closed. I breathe in. I breathe out.

"If you keep hiding from me, you won't end up where you're supposed to."

A cold hand falls upon my shoulder. Then another. The air tightens further. It feels like the walls of this dream are closing in.

"Open your eyes and see your path. If you won't listen to me here, you'll listen to me there."

***

The atmosphere loosens its grip on me. I exhale loudly as if I had been awakened from a nightmare. I open my eyes.

"What did she say?" immediately asks Elise. With her hands on her knees, she looks at me nervously. "What did she say?" she asks again.

"Sh-she said not to hide from her. . .and that if I ignore her in my head, I won't be able to ignore her there."

"Why did you ignore her?"

"I didn't want to trip up. I wanted to force her hand, to try and get her to say something without me asking for it. I want to know if she's really trying to help."

A voice comes from behind the four of us. It's Rosie's. "What do you think she meant by 'there?'"

If you don't listen to me here, you'll listen to me there.

I bite the inside of my lip. "Halcyon?"

"That's the only thing I could think of, too," replies Elise. Tucking her hands against her sides, and under her arms, she looks at the ground. "I don't think there's a way away from this. We won't know this woman's desires until we meet her."

"Once again, let's just keep moving," sighs Marcus, a clear tinge of sadness in his voice. "It's the only thing we can do."

7 May 2192

Elise

It's taken a few days to get here, but there it is. There's the city. My skin crawls. My stomach aches. Yet, my head doesn't dive into the darkness; it remains calm, devoid of the pain formerly associated with that place.

I step past a rotting body face down in the mud. The scent of the corpse forces us to walk faster.

I look to our left once more.

The city looks emptier than before; it seems lonesome—not fearsome. The skyscrapers hide in the clouds while no visible body lurks in the streets. As we pass the outskirts, the eerie silence is almost more piercing than the sight of a decaying corpse.

This area has never felt like this. The unnerving worry that we've all associated with it is practically gone.

"Do you think *they* still exist?" asks Miles from behind Sean and I. "You know, the Lurkers."

"I don't think the group does," replies Sean. "I'm sure several of them are still alive, but they're probably in hiding."

"You don't think someone else took over after Arthur's death?"

"Didn't you see the way they ran away when Elise killed him?" laughs Ella. "They're cowards. They only listened to Arthur because they were too afraid to do anything themselves."

"And with MacMillan dead, too, there's no one in control of them," adds Sam. "They're finally just like we were when we were sent out: alone and afraid."

"Or just dead," I say. "Remember the amount we saw on our return to Nimbus? They were everywhere."

Echoing agreement, Rosie speaks from beside Sam, "I'm glad they're probably gone, but I'm sure we have bigger things to worry about now."

"If we keep seeing those we never saw after the fire, we're in for something far worse than the Lurkers," says Marcus. "Whoever's behind this is intentionally trying to scare us. They're filling us with the fear that we could end up like our friends if we don't stay on track."

"And you think that's the same person I keep hearing in my head?" questions Sam.

"I don't see why it wouldn't be."

"I guess she just hasn't sounded menacing."

"You don't have to sound menacing to be hiding your true self," I jibe. "I've met plenty of people who seemed nice, but in the end were just playing me or Sean to get what we had."

"So, you think this is the work of one person? I mean, Collin didn't speak, and Ted never mentioned a singular person. I just don't think one person can do all this. Plus, the woman said *they* know about Elise and me."

"She could be in charge, sort of like MacMillan," mutters Rosie. "I mean, it only takes one to make a difference."

The darkened grey clouds float above. A small crack of thunder echoes in the distance. I glance back at the city, back at the place I promised Marcus we'd return to one day. "She's right. It only takes one to cause pain, but one is always easier to bring down."

"Until you realize the one you've killed wasn't the only person you needed to worry about," says Sean.

"He's right," replies Miles. "It's never just one out here."

Quiet murmurs fill the air behind me. The conversation continues, but I have no desire to further it. I keep walking forward, but I can't stop peering over at the city. If it's truly empty, maybe we could start rebuilding now, but then again, this woman might take Sam when we least expect it just like Arthur did. She's trying to guide him, which by association guides us. I just wish we knew what she wanted.

Her words are innocuous. The visions Sam's fallen into aren't filled with flames. Everything that's happened almost seems better, but *how? How can someone who's in our heads make us feel comfortable?* That baffles me.

If I've learned one thing about being outside Nimbus it's that you can't trust anyone, and sometimes that includes yourself. So, if she's allowed to be present in our minds, *who's to say she's trustworthy?* I mean, Arthur wasn't.

Yet we keep moving in the direction she guided us because there's nothing that can be said to change our course. We're inevitably going to head toward the person Melanie told us to stay away from simply because we have no other options. If we stand still, she'll forge her way further into Sam's head until he's as weak as he was when I found him in the dungeons. And the second he gets back to that state, he'll give up.

The clouds open up. I pull my hood over my head.

I look over toward the city once more. There's no fire, no cries, no horror, yet everything I said when we left feels like a lie. I thought we could rebuild there. I figured that could be our new home, but just like Nimbus, I don't want to live in a place that tried to kill me.

Sean pulls his hood up beside me. A few of the others stop to put on raincoats or sweatshirts to block the rain. We keep walking.

"Do you feel like we could ever actually go back there?" I ask.

A quick "no" is hurled in my direction from behind me. Hunched slightly forward, Sam uses his backpack to shield the light rain.

"Yea?"

"Just walking past it gives me no desire to go back," mutters Sam. "There has to be something better."

Sean tilts his gaze toward the skyscrapers. "And what if there's not?"

"Then we'll go back."

"There will be. The world is too big to just be what we've seen," I say.

"We can only hope. We didn't learn anything about the outside world. School made it seem like Nimbus was the center of the universe. Heck, it made it sound like Nimbus was the universe," laughs Sam. "Who'd believe that?"

"You guys weren't taught anything about the world beyond the barrier?" asks Sean sharply. Stopping in his tracks, he turns toward Sam. "Nothing at all?"

Caught off guard, Sam cocks his head to one side and stares at Sean. "Nothing," he mumbles.

"I-I don't believe it," stutters Sean. "I know they were horrible at teaching us anything, but this proves that each year they slowed the curriculum. They essentially were dumbing kids down year after year."

"What do you mean?" I ask. "Were you taught about other areas? I wasn't either." I push my jaw out slightly. "You've never made it sound like you knew anything about any other place besides Nimbus."

"I wasn't exactly, but there was one professor who seemed like she wanted to tell us more than she was allowed to. She was older. She was a founder."

"Who?"

"Brooke Hawkins."

"She died the year before I took her history class."

"Guess how," says Sean, his eyes bulging.

"MacMillan had her killed? Wasn't she in her nineties already?" asks Sam.

He nods.

"Is it because of something she told you guys?"

The rain picks up.

Sean pulls his hood further over his head and puts his arms around Sam and I. "Yea," he quietly mutters. "I'm surprised MacMillan didn't have us all executed just for hearing what she had to say."

"What was it?" I ask.

"What's going on over there?" intrudes Marcus. Poking his head in between Sean and I, he pushes out his chin. "Why are you huddled?"

Sean releases his grip. "There's something everyone should know."

We all circle around Sean.

He takes a breath; the rain continues to increase its weight. With his hood held outstretched beyond his head, he speaks. "In 2165, MacMillan refused someone's re-entry. A woman who had passed her exam."

"Who?" asks Rosie as she pulls her bangs underneath her raincoat.

"We weren't told her name."

"What else were you told?" asks Miles.

"That she was sent away to create something new."

"What do you mean? If she was sent away with a chip in her head, wouldn't she be dead?"

"She could be, or maybe they deactivated it. If they wanted something new, they probably wouldn't just kill her off."

None of this feels right. When MacMillan was younger, he preferred to keep the strongest within Nimbus rather than send them away. If he purposefully sent someone else back out without giving them a chance within the confines of the wall, it might not have been his choice.

I shake my head before looking into the rain. Droplets break upon my forehead. I turn back toward the group. With squinted eyes and a furled lip, Marcus slowly glances up at me. Our eyes sync—it feels like we're thinking the same thing. He nods.

"Sean," I muster quietly, almost muted by the storm.

He looks over at me.

"Do you think MacMillan was governed by someone else?"

His cheeks quiver. He looks like he never considered that to be a possibility, like the thought of it has caused him to refute everything he's learned about our world. His blinks become rapid.

I put my hand on his shoulder. "Are you okay?"

"I-I've never thought of that." He shakes his head. "It would make sense. It would explain why he didn't separate a lot of people twice. It would explain why he became more violent as he grew older, as if he knew being near death would allow him to do whatever he wanted."

"If any of this is true, where would that 'higher power' be?" asks Ella before she steps out from the circle and starts to look around the desolate area—like she's waiting for an answer.

I walk toward her. Everyone else follows. "Maybe that's who we're going toward," I say.

"Or maybe that person is the woman Sean said was sent back out twenty-seven years ago."

Gliding toward us, Derrick takes off his hat and squeezes out the rainwater before putting it back on almost like he has no idea it'll just happen again. "If MacMillan refused someone's re-entry, I don't think he would also allow that person to rule him," he says with a voice as deep as a lake—almost unfitting to his clean-shaven, balding appearance.

Juan and Ralph nod beside him. "MacMillan was a prick," grins Ralph. "It would be tough to rule that man unless you had something you could hold over his head."

"That's just it," says Ella. "If someone else was more powerful than him, they'd know something about him. Something he wouldn't want everyone to know. That's why it could be that woman."

"But that's also why it couldn't be her," adds Sam. "Like Derrick said, MacMillan wouldn't want someone else to rule over him. He would have had this woman killed if he could, but he clearly couldn't, or wouldn't. So, it's almost like someone else had him under his or her control. Maybe someone wanted him to send her away to create something else, to create a new society." Sam takes a short breath. "It seems like MacMillan didn't have a choice. If he did, we wouldn't know anything about this woman. She'd just be another failure in the eyes of Nimbus."

"He's right," I say. "I think this woman is just the second piece. MacMillan was the first. We have to find her. We have to know what's going on."

"And what if we can't? What if the woman in your head, in Sam's head, is someone else?" asks Sean.

"We just have to take that chance. We've been guided this far by one person, and we're still alive. Our best bet is to keep moving and hope everything will sort itself out."

Marcus scoffs. "Sometimes I feel like you don't understand this world. Nothing ever sorts itself out. At least not happily."

I grin sarcastically. "And that's why it's so much fun!"

Sam rolls his eyes. "Let's find shelter. We've been in this rain so long that it's made you guys weird."

Everyone laughs. The rain refuses to cease. Readjusting our bags, we turn back toward the open field ahead of us.

With the city fading into the distance behind us, I keep my head up. I just hope what's ahead is better, that where we're going isn't going to be our demise—even if each stride makes it seem that way.

I smile. Sean grabs my hand. A slight inkling of pain runs across my forehead, but I don't think about it. I squeeze his hand tighter and keep moving.

8 May 2192

Sam

The barrier is within reach. Rosie's been on edge since she first saw the field—since she recognized the area she had been trying to forget.

While the 'pop point' isn't physical, the area is more open than that of the forest. The trees discontinued a while back, and all that lies in front of us is open field. There are no houses, no streets, and no signs of life in this barren landscape. There's just a mixture of grass and dirt.

Rosie steps closer to me. "I-I don't see anyone," she mumbles.

I smile. "That probably means we're on the right path."

"You don't think we'll see her, do you?" she asks quietly while fidgeting her fingers.

"If she was guiding you like you told me, then no. She has no reason to stop us now." *I still don't know who she is*, I think.

Rosie perks up. She half smiles and walks over toward Ella.

For all we know, there are two separate women leading us away from Nimbus. One's the lady in my head. The other could potentially be Wesley's older sister. Heck, they could be the same person. We don't know. Everything is a mess, and the uncertainty is killing me. I just want to know we're safe, that the direction we're heading will provide us with some answers rather than end our journey.

I kick a pebble; it bounces along the uneven terrain until it disappears into some weeds.

"Sam," says Elise from behind me.

I turn around. "Yea?"

"How's your head?"

I stop. "What do you mean?"

"You haven't seen this woman since we got out here, have you?" she asks, as she itches her scalp.

"Nope. I haven't seen or heard anything."

"Good. We must be going in the right direction then. I have-haven't hear-heard anything," she stutters. Falling to her knees, Elise thrusts her palms into her forehead.

"What's happening?" shouts Sean frantically. "Are you okay?"

"My head," exclaims Elise. "It feels like it's going to explode."

Marisa hustles toward us.

I fall to my knees beside Elise. I feel a slight trickle of pain scatter across the top of my head, but I don't think anything of it.

Our eyes lock. Hers are wide; tears are beginning to fall. My head starts to ache more. I can feel my eyes begin to water. I can't blink. *Something is happening.*

Elise falls onto her side. Her eyes remain open, but she doesn't move.

I try to move closer to her, but my limbs tighten.

I fall beside her. I can see her quivering cheeks. I can feel mine waver, but I can't move. *This isn't good.*

***

The lights flicker on. The path glistens in front of us. Elise turns her head toward me.

"Sam, what's going on?"

"I think we're going to meet her."

"Who?"

"Me," comes the woman's voice.

"What's your name?" I ask.

"Why don't you come have a seat beside me?" she responds.

"Where are you?"

"Walk to the end. You'll see me."

I glance over at Elise. Her face is flushed. Her eyes stricken with fear. "I thought I wasn't supposed to be here," she mutters.

"You weren't then. It's okay now," answers the woman. "Come, you two."

Elise grabs my hand. We walk past the benches. Each have an illegible word engraved into the back. I step closer, but the words are blurred out, as if we're not supposed to see them—at least not yet.

With each step, the lights behind us fade away. The sea of black consumes everything we've passed as we near the end of the row. Yet, no one sits at the end. The woman isn't here. She's nowhere to be seen.

"I don't see you," I say.

"Turn around," she whispers.

We release our grip on each other and turn around. The void has gone from pitch black to being highlighted by silhouettes of light. Above us, a man stands atop a platform dressed in a light blue robe. He looks down. The lights go out.

A new beam of light flickers on directly in front of us. A woman stands upon a small circular stage with her back facing us. Clad in a dark grey robe complete with a hood above her head—just like the one I saw on the woman in the forest—she rests her right palm atop an all-white cane. There's an object attached to the top of it, but I can't tell what it is. It looks like a bird.

"Welcome," the woman speaks. "My name is Caroline and this is Halcyon."

Suddenly lights populate in all corners of the once-dark space. A crowd erupts in applause. Screams, laughter, lights, deafening thuds fill the arena around us.

I squeeze tighter onto Elise's hand.

***

Our hands are entwined. Everyone is around us. We can move.

"Caroline," I silently moan.

"Caroline," repeats Elise.

"Who's Caroline?" asks Marcus.

"The leader of Halcyon," I answer.

"You mean you guys met her together?" questions Kyle nervously.

We nod simultaneously.

I roll up into a seated position.

Elise does the same. The second she gets upright, she clenches her jaw. Her fingers begin to twitch against her lap. She tilts her head down.

Sean puts his hand around her shoulders. "Are you okay?" he quietly asks.

"Sh-she welcomed us to a place that looked like a circus," sobs Elise. "She welcomed us to my nightmares."

Sean

Elise hasn't been herself for an hour or so now. She's agitated, disturbed, angry. I wish she didn't see what she saw. I wish it were me who fell into those dreams with Sam instead of her. I know the horrors they see would suffocate my mind and make me just as weary as them, but at least it would be me. I'd always rather have the pain fall upon my shoulders because I hate seeing her suffer. I hate seeing anyone I care about in pain.

Every time something happens, I feel like turning around, but we can't. The moment we do, this woman will haunt our path until we're forced in her direction. We're in a pickle. Each direction is pain, but only forward gives us answers.

We'll just have to endure, I think. *It's what we're used to doing anyways.*

"It's around here somewhere," echoes Rosie's voice from ahead. She's been guiding us since Sam and Elise collapsed. Since she's the only one who's been out this far, she's the only one who can let us know when we've truly crossed out of Nimbus's territory.

"Do you think we might have passed it already?" asks Miles.

"Could be. There hasn't been an ache. . .or a shriek," mutters Rosie.

With nothing but open field in front of us, there's a possibility we passed the barrier miles ago. I turn back toward Elise. She remains close to Sam. Both their stares are fixated on the ground. Elise's cheeks are red; she's vulnerable. I can't take this. I turn back to face the empty reality ahead of us.

"Rosie," I say.

"Yea?"

"What do you remember about the 'pop point' as you neared it?"

"Aside from the pain and the shriek?"

"Yea, could you see anything in the distance?"

"Not really. There was just more field. It seemed endless."

"So, you're saying there aren't any physical clues to let us know if we've left the area occupied by Nimbus?" asks Marcus.

"Not that I can recall. Like I've said before, I tried to forget that day," answers Rosie. "It sucked."

"I think I found a clue," shudders Kyle. "L-look over there." With his arm outstretched, Kyle points just ahead and to the right.

I walk over toward him. There, in the grass, lies a woman. Her face is red and covered in scratches. Her eyes are closed. The veins in her forehead are protruding. I step closer to the woman.

"Is she alive?" silently asks Kyle. Awestruck in place, he remains where he spotted the woman.

I take another step toward her. Her chest isn't moving. I get closer. Covered in blood, her neck is marred by the same marking we saw on Ted. The blood's dry and there's no sign that this woman is alive. I kneel beside her.

"Well, is she?" questions Marcus.

"I don't think so," I answer.

"Then, let's keep moving," states Rosie.

Everyone turns their attention back to Rosie as she continues the trek through the field. Yet, I can't help but feel this woman's here for a reason. She has the same mark we've seen and heard about several times already; she's conveniently on our path rather than being somewhere else. It all just feels like there's more to it.

The wind pushes through. The grass moves beside me like an invisible hand is trying to pull it from its roots.

I stand up.

"Marcus," I say.

He spins back to face me. His eyes widen, his limbs seemingly lock in place as his jaw falls open. "S-S-S," he stutters.

The wind stops. A rapid, loud breath consumes the air around me. I look down.

The woman is sitting up.

I don't move. I don't run. My legs lock. I can't tell if I'm afraid.

She tries to speak, but the words don't come. Her throat just releases dry air.

"S-S-S" slurs Marcus once more.

I don't respond to his incoherencies. I turn back toward the woman. She looks up at me. "Are you okay?" I quietly ask.

She opens her mouth once more—the slight parting of her cracked lips pierces my eardrums, while the muted attempts to speak that follow draw me back to my knees. I put my hand on her shoulder.

She turns her head to face Marcus. Her eyes well up.

Marcus remains locked in place, but his mouth is closed, and his eyes are watering.

"It's Marie," cries Ella from behind him. "It's Marie."

Marie?

Those from the library rush toward me, except Marcus. He's frozen to the spot. Elise and Sam stand behind him, both without a visible care to come close.

I walk over toward them.

"Marcus," I softly say.

He doesn't reply.

I wrap my arm around his shoulder and try to guide him toward Marie, but he doesn't budge. I'm not sure what's going on. I've felt fear; I've seen fear, but this is something else. Marcus is almost paralyzed with it. And if it's not fear, I don't know what it is. With all these bodies from the library—from Collin to Ted to Marie—he has to fear for his own life. Someone's going after everyone he knew, everyone he cared for. It has to be eating him.

"Marcus," I say again.

No response.

I walk toward everyone huddled around Marie. She's still unable to speak, but she's trying. She's showing no signs of the breathless body we all saw a few minutes ago. She seems more alive than Ted.

"Ella," I whisper.

Tilting her head back toward me, her eyes respond, "Yea?"

"Something's wrong with Marcus. I can't get him to move or speak."

Ella looks over at him. Gently grazing Marie's shoulder, she gets up and walks to Marcus.

I remain with everyone else. Marisa stands between Marcus and Marie. Undecided on who to help, she remains still—not frozen, but uncertain. I nod for her to come to Marie. She heads toward us.

"When did you get those wounds?" she asks Marie before kneeling between Kyle and Miles.

Marie's hands tremble as they move toward her neck. She grazes the wound, softly pinching the skin around the unevenly cut marking. Slowly moving her hand away from the dry blood, she holds up two fingers.

"Two days ago?" asks Marisa.

Marie shakes her head, "No."

"Two hours ago?"

Marie nods.

"How is that possible?" asks Miles angrily. "Wouldn't we have seen someone bring her here? Wouldn't we have seen something?"

Marie shakes her head side to side once more. She points to herself while trying to mouth her disagreement. "I. . ." she groans silently, airy.

"You what?" asks Marisa.

Marie closes her eyes and tries to breathe. Each deep breath sounds congested, like something is preventing her from speaking volubly.

Moving her hands back toward her neck, she faintly, almost inaudibly says, "I. . .di-did. . .th. . . this."

Marisa leans in. "You carved that into your own neck? Why?"

Pointing to her hand, Marie moves her pointer finger across her palm.

"Paper!" shouts Kyle. "Does anyone have any paper and a pen or something?"

Suddenly engaged and aware of what's going on, Sam raises his hand and comes rushing toward us. Setting his bag beside him, he pulls out a small notepad and hands it to Marie along with a pencil.

Eagerly grabbing the materials, Marie starts to write.

I look around. Ella's gotten Marcus to sit. Elise is seated beside him. They both look horrified. We've all been a part of this nightmare for too long, but something's snapped in them, something's trying to break them harder than Arthur ever could.

I wish I could help, but if I've learned one thing out here, it's that words don't always guarantee life. The only way to help someone who's struggling is to be there, to do anything and everything they require of you.

Itching my neck, I sigh and turn back to face Marie. With the pad held up, it reads:

They made me. They controlled me.

"Who are they, and how did they make you?" asks Rosie.

The light sound of her scrawls echo in the wind. She holds up the pad again while shaking her head.

I don't know. Only heard voices. Only saw darkness and circles on wall.

Pulling the paper close, she starts to write again. This time, the words don't come as quickly. She looks into the sky and takes a breath before showing us what she's written.

They used the chips. They took over my mind. They sent me outside and I wandered here. Two hours ago, they said to start cutting. I couldn't stop. I couldn't fight it.

Tears start to stream down Marie's reddened and lacerated face. Rosie wraps her arms around her. Marie embraces her.

I dig my thumb and index finger into my forehead. *Who are these people? Why would they force someone to do this?* There has to be a reason. There has to be something they want us to know, or to see.

Escaping my thoughts, I clench my jaw and look at Marie. "Was the bottom circle blacked out?"

Marie nods.

"When did they take you and where did they take you?" asks Miles.

Letting go of Rosie, Marie quickly holds up the paper again.

Fire. Not completely sure. Was injected. Woke up.

"Were there others with you?" asks Rosie.

Collin, Ted, and I.

I sigh. "That means she's the last one," I say aloud. "If they only took three of them, she's the last one. Halcyon must be close."

"Why do you say that?" sniffles Rosie.

"It just feels like the three of them were taken for a reason. That they were placed where they were placed to almost guide us."

Marie taps angrily at the pad. I look over.

It reads:

Halcyon?

"You mean, that's not where you came from?" I ask.

She shakes her head.

"You don't know where you were though, right?"

She tilts her head a bit to the side and shrugs her shoulders.

"Then how do you know it wasn't Halcyon?"

Holding up her finger, she motions for us to wait. As she starts writing, her fingers lightly convulse. She looks uneasy, scared to even write what she's thinking.

In the room, the three circles were all lit up when we were placed there. It took a few days before the bottom one went dark. The men who took us kept mentioning the initials, "DZ."

"What else?" I ask.

She scribbles away.

I think we were somewhere dealing with those initials. They never mentioned Halcyon, or Nimbus, or anything. They just kept saying "DZ."

I exhale loudly and walk away. I can't think straight; I can't focus. My brain feels like it's going to explode.

There are too many things going on, too many directions we could go. We finally learned Halcyon is a place, and now it feels like there's more to this world besides another society. I don't know what 'DZ' stands for. It could be a place, a person, anything. We're on one uneven path already; it almost feels wrong to venture down another, or to split up and find out where each one leads.

At this point, I just want to keep moving forward. I don't want to get caught up in any more mystery or misery. I just want to find Caroline.

I hear a slight thud behind me. An audible gust of wind pushes through, finally returning an earthly sound to this field.

"Sean," comes Rosie's voice from behind me.

I turn around to look at her, but I don't reply.

With tears in her eyes, she softly speaks, "Marie said not to try and find the 'DZ' because they'll find us. Th-then she just f-fell over, and stopped breathing."

"What?" I mutter.

"She's dead."

"How is that possible? She seemed fine compared to Ted."

Rosie wipes her cheeks. "I don't know. Whoever had control of her chip must have had more power than MacMillan ever had. It was instant."

I quickly glance toward Marie. Wide-eyed and motionless on her side, she stares into the emptiness, paper still in hand.

I gnaw at my bottom lip and look into the vast field ahead of us. "There's something going on in this world that's bigger than Nimbus and Halcyon."

She doesn't respond. Silence engulfs the atmosphere. The wind has returned to its quiet inexistence; the air feels stagnant. It feels like time has stopped and the only thing that can push us forward is our will, but even that is fading. It nearly died the moment we saw Marie.

Scratching the scruff on my neck, I take a deep breath. I inhale. I exhale. I try to relax.

Yet, the split second of clarity I find is trounced by the weakened voice of Marcus. "Whatever's out there, it's trying to kill us one by one."

I turn to face him. Still sitting in the dirt with his eyes glued to the ground, he doesn't budge. "But it won't kill us," I say.

"It will and there's nothing we can do about it."

"Then why continue? Why move on if you think this is just the end?"

Marcus glares at me, crudely. "Because we're going to die anyways. Might as well do it somewhere new."

His words don't dignify a response. He's not himself.

I ignore him and turn to face the direction we were heading before finding Marie.

"D. . .Z," I mutter to myself. "D. . .Z."

I feel a brush of wind against my shoulders followed by the gentle touch of fingernails. "They don't want to be found," whispers Elise. "We have to find Caroline. She's the only one who can help us, who can tell us what 'DZ' means."

I turn to face her. Her eyes and cheeks are the same shade of red. She wipes her nose.

"Do you even want to know?"

She lightly shakes her head and looks down. "I don't, but we have to. If we don't figure out what's going on, Marcus will be right. . .and. . .and I don't want to die in this miserable world." She wipes her cheeks. "I just want to feel safe for once in my damn life."

I wrap my arms around her.

10 May 2192

Elise

The terrain has changed. There are more hills, grass, plants, trees; there has even been a lake—not a pond—a lake. Those didn't exist in Nimbus, nor were there any on the outside. Streams were all we had. Now, we're clear of that bare and rigid landscape. We're past the 'pop point.' We're beyond Nimbus. We have to be.

And we're still alive.

Where we are feels like a dream. Birds cheerfully sing in the sky, the sun shines brightly, the wind is barely noticeable—everything feels surreal. It almost seems like this locale is happy. Nimbus was always dark grey and eerie where not a second of serenity seemed to exist. It's as if we've crossed from the dark to the light, like Halcyon will be a peaceful oasis compared to the nightmare we've moved away from.

The only problems are, we don't know where this place is and I don't know if I want to go anymore. I still can't get over what I saw, what I felt. Caroline introduced us to the nightmares that have been plaguing me for years. It's almost like I was meant to see that, that only I was allowed to have a glimpse into Halcyon. Yet, I wasn't supposed to know what I was seeing; I was just supposed to be afraid. And now, I almost have to move on like those visions didn't haunt me. I'm supposed to act like everything will be okay the second we meet her.

I want to believe that, but I don't know if I can. Trusting the one person who's been scarring me for years is like befriending Arthur. *Why believe someone can be kind when all they've shown me is misery?*

Trust isn't something I can give out for free. At this point in my life, it has to be earned—you have to prove your value to me. It doesn't matter what you've done, who you've helped, or who you've saved; if you haven't done anything to benefit me, I can't trust you.

It's selfish. It's unfair. But, so is life. There are no second chances out here, so if I want to make it to Halcyon, I have to move forward like this is it, like this could be the end of everything.

I have to push past what I saw, what's eating every fiber of my being, and stay alive. But it's hard. I saw Halcyon when we were still separated from Nimbus. I felt horror that I couldn't physically touch within the confines of the world I knew. And, I don't think that will just fade away. It can't.

And the worst part of all of this is that it's distancing me from everyone, especially from Sean. We're all falling apart, but only Sam and I are seeing fragments of a new reality; only we have some idea of what's coming. But, at the same time, we don't—and this lack of clarity makes me feel isolated. It makes me feel different, but for all the wrong reasons. It scares me. It really scares me.

"Where do you think we are?" asks Miles.

I turn to face him, but the instant I do, the sun shines into my eyes causing my face to contort weirdly. I throw my arm up and turn away.

Sean laughs.

"It's bright," I grin awkwardly.

"Who cares where we are?" retorts Marcus. "We'll all be dead soon anyways."

Like the sun, I glare at him.

Yet, he doesn't care. His self-deprecating sarcasm is unlike him. It's ill-fitting to the one man whom we all relied on to pick us up after the death of our families. Even when he was weak in the forest, he showed strength when it came to putting his life on the line in Nimbus. But now, something's changed that. Something's grabbed ahold of his mind and is continually pushing it further and further into the mud. I wish I could help, but if I know one thing, it's that when you're lost, it's easier to give up. It doesn't matter who's trying to help; if you're struggling, sometimes the only wake-up call is a sobering reality.

"You can't keep being like this, Marcus," asserts Ella. "I'm from the library, too, so are Rosie, Kyle, and Miles. Do you think we're just assuming death is around the corner for us?"

Marcus furrows his brows and huffs, but doesn't say anything.

"I'll take that as a yes."

"He's in shock," adds Marisa. "He has a right to be angry and confused. What we may find next could fix it. It could counterbalance his state of mind."

"What do you mean?" I ask.

"He's seen death too many times lately—more than his mind wants—so if he were to be in a situation of calm, happiness, or ecstasy, he might come out of it."

"And where are we going to find that?" laughs Marcus. "That doesn't exist out here."

"Do you not see where we are?" quips Sam. "Look around you, Marcus. There isn't a city trying to fall onto you, there aren't vagrants trying to poison you, there isn't a madman aiming a gun at your head." Stressing each syllable, Sam throws his hands into the sky. "Look at this! This is as free as it's going to get. Enjoy it before we're back in hell."

"Who says we're going back to hell?" questions Miles unsurely.

I look ahead. Not toward anyone, not toward the path, just into the sky. I open my mouth, but only air slides past my lips. I try again; it's airy. "Everyone."

"I didn't say that," snaps Miles. "I wouldn't have come if I firmly believed death was my only exit from Nimbus."

"We could be wrong," answers Sam. "We could be way off base, but doesn't this place seem too good to be true? Doesn't this warmth, this field, this situation feel unreal?"

"He has a point," I add. "We're walking toward a new place. Are we just supposed to expect solace?"

Becoming more defensive, Miles stops in his tracks. "Why wouldn't we?"

"Because we know nothing of Halcyon. At least nothing about how they live. It could be just as bad as Nimbus. Hell, it could be worse."

Miles shakes his head. "I don't think it'll be worse. I think it'll be what we've been searching for; I think it'll be a world without walls. And the best part is, we didn't have to make it because we found it." His lips form into a smile, but his eyes mock his words. I can tell he wants to believe Halcyon is heaven—we all do—but I'm not moving forward thinking it is. I don't think anyone should.

"There may not be any walls, but that doesn't mean it's ideal," derides Marcus. "No amount of beauty can conceal suffering. You can't cover up lies with words people want to hear. Whatever lies ahead is fake. Death is the only thing that awaits us, and the sooner you get that through your head, the better." Shaking his head, Marcus tightens the straps of his backpack around his shoulders and starts to move forward.

Kyle and Marisa follow.

The rest of us stay still. No one knows what to say. No one cares to add any more words to the searing wound Marcus has cut upon each of us. It doesn't matter if we choose not to believe his absurdity; we all know he could be right. There's no way to prove him wrong, and there's no way to prove any of our ideas right. All we know is what Caroline's shown Sam and I—and that's not enough to build on.

I grab onto Sean's hand and pull him forward. We forge ahead, following the one man we're unable to help.

Hours pass as the trek yields no sight of anything or anyone. The field seems unending, and the scenery seems unwilling to change, minus a hill in the distance.

I hope this isn't all that's out here.

"Sean," I say.

"Yea?" he responds.

"What do you think about all this? Do you think Halcyon is even real?"

He itches the scruff on his chin. "I don't know why I wouldn't. You guys have seen enough to prove it is."

I take a quick glance back. Sam's fidgeting with his pinky, Rosie's handing her canteen to Ella, Miles is staring off to the side, the men from the Guard are laughing about who knows what; everyone's different. No two people have the same frame of mind or the same emotion. Everyone seems to cope differently.

I turn toward Sean. "Sometimes I don't know if I can trust my head," I say pessimistically. "And before you say anything, I know Sam and I have been seeing the same things, but who's to say any of that is real?"

He looks back at me. His stubble looks rough; his dark, marble-green eyes look tired. I know he's hurting, but he hides it better than the rest of us. "You are," he answers.

"Why me?"

"If it wasn't real, it wouldn't scare you."

"Nightmares aren't real and they still scare me."

He squeezes my hand tighter. "That's because in this world, everything has a chance to be real."

"Why do you say that?"

"We've seen everything. We've felt everything. It's tough to rule out anything anymore because we never know if we'll encounter it."

I bite at the inside of my cheek. *He's right.*

We approach the hill. Sam tugs at the back of my shirt.

I turn around.

"Do you feel that?" he asks, his lips quivering. "Do you feel a tingling sensation in your fingers?"

I try to focus on my hands, but I feel nothing. "I don't feel anything, Sam. Are you okay?"

"Something's not right. It just started. I've never felt this before."

"What does it feel like? Just tingling?"

"Like someone's pulling me down. It feels like someone grabbed onto the ends of my fingers and is trying to pull me into the ground."

"Is it worsening the farther we go?"

"Yes," he murmurs. "I think we're close."

"Guys," comes Kyle from ahead. "You need to get up here."

Sam's eyes link with mine. His pupils dilate.

"We're here," he murmurs.

I spin around to face the top of the hill. The others stand with their backs to the three of us. Nobody flinches. Nobody turns around to tell us to hurry up. Nothing. I know what's ahead, but I don't want to get any closer if it's going to make Sam physically anxious, or worse, hurt.

"Sam," I whisper. "Are you going to be okay?"

"I-I'll try," he shakes. "I have to."

I reach for his hand.

"Let's go," says Sean, his face empty of emotion.

We stride to the top of the hill. Sam's hand grows damp with each step; his nerves are becoming tangible. "Sam," I say, turning toward him. "Breathe."

"I am. I am," he mumbles.

His grip loosens on my hand; I squeeze tighter.

"I can't believe what I'm seeing," mutters Marisa.

The three of us squeeze between Kyle and Marisa—and that's when it jumps into my line of sight, that's when Halcyon becomes apparent.

It's a city.

Yet, it's not like anything I've ever seen. Unlike the one we escaped, this one is small in stature. There are less than ten buildings in front of us. The tallest is, maybe, ten stories. The others sit tightly together—five on each side of the street. The street is entirely made of brick. But something's off, something's familiar.

I take a step forward.

The brick continues toward us. The path grows more visible. Lampposts are interspersed between benches. Shrubbery conceals the bottoms of each and every post. Everything's immaculate, but I know it. I've seen it. Sam's seen it.

I take another step forward.

I can feel a tingling sensation in the tips of my fingers. I take another step to ensure it's not in my head—that I'm feeling what Sam was mentioning. Each step yields the same bodily response. *I know this place. I've been here.*

"Elise," groans a voice from behind me.

I turn around. Sam's facedown in the grass. The sensation in my fingers starts to vibrate up my hands and into my arms. Even as I stride back toward Sam, I start to feel weak. My limbs tremble. My lips shake. The sky is becoming black. The ground is opening up. I know what's happening, and I can't fight it. I never can.

***

"Don't say a word," she says.

I try not to think. I try not to speak, but it's impossible. I can't be empty; I can't be thoughtless.

"Don't say anything," she says again.

My jaw clicks open, but I don't speak. Air glides off my tongue and into the opaque, but no syllables follow.

"I know you want to speak, but you need to listen to me."

I look around, but I don't see anything. Everything is pitch black; not even a faint silhouette of light hovers in the distance. I've never been trapped in something so uncomfortable, so barren.

"They're coming."

"Who are they?" I ask.

"The followers."

"Followers of who?"

"Caroline," answers the voice.

"You mean, you're not Caroline?" I ask.

"No, I'm—," she cuts out.

***

The sky juts back into my vision, along with a few faces. Nearly everyone's hovering over Sam—only Ella stands over me.

"He's not breathing," she quietly whispers.

I hop to my feet. My skin's not shivering; my hands aren't shaking. Everything feels *normal*. . .but what I heard wasn't.

"Why isn't he breathing?" shouts Sean, his words directed at Marisa.

"I don't know. He still has a pulse. He's here, but he's also not."

"What do you mean?" I ask.

"He's trapped. Was he not in your headspace?" she questions.

I shake my head. "It was dark. I couldn't hear or see anyone," I lie.

"Could you feel anything?"

"No."

"We need to get him out," shouts Sean, as he grows fidgety. "He's not breathing for crying out loud. This hasn't happened before." Pacing around Sam and Marisa, Sean's footsteps become heavy.

Sticking her hands underneath Sam's head, Marisa flags me over. "Elise, I need you to get into his head."

"What do you mean?"

"Like you did in the past. Talk to him. Do whatever you can to make him aware that he's okay, but you have to move fast."

I drop to my knees. "Sam," I whisper. "Wake up. We're here. Everyone's here. You just need to wake up."

"Keep going," musters Marisa—her hands still behind Sam's head.

I continue to whisper. "Breathe, Sam. Breathe." As much as I want to shout, to shake Sam's body, to throw water in his face, I don't. Marisa's a doctor. I'm not.

"It's working. Keep talking."

"Open your eyes, Sam. It's not real. Nothing in there is real."

Quickly yanking her hands out from behind Sam's head, Marisa looks at me. There's blood on her fingers. She immediately wipes her hands on the grass and mumbles, "He should come to."

"Why is there blood on your fingers?" I ask.

"I had to finagle with the scar where his chip was," she quickly answers.

I don't say anything else.

"When will he come to?" frantically asks Sean, as if he didn't notice the blood.

A loud inhale silences the air around us. Sam's pupils dilate. His chin nearly touches his chest as he gasps for air.

"Slowly," hushes Marisa. "Breathe slowly."

Wide-eyed and distraught, Sam ignores the nurse; he breathes quickly and loudly. "What hap-happened?" he babbles. "I saw nothing. I felt nothing. Wha-what happened?"

"I-I'm not sure," responds Marisa, bemused. "I can't figure out why or how you weren't breathing. You had a pulse. Your heart was beating. It. . .it doesn't seem right."

"That's because it isn't," howls Sean.

I open my mouth to speak, but I change course.

It doesn't matter what I have to say, or what I want to say. This doesn't make sense, and Sean's not looking for a direct answer to how Sam's still alive—he just needs to be certain it won't happen again.

Nervously looking at me, Sam speaks dryly, "Why wasn't I breathing?"

"What did you see?" I ask calmly.

"Nothing. I heard you say something once, but that's it."

"Could you hear the person who was speaking to me?"

"No." He licks his lips and pulls a water bottle from his bag. "I could only hear you."

"You said you didn't hear anyone," chides Marisa.

I run my hand through my hair. "It was just the same as before; it's nothing."

She looks at me, puzzled.

I turn back to Sam. "Why weren't you breathing?"

"I felt like I was," he mumbles. "I felt fine."

Sam glances over at Marisa; she wipes her hands on the grass once more. "Why does my head feel so light?"

"I had to check your scar to ensure there wasn't an issue from your chip," she replies, as her fingers tug on the ends of the grass. "That's why you might feel a little blood drip down the back of your neck."

"What would my chip have to do with this?"

"Your head's so used to having it, that without it, incidents can occur."

"How come nothing has happened to anyone else?"

"It's rare."

Searching for air, Sam closes his eyes. "If it happens once, does that mean it will happen again?"

Marisa's eyes search the field. "I doubt it. You should be fine."

"I'll never be fine," grimaces Sam. "I haven't been fine since I was separated."

"None of us have," adds Marcus. "We're all just dying a slow death."

I wave off his absurd response and turn back toward Halcyon. Now, the image of the city doesn't give me anxiety; my fingers feel fine. So, I start to walk toward it. Yet, just as I do, the sound of footsteps echoes ahead of me. I keep walking, but I don't see anything.

With each step, the footsteps grow louder. It sounds like they're running, or clomping, like horses are afoot.

I stop.

The sound continues.

It grows louder and louder until a group of five people clad in light blue—almost vibrant blue—robes step into my line of sight. Each person is walking with his or her head down, a hood draped over his or her hair. I can't see any faces. They keep walking forward without so much as an attempt to look up.

I turn around. Everyone else is staring. Nobody's moved closer to me. They're all still atop the hill in awe.

I turn back. The figures have stopped moving.

The one in the middle takes a step ahead of the rest. "Hello," comes a deep baritone voice. "I'm Noah." Slowly lifting his head, he removes his hood. His dark skin carves way to his visible cheekbones, scarred forehead, and piercing green eyes. He brushes his shaved scalp and nods. The others lift their heads, but don't speak.

"I-I'm Elise," I stutter.

"It's nice to meet you, Elise. Welcome to Halcyon."

I don't reply. I'm not sure what to say.

Noah glances up at the hill. "Elise, would your friends care to join us down here?"

I wave them down. They slowly make way toward us.

"Thank you. I'm sure this is all quite confusing to you, so I'll take it slow," smiles Noah. "These people behind me," he says, gesturing from the left to the right, "are Katrina, Ahmed, Nicholas, and Maya. We all work for Caroline and ensure Halcyon operates smoothly and effectively."

"Where is Caroline?" I quickly ask.

"She is waiting."

"Where?"

"You'll see if you follow me."

My heart says not to follow him, but my mind says otherwise. We've finally found Halcyon; it only makes sense to indulge Noah in what his world has to offer us.

"Where?" Sam repeats my question. "Where is she?"

"And who are you?" softly asks Noah.

"Sam."

"I've heard a lot about you, Sam," smiles Noah awkwardly.

Sam steps back. "How?"

"Caroline has told us. We've been looking forward to your arrival. Please follow me."

Sean steps ahead of me. "We're not following you until we know where she is. We came here to meet her, so we want to meet her now."

"Caroline doesn't come out this far. If you want to meet her, you have to follow us."

Halcyon

"Not until you tell us where."

"The edge," answers Noah.

"The edge of what?" I ask.

"Halcyon."

"What do you mean?"

"We're wasting time here. Please follow us. You don't want to keep Caroline waiting."

"Why not?" irritably asks Sam.

Noah feigns a smile. "If you keep her waiting, the consequences will be, shall we say. . .painful?"

"I say we turn around," barks Miles.

"It's too late for that," I mutter.

"Exactly. Now, come this way," says Noah.

"How is it too late?" adds Ella.

"We're already here," I answer.

"She has a point," chimes in Marisa.

"If you quarrel for too long, nightfall will be upon us," creepily smiles one of the others whose name I've already forgotten.

"And then you'll have nowhere to go," adds the girl at the end, with a slight accent, and an equally uncomfortable grin.

None of this feels right. At least in Nimbus, everyone was fairly normal. Here, it seems everyone is brainwashed, or just crazy. *But she's right, we have nowhere else to go.*

"Let's just follow them," groans Marcus. "At least that might get us some shelter."

"It will," responds Noah. "We will accommodate your stay adequately."

Kyle shrugs his shoulders and looks at me. "Let's do it."

"Well, then come on. We really don't want to keep her waiting any longer," says Noah, the scars on his forehead tightening as he raises his brows.

I take a step forward. The five of them turn around.

I grab ahold of Sean's hand. We step onto the brick path—the same path I see every time I close my eyes. It's eerie and uncomfortable. Yet, everything looks exactly like what I've seen; not a single object is out of place. The only difference is that I'm not shrouded in darkness. I can see everything ahead of me rather than the black that has previously consumed my vision.

I step toward a bench. Placing my hand on the iron armrest, I take a seat. Something's come over me. Something's sending my unrested mind into a frenzy. *This place is evil. This place is death. This is the end.* These phrases keep encircling my brain; they're clouding any pure thought I want to have. I can't take it.

"Get out of my head!" I shout.

Sean slides beside me. "Elise?" he says softly.

I look up, but not at Sean. I can feel my cheeks warming. Sam's staring at me. His eyes are welling and his hands are trembling. "Look," he mutters. "Look at the bench."

I'm confused. I don't know what he means. I can already see—heck, I can feel—how real all of this is. I wipe my eyes and look at the bench in front of me. The only discernible difference between reality and my nightmares is the word, 'We.'

"There's just one word, Sam," I reply.

"Look at the first bench."

I look. It contains the word, 'In.' I move my eyes over to the second bench. It says, 'Peace.' "In peace we. . ." I quietly spit out. I know what the last bench says, but I don't want to see it. I don't want to read it.

Before I have a chance to look at it, Sean stands up. "That's the slogan of Nimbus."

An ensemble of voices follows. Marcus, Kyle, and Ella are reading the benches aloud, starting on the side I'm sitting on. "In harmony we live, in peace we thrive."

"Noah!" I yell, my voice shaking.

He turns around from a few dozen feet ahead of us, as if they didn't notice us stop. "Yes?" he loudly answers.

"Why are these words here?"

"That's the slogan of Halcyon."

"That's the slogan of Nimbus," retorts Sean.

Raising his left eyebrow, he glares questioningly at me. "That's odd."

"Why are they the same?" asks Sean angrily. "Why would two separate places that don't even seem to know about each other have the same damn slogan?"

"Calm down," speaks Noah. "It's probably just a coincidence. Nothing to worry about. Shall we keep moving?"

"Let's turn around," scowls Miles. "This place is too much."

"You can't turn around now," laughs Noah. "You're already in Halcyon."

Shaking his head, Miles glares at Noah. "All we have to do is take a few steps backward and we're out of here. There's no wall. There's nothing stopping us from leaving."

Those behind Noah sneer.

"Turn around then. See if you can leave."

I turn my head to the right. A wall of cerulean cloth shields the hill. At least three dozen individuals dressed in the same outfit as Noah and the others now stand behind us.

I stand up. "Who are they?" I ask, my question directed to Noah, but aimed at the people behind us.

"They're one of us."

"And what are you?"

"We're followers of Caroline. We don't have a collective name because we believe each person has a role."

The followers.

"But you all dress the same?" chides Marcus.

"The sea moves as one," calmly replies the girl next to Noah. Katrina, I think was her name. But just like the others, I don't intend to remember it.

The air around us thickens. Nobody knows what to say. *We're trapped. This is the end*, I think.

". . .this is where we're supposed to be," I murmur, almost inaudibly. "This is where we're supposed to be," I say again, louder this time, in an attempt to reassure myself about our path.

"That's right, Elise. This is where you belong," says Noah. "Now, don't be afraid. Follow us, please."

It's impossible not to be afraid. This society is new, and we know nothing of it. We just know that Nimbus and Halcyon are related somehow. It seems we never have enough to go on, but we keep moving, we keep fighting for each breath. If we don't, we'll drown in our suffering. And I refuse to let this sea of pain consume me. "Let's go," I answer.

Sam

This place is uncomfortable. The street seems long and unending, not to mention how empty it is. There are various buildings on both sides of us, but none have noticeable names or visible activity occurring inside of them. They all just have red and white 'closed' signs hanging on the door.

It makes me believe people live here, that a society exists here, but there's no physical proof. The only proof we have are Noah and the others, and their cloaked existence is more frightening than ideal.

I itch the end of my pinky; my nail catches on the edge of the scar. My finger starts to bleed. I shake my hand before putting my finger into my mouth. Marisa looks at me, but doesn't say anything.

"How far away is Caroline?" asks Elise.

"Not too much farther," answers Noah without turning around.

"Where exactly is she?" asks Rosie.

"You'll see."

"Why can't you just tell us where she is?" I spit out.

Noah stops. The others do the same. With his head cocked to the side, he speaks. "You already know where she is, Sam." He turns his head back forward, and proceeds to move again.

I look at Elise. "What does he mean by that?"

She looks back at me. "The circus," she mumbles.

"Then why did you want to follow him?" I ask angrily, my pinky irritation causing me to nearly shout my question.

Marisa hands me a bandage. I wrap my finger.

"Because my fears aren't why we should stop. We're supposed to be here."

"We're not supposed to be anywhere," I grumble.

Our conversation ends. We keep moving. Nothing I can say or do can change our fate. *I just have to be stronger.*

"We're nearly there," mentions Noah from ahead.

The street is coming to an end. The buildings are behind us and the road is seemingly about to disappear. It looks like the edge of the world.

"Watch your step," says Noah.

Yet, I don't see what I'm supposed to watch. We're mere feet from the end of the road; it looks like we can't go any farther.

"What do you mean?" I ask aloud, just as one of the girls turns to face us before disappearing off the edge of the road—her arms crossed across her chest as she falls backward.

Ella shrieks. "Where'd she go?"

The other three follow as Noah turns to face us. "This is the edge. Close your eyes and fall. If you don't, your journey ends here." Then, he disappears from view.

Elise

They all fell.

It looked easy. It looked peaceful. They weren't afraid, yet here we all stand, uneasy about what just happened.

"I didn't come this far to jump to my death," fumes Miles. "I mean, what the hell was that?"

I step forward. I can hear footsteps inching closer behind me.

I take another step. And another. Eventually, I'm at the threshold. *This is where they fell.* I look down. Nothing but black lines my sight.

It looks like a fault, but the other side is obscured by an oncoming storm. And if it's not that, then there's more to why Noah kept referring to it as 'the edge.' It could be where the world ends, but it could also be where it begins.

I take a small step forward—my toes hang off the edge of the cliff. Sean grabs onto the back of my arm. "Watch your step," he mutters.

"They wouldn't lead us this far to kill themselves," I say as I wriggle off his grip. "Halcyon is down there."

The footsteps behind us grow louder. I turn around. With my back facing the chasm, I cross my arms and lean backward. Sean fades from my sight. The cloaks of those behind him amalgamate into the sky. A light blue is all I see as I fall.

Soon the light fades.

I close my eyes. *I hope this isn't it.*

Then, it's over. I roll off a net and onto the ground. Noah and the others stand in front of me. A guided path of lights—similar to the one on the road above—illuminates the space behind them. *I survived.*

"Why did I have to come down here?" I utter uncertainly.

"This is where we live. This is where Halcyon thrives," responds Noah.

"But why in this chasm?"

"Misdirection creates solace for the ideal."

"What do you mean?"

Noah smirks. "We thwart our enemies with the city above while we live peacefully below."

"So what's up there is essentially a disguise, so you can function without interruption down here?"

He nods.

A loud, girlish scream echoes behind me. Sam rolls off the net beside me.

"What the heck was that about?!" he grunts.

"That's how you get to Halcyon," I answer.

"But why like that? Why not stairs, an elevator, or something better than falling into a pit?" he stammers. "I mean, how do you get back up?"

"That's not important," replies Noah. "Where are the others?"

"Still up there," responds Sam, as he tries to catch his breath.

"Are they coming?"

"I don't know. The people behind us were getting closer, but everyone was afraid. Derrick punched one of them, but the guy didn't flinch. He just took it. Blood gushed down his face, but nothing changed."

Noah takes a deep breath. With his eyes closed, he exhales.

Another scream echoes behind me. Rosie rolls off the net. She's followed by Ella, Marcus, and Miles.

"What's going on up there?" I ask, as I help Miles off the net.

"Chaos. The people behind us were getting closer and closer. Eventually, the four of us just jumped. Derrick punched one. The guy didn't move, so after Sam jumped, Derrick punched another one. Same reaction."

"Are the others coming?"

Rosie pulls her bag tighter around her shoulders. "Kyle and Sean seemed afraid. The other three appeared ready to fight."

A deep cry resounds above. Kyle lands on the net. Marcus helps him off.

"Are the others coming?" asks Marcus.

Stuttering, Kyle looks at the ground. "Th-they k-killed Derrick."

"How? Why?" questions Miles in a daze.

"He kept hitting them. Eventually, one sliced his throat."

I reiterate Marcus's question, "Are the others coming?"

Kyle looks up at me. He's shaking; his thin lips quiver against each other. "They were afraid," he mutters. "Sean didn't look like he could jump."

I turn to face Noah. "If they hurt Sean, I will kill you." The words flow out like water—effortless.

Noah grins sarcastically, almost vilely. "He's coming."

I face the net again. The air around us thickens, yet no cries echo.

When Sean and I were together outside Nimbus, he never mentioned any fears. We were both vulnerable, but he didn't show it. He moved through the outside like he knew he'd survive, like he knew what he was doing. He never mentioned a fear of heights, or falling. The wall wasn't tall enough for him to be afraid up there, but this drop is several times higher. It's quick, but it's still a ways.

It doesn't feel right. *Something's keeping him up there.*

"Where is he?" I shout, unable to control the anxiety coursing through me.

Silence strangles the life out of me. My body feels empty.

I move toward Noah. With my hands outstretched, I reach for his neck. He doesn't stop me. He doesn't push me away.

His cold skin presses against my fingertips; I claw into his neck, yet he shows no fear. As if he isn't afraid of death, he looks at me. "Are you done yet?"

"Why aren't you afraid?"

"You're weak."

Sam pulls me away.

I feel nothing. Any time something happens to Sean, I crack. I'm powerless. The only emotion within me is fear, and I hate it. It consumes me. It makes me dependent on others. It makes me someone I'm not.

I've lost control, *and for what?* Nothing. Sean's stronger than anyone I've ever met. He'll probably be down here shortly.

I take a breath. And another. And another. I need to push away the doubt.

The air remains stagnant. No sign of life tumbles through the skies.

Rosie grabs onto my hand and turns me around. "He's coming," she promises.

Sean

I'm afraid. I won't say it aloud; I won't even show it in my face. But I'm terrified.

The followers of Caroline have been inching closer and closer every minute since they killed Derrick. Juan and Ralph are at my sides; they're each holding a gun toward the group, but they're not firing. I can sense they're too afraid of what would happen to the others if something happened up here. I can see their fear. Hell, I can feel it. Derrick was our friend, but they ended him as quickly as one could snap a twig. It was effortless. It doesn't matter that we could retaliate. We shouldn't.

Derrick's blood soaks the dirt behind those pushing us toward the edge. His body is limp; his eyes stare into the oncoming storm.

I hate this. I need to jump. I need to fall. I need to see if the others survived, but I can't. My body is stuck. I feel helpless. And the longer I stand here, the more I can see my demise—the more I can see myself beside Derrick, eyeing mother nature's fury.

"We gotta jump, Sean," states Ralph.

He jumps before Juan or I respond.

The followers lunge closer. My heels kick dirt into the crevice.

Noah made the fall look peaceful, yet the others up here make it seem like it'll kill us.

They're essentially pushing us toward the edge. If the fall really is safe, I have nothing to fear; yet with each passing second, I feel more and more like the bottom is just a rock. And some deep, angry part of me believes everyone jumped to their deaths—even Noah and the others. It's irrational. It's unrealistic, but it's how I feel—and I can't change it. I can't just fall into oblivion believing I'll land on my feet.

"We have to jump," shouts Juan. "Either we do it ourselves, or we die like Derrick."

But why would we die? They're pushing us to the edge. They're not trying to hurt us. *They're trying to show us.*

I jump.

Elise

"What took you so long?" I angrily toss my words at Sean.

"Nothing." He shakes his head.

It's something. The Sean I know wouldn't have waited that long. He would have been the first into the abyss, the first into the shadows to ensure it's safe for others.

"Now, you're ready to see Halcyon," speaks Noah.

I turn to Sean again. I can see in his eyes that something's off. I doubt it has to do with Derrick's death; I doubt it has anything to do with the fall. There's something going on in his head. Something he's too afraid to say, or maybe to even think about.

He squeezes my hand.

I can't say anything. My head's just as torn apart as his, if not more. I don't know what's going on, what's going to happen to us, or if this might be the last time we see each other. All I know is that something was pulling us here for a reason. We're supposed to be in Halcyon. I know it. I just don't know if I want to believe it.

"Follow us," calls Noah from ahead.

The path is the only source of light around us. There's a slight red hue in the distance, but I can't make out what it's emitting from.

"Where are we going?" asks Marcus, his voice fraught with uncertainty.

"You'll see," responds Noah.

"Why can't you just tell us?"

"That takes away the fun."

Marcus stops. "Tell us, or I'm not taking another step."

"You already know."

"What, is it Halcyon?"

Noah nods.

"Then, what's this around us? Is this still 'the edge?'"

Noah's face remains forward. The light's growing larger ahead; it softly highlights Noah's cheek. "This is the sea."

I clench my jaw; my eyebrows fall toward the ridge of my nose. "What do you mean?" I ask, the words slowly exiting my lips.

With his head still facing the distance, Noah exhales. "The sea swathes the city. It protects us."

I look at my feet—or what I can see of them—and it's clear they're in dirt. Not water, not any other liquid, dirt. *That's not a sea.* I squeeze Sean's hand. He coughs.

"Noah, how is this a sea?" he asks.

"It's endless." He continues forward.

It's gotten to the point that asking Noah anything seems like a waste of time. He shrewdly skirts around the answer to just about everything we ask. The followers don't have a name; we fell off 'the edge'; we're currently in a dark 'sea.' None of it makes sense. Halcyon still isn't visible, and at this point it feels like we jumped into this fault for nothing.

Marcus shakes his head and slowly treads behind Noah.

We do the same. The lights get brighter. They become a mixture of red and white with the pale vibrancy overshadowing the red. Yet, the area around the brightness remains dark; it's vapid, empty, full of nothing. The lights are the only things breathing life down here. It feels like we're on a stage.

My head starts to ache. My body starts to tremble. I know what's ahead, but I don't want to think about it regardless of how inevitable it is.

We keep walking. The lights along the path darken the closer we get to Halcyon. Yet, while they fade, the city illuminates. *The circus shines. The stage extends.*

Eventually, the path ends, and everything changes. The world in front of us has become visible. It's become something entirely different than a dark diversion: it's a city. But it's not like the one in Nimbus; it's alive, and its reality instantly grabs ahold of me.

Unlike the city in Nimbus, it's not pulling me into the shadows. It's pushing me into the light.

I sprint across the street, oblivious to the physical presence of others. Everywhere I look, beautifully designed buildings consume my line of sight. And it's not just the architecture, it's the set-up. Halcyon looks like a world I've read about and seen a few times in old films from my childhood. It looks like the 1920's—almost as if that era was perfection, to some degree, in the eyes of its creator.

There are little shops everywhere with apartments above them. Lampposts illuminate the street as far as the eye can see. A few of the shops have small, incandescent bulbs dangling across the windows showcasing the antiquated font upon it.

Big Jim's Deli. Threads by Tallulah. The Halcyon Herald. City Hall. I.E.M. Library. Every business's name is clear. Whether it's printed on the window or shining atop a roof, it's within eyesight.

Signs flash in the distance.

I stop and stand still. I take a breath. I exhale.

Noise begins to penetrate my eardrums. The streets flood with pedestrians; passersby walk past me without so much as a glimpse. They don't bother to stare, or even speak. They walk in stride.

I continue down the street. I don't care if anyone's following me or not. This world is too unbelievable to sit back in awe, gawking at the beauty of our predicament. It needs to be explored, to be seen, to be felt. Halcyon is unlike anything we could imagine. It's more than I thought could be possible.

But despite its beauty, it's still surrounded—it's not a world without walls. It's not exactly what we want, but it's enough. . .at least for now.

A slight pulse shifts across the top of my head. I itch my scalp and keep walking.

The flashing red from earlier hops into my peripherals. I don't chase the light; I chase the city.

I seek what brought me here, what decided this was where we all needed to be. I don't think Caroline will magically appear in front of me, nor do I believe the circus will present itself out of thin air.

All I know is, this place is surreal. I want to enter all the shops; I want to run through the streets from beginning to end in search of nothing in particular, but to instead find myself immersed in desires I never knew I had. I want to find something new. I want to touch something soft; I want to be here. *I really do.*

Even if this place ends up changing its course, I finally feel at home. It's strange. It's almost unrealistic, but something inside me is quickly becoming attached to Halcyon.

I feel alive.

I feel free.

I'm in a state of pure euphoria.

But like every good thing in this world, it won't last. I'm certain this ecstasy will fade over time, or be lost in a moment. At the snap of my fingers, Halcyon could fade to black and this could turn out to be another dream, or another painful nightmare that's tricked me into its ephemeral charm.

At least, that's how it usually seems to work.

I wander farther down the street. More signs punctuate various windows. People continue to walk past. They're all heading in the same direction, too—and I almost want to follow, but at the same time, I don't. I'd love to have everything to myself, or at least to share with Sean.

A neon green hue blinks to my right. I turn to look at it. It reads: MYSTIC.

What's that all about?

I step toward the flashing light.

People bustle past me quicker and quicker. I can feel the wind from their movement chilling the air around me.

The sign grows brighter the closer I get; yet, before I can reach the door beneath the illumination, someone grabs onto my shoulder.

I turn around.

Everything goes dark. The neon disappears. The world starts to swirl around me. I can't see Sean, Sam, Marcus, Rosie, anyone. All I can see are the bottoms of shoes, almost as if the city is walking over me, ignorant to my existence. I feel helpless.

Am I dead?

Sam

Where am I?

The last thing I remember, Elise had ventured into the streets of Halcyon. She wandered away from the rest of us—even Sean didn't chase after her. It seemed we were all too caught up in the allure of a new city, in the beauty of something brighter and more appealing than the rundown city outside Nimbus.

Yet, the longer we stood around and watched pedestrians flood down the street, the more light-headed we became. Or at least I did. I'm not sure what happened. One minute I was lost in the beaming signs overlooking Halcyon, the next, I'm surrounded by darkness.

I'm not in a dream, nor am I above. I'm not in the 'sea,' or standing on the 'edge.' This isn't Nimbus. This isn't the city. I can't tell what it is.

The only thing I can see is a thin blue light in the distance.

I reach my arms toward the color, but an invisible barrier blocks them. I pull back before stretching my arms toward the barrier once more. I start to push. It doesn't budge.

My heart starts to pound against my chest. "Sean!" I shout.

"Sam!" comes Sean's voice, clearly. It sounds like he's right next to me.

"Elise!" I yell.

No response.

"Marcus!"

His voice bounces off my surroundings. It's followed by Kyle's. And Rosie's. And Miles's. It sounds like they're all near me, if not next to me.

I reach left. The ends of my fingers grasp onto fabric; it feels like a t-shirt. I grab onto it.

Ella shouts. "Who's grabbing my shirt?"

I reply, "I am."

She extends her arm and clutches at my shirt.

"Sean, where are you?" I say aloud.

"He's right here," mutters Ella. "He's got my other side."

"Elise?"

No answer follows.

"Elise?" I say again.

Still nothing.

Where is she?

I feel around again, hoping to be able to find Elise and pull her close to the rest of us. My fingers glide against the barrier in front of me as it starts to shake. I step back and begin to rub the back of my head. Instantly, my fingernail catches on my scar. It feels wet. I glide another finger against the opening. Still wet. *Am I bleeding again?*

Closing my eyes, I take a deep breath and press my pointer finger into the wound. The liquid smears against my finger and sends a searing pain down my neck and into my spine. I quickly let go, cringing. I fall to my knees.

The floor begins to vibrate.

The walls rattle.

The light disappears.

Elise never answers back.

Elise

The back of my throat is dry. I don't dare yell because my cries will go unheard. There's nothing I can say to be reunited with everyone else. Hell, there's nothing I can do.

I knew the city was just another lie.

I lick my lips and swallow. The ground starts to shake.

A radiant burst of white illuminates the air above me before fading to nothing. It's followed by red. A few more times, the colors bounce above, brightening my position; showing a cloaked person beside me.

Where is everyone else? I think.

Then, the lights stop, and a cerulean blue line appears around me. I close my eyes.

The shaking stops.

"Welcome!" shouts a loud female voice. The words echo. I don't move. I don't open my eyes. "My name is Caroline and this is Halcyon." The last syllable rings loudly in my ears; a mass of applause consumes me.

I take a deep breath and turn in circles. Caroline continues to speak, but remains out of sight.

"I'm sure you're all wondering how you got here." A slight chuckle can be heard in an otherwise silent arena. "If you're not then I'm sure you're confused about why you're here, and what's ahead." A spotlight flicks on. Yet, it shows no one. "I can assure you, you're safe in Halcyon."

"Then why were we knocked unconscious and awaken in this dark arena?" I shout, unable to control the pitch of my voice.

"Not everyone comes to . ." she trails off, the air around me thickens, ". . .the circus by choice."

I jump back.

It doesn't matter how many times I've seen the circus; it doesn't matter how long I've known our journey would lead us here.

It doesn't matter that just moments ago I felt nearly as safe as I've ever felt. Hearing those words fall from Caroline's lips have sent my body into another realm—one I can't control. I can't stop it. I can't calm the tingling sensation running down my shoulders and into my palms. My breathing becomes rapid. I fall to my knees.

"Yes, that's right," echoes Caroline. "You've made it."

The spotlight enlarges; a woman—most likely Caroline— emerges dressed in a long, grey cloak atop a stage. Unlike the ones worn by Noah and the others, Caroline's cloak is smooth. Its silk-like appearance shines in the spotlight.

Slowly stepping down from the stage, she begins to move toward me. With her head held down, and a white marble cane at her side, she glides toward me like the Grim Reaper.

Yet, I remain still, unable to fully process what's happening.

Caroline keeps moving. She doesn't look up.

It feels like we're the only two people in the world. I don't know where Sean and the others are. The cerulean blue light has faded. The only spectrum of color outside the black is the spotlight guiding Caroline toward me. Everything else is invisible.

"Stand up," mutters Caroline as she approaches me.

I don't budge.

"Stand up," she says again, her black shoes poking out from underneath her robe.

I remain seated, my body's depressive state preventing me from standing.

Caroline leans toward me. With her arm outstretched, she grabs onto my fingertips; her face remaining concealed. "Slowly. You can stand up," she whispers with an almost friendly tinge of support, like we've known each other for years.

I lightly grit my teeth.

She pulls. I lift off the ground. The feeling in my body remains stagnant.

"See, that wasn't so hard," she says, releasing my fingers.

Standing in front of me with her neck craned forward, Caroline reaches her hands toward her hood. Pinching the ends of it, she slowly pulls it back, revealing a gorgeous smile. Unlike MacMillan, her teeth shine brightly in the spotlight and don't reek of alcohol. Her bright blue eyes pierce the light. Her shoulder-length brunette hair that curls up at the ends once again reminds me of the era Halcyon seemingly exists in.

Nothing about her appearance puts off an aura of evil; instead, it paints her as a beacon of hope. She looks like the opposite of what I imagined.

Caroline smiles; then, winks.

Taken aback, I stop grinding my teeth, and force a half-hearted smile.

"Would you care to come up to the stage with me, Elise?"

"Why me?"

"You'll see, my dear."

Uncertain of her proposal, I lift my hand. She takes it.

As we move toward the steps leading onto the stage, I aim my attention on the area around me. It looks empty. Nothing but the loud cries of a crowd encircle me. It feels like I'm the main act of a show, like my presence is why everyone showed up.

Caroline turns to face me; her lips murmur an inaudible phrase—one I can't decipher while my focus remains on my surroundings. Her muted lips continue to move, but nothing enters my ears.

Slowly sliding off her robe, she walks up onto the stage. Now, with the cloak behind her, she sports a dark blue suit accompanied by the same glistening ivory-colored cane. The suit's different than the color of the followers' robes in that it's enough to make her stand out. It shows Caroline's in charge. As for the cane, the handle appears to have an animal—one I can't quite see—as the grip, while faint strips of blue coalesce into the white.

I take a step closer to her.

The cane becomes clearer. It almost looks like an inanimate waterfall.

She cocks her head to the side and smirks at me.

I don't say anything. I'm unsure what's happening. I don't know what to focus on.

Then, before I get a chance to speak, the lights come on. The darkness becomes illuminated by an audience—by my friends. Standing in a glass case above the crowd, they huddle together— everyone looking as confused as the person next to them.

What's going on? Why are they up there?

Suddenly, Caroline grabs me from my trance. Her words become clear: "Who shall go first?" she asks to loud applause.

Go first? On what?

Uncertain of what's going on, I take a step beside Caroline. My ears start to ring.

I close my eyes. My legs start to feel weak again. *What's going on?* I think to myself. *Why are they up there?*

The shock makes me unsteady. I fall onto my knees and look up at Sean. He's holding onto Sam while Marcus holds onto him and Kyle onto him and Rosie onto Kyle, and so forth. They're all tightly gripping each other as if the confined space they're in is about to fall, as if it's about to shatter and become the end of our journey.

I yell nonsense directed at Sean.

His body doesn't budge. He doesn't look at me.

"They can't hear you," says Caroline. "I'm the only one who can. Now choose."

"What. . . ?" I softly mumble. "Choose. . .what. . .?"

Everything around me goes silent once more. The lights dim. The world closes in on me.

I wish I could understand. I wish I could see what Caroline wants me to see, but I can't. It's like my perception is obscured, as if it's chosen to be blinded in the light.

"Choose! Or, do you not want to?" echoes Caroline's voice.

Stranded in a wary mind, I try to focus, but I can't.

Caroline grabs onto my wrist.

"Elise," she angrily whispers in my ear. "Choose who goes, or I will."

Befuddled, I blink. I try to focus on what she's seeing, but I can't. My mind has blocked whatever abhorrent circumstance lies ahead. Thus, without control, my tongue slips past my dry lips and murmurs, "Ralph."

"Then Ralph shall go first."

The words ring loudly in my ear, essentially overcoming the silence that has taken control of me. "Go first on what?" I ask, glossy-eyed and unsure.

"Cirque de Chance."

"What's that?"

"The circus of chance," she grins.

"Why don't you just call it that?"

Caroline bites her bottom lip and looks into the glaring lights. "Because, Elise, the latter sounds more intimidating. The former sounds more exciting."

Gently tapping her cane atop the stage, the lights disappear. The entire arena goes black.

She taps once more.

The cage above turns green. Ralph is pulled off the others and pushed onto a platform by one of Caroline's followers.

Caroline's voice echoes once more. "Welcome, Ralph, to Cirque de Chance. You are the first outsider to ever attempt this feat. With that, we'll even allow you to choose who goes second. Normally, it's random, but this will make it more fun."

A smaller spotlight forms on Ralph. He's shaking. He's been stripped of his weapons and his bag. I can't discern his facial ticks from where I'm standing, but by his jittering hands, I can tell he's terrified.

Eloquently continuing her speech, Caroline speaks, "Who would you like to follow you in this endeavor, Ralph?"

Ralph turns to face the glass cage. He doesn't speak, nor does he motion toward anyone. He just shivers.

"Ralph, it's okay to choose. Elise chose you. She struggled, but she did it. Now, you pick someone else. It's that simple."

Everyone's still huddled together; no one's looking at Ralph—who's still visibly shaken by what's going on. Far from the burly, tough guy he was in Nimbus, Ralph's been broken. He's been stripped of his dignity, his control over his fate. I hate that it's my fault. I hate that I could have sent him to the gallows simply because I figured whomever I chose would be subject to something, and I didn't want it to be Sean or Sam.

I can't look.

"If you don't pick someone, I'll have the audience choose. . .and they love to choose. They usually make the right pick."

"Ky. . ." stutters Ralph.

"Ky?" repeats Caroline.

"Kyle," stammers Ralph. "I pick Kyle."

I keep my head held to the side, all while my eyes try to sneak a peek at the cage above.

"Kyle, would you step forward," echoes Caroline's voice.

The air is silent. There's no applause, nor is there a sound from above. It feels like time has stopped.

Kyle's not moving, I think, but don't look.

"Please step forward, Kyle," reiterates Caroline. "If you don't, you won't like the consequences."

"Just move!" I shout without looking.

The audience starts to clap. *He must have stepped out*, yet I still refuse to look. Everything that's transpiring above has to do with my decisions. I'm down here. I'm seemingly safe, and in control. It's unfair.

The applause loudens.

"See, that wasn't so hard," says Caroline. "Now, will both of you step to the edge of the platform," she states, rather than asking.

"I thought only one went at a time?" I mutter under my breath.

Caroline taps me on the shoulder with her cane. "Why don't you come stand beside me and watch, Elise? The show can't begin until you're ready."

"Why?"

"After all, it's your show," she smirks—her blue eyes glistening in the light.

"Why?" I ask again.

"Just stand up and you'll see."

I oblige. I fear that if I don't listen to her, something worse will happen. And I can't let my anxieties get in the way of someone's life.

"What you're about to take part in is something that's been a tradition of Halcyon since I founded this place twenty-seven years ago." She pauses and looks around. The lights still remain limited to her—with a faint glint upon Kyle and Ralph. "I call it Cirque de Chance, but those who have passed it call it the 'Devil's Game,' while those who have failed are simply unable to label it as anything," she smirks.

Twenty-seven years ago, I think. *2165*. The year sounds familiar. I glance up at Sean. For once he's not focused on the group—his eyes are glued to me. I bite my bottom lip and widen my stare.

He steps to the edge of the cube and presses his face against the glass.

I mouth, "What are you doing?"

He doesn't intimate anything. He just stares.

Unfazed by Sean's sudden intrigue, Caroline starts to speak once more. "This isn't a choice for newcomers. You must attempt it. In order to become a follower, you must succeed. Those who perish are forgotten. Those who don't attempt look on—but like I said, that's not an option for you."

Caroline looks over at me. Her enlarged pupils playfully watch me in a manner inconsistent with her words. It's like she thinks this game will make us closer, like this peril will create a bond. I don't get it.

With her eyes glued on me, she continues. "Now, we must decide which one of you goes first."

"On what?!" shouts Kyle from above. "There's nothing in front of us!"

Caroline grins, "There is. You'll see shortly."

The air around us thickens.

"Elise," says Caroline.

I don't reply.

Leaning toward me, she inches closer. With her head down, she whispers into my ear, "In this world, you don't choose your fate. It's chosen for you." Pulling her head away, she half-smiles and raises her arms.

The audience starts to stomp their feet. Like a collective orchestra, they stomp twice, pause for a second, and stomp again. The process repeats itself over and over until Caroline slowly moves her arms toward her sides like a bird closing its wings.

"Noah, will you select our first competitor," shouts Caroline.

"With pleasure," responds Noah.

The arena goes dark.

The deep, gut-wrenching scream of a man falling consumes the shadows.

"What's happening?" I shout, unable to control the words from spewing out behind my lips like a sickness. "What's happening?" I angrily ask again.

An aura of silence stagnates around me. Caroline doesn't respond, nor does the voice of Ralph or Kyle. The audience is remarkably quiet—there's no stomping or clapping. Everything has truly gone dark.

Halcyon

My teeth clatter. *I don't like this.*

"Caroline!" I shout again.

The whole arena alights.

I jolt my head upward. Kyle is still standing. Ralph is gone.

"Noah," echoes Caroline. "Would you care to make the invisible. . . visible?"

"My pleasure," he loudly answers.

As he quickly snaps his fingers, the empty space in front of the glass cage—where I was uncertain if my head was blocking an image, or if nothing was actually there—becomes the opposite. Like magic, it goes from being clear to showcasing a large chasm in the earth.

I run toward it. There, at the bottom, encircled by rough, jagged rock, sits Ralph. Lying on his back atop a mat, he has his hands on his forehead.

"Caroline! What is down there?"

"Just wait," she slyly grins.

"Answer me!" I shout.

She doesn't reply. She remains tall behind me, her hand resting atop her cane.

Nobody speaks. Sean, Sam, all of them above me are muted by the glass. Noah and the rest of the followers seem not to speak unless provoked, or spoken to by Caroline.

I look back down. Ralph's hands are at his sides; his eyes are closed.

"Are you okay?" I shout.

"I'm not sure," he softly responds. "Where am I?"

"In a pit," I reply.

"Why?"

I don't answer. We both know why.

Resting my hands upon my scalp, I take a deep breath. *This is unlike any circus I've ever seen. What sort of carnival sends a man into a pit while an audience looks on?* No matter how I look at it; no matter how I try to reason with myself, all that will ever make sense is that whatever I saw in my head, wasn't the true horror I'd witness in Halcyon. It's almost as if it was a diversion—a nightmare devised simply to frighten me, but not to the extent that I'd fear even moving.

Whatever's going to happen to Ralph is far worse.

119

Sean

I can't exactly tell what's going on.

I see Ralph. I see Elise. I see Caroline, but I can't tell what's happening below us. With my forehead pressed against the glass, I try to lean farther forward, but I can't. There's only so much pressure I can take before it's hard to breath.

"What's going on?" I ask aloud, hoping my question will be answered by Noah.

But he doesn't respond.

"Tell me!" I shout—the veins in my neck pulsing against the glass. "What is going on?" My words grow louder, but my stature lessens. I fall to my knees. *I hate this.* "You piece of shit," I softly mutter. My head falls into my hands.

Noah doesn't move. He's simply unfazed by my words. He remains still on the platform; like metallic art in a lightning storm, he doesn't move. He lets the questions fall unto him, uncaring of their intentions or meanings.

Then, he pulls up his hood. As do the others.

The spotlight shifts to the crevice.

Ralph screams.

"The first task has begun," echoes Caroline's voice. "Start climbing."

I glance at the chasm. Ralph's running toward the back wall. I can see his hands holding onto the rock.

Caroline continues. "If the water gets above your chest, you fail. If you sit and allow the water to push you to the top, you fail. The only way to escape is to climb to the top and get out. If you fail, you will die. . .good luck."

I stand back up.

Everyone behind me rushes toward the glass. Sam, Marcus, and Rosie stand beside me. Kyle remains immobile on the platform in front of us.

"Do we all have to do this?" asks Sam, his voice cracking.

"I'm not sure."

"I think we do," answers Rosie. "I think this is the test."

"Do you think this is all we have to do?" questions Miles from behind us.

"Who knows," I reply.

"I hope so," he mutters.

I arch my neck upward. From what I can see, the water is several feet deep. Ralph's holding onto the wall for dear life, but he's not moving. The water is up to his knees and he's not moving.

"Ralph!" yells Juan. His words do nothing. They merely bounce around this glass contraption we're in.

Elise stands beside the widened crevice—which is more like a diamond-shaped slit—and leans forward. Her hands are on her knees. I'm sure she's trying to help Ralph. Maybe by pointing out larger rocks to grab onto, or by just telling him he can do it. Whatever she's doing, I know she's hurting.

Hell, I am, too.

We might all die here. But Elise might not. She's down there rather than up here for a reason. Whatever this world wants to do with her, it's become harder for me to protect her. Not like she needs it, but I want to provide it. I'd rather lose my life than Elise lose hers.

Running to the other side of the pit, Elise lies on her stomach and extends her arm. Immediately, Caroline runs over and hits her on the back with her cane. "Stand up!" she shouts. "Let him do this alone!"

The water continues to rise. Ralph's moved a few feet upward, but the water's pace has shifted. It's now up to his waist and he's still barely moving.

He's not prepared for this, I think. *None of us are.*

We're just trying to live, but now we're forced to survive. And it's harder to survive when you don't know how to perform the task. I've never rock-climbed before. None of us have. The physical tests outside Nimbus never involved that. It's essentially just a game of chance; an improbable game that the audience devours.

The water gets higher, and higher, and higher.

Ralph's moving, but not quick enough. His right hand slips. He holds tightly onto the rock with his left, but I can see it sliding loose. The moisture is pushing him into the water.

He swings his right hand back onto the rock, but before he knows it, the water's too high.

Caroline quickly waves her cane into the air. The lights fade. The audience starts to stomp again.

"Looks like he wasn't ready for Halcyon," rings Caroline's voice. "Hopefully tomorrow, Kyle is."

The lights turn back on. The audience goes silent. The chasm has faded from sight, as if the ground closed atop the gap, or if it wasn't real. Elise lies on her back on the ground with her hands covering her eyes.

Her mouth is agape, but nothing comes out.

Caroline looks up at us. "Tonight's game has concluded. The rest of you shall join me at dinner in an hour." Flashing a slight smile, she continues. "Noah will guide you to your chambers, where a shower and a new set of clothes awaits. See you soon."

Juan pounds his fist into the glass. Everyone else sits in silence around me. *What just happened?*

One minute Ralph was chosen. The next he's gone. Dead. And now, we're supposed to act like nothing happened—like his death was meaningless. I've feigned my way through pain before, and I can do it again, but eventually it's bound to catch up.

I stand up.

"Guys," I mumble, my head spinning.

"Yea?" answers Marcus, his whisper nearly silenced by the heaviness of his sigh.

"Stand up."

"Why?" responds Sam.

"We have to show Caroline we're not afraid."

"But we are," mutters Miles. "He wasn't given a chance."

"We can't show that," I state. "She'll pick us apart one by one if we keep showing that we're vulnerable."

"He's right," adds Rosie. "We need to stand up and face her."

"H-how?" stutters Miles. "Our backs are against the wall."

I close my eyes and curl my lips in. Tightly pressing them together, I lean my palms against the glass. "We have to act normal."

"Normal?" laughs Marcus. "That's impossible."

I grit my teeth. "Fake it."

"And what if we can't?"

"Then you're as good as dead."

"He's right," mutters Sam. "We have to smile through the pain."

"We've done it before," adds Ella. "We might as well do it again."

Everyone stands up.

Noah snaps his fingers.

Sam

The silk shirt sticks to my back; the remaining moisture from the shower presses it into my skin. This outfit, white pants with a white button-up, feels like pajamas. It even looks like pajamas. It's weird. It's not what I expected.

None of this is. Caroline's been all over the place. Each moment with her presence before Halcyon felt justified; it felt like we were supposed to be here, like this was the fresh start we were looking for. But we were wrong. She's deceived us.

Unless, she hasn't.

Maybe Ralph's death serves a greater purpose. Maybe our place here was never in doubt. Maybe everything will work out. This world's always been full of 'maybes,' and rightfully so. They're the only thing we can cling to.

Sitting on the edge of a dimpled, dark green chair outlined by streaks of brown, Sean pulls the equally unappealing white slippers over his toes. With his head down, he asks, "What are we doing here, Sam?"

For the first time, I don't know how to answer that. I thought I knew. I still think I know, but I'm not sure if I should say anything. It's not the 'what' that would bother Sean, it's the 'why.' He's headstrong; he's tough. Whatever tasks could be put forth in Cirque de Chance, I know he'll succeed. But if Elise is always on the outside looking in, he could become more irritated, more prone to failure.

I scratch my head, being sure to avoid the scar. My stare catches the large oak door being pushed open.

"Sam. Sean," says Noah.

Our eyes meet. Neither of us replies.

"Caroline's ready."

I pull my shirt off my back once more, but even as the moisture lessens, the fabric still sticks to my skin. I shake my head and step into the hallway.

Dimly lit chandeliers hang from the ceiling. The walls are covered in a forest green wallpaper that's similar to the color of the chair in Sean and I's room. It makes this hallway feel like a forest—one lined with large doors every five or so feet.

Marcus and Miles step out of a door to our right. One of the five followers from before is pulling it closed behind them.

Ella and Rosie step out of room across the way. A follower is standing behind them.

Juan and Kyle hop out of the next room on our walk. Another follower is waiting.

We're all wearing the same pale white outfit, making our walk through the hall more of a cult march rather than a jaunt to a meal.

"Where's Elise?" asks Sean, his head remaining forward.

"She's with Katrina," answers Noah. "You'll see her at dinner."

Sean doesn't respond.

Nobody speaks, and nobody stops moving. The hallway seems endless. Each door looks the same as the one before it. The only obvious differences are the tables between them. No two are the same, but they're all of similar architecture. The one between Sean and I's room and Marcus and Miles's is short in stature, but the designs upon the single leg are surreal. Two men are carved into the wood to appear as if they're holding the table up. Then, atop the table sits a vase. It's clear and empty. It feels unnecessary.

The table outside Rosie and Ella's room has four legs and seems more worn than any single piece of furniture in the farmhouse outside Nimbus. Each leg has a variety of ocean-related objects carved into it. From seashells to crabs, to Poseidon himself, it has everything, but it feels just as out of place as the others before it. And just like the ones near it, an empty vase sits on top.

We quickly approach another large wooden door. Unlike the others, it has no handle. Nor is it arched. It's rectangular with a small window on top. The window is circular with an 'X' through it, but that's it. There's no light shining through; it's seemingly pointless.

"Proceed," says Noah.

I push the door forward.

"Come in," softly rings Caroline's voice.

I step forward. Sean follows. Like the hallway, this room is the same shade of green, but with a more unique style upon its walls.

The dark green is brush-stroked with lines of white to look like wave crests. Every few feet, there's a curved strip of white before it peaks and the color fades down the opposite side. It's odd considering the room isn't blue—like the waves are misplaced. Sort of like us.

In the middle of the room sits an elongated wooden table. Like everything else in this place, it's the same color, material, and aesthetic. Whatever era Caroline's going for, she's got it.

"Each of you has an assigned seat," utters Noah, as he steps in front of us.

"You're not going to be seated by someone you're extremely close to," speaks Caroline from the end of the table. Standing with broad shoulders, she smirks. "There will be no love birds side-by-side here."

"With that said, Sean, you will be seated to the left of Caroline." Gesturing toward an open chair, Noah directs Sean toward it. "Beside Sean will be Rosie. Next to her will be Juan, then Kyle."

They all take their seats.

"Now, for the opposite side. Next to Caroline on her right will be Marcus. Beside him will be Sam. Next to Sam will be Ella, and Miles."

We all sit.

"Lastly, Elise will sit at the end of the table facing Caroline."

The sound of her name makes Sean uneasy. He looks every which way, but she's nowhere in sight.

"Where is she?" he asks, his voice shaky and bouncing in frequency.

"She's coming," quietly responds Caroline.

"When?"

Caroline doesn't answer. She merely keeps up the façade she's been using since we met her. Her lips fold into a smirk, but her eyes remain indifferent.

A slight ache runs across my forehead. I try not to think about it.

It quickly fades just as the door we entered through flies open. Out steps Elise. Cloaked in black silk, she doesn't make eye contact with any of us. She simply steps into the room and is directed to her seat by Katrina, at least I think that's her name.

"Now that you're all here, I want to try and help you further understand Halcyon," announces Caroline. "I don't want you to be frightened by the tasks at hand; I want you all to flourish, to prove that your murder of MacMillan wasn't a fluke."

Miles stands up and angrily interjects. "How could murder be a fluke?"

"Just like death can."

He sits back down, unsure how to respond.

"Now, to help you better understand my world, I will give you each two questions, excluding Elise. We'll start with Sean."

Befuddled, or at least uncertain, Sean blurts out a question. "Why did Elise have to choose who went?"

Caroline folds her hands into her lap. "Elise was chosen by a higher power. That's all I can say on that matter."

Sean fires back. "Will she have to take this test?"

"She will not."

"Why not?"

"You already had your two questions," answers Caroline. "Rosie, what would you like to ask?"

Rosie picks at her nails. Sean looks over and speaks again, "Why won't she have to take this test? What are your plans for her?"

"One more word out of turn and you will go first tomorrow," retorts Caroline.

Sean huffs and slams his back into his seat.

"Rosie, what would you like to know?"

She grits her teeth, her hesitant glances going from Caroline to Marcus. "Is the test Ralph did our only test?"

"No. There are four," Caroline answers tersely.

"What are the other three?"

"I can't answer that."

Rosie opens her mouth, but nothing comes out. She rests her back against her chair; her eyes quickly looking at Sean before going back to the table in front of her.

"Juan, what would you like to know?"

With his hands clenched at his sides, Juan stands up and slams them into the table. "I want to know why you killed my friends."

"That's not a question," Caroline calmly responds.

"Why did you kill my friends?" he asks, his words full of vigor.

"I didn't kill anyone. They chose their fates. They failed. What else do you want to know?"

His knuckles crack against the table. "How many tests do we have to take per day?"

"Just one. Everyone will attempt the same test Ralph failed, tomorrow." Moving her stare to Kyle, Caroline leans forward. "Now, I know you're first to go tomorrow, but that doesn't mean you should be frightened. Since you're on the hot seat, I will allow you three questions, Kyle. Ask wisely."

He instantly fires his first question. "Are all the tests individual?"

"Yes."

"Why?"

"You all made it here by surviving Separation collectively. In Halcyon, we separate you from others to truly find out who you are, and what you're capable of." Caroline leans back in her chair. Crossing her legs, she holds up her pointer finger.

"Why did you say that not everyone has taken this test, but we all are required to partake?"

"Good question. Not everyone in Halcyon has chosen the route of becoming a follower. Those who decided against the Cirque de Chance are now the foundation of this society. They're the workers who enable this world to thrive." Pausing before continuing eloquently, Caroline looks over at the walls—her focus primarily on one of the larger wave-like designs. "They work fourteen-hour days every day to ensure Halcyon functions at the highest level while myself, Noah, and the other followers watch over and protect our world. If everyone took the test, this world wouldn't be as vast as it is. It wouldn't have the appeal I've sought after since escaping Nimbus."

"You were in Nimbus?" mumbles Kyle.

"It's not your turn to ask. The question is forfeited. Marcus, what would you like to know?"

"When were you in Nimbus?"

Gritting her teeth, but holding her smile, Caroline mutters, "That question was forfeited. You have one more question."

"Why won't you answer that?" he asks, his cheekbones tightening.

"Because I'm here to help you understand Halcyon—not my past. Your turn is over. Sam, proceed with your two questions."

I don't want to waste my questions like the some of the others and I don't want to pry at a past that won't save my life.

"Did you meet a girl from Nimbus recently named Melanie?"

"I did. She was very sweet, but very frightened."

"How did you meet her?"

"Are you sure that's what you want to ask?"

I shoot a look at Elise. She quickly shakes her head. "Let me think for a second."

"Take your time. I don't want you to waste your questions like some of your friends."

"Where's Marisa?"

My question makes everyone lean forward, their collective eyes focused on Caroline like an audience entranced by a flawless ballet.

I run my fingers across my scar.

The edges of Caroline's mouth tighten. She softly exhales. "Marisa's busy."

"That's not a fair answer," shouts Elise. "Tell them what you told me earlier. Tell them the damn truth."

All our eyes shift to Elise then quickly back to Caroline.

"They don't need to know."

"But I did? I needed to know that Marisa was working for you the whole time? That she led us to you!"

"Enough!" sharply interrupts Caroline. "You need to know how everything works. They," she says emphatically, "do not."

"Why does Elise need to know everything?" asks Ella, in turn.

For the first time, Caroline looks irritated, completely baffled by Elise's words. Yet, she remains focused, or at least tries to, and turns to face Ella. "That's not important."

"But it pertains to Halcyon. She doesn't have to compete. She's here, but she's not on the precipice. I ask again," she says firmly. "Why does Elise need to know what's happening and we don't?"

"That's two questions, my dear. Your turn is over. You've asked more than allotted."

Ella rolls her eyes, but doesn't say anything.

"Just answer them," cries Elise. "Tell them what you told me. Tell them why I'm wearing black and they're wearing white. Tell them everything. I'm your pawn; the devil's puppet unable to fight back for fear of suffering. Tell them what they need to know, or I will."

Elise's face has gone red. Her cheeks are saturated with tears. Her hands shaking against the table, she clenches her teeth.

"You can't say anything if you want to live, Elise. You know why you're different. They don't need to know." Then, she snaps her fingers, and Katrina grabs Elise's forearm and yanks her out of the chair, flinging her to the floor. There, Noah grabs her by her wrist, as Katrina takes the other and lifts her up.

She doesn't fight back.

But Sean does. "Let go of her!" he shouts as he angrily stands up—sending his chair reeling into the wall.

"Sit down, Sean," utters Caroline. "If you so much as try to follow them out of the room, you won't like the consequences."

"Listen to her," cries Elise.

Sean heavily exhales and looks away.

Noah and Katrina carry Elise out of the room.

"That's enough for today. Dinner has been ruined and no more questions will be asked," says Caroline as she stands up. Turning her attention to Miles, who was next up in the line of questions, she speaks. "Sorry, Miles, you can blame your friends for ruining this evening. I will see everyone tomorrow morning," she continues as she works her way toward a door at the back of the room. "Goodnight."

Elise

I don't know where the hell I am, or what in the world I'm doing. All I know is that Caroline is a monster. Everything I saw in my head, everything Sam saw in his, was a lie. We saw what Caroline wanted us to see, what she wanted us to believe: that Halcyon was a safe haven, a blissful escape from the rigors of an unknown landscape.

And we were all foolish enough to believe that those visions were true.

I kick an end table across the room; a vase wobbles and shatters on the floor in front of me. I pick up a shard and chuck it at the wall.

My hands are shaking; they're becoming numb. I pick up another piece and throw it at the ugly dark paneling. And another. And another. I can feel the glass cutting into my palms, but the warmth doesn't concern me. The blood dripping onto the floor doesn't faze me. Angrily and rapidly, I keep throwing the pieces.

Then, I stop.

Every bit of rage flowing through my veins feels like the poison in the city. It feels like my skin was pulled back, and an iron was pressed into my tendons. Not a hot, scalding iron, but a tepid thickness pressing into my insides. It's gross. It's frightening. I want to scream, but I can't.

I throw my back against the wall and slide down onto my backside.

My hands continue to bleed, but I don't do anything. I lean into the wooziness. I fall toward the sudden lightheadedness.

Everything that led us here is part of a bigger picture—one not even Caroline seems to know everything about. All she told me was that the DZ runs the world and Nimbus, Halcyon, and another society are under the order of that place. She didn't tell me what the

DZ does, how they rule, or anything that could help. All I know is that there are three circles, but the fourth, well, that's mine.

Caroline doesn't care about the other circles, nor does she care about Sean, Marcus, or any of them. She only cares about me. The DZ cares about Sam, but Caroline's focus is solely on me. I'm supposed to study under her; I'm supposed to 'learn' how to create the perfect society, how to devise a system that inherently favors the strong. *Because that's all a world needs to survive, apparently.* For whatever reason, the DZ chose me to be the next leader.

I press my palms into the floor. The boards creak beneath the pressure.

From how I see it, there are two ways to look at my current situation. One: It guarantees my survival for the immediate future. Two: It kills everyone I care about, leaving me with nothing but scars.

My survival isn't paramount. My fate doesn't matter—at least, to me. I can't imagine a world in which Sean, Sam, Rosie, Ella, all of them, are dead. I can't. I've lost enough people in the past ten years that the thought of losing all that I have left eats me. It furthers the iron upon my skin. It presses, and presses, and presses until my bones crack.

I let out a slight cry. One soft enough not to alert Katrina—assuming the previous noise hasn't already.

Tilting my head against the wall, the faint echo of my scalp hitting the plaster reverberates through my body. Then, it hits me.

I still have a chip.

Sam does, too.

MacMillan got into our heads through the chip. Caroline did as well. There's no other excuse.

I reach for the scar atop my scalp. About an inch long, I glide the tip of my finger against it before digging my nail into the slit.

Shit! I shout internally, as the sensation quickly eliminates feeling in my fingers.

I let go.

Caroline told me Marisa works for her, and she has the whole time. She was the doctor we so freely welcomed back into Nimbus after killing MacMillan. Though, we didn't know she was an outsider. We just knew she was a doctor; we knew she could help. Dr. Tierney didn't say anything either. It's almost as if there was some collusion that brought us here.

Does that mean the others' chips were taken out? Or, like Sam and I, were their chips adjusted to allow Halcyon, or the DZ, complete control of our minds?

It's a question I can't answer. It's a question I don't want to answer. I just want to be free from the stressors pitting me against those I love.

I lift my hands from the floor. The blood is drying, but the tips of my fingers are covered in a fresh batch. My head grows unsteady; I fall onto my shoulder atop the floor.

The door bursts open. Legs hurry toward me, blurring the closer they get. I close my eyes.

Sam

"Did you hear that?" anxiously asks Sean.

"Hear what?" I reply.

"That thud. It sounded like a door smashing into a wall."

I shrug my shoulders. Unfortunately, whatever paranoia Sean has, isn't shared with me. I'm frightened; that I can admit, but I'm not falling apart inside. Sean is.

Ever since dinner, he's been growing more and more agitated. His head is constantly in his hands; when he speaks, it's upsetting or tough to comprehend. Whatever grip Caroline has on him might be stronger than the one she has on Elise and I. Either that, or Sean's truly at a loss without Elise. It's almost like she died, but she hasn't.

We've both experienced death. We've both survived and continued forward, but this is different. He knows Elise is alive, but he can't stop treating it like she's not. I'm worried.

He's my brother and I love him, but I'm afraid I might not be able to help him.

I take a seat on the edge of the bed. "Sean," I mutter.

He relocates his hands from his face to his knees, but he doesn't look up. I can see the scars from his eleven years; I can see what Separation did to him. His palms tremble against the silk—causing the pant legs to glide back and forth like he's sitting atop an air vent.

I continue. "What's on your mind?"

I know it's a dangerous question, but he's also in a position I've been in.

He tilts his head slightly upward, making only his eyes visible. Then, he whispers, "What if I never see her again?"

The hair on my arms stands up. The words linger across my forehead like a vicious headache—one I can't do a damn thing about. I move my hand onto my forearm, slowly moving it up and down. "You will see her," I mumble.

"In what capacity?"

"Outside of this place."

He slumps his head back into his hands, as if he doesn't believe me.

"We're going to get out," I quietly say. "We're going to escape."

Muffled, he says, "We're not. We had all the chance in the world to take a different route, yet we came here. We're not going anywhere. We're all going to die here."

I stand up and walk across the room until I'm a mere inch from Sean's face. Then, I slap him.

He instantly leaps forward and pins me to the ground. "Do you not see how there is no escape, Sam?!" he shouts at me, his spit flying into my eyes. "There's no way out except victory. If we don't pass Caroline's tests, the only way I'll see Elise again is in the clouds."

I try to pry his arms off, but he's far stronger than I am. "Stop it! Stop it! Stop it!" I cry. "You sound like Marcus and that's not where you need to be right now."

His grip lessens, but he keeps me pinned. "It doesn't matter what I sound like, Sam." His hands start to shake. "I'm absolutely lost. I've become more reliant on Elise than I ever expected I would. I love her more than myself."

I take advantage of his weakened state and roll out to the side. Hopping onto my feet, I move back to the bed. "And you don't think I loved Abby?"

Sean doesn't answer. He remains on all fours.

"I may not have had as much time with her as you've had with Elise, but that doesn't mean anything. She was with me since the day I turned fourteen, and she still is. I never get to see her again—not in any capacity." My words start to become hushed. "We can still get out of here, Sean. You can still be with her here. . ."

He bites his bottom lip and slumps his head further toward his chest. "Sam," he utters beneath his breath.

"Yea?"

"I'm sorry."

"It's okay."

"It's not." He moves back to the chair. "I always try to be the tough guy. I try to be the leader, but I might be more scared than everyone else."

"There's nothing wrong with that."

"Until fear blocks your other emotions. Until it becomes the only thing you feel."

"That's why you can't let it," I mutter, knowing good and well that fear still plays a part in my life. It's why I couldn't move in Nimbus to give my parents a chance to breathe again; it's why Ann died. It's why Abby died. Fear is all I feel, but I can't tell Sean that. I can't lean into his suffering. It would just further mine, and at that rate, we'd both be dead quicker than Ralph.

"It's harder than it sounds," he replies. "I can't keep faking my way through everything."

"You might have to."

"I don't know if I can."

"It's gotten you this far," I state. "Keep doing it until we get out."

He closes his eyes and rests his head against the back of the chair. "I'll try, Sam. I'll try."

I hate seeing Sean like this. I hate seeing anyone like this, but I'm sure they all feel the same about me. I'm always the one with the short stick, forced into situations I failed to personally choose. But the reality is, this world doesn't want you to feel anything, yet we all do—and we will all continue to.

Nimbus wanted us to become heartless, cold-blooded killers. Halcyon wants us to eliminate any emotion blocking us from succeeding in rigorous, near-impossible tests.

Whoever the 'higher power' that chose Elise is, I'm afraid they may want us to become more robotic than anything we've ever seen—if we even get that far.

I fall onto my back atop the bed.

Speaking toward the ceiling, I faintly say, "Who chose Elise?"

But before Sean can do so much as open his mouth, Noah pushes open the door. "Lights out."

"I'm not tired," I retort.

"Halcyon decree number three states that all lights must go out at 10 p.m. each night or the perpetrator faces Cirque de Chance the following day."

I laugh. "Well, we face it anyways."

Noah's jaw becomes rigid. "Doesn't matter. Lights out." Then, he flips the switch and slams the door.

11 May 2192

Elise

To my right, my left, and in front of me sit at least a dozen black iron-framed beds. Each one is covered in off-white sheets with the ends tucked under the mattresses, while mildly dusty pillows rest against the part of the frames nearest to the wall.

I'm the only one in here.

My hands are bandaged and I'm halfway under the sheets. The room is freezing and the only visible light is a flickering bulb in the hallway just outside the open door.

Where am I?

I pull the blankets off; my hands throb as I do so.

Turning onto my side, I swing my legs over the edge of the bed. My toes nick the cold tile. I let out a slight yelp of displeasure.

"Sorry this room is so cold," echoes Caroline's voice.

I look every which way, but I don't see anyone.

A light turns on behind me. I look back.

Perched up on a bed adjacent to me but three rows over, Caroline smiles.

"Where am I?" I ask.

"The hospital."

"Why?"

"Don't act like you don't know why," she smirks.

I press my hands into the mattress as I try to situate myself to face Caroline. With each subtle movement, I press my lips tightly together, trying to hide my obvious pain. "How come nobody else is here?" I ask in an attempt to blind her from my discomfort.

"The hospital is only used for followers and myself. Others aren't welcomed."

"How do they get help if they're hurt or ill, then?"

"They don't."

"Why not?" I angrily retort.

"Because they chose not to take the test. In doing so, they knew they wouldn't receive the same luxuries as those who completed it."

I bite my tongue. I know that if I try to tell Caroline her vile methods will be the downfall of her society, she won't listen. She'd rather laugh at the suffering of others than be told she's incorrigible. And being that I'm currently wounded, my words hold no traction. So, instead, I ask, "Are there any doctors here, then?"

"Yes, one."

"Where?"

"Right outside. Why? Do you need her assistance?"

"I'd like new bandages," I murmur. "I think one of my cuts opened up."

Caroline snaps her fingers.

In steps Marisa. Wearing the same cerulean blue robe as Noah and the others, she offers no attention to me.

"Marisa, would you fetch some new wrappings for Elise?"

Marisa nods, but before she can leave I grab onto her robe.

She slaps at my hand, but I don't let go. My hands have become tremulous; the pain is now searing, but I don't release. "Why did you do this?" I swallow. "What did we do to you?"

"Let go," she replies.

The pain worsens. I can see blood soaking into the gauze. "Answer me!" I shout.

She doesn't respond. She knows I'm weak.

"Marisa, continue along. We don't want her to pass out again," voices Caroline.

I let go of the robe. Marisa storms out.

"I want a different doctor," I whisper under my breath.

"Sorry, that's not an option. Unless you want the same treatment as the failures, you will deal with what you've done."

"The failures?"

"The foundation," she simply answers.

I don't want to be here. I need to get out.

I fall back onto the mattress—a slight bit of dust bounces into the air then fades into nothingness. I slam the back of my head onto the pillow and roll onto my stomach.

"Why are you angry?" Caroline asks genuinely—but not enough to the point that her words are endearing.

I grab the pillow and wrap it around my head.

She continues to speak, but her muffled speech doesn't penetrate the fabric, nor the feather.

I need to run. I need to find Sean and just run.

I hold the pillow tighter against the back of my head, while not allowing myself to limit the pressure due to the pain in my palms. The end of the bed sinks in. I know it's Caroline, but I don't move; I don't yield to her incessant questioning.

She inches closer to my waist. Then, toward my chest.

I don't budge.

She doesn't care. She puts her hand on the nape of my neck before gliding the nail of her index finger onto my scalp beneath the pillow cover. Then, she presses into my scar.

***

"Elise," rings Caroline's voice in my eardrums. It's loud. It's like she's everywhere, like she's projecting the sound directly to my brain. "You need to listen."

"I can't," I cry, the words deafening my senses.

"Come out, or I'll place your mind into complete darkness and leave you there until everyone's dead."

"Come out of where?"

"Don't bullshit with me."

I open my eyes, but I'm still here. I'm still stuck in this darkened corner of my mind. "How do I escape?"

"You can't until you tell me you'll listen."

"I will," I shriek. "Please get me out of here!"

***

"You're going to listen now?" asks Caroline.

I roll onto my back and throw the pillow across the room.

What the hell was that?

"Elise. . .?" Caroline says, staring at me.

"Yes," I mutter.

Marisa enters.

I glare at her indignantly.

"Marisa, dear, would you please unwrap Elise's hands and tell her why you did what you did?"

What? I think.

Marisa looks at me begrudgingly. Her hands lightly shake as she starts to unravel the bloody gauze upon my palms. She must know she shouldn't disobey Caroline. "I. . .I brought you here because it's your destiny," she mutters, her tone completely unreadable.

"That's not all," says Caroline.

Marisa pulls the wrappings off my left hand—my blood-soaked palm is unrecognizable; there are cuts in all directions making it look more like a spider web than a hand. "You were brought here because Nimbus was no longer safe."

"I chose to leave Nimbus," I rebut.

She starts to blot at the blood. "You were directed out."

"How?"

"Caroline just showed you."

I yank my hand away from Marisa and jump back into the iron frame. "No, I chose to leave. We all chose to leave."

With her head down, Marisa reaches for my palm again. I oblige, but not by choice. The pain has become too unbearable not to be mended.

"In some sense, you chose, but in reality, Caroline has always been guiding you."

I turn to Caroline, my eyes pushing Marisa's statement onto her.

"She's right. Why do you think you always had those circus nightmares?" calmly states Caroline. "Do you really think those were just some coincidence?"

"But the circus here is nothing like what I saw."

"I couldn't show you Cirque de Chance, dear. I couldn't let you see everything. I just needed to give you a clue."

"How was that a clue? Those nightmares ate at me. They still haunt me," I retort, accidentally pulling my hand from Marisa this time.

She quickly grabs it back before rewrapping it and moving onto my other hand.

"But you overcame them. You beat the fear that was trying to break you, and now look where you are," she smiles. "You're in Halcyon, safely away from Eldridge's horribly inadequate world."

"You knew MacMillan?" I quickly spit out.

"Where do you think I was twenty-seven years prior to founding this place?"

I don't answer.

"I was surviving Separation just like you. So, of course I knew that old bag of bones. Good riddance," she smirks.

I stay quiet.

"Like I was saying, his world was inadequate. Halcyon isn't. This is why you're here. This is why you need to pay attention. Halcyon will show you the true distance man is willing to go before he breaks."

"But why me?" I ask, uncertainly.

"Because you were chosen by the DZ, Elise. You were chosen by the people who created everything you know."

"Who are they?"

"They're the highest power. They sent Aldous to make Nimbus. They sent me to make Halcyon after I easily survived Separation. Then, they sent Vincent to your next destination."

My head is spinning. "Who. . .what. . .why. . .how?" I achingly mumble.

Caroline bites her bottom lip and half smiles at me—her eyes almost menacingly staring at me. "You'll understand everything in due time."

Marisa tapes the gauze around my right hand and exits the room.

"I want to understand now. I want to understand everything. Why can you get in my head? Why do I still have a chip? Why does everything here look like it's over 250 years old?"

Caroline stands up and starts to pace back and forth. Her shoes click upon the floor, causing a faint echo with each step.

"One: I need to know you're paying attention. Two: Same answer as one. Three: It's my favorite era. It was a time when the world hadn't learned all it knew by 2105, yet despite its shortcomings in technology, it made up for it with its efficiency. Plus, the style, the aesthetic, the colors, were quite gorgeous."

"So why don't you dress that way too?"

"The temperatures and dirt in a fault aren't conducive to achieving everything that era had. Plus, classes here need to be recognizable, so by dressing certain ways, we know who belongs where."

"Then why am I in this black silk?"

She smiles and makes her way back toward my bed. With her hands outstretched, she gently places them on the end frame and leans toward me. "You're my apprentice. You need to stand out."

I bite my tongue. I know that's not why. I'm the Princess of Death—the lesser-known evil to the Queen of Darkness.

With her eyes still focused on me, Caroline smiles. "Now, are you ready to go?"

"Only if you don't hurt my friends."

She steps toward the door; her back to me, she exhales, "Oh, I won't hurt them. You will."

Sean

I don't want to do this. They can't make me do this. My mind is pushing fear-based phrases deep into my psyche; they're causing me to feel a new kind of pain, a pain I've never had the desire to feel. It's more than just dread; it's trying to become full-circle depression.

But I won't let it. I pull my t-shirt over my head.

"Are you going to be okay?" asks Sam, as he throws off his white slippers and slides on his tennis shoes.

"Yea, I'll be fine," I reply.

"Are you feeling better than last night?"

I pull my shoes on and nod.

Sam hops off the bed and walks over toward the door. Running his injured hand around the scratched charcoal doorknob, he speaks. "Do you think Noah is always behind this? Or do you think if we opened it in the middle of the night, we could make a run for it?" He jiggles the handle.

"Maybe."

"You couldn't," permeates Noah's voice through the wood.

The door flies open—sending Sam reeling backward into me.

"You could try to run," he continues, "but you wouldn't even know which door to exit through. Nor would you be able to get past any of us."

"Do you not sleep?" chides Sam from the floor.

Noah just smiles, but not a friendly smile—a fake one. He then looks over at me and says, "Just so you know, the order for today has already been decided."

"How?" I ask, grinding my teeth.

He doesn't answer the question. "Today's order is Kyle, Rosie, Sean, Ella, Sam, Marcus, Miles, and lastly, Juan."

Third. I shake my head. But at least that's better than choosing who goes after me. Picking a friend to face death is an incomparable task. Nothing can prepare you for it, and nothing can make your decision easier. I guess we got lucky in the fact that someone else chose our order.

"Are you ready?" smirks Noah.

I stiffen my jaw. "What about this is humorous to you?" I snarl back.

"You're all weak. None of you show any desire to succeed. You reek of failure."

His sudden change in tone makes my muscles tighten; I want to punch him. I want to strangle him. I want to kill him. But I can't. If I let my emotions control me, I'll die and they'll kill Elise, Sam, and the others. I can't have that; I can't let my sorrow be theirs. So, I half-smile, lift my hand toward him, and ask him to lead the way, closemouthed.

"This way," he responds, indicating for us to follow someone else.

We move into the hallway. The follower takes a few steps ahead of us while Marcus, Kyle, Rosie, Ella, Miles, and Juan step in behind us. Noah and the others remain steadfast in the back.

"Conveniently, the entrance to Cirque de Chance is at the end of this hall," speaks the woman.

"So, our only real escape is this test?" says Marcus from behind me, as he cracks his neck. The soft grinding of his bones bounces off the walls before fading back into the inimitable silence of Halcyon. "I knew those nice rooms were too good to be true."

"I guess you could say that," she answers.

We slowly move past unopened doors, more empty but intricately designed vases, and a mass of artwork. Each painting hangs above a vase of corresponding color. Beneath a painting of a ship stranded at sea during a storm sits a dark blue vase with gold streaks down its sides. Below a portrait of a sulking woman clad in a red scarf with a white blouse sits a vase akin in likeness. It's entirely white with a crimson line wrapped around the top.

I turn around and reach for Sam's hand.

He keeps his attention on the photo of the crying woman, but manages to find my hand amidst his infatuation.

As I look back, I catch a glimpse of everyone. Marcus looks pale; he's showing no emotion. Behind him, Kyle looks lost, distraught, every word anyone could use to describe unwilling and frightened; yet, next in line is Rosie and she looks eager. Ella looks prepared. Miles looks angry. Juan looks like he did every day on the Guard: unenthused, but prepared to do what he needs to do to survive.

Everyone is different. Hopefully that doesn't mean that we lose another in this task.

Our walk slows to a halt.

"Are you ready?" asks Noah, as he pushes past us to a stance in front.

None of us answer. It wouldn't matter if we did. Our fate's been chosen.

I squeeze onto Sam's hand. He squeezes back. The door flies open. A bright light shines upon us, instantly blinding our path.

"I bring you today's competitors!" echoes Caroline's voice around the arena.

We walk in to sheer pandemonium. Unlike yesterday, the crowd is on their feet screaming, cheering, yelling whatever comes to mind. I press my lips together.

Sam's fingers become moist.

"We've got a great show for you today!" continues Caroline, "Our first competitor will be Sean Martin!"

My knees buckle. My hand slips from Sam's grasp. Noah and another catch my elbows before I fall; Noah's heartless smirk angers me. "Sorry, did I get the order wrong? I do that sometimes."

What the hell?

I don't bother to fight back. Fate's chosen me and there's nothing I can do about it.

Elise

"You said he wouldn't go first!" I shout into the glass, as Caroline walks on the stage beneath me.

"Caroline likes to have fun," responds Katrina from behind me.

"This is fun to you?" I retort; my fists pounding into the glass.

She doesn't answer.

I turn around and say again," Is this fun to you, Katrina? Is watching people suffer for your own amusement fun?"

She steps toward me. Her dark brown eyebrows descend toward the ridge of her nose; her eyes mock me with a haunting glance. Then with her voice low, her words come out quieted and breathless, "This is everything to me."

I reach for her throat. She reaches for my wrists. My hands can't sustain the force. She pushes me back.

"You're weak, Elise. You're just as weak as them. Now stand up and watch him die. . .watch them all die."

Sean

My vision is glossy. Everything above me appears as if I'm looking through the wrong end of a magnifying glass. I can't hear any voices, nor can I feel the presence of another. The only thing around me is rock, and this mat.

Before I get a chance to find a moment of comfort or to plan my exit, the stomping starts. Two stomps followed by a pause; two stomps and a pause. It keeps going and going, like an unsteady heartbeat. Then, comes the voice.

"Le cirque commence," rings Caroline's voice.

I wipe my eyes. My toes become wet.

I can't hear anything but the sound of water pouring onto rock. I rapidly blink, trying to clear my obscured line of sight.

My toes feel the cold chill.

I look up.

Directly above me, I see her. She's pounding on glass. I can see the redness of her cheeks, the swelling beneath her eyes.

The water moves up toward my ankles.

Climb, I think. *Climb!*

Despite knowing the task at hand, my body hasn't chosen to move. It hasn't had the desire to fight back. Unlike storming Nimbus where I was fueled by anger, there's nothing pushing me here.

I'm angry, but not that way. I'm scared, but not like I was.

I look back up. Her fists are slamming onto the glass. Someone pulls her back.

My calves start to soak.

Then, a voice hits me. It's Abby's. My mind floods with her. The vase. The picture. The library. I can see her face. She reaches for my waist. *"What's this for?" I ask. "For everything. Thank you for protecting us. . .for keeping us alive," she responds.*

And she's gone; she's gone to a world I'm not ready to see. My legs are becoming cold. I jump toward the rock.

Digging my fingers into the stone, I look for an opening—a small crevice where I can lodge my fingers.

I don't see anything.

I look left. Nothing. I look right. Nothing. I reach up in hopes that I'll find something to grab onto, something to pull myself higher. My fingers nick shards of rock into the water—the splash ices my back.

I fall back into the water, which is now above my knees, as I search for a better route to the top. And that's when I see it: a path of jagged rock seemingly building a stone ladder to the surface. I run toward it and jump upward, completely clearing myself from the water.

Left, right, left, right, I slither upward like a lizard scaling a mountain. Yet, with each movement, my hands grow more and more moist.

Keep going, I say to myself. *Keep moving.*

But I can't. My hands have become covered in sweat. Just holding myself here is difficult—not from the weight or exhaustion of the climb, but from the fact that I'm slipping.

I reach for the surface. My right hand plants itself atop the ground. I try to pull myself higher, but I can feel my hand sliding back toward my shoulder. I struggle to keep it firm and in place as I lift my body.

Then, it happens. My hand slips off the top. My left forefingers slide down the only rock holding me in place.

This is it.

Elise

"No, no, no!" I scream in Katrina's arms as she squeezes my stomach from behind, pulling me away from the only window to Sean.

"He's dead!" she shouts back. "Accept that and move on!"

I won't accept it. I won't believe it.

Sean wouldn't fail on a physical test; it's not in his nature. Even if he slipped out of reach, he hasn't fallen in. No stomping has begun.

I settle myself in Katrina's arms; her grip loosens.

"See how much easier it is to accept it?" she mocks. My breath slows. She lets go.

"I won't accept this world," I say softly, my voice ridden with palpable rage.

"What was that?" answers Katrina.

I clench my fists and don't answer. The cuts ache, but the pain doesn't bother me. I can feel the air around me thicken as Katrina tries to reach for me again, but before it gets too tight, I spin 180 degrees forward. Face-to-face with Katrina, I cock my arm back and jump toward her—smashing my wrapped knuckles into her jaw. She launches back into the glass, blood dripping from her mouth.

"You shouldn't have done that," she grins, the red smeared across her teeth.

Still clenching my other fist, I swing it toward her cheek.

She catches it. Instantly crushing my fingers underneath hers. I try to pull my hand away, but I can't. The pain starts seeping through the gauze, but she doesn't let go. She only squeezes harder.

"Let go!" I cry.

"I'm going to break your hand," she laughs, the blood now dripping down her lips and onto the floor. "I'm going to make the pain you're experiencing now feel like a pinch compared to what's next."

The stomping begins.

My legs crumble. Katrina hasn't let go.

"Katrina," echoes Caroline's voice through the arena. "Please bring Elise closer to the glass."

"Stand up," angrily spits out Katrina. "Stand up."

I don't budge.

It doesn't bother her. She drags me across the room; the agony in my hand has disappeared enough to the point that this movement doesn't faze me externally. It just annoys me.

"Stand up or I'll break your hand and pull you up."

I don't move.

The pressure grows tighter; my fingers are folding into one another, as the cuts are torn open. The pain resurfaces. I've never felt anything quite like this, but I still refuse to stand. I'm not going to watch them show me his corpse. I'm not going to yield to the suffering just to be given a pat on the back for doing so. No. I won't become what Caroline wants me to become.

The stomping continues.

"Katrina. . ." says Caroline caustically.

"Get up!" Katrina grits through her teeth, trying to hide this struggle from Caroline.

"I thought you were going to pull me up," I cringe as my pinky folds at an awkward angle into the center of my hand.

She bitterly sighs aloud. "Just remember, this is what you wanted," she says as she yanks my arm upward in such a motion that my shoulder dislocates. Yet, there's no quick pang of irritation, no sudden discomfort. I can't move my arm, but it doesn't hurt.

Now that I'm on my feet, I look down to see Caroline smiling. She either can't see what Katrina's done, or she doesn't care. My belief is the latter.

"I don't know what took you so long to come here, Elise. I figured you'd be happy to see Cirque de Chance's first success in a month."

What?

I lean my head forward. Standing beside Caroline is Sean. He's out of breath and his hands are bleeding, but he's alive.

Caroline continues. "I know it's only one round, but it's been awhile since even one round has been successfully completed.

Congrats!" she sarcastically declares to the audience. "Now, up next will be Kyle."

"I thought the stomping meant death," I mouth.

"It just marks the beginning and the end, and the end doesn't always equate death," responds Katrina.

A deep, tingling sensation starts at the back of my head. It glides down my neck, across the top of my shoulder, and into my motionless limb before it fades to nothing. The whole extremity has gone numb, yet blood continues to seep through my bandages and onto the floor.

Katrina doesn't care. She simply moves to the back of the room, probably awaiting my fury.

But I don't give it to her. I just keep looking forward.

Sean survived. That's all that matters right now. But Sam still has to go. And if I couldn't handle the slip of a finger from Sean, I don't know how I'll manage to watch Sam. He's just a kid. He shouldn't be here.

The pain worsens. It's like my body's finally realized my arm is dislodged from its normal place. I reach for it with my opposite hand.

There's a slight bump from the top of my clavicle to my shoulder, but it's not enough that it's the worst thing I've ever felt. At least I wasn't stabbed again.

"You know Caroline won't like what you've done to me," I mutter, knowing good and well that Caroline could probably care less.

Katrina huffs. "You got what you deserved. You were chosen for a reason, so you should be tougher than that."

I scoff. "Tough enough that getting my shoulder pulled out of place doesn't hurt?"

"I dislocated mine on the first test and still made it out without the water getting higher than my ankles."

"And how'd you get it back in? Caroline said the hospital isn't open to anyone who hasn't passed the tests."

"Just like this," she wittingly replies, as she steps toward me, grabs my arm by the elbow and quickly, almost unnoticeably, forces it downward. The bones click, and the agony of the injury lunges through my tissue and into the entirety of my body. Almost as if she had cracked every bone in my body simultaneously, the discomfort comes full force.

But. I can't show it.

I keep my face straight, concealing the uneasiness of my ever-changing unhappiness.

"You handled that better than I expected," she says contemptuously. "I figured you'd be on the floor crying."

"I'm tougher than I let on," I bite back.

She grins, her dark, seemingly colorless eyes mocking my words. "You better start proving it then."

My fingers tingle. My shoulder is starting to swell. I can feel it. I can feel the muscles bulging, trying to break the surface of my skin just to breathe. But I have to keep up this façade. I have to smile through the pain if there's any hope of getting out of here alive.

Sam

I'm not watching any of this. I can't watch this.

There are nine of us here, but after today there could only be two. Elise doesn't have to compete. Sean survived. That leaves seven of us to drown.

Stop it, I think. *Stop thinking about the worst.*

But I can't. No matter how many times my emotions go from happy to angry to unsettled to furious, I can't control it. I can't fake my way through everything we've been through. I've tried, and it hasn't worked. It might work for others, but then again, most of them spent more time outside Nimbus after their Separation than I did; they've learned how to handle these emotions. I haven't.

Noah opens the door at the far right of the glass. He motions for Kyle to come forward.

Kyle doesn't move. He remains still in the opposite corner away from Noah, his hands trembling on his biceps.

I slide down the wall and onto my butt. Crossing my arms, I wrap them around my knees, and rest my head on my forearms. *I don't want to be here. We shouldn't be here.* A faint voice in the back of my head laughs at my thoughts.

I shake my head.

"You have to go," mutters Marcus. "I know this is absurd, but if we fight back we'll die here rather than there."

"I'd rather have that," responds Kyle, nearly inaudibly.

"I doubt that," adds Noah. "Come forward now."

"You have to do it. We all do," says Marcus.

Moving his face closer to Marcus's, Kyle whispers something inaudible. They embrace.

Rosie, Miles, and Ella join.

"Enough of this," scowls Noah. "Get out here now."

"You got this," murmurs Rosie.

"We believe in you," half-heartedly grins Miles.

Slowly releasing his grip on Marcus's shoulders, Kyle steps through the others toward the opening. Noah grabs his arm and throws him onto the platform.

The stomping begins.

I bury my head in my knees.

Sean

Kyle: Dead.

Rosie: Alive.

Ella: Alive.

Now, it's Sam's turn. I don't want to add his name beside Ralph, Derrick, and Kyle. But I'm not in charge. I have no say in how he fares in such a ridiculous game.

"Next up. . ." echoes Caroline's voice, with a richer, more enthused tone attached to it, ". . .we have Sam Martin, younger brother of our first successor, Sean." Then, taking a quick glance at me, complete with a childish wink, Caroline taps her cane on the ground, and slowly glides around the pit.

The audience is on edge. I can see people leaning forward in their seats, as if they've never seen familial relations play a role in this sport.

Continuing her speech as Sam trembles above, Caroline doesn't look his way, but speaks at him. "Sam, are you ready?"

Sam doesn't respond—which is probably what Caroline expected.

"Well, you should be. You've had your time to watch. You've had minutes to gawk at the successes of three, and the failure of one. If that's not enough time to prepare yourself, then you're going to have a really hard time with your task."

Then, almost invisibly, Caroline double-taps her cane on the surface of the arena. The lights completely disappear. Ella grabs onto my arm.

"Sean," she mumbles. "Do you think she's going to make Sam do something else?"

"I don't know," I silently murmur. I don't see why she would, why she would see fit to make Sam face a tougher task than what already lies ahead.

Held in a glass capsule similar to the one we were in prior to our test, the three of us rest arena-level, but are far enough away that we can't see if any changes occurred in the pit. Plus, the darkness doesn't help.

"Halcyon," reverberates Caroline's voice through the darkness. "What do we do when we have two consecutive victors?"

The crowd starts to stomp. Not twice in a row, but three. Three stomps followed by a clap. Three stomps then a clap. There's no silence now, but there's also no visible answer. I move closer to the glass. Rosie and Ella do, too.

Rosie taps my shoulder.

"Yea?"

"I think I know what's going to happen."

"What?" I reply, my face on the glass.

"They're going to set a time limit."

"Why do you say that?"

"How long did it take you to get out?"

I avert my eyes down toward my hands. I can feel the dry blood in my fists, but I can't see it. "I don't know," I say. "Nobody told me when I got over here."

"It was at least a few minutes. I bet they give Sam less time. They make the water flow in faster, or something."

Then, before I can so much as I try to fathom the possibility of Sam getting less time than the rest of us, the lights turn back on. And there, inches from the hole, stands Caroline, with her arms outstretched. "Katrina!" she shouts. "Please start the timer!"

A giant, pulsating cerulean three appears in the blackness above the audience.

It starts counting down before Sam's even in position.
2:59.
Sam falls in.
2:56.

I can't see him. None of us can. That's the worst part about being over here. My hands are sweating profusely, but there's nothing I can do about it. I wipe them on my pants, staining them with refreshed blood.

The clock falls to 2:40.

"Sam!" I shout at the glass. "Sam!"

It's no use.

I glance up at Elise, hoping she can provide me with some answer to the welfare of my brother. But she doesn't. She's just as entranced as the audience.

2:30.

"I can't take this," I say aloud, my voice shaking with each word. "I can't take this. The time limit makes it worse. It makes it way worse."

"He'll make it," says Ella reassuringly. "He'll make it."

But my mind won't allow my body to believe it. The nagging voice of doubt trounces any reassurance from those I trust, and I can't stop it.

I look up at Elise again. She's still locked in a trance.

I look over at Rosie and Ella. They're both glued to the glass even though nothing is visible in front of us besides Caroline.

2:00.

Caroline continues to waltz around the opening showing no indication that Sam's close to the top.

I look back at Elise. Still, she doesn't look toward me.

He should be done by now, I think. *He should be at the top.*

"Where is he?" I shout, as my thoughts grow darker, more jumbled by the situation.

"Give him time," answers Rosie. "None of us did it that fast."

1:45.

"That doesn't mean he can't," I retort.

She doesn't say anything, nor does Ella.

My skin feels like it's on fire. Every ounce of my body feels like it's covered in hot coals. I wipe my forehead.

C'mon, Sam. C'mon, I whisper internally.

But he hasn't appeared.

I step away from the glass and start to pace around the room.

Rosie and Ella remain focused.

I can't let myself succumb to the thoughts trying to eat me. They're what almost killed me when I attempted this test; they're what almost killed me when I was separated for the second time.

I just need to breathe.

The last thing this group needs is to lose a leader.

I move back toward the glass.

The clock strikes 1:00.

I clench my fists, trying to force the anxiety away, or at least trying to halt its reach.

"Any signs of Sam yet?" I ask.

"Nothing," answers Rosie.

I step back again, and continue to pace around the limited space we have to roam.

"Wait," mutters Rosie. "Elise is moving around up there."

"That can mean anything," I reply.

"It can also mean he's close."

0:40.

C'mon, Sam. I need you. Elise needs you. We all need you.

I glance at Elise. Her back is now facing us. I pound on the glass, "Elise! Is he close?!"

She can't hear me. Sam can't hear me. Only Ella and Rosie can.

"Thirty seconds," rings Caroline's voice.

Time needs to speed up. But at the same time, this could be it. These could be the last thirty seconds Sam's alive. And the worst part is, there's nothing I can do to help. Moping around in here won't solve what's out there; screaming for a resolution won't provide it any quicker.

I walk back toward the glass, just hoping to see some part of my brother. Anything.

0:20.

I take a deep breath in. I exhale. I take another breath. Anything I can do to alleviate the stress Halcyon has put on me.

0:15.

0:14.

0:13.

0:12.

0:11.

"Sam," I faintly whisper toward the glass.

"Audience," shouts Caroline. "Start the countdown!"

"Ten!" roars the crowd.

"Sam," I mutter again.

"Nine!"

"Please," cries Ella.

"Eight!"

"Sam!" clamors Rosie.

"Seven!"

A sudden reprieve jolts in front of us as Sam's hand appears. "Six!"

His other hand follows.

"Five!"

Soon, his face is visible.

"Sam!" the three of us shout. "Sam!"

"Four!"

His chest appears. His shoulders lift higher as his arms push into the ground.

"Three!"

He falls onto his stomach, his legs still dangling in the water. "Two!"

He starts to pull himself further from the rising waters. His face is battered; his stubbed pinky is gushing with blood.

"One!"

And he's out.

The stomping begins.

"Well now, Sam," says Caroline. "In the history of this test on Cirque de Chance, we've never seen a tighter finish. Thank you for putting on such a show! Up next is Marcus! And just for fun, your time limit will be two minutes and forty-five seconds!"

I look up at Marcus. His demeanor doesn't change. He doesn't show any emotion; he's seemingly unfazed by Caroline's insolence.

Noah waves for him to step onto the platform.

Marcus obliges.

Caroline starts to speak, but her words glide past deafened ears like the wind. For, I can't take my eyes off Marcus.

With his arms outstretched, he rolls his fingers toward his palms—all but his middle ones. Then, he falls backward into the pit.

Marcus: Alive.

Miles: Alive.

Juan: Dead.

12 May 2192

Sam

The chocolate chip muffin stares at me. I rip off a piece from the side and curl it into a ball before eating it. For putting us through hell, Caroline feeds us like we're human—probably the only time we'll feel that way. After all, Kyle and Juan's deaths meant nothing to her. I doubt the rest of ours will, either.

I push my breakfast tray toward the center of the table, nicking my glass of orange juice. It spills across the surface of the wood.

Sean rolls his eyes at me. "You should probably eat, Sam. Who knows what the next test will be like."

He's right, but I don't care. The next test isn't for two days.

Rosie pushes her tray to the center, too. "It's hard to have an appetite after yesterday."

Beside her, Ella nibbles on the edges of a cinnamon roll; Marcus pokes at his toast with a fork, but doesn't eat anything; Miles didn't even get a tray. It's impossible to be hungry when you're constantly on edge, uncertain where your next step will take you.

Sean lifts up my orange juice glass before digging back into his eggs.

"What the hell are we even going to do today?" aimlessly asks Miles, his fingers gliding against the sides of the table.

"I thought I heard Noah mention something about a tour," mutters Ella.

"A tour of what?" I ask.

"Halcyon, I guess," she shrugs.

"What is there to see here?" angrily chides Marcus. "We've already seen all Caroline cares about, and it's killed three of our friends already. There can't be anything else to see." He pulls his fork from his toast before shoving it into his pocket.

"Except the area outside the circus," I grumble. "She said those who choose not to participate in Cirque de Chance are forced into manual labor to keep Halcyon afloat."

"The last thing I want to see is someone suffering through that sort of mental anguish," replies Marcus.

I refrain from shaking my head at his response. Of all of us still alive, nobody has shown more signs of shock and mental anguish than Marcus. He's not the same person we met at the library and I doubt he ever will be. The protective bubble he hid in for eight years popped and he still hasn't adjusted to the air around him.

Then again, nobody really has. Even Sean has struggled. And I have no idea how Elise is faring. I just hope Caroline hasn't gotten into her head; I hope she hasn't made Elise into someone she's not.

A door bursts open behind us. Noah strides in. "If you're done with breakfast, then follow me."

"What if we don't want to?" asks Marcus in a monotone, hushed voice.

"That's not a choice. Just think of it this way: no test today."

I bite my tongue before my brain makes me spit out words that Noah would just laugh at.

"Let's go," comes a voice from behind Noah. "Caroline doesn't like waiting."

"Who cares what she likes?" jokes Marcus.

Showing no teeth, Noah smirks. His eyes are fraught with petty rage he probably wishes he could release on Marcus, or any of us, really. "This way," he says gesturing toward the open door.

I fidget with the end of my lacerated pinky. The skin's healing over the wound, but I can't stop gliding my finger against the scarring. It's light enough that, at times, when I touch it, I can feel the rigidness of the bone. But, if I hit it wrong, it stings; though, that reminds me of how far I've come.

"Will Elise be going with us?" asks Sean as he stands up and polishes off his glass of water.

"Unfortunately, yes," answers Noah. "She's waiting outside with Caroline."

Sean moves toward Noah, while the rest of us slowly get up from our seats.

We're quickly taken through a series of hallways, each with the same color scheme of every room in this place: green and brown.

161

Yet, nothing unique jumps out, making these corridors seem as if they're merely walkways rather than areas of the building with architectural significance.

We go right. We trudge forward. We go left. Right. Left. Forward. Through a door into some sort of den, and out the other side. Right. Right again. It appears to be a zigzag of a maze made to confuse us so we don't try to escape.

Ushering us through another room—this one complete with two working fireplaces—Noah guides us under a walnut-colored archway and into a small room. There, he pulls a short rope on the ceiling, in which a hatch opens above us. He reaches upward. A ladder slides down onto the floor.

"Follow me," he says with one foot on the steel.

Sean goes first. Rosie follows. Then, I go.

The ladder takes us to another dark room. In there, Noah claps. A bulb flickers on, illuminating a room made entirely of cement. It feels familiar. Too familiar. My face starts to dampen; the area around me starts to pulse.

If you believe in the shadows, your eyes will see fine.

I shake my head and wipe away the sweat.

"Are you okay?" asks Rosie.

"I'm fine," I mutter.

"Are you sure?"

"It's nothing," I bite back.

"You're not convincing when you say it like that," she says.

"This room is just familiar," I mutter.

Rosie gently puts her hand on my shoulder before sliding it off.

I half-grin.

"This way," comes Noah's voice.

I turn around. A block of concrete extends outward into a puddle. I step outside.

We're close to where we came in. The sky is visible hundreds of feet above us, while lanterns lace the pathways in front of us. Benches are sporadically placed about, as well.

I take a look back. Nothing but a large square block of concrete stands in front of me, making me all the more wary how far down Halcyon truly goes.

"Where's Caroline?" asks Sean.

"She's meeting us at the library," answers Noah.

"The what?" hisses Marcus.

"You heard me."

Marcus takes a stride toward Noah. I grab the back of his belt.

"Let go, Sam." He grits his teeth at me. "Let go."

I don't.

"Marcus, take a breath," says Sean calmly.

He shakes off my hand and takes a step toward Noah. He takes a deep breath, puffs out his chest, and glares at him.

Noah doesn't flinch. "You might want to take a step back, or it could get ugly."

"How ugly?" snarls Marcus, as he yanks the fork out of his pocket before slashing it across Noah's face.

Noah dabs two fingers into the cuts. He looks at the blood and smiles. Then, swiftly, and almost unnoticeably, he throws his leg behind Marcus. And with one continuous movement, he slams the heel of his palm up into Marcus's chin.

Marcus yelps and stumbles backward into the mud. He tries to stand up, but ends up falling back down.

Rosie and Miles reach for his hands, but he refuses their help.

Noah smirks. The other followers' mock Marcus with their eyes.

Marcus dabs his index finger on his bottom lip before wiping the blood on his shirt. He doesn't speak, nor does he make eye contact with anyone.

"Let's go," declares Noah. "Caroline doesn't like to be kept waiting."

Noah starts to move along the path. The other followers stay close behind him.

I look back at Marcus. He remains on his backside.

"Where is the library?" asks Rosie as she steps in behind them.

Sean follows behind her. Miles, too.

"Just ahead," answers Noah.

I divert my eyes to the fork now halfway buried in the mud.

"Are there any good books there?" continues Rosie.

Marcus stands up. I keep my attention on the fork.

"Sure," comes a laugh from ahead. "If you like reading."

I brush my finger against Rosie's. She speaks once more. "Yea, books suck," she says, her tone undoubtedly sarcastic, but not enough to alert one of the followers.

The path grows brighter.

Marcus steps beside me.

"Now, now, Marcus, you don't want to die out here, do you?" comes the soft, unmistakable voice of Caroline.

Beside me, Marcus drops the fork. "I don't even care anymore."

"Hush," says Caroline. "You don't mean that. You want to die with honor. . .if you're going to die."

With his shoulders slouched, Marcus huffs. "Sure."

"That's better," laughs Caroline with a laugh that feels carefully thought out, like she's practiced feigning emotions—something I wouldn't be surprised to learn was true.

She then strides ahead of us. We follow. We turn onto the main street—the same street we saw before being forced right into the circus. But this time, I can see everything. There are grocers, sandwich shops, clothing outlets, a newspaper, a library, bars, restaurants, even a city hall. This place has everything, but none of it makes sense.

"Hey, Caroline," I mutter.

"Yes, Sam?" she eagerly replies.

"Do non-followers work at all the shops on this street?"

"Good question. The original eleven work those shops. Their kids man them as well."

"What do you mean, the original eleven?"

"The eleven I was granted when I created Halcyon."

"By who? Where did the rest come from? What does the eleven mean?" My mind just keeps spitting out questions.

"Slow it down," she laughs. "That's too many questions. Just follow me into the library, and anything that I won't answer, maybe you'll find in a book."

I grab onto the back of Sean's shirt.

He keeps walking forward, but he tilts his head back to listen.

"Why is that number here, too?"

"It's probably a coincidence," he whispers back.

I shake my head. It can't be. This world is too big for everything to just be a coincidence. There's depth behind everything; there's meaning to everything. I just need to find it.

We near the library; it's smaller than the one in the city outside Nimbus. It can't be more than two stories tall, nor can it contain many books. From the outside, we can see slightly behind the sign on the window that, with scratched off letters, reads 'I.E.M. LIB—RY.'

"What does I.E.M. stand for?" asks Ella ahead of me.

"You'll figure that out eventually," responds Caroline.

My legs go forward, but my head remains transfixed on the mysteries around me.

"Sam, dear," Caroline says.

I hum a slight 'mmm' before responding, "Yes?"

"Stop looking backward. You're in Halcyon to go forward."

Bullshit.

Elise

They're here.

I want to hug them, but Caroline gave me strict instructions not to do so. I fear that if I give in to what I want, she'll kill them right in front of me. Instead, I flash a weak grin, but it doesn't matter. Sean's eyes are glued on my sling.

"Elise," he tries to say my name loudly, but it comes out like a whisper.

I nod that it's okay.

He takes a few steps toward me, but Katrina appears out of thin air like a ghost interrupting a conversation about her past life.

"Uh uh uh," she says in a higher pitch, waving her finger in Sean's face. "Elise is off limits. She will be with us on this trip, but if you try to speak to her, well, let's just say she won't be the only one in a sling."

Sean's face reddens; he tries to take another step.

"One more step and you'll regret it," she reaffirms.

"Listen to her, Sean," I murmur.

He angrily gnaws at his bottom lip before looking away.

I maneuver my hand onto my sling. I look down. As much as it sickens me to have to play coy to Sean, I have to. It's a matter of life and death. Not everyone is granted the same safety that I am, so it's best if I don't try and abuse the one liberty I have.

None of us have to die. There's a way out of here. . .somewhere.

Caroline moves to the center of the room.

Unlike the library in the city, there's a limited selection of books here. There's a whole section dedicated to management, another to farming, and one titled, 'etc.,' which I assume is where literally anything and everything else is. However, it's the smallest area here. There can't be more than a dozen books; all the shelves beneath the ones containing the literature are barren. Cobwebs drape over the wood like the whole concept of fiction is a lost art in Halcyon.

"As you can see," mutters Caroline. "Our library consists of only important literature." She walks toward the management shelves. "Here, you can find what I.E.M. stands for." Stepping toward farming, she continues, "Here, you can learn how to feed more than yourselves." And that's where she stops. She completely neglects the other section.

"Caroline," coughs Sam.

I look up.

"Yes?" she replies.

"What's on the 'etc.' shelf?"

"Nothing of importance," she answers callously, like the question offended her.

Sam steps toward the 'non-important' books. Marcus joins.

"Why are we here?" questions Sean. He glances over at me, his eyes sullen and full of more misery than I'm accustomed to seeing on him.

I avert my eyes away.

"This is the first stop on the tour," answers Caroline.

"But really, why here? You know how most of us feel about a library."

Almost angered at Sean's words, Caroline snaps back. "Your past means nothing to me."

"It means something," murmurs Ella. "That's why we're here when this is of no importance to us."

"Except it is. . .if you survive," she retorts.

Ella shakes her head. "What's that supposed to mean? That these books don't matter now, but when we pass your ridiculous tests they'll suddenly become instant classics?"

"You could say that."

Ella exhales and turns her attention to Rosie. She mumbles something under her breath. Rosie grabs her hand.

Marcus pulls a book from the 'etc.' section. Sam does the same.

"What's Numerology?" mumbles Sam, as he wipes the dust off the cover of a large, gold-embossed black book.

"Put that down!" shouts Caroline. "Nothing in here is for you until you pass. For now, pretend everything you see today is an artifact at a museum."

Startled, Sam drops the book. As he bends down, he rubs his thumb across the top of his pinky while focusing his attention away from Caroline. Now split at the binding, the book lies open facedown on the floor.

"What did you do that for?" angrily chides Caroline.

"I didn't do it on purpose. And I thought we could read here; you made it seem like we could. Plus, I doubt this means anything to you."

"Not yet. And that word means nothing to me, but it might to you. Now, put it away and come over here."

Sam obeys. Marcus remains still by the shelf. Caroline doesn't say anything to him.

Caroline takes a breath, then, unnecessarily loudly, she says, "Noah, would you explain today's itinerary?"

"Yes, ma'am," he responds with a smidge of fright in his voice.

As he starts speaking, Caroline steps toward me. She tightly wraps her arm around mine, and guides me to the back of the library. There, she pushes open a door to the outside. We both step out. It's an alley. The only light is that of a flickering lantern, aside from the muted blue above.

"Elise," she says calmly—a tone she seems to only really use with me.

"Yes?" I quiver.

"You need to stop looking at Sean. You need to stop thinking about Sean. You need to focus on why you're here, not what brought you here."

I don't concede to my emotions. I know if I do, Caroline will reprimand me in a manner I don't care to see. And if she doesn't, Katrina will. I let out a soft, "Okay."

"It'll take more than that to convince me," she sighs. "He's a detriment to your future. The sooner you get him out of your life, the better."

"You can't just stop being in love," I retort bitterly.

"You can," responds Caroline.

"How?"

"If you want to survive, you'll do anything to prove it."

Hmm. I want to pry into her words, but I can't figure out exactly what to say, or how to say it. Plus, I'm not sure if she's telling the truth or if she's just playing me to gain sympathy. To further right the ship, I just say, "Was it worth it?"

"Look at what I've created, Elise. What do you think?"

I smile.

She smiles back.

Hers is real. I can't tell if mine is.

We dawdle in the alleyway. A sign reading 'bar' with an arrow to the left flickers near the street. I step closer to it. "Caroline."

"Yes?"

"Are the others allowed access to the shops manned by the original eleven?"

"Yes, why wouldn't they be?"

"You don't allow them a hospital, so I don't see why you allow them other things."

"If I stripped away all their rights, nobody would work."

"But don't you force them to work long days and threaten them with death if they try and leave?"

Caroline grins. "Where did you hear that I threaten them with death?"

"It was just a guess," I reply. One I'm now convinced is true.

"Halcyon thrives because of my rules, because of proper, strict management. Now, let's go back in. I'm sure they all know the agenda by now."

I ignore her and move toward the sign at the end. "If you allow them these places, how come nobody is at them now?"

"That's because they're working, my dear." She says 'my dear' like a witch—one trying to undermine any question I have about her dealings.

Really, she knows why they don't come up here. They slave too hard to keep Halcyon afloat that when they have a moment of reprieve it's spent sleeping, eating, or with family. When you work fourteen-hour days, I doubt alcohol can provide the same release.

These shops are useless. They're just another façade like those on the edge. Everything down here has been created to make us feel like this could be our home, but in reality, it never will be. It never can be. The only time we've seen others in this hellish chasm was when they were on their way to the circus—which, at the time, we didn't know. We, or at least I, assumed they were out shopping, living, being happy, but in reality, they were heading to watch us suffer.

I take another step toward the sign. The 'A' and 'R' fade to black. The neon red sign now reads, 'B.'

'B' what? Be me? Be free? Be everything taken away from me?

"Elise," echoes Caroline's voice.

I walk out onto the street. It's not bustling. It's quiet enough that I can hear the earthworms wriggling in and out of the mud.

"Elise," repeats Caroline.

What do you want? I say to myself.

I keep walking. The cobblestone pathway reminds me of the streets of Nimbus, but unlike there, where there are houses every which way, this place is littered with cover-ups. It looks like the era Caroline loves, but it feels like a prison.

And who wants to be a warden in hell?

"Elise, stop." Her voice loudens.

I come to a halt.

"Turn around."

"Why?"

"Turn around," she says firmly.

I oblige.

"Now, come here."

I listen once more. I can't keep wandering away, fighting back, and throwing my rage every which way. If I keep doing this, if I keep yielding to the strings pulling me away from what Caroline wants, she'll more than likely kill Sean.

I scream internally and force my legs to move toward Caroline.

"Listen, Elise. Do you think I chose to leave Nimbus once I passed my re-entry exam?"

"Since you're asking, no."

"You're right. I didn't want to leave. I was ready to spend more time with my family. I was ready to settle down and start my own family, but I wasn't granted that privilege."

"Why not?" I respond, full of false intrigue.

"Eldridge said I was chosen. He told me I had to leave."

"Did you fight back?"

"Yes, but what I did didn't matter. He took my anger as a reason to throw me out sooner." She sniffles. "Like you, having a predetermined role in this world wasn't my choice. Someone made it for me, and I knew if I didn't respect it, there would be consequences."

"Like what?"

"The deaths of anyone and everyone I've ever known or cared about."

"By who?"

"The DZ."

"Why would they kill when they need people to create these worlds?"

She wipes her nose. "Because that's how they maintain order." Putting her hand on my shoulder, she leans in, "Like you, I tried to shy away from the choice that was made. I tried to hide in the city, but after a week, they found me."

"How so?"

"I don't know, but I awoke to a pair of gauged eyes next to me where I was hiding. No matter where I went, they followed, so I listened."

"How did you know to come here?"

"Whenever I awoke to solace, I knew I was on the right path. It was only a matter of time before I ended up here."

"And how did you get here?" I ask, motioning my one available arm in a circle above me.

"When I first saw this opening in the earth, I thought it was the farthest I could go, and if I didn't go any farther, I would be killed." She takes a step closer to me. "So, I climbed down."

"How could you see?"

"I left Nimbus with a few essentials, but it didn't matter. When I got down here, there were eleven people waiting. They had built this street. They had built me a small home—one I've improved upon over the years. The DZ was prepared for me to build a new community down here. This is what they wanted."

"But why here? Why in a pit?"

"That's a question I've never asked."

"Why?" I stammer. "Don't you want to know why you sleep with the bugs?"

She chuckles. It's playful; it doesn't sound rigid like her fake laughs around the others. "If I keep prying into my destiny, the DZ will make it harder for me to survive. They'll make it harder for Halcyon to survive."

I close my eyes and twist my neck to the side. Then, to the other side. "So let me get this straight: They wanted you to create Halcyon no questions asked, but if it failed to yield the results they wanted, you would suffer for asking why?"

She nods. "They're in charge for a reason, Elise. They function above for a reason."

"Where? Where do they function?"

Caroline looks away.

"Where, Caroline? Can't we go and stop them? Can't we make our destinies what we want them to be?"

She tightly turns to face me. Stiffly, she says, "No."

I move closer to her. I put my arm on her elbow. "Why not? You don't seem to like them either."

"It doesn't matter, Elise. This is MY home," she states, her enunciation growing more firm. "I will never leave what I control."

"You don't control this. You basically just said that."

She laughs. Yet, it feels like a thinly veiled guise for how she truly feels. "I get to control life and death in Halcyon. I couldn't do that in Nimbus. I could only do it outside Nimbus, and now, I can do it at will." She smirks at me. "You don't understand the power, the rush, the excitement of what I do. But, you will. In due time."

And without so much as another word, she turns toward the door, throws it open, and whistles for me to go back inside. Yes, whistles.

Sean

Heavy floodlights beam down upon the fields. Stripes of white sit even closer to the crops. As we step forward, the white becomes more apparent; the glow shines brighter. Mixed with hues of red and orange, hundreds of heat lamps sit about a foot above the plants. Not close enough to burn, just close enough to do what the sun can't this far down.

Caroline waves her arm. We follow her into a row of peppers. Orange. Green. Red. Yellow. Every color, every size, every shape, they're all perfectly matured despite the lack of pure sunlight. A few other vegetables step into my peripherals, but I can't make out anything more than green beans and the tops of onions.

We move farther down the row. A small, gated-in section containing dozens of grapevines jumps into our sight. Within the confines of the area, a tall, redheaded woman tends to the fruit.

"Hello, Lucille," says Caroline, in a friendlier tone than she uses with us.

Quickly standing upright, Lucille flashes a grin. "Car-Car-Caroline. Hello," she replies.

"Would you care to explain what it is you do here?"

"Sure, sure, sure," she stutters.

"Well, go ahead," says Caroline callously.

Lucille gently wipes her hands on her apron and turns her head away from us. She motions it leftward three times before turning back to face us. "Well, here I plant, grow, and tend to the grapes for Caroline's wines. She has a vast collection ranging from—"

Caroline interjects. "That's enough, Lucille."

"Okay, okay, okay," she repeats before wiping her fingers on her apron once more.

I look over at Rosie. She throws back a confounded look. *What's the point of this?* I mouth at her.

She shrugs her shoulders.

I turn my attention to Elise. I can see her looking at me out the sides of her eyes, but she doesn't turn her head.

Caroline directs us forward once more. I glance back at Lucille. With her head facing away from us—to the left—her neck convulses thrice. Like she's trying to turn her head farther than it allows.

Is she okay?

Yet, before I can so much as allow myself to feel any additional sympathy for Lucille, or the rest of the workers, Caroline turns onto another path. With sporadic lanterns guiding our way and members of the foundation working the fields, the area feels relatively empty. For such a nice development back by Caroline's home and the circus arena, everything out here is pure rot in comparison.

I slide my fingers into my pockets.

"Up next, we have our school," echoes Caroline.

"Where?" asks Ella.

"Take a step forward, dear," she answers.

Ella steps to the right.

I step to the left ahead of Noah.

About one hundred feet in the distance sits a decrepit, muddied, white building. But it's less than a building; it's a glorified shack. It's maybe a few feet larger than where Elise and I hid in the outside. But unlike the shack we hid in outside Nimbus, this one's windows aren't broken—and that's probably the only positive discernible difference.

It's so small in stature, the fact that I couldn't see it over Noah—who's maybe two inches taller than me—shows how little Caroline values anything, and anyone, outside of herself.

"Can we go in?" asks Sam.

"We best not," remarks Caroline.

"Why not?"

"It's early. School is in session and we don't want to disturb them."

But it can't be. There's no visible light in the building. It's most likely there to make Caroline feel like she does something, when in reality, she doesn't do anything but force an ill woman to make her

174

wine. Like MacMillan, I bet if I got close enough, I could smell the alcohol on her breath.

She's no better than that lying, power-hungry lunatic, even if she thinks this tour will make us feel otherwise.

I turn to Sam. He rolls his eyes and looks over at me. I know what he's thinking, and he knows what I'm thinking. We don't need to say anything. *Caroline's a monster.*

Sadly, it does nothing for us to dwell on the evils she's deluded herself into believing. They aren't kindhearted gestures to those who choose not to compete in the circus. They're atrocities, on par with forcing us to partake in her cruel game.

Caroline turns left. We walk beside the fields. Some rows' lights are off, others have miniature irrigation pipes above them watering the plants, while a few others are illuminated brightly enough to the point that it's surprising the vegetation hasn't caught on fire yet.

Our tour guide stops once more. She speaks, but I don't listen. On our right, several feet deeper than where we currently stand, lies a shantytown. Dozens of small fires are lit with hundreds of people standing around them. Behind them are small, rusted homes made from what looks like scrap metal and damp, rotting wood.

And yet, farther in the distance there's a statue. Its front is unrecognizable from here, but from the back, it's clear it's a person. Who, though, I'm not sure. The stone features are obscured by the darkness of the surrounding earth, so unless I can get out there, I'll never know.

It's probably Caroline.

I glance back at the people in the makeshift, shoddy community.

"What the hell is this?" I ask aloud, unable to stop my thoughts from exiting out my mouth.

"This is where the foundation thrives," answers Noah.

"Why does it look like hell?"

"It doesn't," he responds. "This is how they've chosen to live."

"Nobody in their right mind would choose to live like this when they're the ones who built the world you think so highly of."

"That's where you're wrong, Sean," says Caroline. "They've chosen simplicity over gaudy. When you work like they do, you don't need to live like we do."

I rub my thumb and index fingers against my forehead. *What kind of answer is that?*

"You'll understand why our lives are of greater importance if you pass the Cirque de Chance," continues Caroline.

"How? How can our lives ever be more important than someone else's?"

She doesn't respond. She only smiles.

I take a deep breath and try not to let my emotions get the best of me. The last time I was furious at a so-called leader, I head-butted my way to the edge of death.

I don't need to do that again.

But, not everyone has the same control I'm forcing myself to exhibit. Marcus, for example, doesn't care for Caroline's petty response. With his fists clenched, he steps closer to her. "He asked you a question, Caroline. Why can't you answer it?"

Caroline smiles, but shows no teeth. "Just like right now, my life is more important than yours."

"How?" he angrily retorts.

"Unlike you, Marcus, I can control my emotions. You were such a kindhearted kid outside of Nimbus. Now, you're a blubbering fool like all those who can't handle death."

"How do you know how I was outside of Nimbus?" he quickly responds, his tone calmer than his initial questions.

"There's a lot to this world you don't understand," she answers.

"Like what?"

Caroline smirks and tries to say something, but before any sound can penetrate my eardrums, Elise speaks.

"Stop asking, Marcus!" she shouts. "This world will kill you for asking."

"She's right, you know," gibes Caroline. "It's best you don't know more than you already do."

My mind grows weary; my thoughts become terse.

I bite down. I glance over at Elise. Her eyes are wide. Her lips are quivering. *She knows something.*

We all know there's more to this world than Caroline's let on. There's more than we've seen; there's more depth to why everything is the way it is. But we can't ask, and that's almost a good thing. It's almost better if we figure it out on our own; it might work in our favor to discover Halcyon's secrets without them being blatantly thrown in our faces. At least then the truth won't be obscured.

Marcus steps back beside Ella. He doesn't ask anything else. He simply analyzes his surroundings, as if he, too, has run into the same train of thought I'm now trying to breathe life into.

I get closer to him.

Caroline starts to move forward again.

"Marcus," I whisper.

"Yea?" he murmurs back.

"We need to get to Elise."

"What do you mean?"

"I have to find out what she knows."

"What are you two bickering about back there?" interrupts Caroline.

"Nothing," I quickly fire back.

"Sure, sure, sure," she laughs.

I glance at Marcus. He looks away, but he steps closer to me. With his focus on the foundation, he softly says, "I know how we can get to her."

"How?"

He turns to face me, but keeps his stare in the distance. "I heard her through the vent in my room the other night."

"Is it big enough to get through?"

"Would you please be quiet," interrupts Caroline. "I don't need you two getting any closer to each other." Then she turns her attention to Rosie, Sam, Ella, and Miles. "You all need to treat each other like you've never met. That way, when someone fails, you won't feel anything."

Marcus swallows. He wants to speak, but he stops himself.

Instead, Sam does. "Why do you hate everyone?" he asks with an innocence I've never seen upon him. He knew MacMillan hated everyone, and I thought he knew Caroline was essentially the same, but the way he asked makes me feel like he believes she's not who she claims to be.

Caroline halts. Two followers step aside. Caroline steps toward Sam. "Dear boy, I don't hate everyone. I just know where true strength lies." She crouches and points to Sam's chest. "True strength lies in one's ability to deceive the desires of the heart."

"Why would anyone do that?" he asks, the air of innocence unwavering.

"Because the heart is what kills you. Just ask your brother."

Sam looks over at me, a wide-eyed look of confusion. "What does she mean?" he asks.

"I-I'm not sure," I stutter.

"How did you get that bullet wound in your chest?" asks Caroline.

"I was shot trying to protect them."

"Why were you protecting them? Do they not look capable of protecting themselves?"

"MacMillan would have killed them if I wasn't atop the wall looking down."

"Seems to me he didn't kill anyone—except that poor girl—and all you did was kill some lousy henchman."

My mind wanders. *How does she know all this?* But I don't ask her. I keep answering her. I keep yielding to her absurd speech. "If I didn't kill him, he would have killed them."

"Alas, you were shot, and your heart was almost the death of you. Your longing to protect everyone without looking out for yourself first proves my point. The heart is what will kill you."

"But it didn't kill me then and it won't kill me now," I stammer back.

Caroline strides even closer to me. Her cloak rises briefly as a faint wind brushes through, displaying a small tattoo on her right ankle. But, I can't make out what it is; it sort of looks like a bird.

"Oh really?" she asks apathetically.

"Yes," I firmly reply.

"Noah, grab Sam."

What?

But before I can so much as verbally or physically fight back, my brain tells my body not to. Instead I stand still, determined to prove her belief is ridiculous.

"Bring him next to me," she continues.

Sam struggles. I don't move. I stare stiffly, like my face is covered in a plaster mold.

"Cut off the rest of his pinky," she asserts.

Noah pulls out a knife.

I can feel my insides tensing up as my body grows suddenly warm. But I don't move. No matter how horrible this could be for Sam, I can't prove her right. And he knows that. Even if he can't admit it right now, he knows this is what I have to do.

"Nothing, Sean?" Caroline maliciously taunts.

"What do you want me to do?"

"Exactly what your heart wants you to do."

I shoot a quick look at Elise. She subtly shakes her head.

"It's not saying anything," I answer.

"We'll see about that," she grins. "Noah, slice it off."

Noah holds Sam's arm outward. Another follower steps beside Sam and grabs his other arm. Pinning it against Sam's back, he glares at me.

"Are you sure there's nothing you want to say?" Caroline asks.

"Are you just going to let her do this?" exclaims Rosie. I turn to face her. Her cheeks are the color of her namesake; her eyes are misty. "Well, seriously, are you?"

My mouth falls slightly agape. The heat furthers itself through my chest and into my core. I'm sweating. I don't say anything.

"Wow," she mutters. "Then I'll do it." She steps up to Caroline. Face to face with her, Rosie nods. "You're right. The heart is weak, but it's also the same reason we're all still alive."

Caroline smiles. "See, Sean. That's all you had to do. Admit it."

Rosie spins back to face me. As she does, Caroline's lips widen outward. They form an almost malevolent smirk—one I've only ever seen in my dad's old comic books.

"Now!" she shouts.

And just like that, Sam's pinky falls into the mud. Blood pours from his hand as he screams into the skies.

13 May 2192

Elise

It's 5 a.m. The grandfather clock rings in the hallway.

My shoulder aches.

The lacerations on my hands run across my palms. Some cuts are worse than others; some are already fading and have become barely visible. But the fact remains the same: I did this to myself. I let Caroline win.

And I had a choice.

Sam didn't.

Noah took off Sam's finger in an instant. Nothing could have stopped him from obeying Caroline. It was almost as if he got a thrill from it. Blood even splashed his arm; it bled through his cloak, but he didn't care. He just kept smiling.

He made sure we all felt Sam's pain.

I attempt to clench my hands into fists.

"You shouldn't do that, Elise," mutters Caroline while hovering over a glass display case.

"Why not?"

"You don't want to make the wounds worse. It seemed to me that you didn't care for the hospital the first time around, so why would you send yourself back?" She still doesn't look back at me. She's too focused on the case, and I'm not sure what's in it. I'm not even sure what this room is.

Unlike my bedroom, which consists of a canopied bed complete with the plushest blanket I've ever slept with, an oddly colored green armchair, and a wet bar, this room is more of a museum. There are framed documents upon the wood-paneled walls, display cases diagonally placed in each corner, and one unnecessarily large chandelier hanging in the middle. The diamonds on it alone were probably once worth more than all these artifacts put together.

But now, it's all useless. Money doesn't exist in Nimbus, and I'm not sure if it does here.

It just never made sense to place a monetary value on something in Nimbus. When you live in a society where everyone's working to help each other—with the exclusion of Separation itself—you thrive on social niceties to get by. If you wanted two apples, you would just go to 'Joanna's Fruit & Veggie Supply' and get two apples. No bartering. No money. Just don't be rude. You took what you needed to survive. We were all in it together, so there was no reason to monetize worthless paper when it would just tear everyone apart.

In essence, everything within the confines of this mansion is worthless in some capacity—but maybe not to Caroline. She wouldn't have this world set up the way it is without a reason, without some sort of personal value in each and every artifact.

Though, living in a world where you're governed by emotionless followers of a deluded woman, it's odd that anyone would place value in anything.

I turn to my left to look at Caroline. The brown leather of the chair makes a sound as I do so.

"Why did you bring me here?" I ask.

"To show you something."

"What?"

She remains fixated on a particular object; it looks like another vase. But it's different than the ones in the hallways. I lean out a bit more, trying to get a better glimpse. It looks like it has two birds on it. They're both blue—the same blue-ish color prominent in Halcyon—with a light orange breast. The birds' beaks are touching, while in the background a calm sea awaits. One of the birds seems to be sitting upon a nest, but I can't quite make it out. Regardless, I don't see the importance; I don't see why such a thing is on display rather than randomly placed in the hallways like the others.

"Come here."

I oblige.

As I get closer, the image drawn upon the vase becomes more visible. The bird sitting atop a nest has a tear falling down its cheek. *Huh?*

"The painting on this vase represents Halcyon."

"What do you mean?"

"There was a myth thousands of years ago. A myth about a woman who killed herself after her husband drowned at sea."

"So what do these birds have to do with it?"

"Allegedly the gods turned the woman and her husband into these birds because they found her sacrifice and commitment admirable." Caroline keeps her eyes still on the vase. She never turns her visual attention to me. "And despite this newfound life as birds given to the couple to make them happy, the gods then decided to make sure the female's eggs were always swept out to sea, so they could never truly be happy."

I itch the back of my head. "Again, what does all of this have to do with Halcyon?"

"It's the message. The message that love never wins."

"Why does Halcyon have to be built upon the foundation of no love?"

She finally turns to face me. Her eyes widen. She forces a smile without revealing any teeth. "Because that's how you die, Elise. Attachment can lead you down many paths: One where you take your own life because of another, one where being with someone doesn't yield the life you deserve, and even one where another hand at play ensures you're always miserable." She briefly looks away. "I like to think of myself as the last one."

"But why should any of that matter to you? Why should the happiness of others have any impact on society?"

"Because love makes you weak. It changes your brain function and puts someone else first. And if you're not first, you're dead. Halcyon is strong because the followers and myself put our individual selves first. We don't sink into that confounded misery of our foundation. We know the priorities of a functioning world versus one where love reigns supreme and slows down the advancement of life."

"So how can your world grow and expand if love doesn't exist?"

"I never said it doesn't exist."

"Where does it exist?"

"The foundation."

"You're saying the population of Halcyon is dependent upon your workers, the people that live in that shit heap of sheet metal and rotting wood outside of the fields? The same people who aren't granted access to a hospital, or even one nice thing?"

Caroline drags her hand across the top of the display; her nails leave slight marks on the glass.

"That's their prerogative, Elise. If they want to truly survive, they know what they have to do."

I roll my eyes. "So why do you even let them live here to begin with if you hate the way they live?"

"Without them, I wouldn't have any of this."

"You couldn't do that yourself? You couldn't have your lackeys do it for you?"

"There's no reason to get so defensive, Elise."

Stop saying my name.

She continues. "Every world needs a foundation. You don't have to agree with how it was built; you just have to reap the benefits of its existence—," she waves her arm, knowing good and well that I was going to interject, "—and who better to reap the glory than those who know how to keep the world alive, those who have chosen to sacrifice everything to lead?"

"What exactly are you sacrificing, Caroline?"

"I told you: love."

"Do you even want that? Do you even know anything about it?"

"I know more than you ever need to know, Elise."

"It seems to me that you don't know anything; it seems that you're choosing to make some nonsensical idea the basis of this world." I don't stop to take a breath. I let the anger inside me boil to the surface. "Everything you've just said to me is ridiculous. The fact that some story, some fable, has given meaning to your existence is absurd. No society should exist in which love is deemed evil."

"Sit down, Elise," Caroline softly whispers.

"No. Why should I?"

"Sit down before I make you."

I angrily glide back toward the dark brown leather chair. I take a seat on its arm.

"Do you want to know why I've created MY—" she emphasizes this word strongly, harshly, "—world this way? Do you really want to know why I've chosen limited relationships, limited connections, and one primary source of power?"

I nod.

"It'll eat your heart out. What I'm going to tell you will show me how weak you truly are. It'll prove to me that the DZ's choice in your for our fourth circle is illogical because you're too enriched in the fibers of love, of mediocrity."

She disrobes from her cloak and drapes it over the back of a couch that is similar in appearance to the chair I'm currently sitting in. Yet, before she takes a seat, she walks back toward me. Not quickly, not normally, but slowly and lethargically. Like she's trying to drag out what she's going to say, or do.

I fall into the seat.

Caroline rolls up her sleeves.

"What are you doing?" I ask.

Slowly, and meticulously rolling the sleeves of her red nightgown up to her elbows, she takes a stance directly in front of me. Once the final sleeve is tucked into place, she crouches. Her breath is rancid. It's like onions and red wine—and it's 5 a.m. *It wasn't like this when we first met.*

"What are you doing, Caroline?" I ask again.

"Showing you."

But before I can so much as say another word, Caroline digs her nails into the back of my head, and my body goes limp.

***

I'm back.

I'm inside Nimbus. But it's considerably smaller than the last time I was there. It's even smaller than it was over ten years ago. *What year is it?*

I take a few steps forward in an attempt to gauge what's going on. I mutter her name under my breath. "Caroline." But nothing happens. I do it again. Same results. "Is anyone here?" I ask, this time with some volume.

The sky instantly goes dark, but Nimbus remains the same: empty.

I move forward again, uncertain of why I'm here.

"Caroline, what's going on?" I ask aloud, hoping she'll appear to guide me. But she doesn't. Nobody appears. Nimbus is a ghost town.

I start walking. The only way to understand my presence in this place is to walk around; it's to see something that Caroline wants me to see. I move past the hospital, the grocer, Joanna's, an antique shop that never existed when I lived in Nimbus, and a blacksmith, while making my way toward the most recognizable landmark here: the iron gates in front of the empty field of the Founding Festival.

The gates don't creak. There's no wind to recreate the annoyance of their structure. I step underneath the wrought iron slogan—the same words that seemingly represent Halcyon. *In Harmony We Live, In Peace We Thrive.*

But I still see nothing.

"Caroline, why am I here?" I shout. "If you want to show me something, show it!"

And for the first time, I can feel pain in this realm. My scalp starts to pulse violently. The back of my head feels like it's being sliced into thin strips slowly and painfully, until I collapse—until I die. I scream.

Then it disappears. The ache fades like it was never there.

I reach for the back of my head. Everything's still there. There's no blood. My brains aren't spattered on the fields. Nothing's changed but the world in front of me.

The stage is in sight, and a man, probably in his sixties, walks across it. His boots click.

MacMillan?

Clad in a unique jacket—dark brown leather with a fur collar, gold zipper, and two buttoned front pockets—he strides back and forth. Also sporting a pair of aviator sunglasses and dark grey pants tucked into his clashing black boots, the man—whom I presume to be a younger Eldridge MacMillan—walks back and forth. He never yields; he never speaks. He just keeps walking. Like the second hand on a clock, he doesn't stop.

Then, a scream echoes behind the stage.

Two men carrying a woman who's kicking, screaming, and trying to claw her way out of their clutches show no signs of stopping. MacMillan snaps his fingers. The men push the woman onto the ground.

I step closer, unsure if they can see me.

The woman's moving her head from side to side screaming incoherent words. I try to reach for her, to touch her, to feel her

185

suffering, but before I can, MacMillan pulls out a gun and fires. She goes quiet.

I become empty.

***

"That was my mother," says Caroline.

I don't say anything. My neck feels wet. I reach my hand back. It's wet with blood.

Caroline doesn't say anything.

I finally speak. "H-how do you keep getting into my head like that?"

"Magic," laughs Caroline.

I glare at her.

"How I do that doesn't matter, Elise. What matters is what I just showed you."

"How you make me fall into my mind by just touching my scar means something, Caroline."

She doesn't say anything. She just smiles awkwardly.

"Caroline, answer me!"

She doesn't.

I angrily gnaw at my upper lip before closing my eyes. *Ugh.* "Why was she shot?" I ask while slowly wiping the blood on the back of my shirt.

"For treason."

"What did she do?"

"She wanted to escape Nimbus, but my father wouldn't allow her to."

"How did MacMillan find out?"

"My father told him."

I pat my shirt against the back of my head.

"Why?" I ask.

"You know why."

"I don't."

"Think."

"Because there's no such thing as love," I spit out, knowing it's what she wants to hear.

186

"Exactly. When I got back from my Separation, MacMillan brought me to that field to watch her execution. Then, I was immediately ushered back out. Told I was chosen, and that was it."

"Why would he execute her then kick you right back out? That doesn't make sense."

"That's why I'm in charge of this world and you're my pupil, Elise. Suffering only makes you stronger."

"But how could you suffer if you didn't love her?"

"She was my mother. I will admit I cared when I was fourteen, but by the time I survived my eleven years outside those walls, I felt nothing. . ." she trails off, and walks back to the display case with the symbolic vase. "The outside erases emotion. Fighting for survival for eleven years, you learn what's important. And I'll be damned if I didn't learn how to cut off attachment, how to fend off my mind's trickery."

"What happened to you outside of Nimbus, Caroline?"

She turns back toward me, the blood from my scar dried upon her fingers, and laughs. "Nothing. I just woke up."

"How so?"

"You will see tomorrow."

"What does that mean?"

"Tomorrow's task will show you."

"What is it?" I scowl.

"Exactly what I've showed and told you: cutting off attachment."

I angrily stand up; my veins pulsing against my arms. "What are you going to make them do?"

"Prove the heart wrong."

"And what if they fail?"

Caroline's jaw stiffens. "Unfortunately, death won't come from this one, but failure will have a consequence."

"Of what?"

She loudly exhales. "No more questions. Just watch and learn."

14 May 2192

Sam

I'm at war with myself.

A part of me knows Sean was right.

Another part hates him.

But neither side matters when the reality will forever remain the same. I'm down to nine fingers. My skin is still raw around the knuckle; the lack of blood flow has left the area pale.

I scratch my head with the opposite hand.

We all wait in line outside the arena for the next task.

I rewrap the bandage around my injured hand. For whatever reason, Halcyon doesn't seem to have a hospital, so all I have to ease the pain is this gauze—and all it does is stop any more blood from spilling. There aren't any painkillers here. There's not even ice.

All I can do to rid the ache is avoid thinking about it in hopes that maybe it'll subside over time.

A follower reaches for the doorknob in front of me.

I'm up first. Unlike our last task, we're all sent into this one alone. The others aren't even allowed to watch.

And we don't know what it is.

"Sam," whispers Marcus from behind me.

"Yea?"

"This is the last one."

I gaze at him, confused.

He repeats himself.

The door opens.

I'm thrown out.

A singular beam of light climbs from the top of the stadium down to the gravelly floor. There's no one in sight, and no noise echoing around me.

I look back. Everyone's gone.

I just wish I could see Marcus to gain some clarity about what he said. Caroline said there are four tasks. This can't be the last one.

I keep moving. A phantom ache races through my nonexistent finger.

"Come, stand in the light, Sam," rings Caroline's voice.

As much as I want to disobey, I have nowhere else to go.

"The light won't hurt you," she says. "It will show you."

This feels like the opposite of my nightmares outside Nimbus. Rather than being thrown into a realm of fire and confusion, it's like I'm being pulled into a brighter one—one that might end in triumph rather than tears.

I make it to the light. The beam extends at least five feet in every direction around me. "Now what?" I say aloud, unsure if anyone can hear me.

Then, the light gets brighter. And brighter. And brighter. I'm forced to close my eyes. I throw my forearm in front of my face to further block the light.

In an instant, it's gone.

The only thing in front of me is the farmhouse.

The same farmhouse Elise, Abby, and I stayed in for weeks. The same decrepit, hidden place we called home until the Shadow Lurkers took me away, until they kidnapped me and threw me into that dungeon.

A flash of being chained to the crumbling cement wall skids across my mind. I shake it away.

"Is this real?" I audibly ask to anyone and everyone who can hear me.

There's no response. Meaning, the best way to determine the reality of what's happening is to approach it.

Or should I stand still? This is a task, after all.

Enshrouded in complete darkness, the farmhouse is the only illuminated thing within eyesight. Nothing else is present in the vicinity; at least, nothing I can see. I move toward the house.

The front door is the same: rotted, broken, and covered in scratches. The paint's just as worn as I remember, and the screen door has the same sporadic holes spread about it. Broken steps make way toward the front porch and front door. I take a step toward them.

I stand mere inches from the steps. The chipped white paint is exactly as I remember it. Every last detail is the same. Nothing is out of place, and nothing new has been thrown in.

How is this happening?

I bend down onto one knee. My hands become moist.

I don't want this to be real. I don't want to be taken back to that world. Everything that happened in that farmhouse led to the suffering I endured at the hands of the Lurkers. Even when I felt safe, fate was planning my future. And now that I know what this place means to my past, I don't want to see it again. I don't want to touch it again. I don't want anything to do with it.

But, at the same time, I can't resist *her.*

If the farmhouse is here, if this is real, Abby's in there. She has to be.

And with one fell swoop, I glide my fingers against the wood. *It's real.*

I stand up, and take a step upward. I'm on the porch. I reach for the chipped handle attached to the screen door. Quickly, and almost reluctantly, I pull it open. Then, I push the front door open.

"What are you doing over there?" comes a familiar voice from ahead of me.

"Abby?" I softly mumble, almost muted.

"Who else would it be?" she answers. "Can you shut the door? It's cold."

Huh?

I turn back. It's snowing. The fields around the farmhouse have been recreated seemingly out of thin air. I shut the door.

"How is this real?" I ask once again, nearly silent.

"You need to stop mumbling, Sam. I'm sure Elise will be back with some firewood soon."

"Yea, yea, I know," I answer, this time loud enough for her to hear.

"Why are you standing over there anyways? Elise will be okay. It's just a little snow."

"I just felt like moving around," I reply, trying to give off a vibe that I'm not as lost in what's happening as I actually am.

"Oh, well, you should come sit down by the dying fire with me. I'm cold," says Abby somewhat cheerily despite the circumstance.

"Okay," I say.

I walk around the end of the couch. The fading firelight bounces up and down on the walls. And, there, she sits—directly in front of the fire. For the first time, I can truly see her. The crimson red scarf, black jeans, grey jacket; it's all there. Her dark brown hair is draped down to her shoulders; her hands are extended toward the embers. *It's really her.*

She turns to look at me. "What are you looking at?" she asks. *You.*

In all the time we spent together before she sacrificed herself to save Elise, I never truly noticed her beauty. I'm still a kid. She's still a kid. Everything about this makes me miss her more. My body aches.

"Sam?" she coyly asks.

"Yes?"

"You didn't answer my question."

"N-nothing," I stutter.

Before she can pester me again, I take a long stride toward her and sit down. And that's when it hits me, *this is when it happened. This is when Abby told me she could see us falling in love like Elise and Sean. This is when my heart first skipped a beat.*

"Abby," I mutter under my breath.

She turns to look at me. Her eyes mirror the fire. Her skin glistens in the light to a point that almost seems abnormal. Almost as if, rather than a recreation of Abby, it's something else, something projected. "Yea?" she replies.

Yet, no words escape my lips. My skin tingles. My brain feels like it weighs a million pounds. I just want to hug her. I want to be with her. I never want her to leave me again.

But, before I impulsively reach for her, I stop myself.

I need to know if this is real.

But how?

She speaks again. "You were saying?"

"Nothing," I murmur.

"Sam," says Abby, softly.

"Yes?"

She looks away. Her voice quiets. "Do you think we'll end up like your brother and Elise?"

"What do you mean?"

"You know. . ."

"Closer?"

"In love," she replies, her eyes still focused away from me.

"Maybe. . ." I answer.

"Why just maybe?"

I gnaw at my lips. The cracked skin falls to the floor. *Because you're dead*, I think to myself. A searing pain starts in my waist, runs up to my heart, and trickles to a halt at my shoulders. *Because you're dead.*

"Sam," she whispers. Just hearing my name cross her lips makes my hands shake.

I can't take this anymore. I need to get out of this house. I need to stop seeing her. She's dead, and this torment only makes knowing she's gone that much harder.

"What?" I angrily reply, as my emotions take hold.

"I think I love you."

The words bypass my eardrums.

This can't be real. She's dead.

"I don't know you. You're not Abby, and you'll never be Abby."

"Sam, why would you say that?" she says defensively, tears welling in her eyes.

"Because you're dead!" I shout before storming toward her.

"Don't say that!" she shouts.

I extend my arm toward her. It goes right through her. I reach out my other arm. Same thing.

Then, she's gone. A light shines through the windows. It gets brighter. And brighter. And brighter.

I fall onto the gravel.

The light fades. A blue beam appears around me.

"Well done, Sam!" echoes Caroline's voice around me. "You've succeeded in the emotional task of Cirque de Chance."

"What do you mean?" I ask aloud.

"This task was set before you to test your emotional endurance. While you desired to believe it was real, you didn't allow yourself to succumb to the memory."

"But why did I have to go back there? Why did I have to see her?"

"You will know tomorrow."

"What's tomorrow?"

The blue fades; the area becomes black. Someone grabs onto my arm and pulls me away.

Sean

Caroline's voice echoes just beyond the bolted door. Rosie, Ella, and Marcus stand behind me. Miles has been outside performing the task none of us know anything about, and Sam. . .Sam hasn't come back. I don't know if he's dead or what—but I can't think about it. I'm up next.

I'm not ready.

It's one thing when you see someone compete in an event, and it's another when you go into it completely blind. All I can do is hope this task can't result in death, that whatever I have to do won't kill me. *And that it didn't kill Sam either.*

But with the way Caroline works, it seems death is her favorite part.

Noah pushes open the door. "You're up, Sean."

"Where am I going?"

"Out there."

I step beyond the door. He slams it shut behind me. *What the hell?*

"Sean, would you please step forward," comes the unforgettable voice of Caroline over the airwaves.

I take one step. Nothing happens. I take another, and another, and another, until eventually a sweeping ray of light shines down from above. It blocks out my surroundings, making it impossible to see anything.

"What is this?!" I yell, hoping my question yields an answer.

Yet, nothing changes the brightness casting over me.

I close my eyes. The light pierces through my eyelids; it barrels through my skin and slams into my retinae—in turn sending a sharp pain up and into my forehead. I bury my palms into my eyes, but the more pressure I apply, the less it matters. This light won't be fazed.

But then, it's gone. And I still can't see.

I rapidly blink several times, but my vision is spotty at best. So spotty that it looks like my home in Nimbus stands in front of me, and I know that's not possible.

I wipe my eyes a few more times, but no matter what I do, the image in front of me doesn't change. The number 2156 jolts out at me like a strike of lightning running across an overcast sky.

"What's going on?" I ask aloud.

Nobody responds. Not a word is uttered around me.

I must be hallucinating. There's no way this can be real. It's the house I grew up in, and it's right here in front of me despite the fact that's it's definitely dozens upon dozens of miles away.

I shake my head.

The vision doesn't change. The house is there. Replete with blue shutters, windows that need a good wiping, the rusting door handle and doorjambs, everything. The particular worn-white coloration makes it all that much more real. No other house in Nimbus looked like this. No other house had that number, or that look. This *is* my home, and now it's right in front of me in another society. *I don't get it.*

A part of me wants to see if the inside is the same, but the other's clawing at my back telling me this is just the game, and if I avoid entrance, maybe I'll pass. There has to be something behind the door that Caroline wants me to see, and if I just stand still, she can't win.

As boring as it is, I do just that. I cross my legs and sit down.

The eerie calmness passes over me as the silence makes me tired.

Minutes pass without any attempts by Caroline to force me through the doors and into that house. No followers step out to coax me into the task; Noah doesn't saunter out and threaten me to compete; nothing happens. The silence remains, and my participation stays nonexistent.

I'm not sure how long my choice will last, but I have to stick by it.

I look around. Nothing but pitch black encompasses my surroundings. I don't see a visible audience, nor do I see Caroline or Elise. It's as if the only two things in the world right now are me and this house. It's not comforting.

"Is anyone here?" I ask out loud.

Still, silence responds.

Who knows how long I can do this. Eventually, Caroline's bound to find a way to get me to see what she wants me to see. I don't know how she'll do it, but I just know she'll try anything to make me take part in her game.

There's no way any of us can avoid her circus. We haven't seen a way out anywhere. This fault goes on as far as the eye can see; the only light—aside from the lampposts and lanterns that illuminate this world—is the sun, and even that barely creeps into this chasm. I'm yet to see a ladder, stairs, or even an elevator to the top. But the thing is, a way out exists. Noah and the others met us in that façade of a city above Halcyon somehow. They didn't just fly up there or teleport; they used another means of transportation—one that we need to find because if we don't, we'll have to keep playing until we're all dead.

I rub my hand against the back of my head. The darkness tightens around me. My blinks become heavier.

I try not to let my eyelids fall, but the longer I sit, the harder it becomes.

I've barely slept lately, and now, with nothing pulling me into that house and no one around me yelling for me to do something, I feel calm. Even though Caroline's given us a better setup than any of us could have ever dreamt of, sleep hasn't come naturally. We know when we wake up we're subject to death. And it doesn't help that I don't have Elise beside me.

"Hey Sean," comes a resounding, yet familiar voice in the distance. But it's not Caroline. It's too deep. It sounds like a man.

I don't allow myself to answer.

"What are you doing out there?" asks the voice.

Still, I avoid response.

Then, the front door of the house opens.

My body goes numb.

The voice grows louder. "C'mon, Sean, why don't you step in? It's a hot one out there today, and there's lemonade inside," cajoles Dad.

"But it's May," I quietly respond, my vocal chords nearly muted by my confusion.

"Did you say May?" he laughs. "It's October, Sean, and it's weirdly hot for that time of year, so come on in."

October? What is this?

"Come on, son," he continues.

This can't be real. I bite my lip. "I have to go back to work," I answer.

"You just got off, Sean. Now, come inside."

"I can't."

He steps out onto the porch; the wood creaks beneath his feet. "Are you okay?"

"I'm fine. I just can't come inside right now."

He takes a few steps forward until he's on the ground, eye-level with me but still several feet away.

Neither of us speaks.

I don't know what to say, or what to do. This feels like a dream—one that has a thicker dose of reality in it than any other dream I've ever seen. I feel that if I took several steps forward, I could hug him; I could touch him. But I can't. I won't. Because this can't be real. None of this can be. It's impossible. *He's dead.*

He finally opens his mouth. "You don't seem okay, Sean."

"I'm fine," I counter.

"Is this about Sam being separated?"

"What do you mean?"

"You've been different since he was separated over a month ago. He'll survive, Sean. He knows who he has to meet, and from what you've told me, Elise will ensure he knows. . ." he cuts off. "But let's go inside and talk about this. You never know who's listening out here." He awkwardly looks around, like there's someone standing close to him or I despite the fact that there's no one remotely near.

"I'm fine, Dad," I reply.

"Then come inside."

"I'm not going to do that."

He sighs. "Your mother wants to see you, Sean. She misses you."

My eyelids become heavy once more, but not with exhaustion. I keep myself from crying. I stop myself from becoming attached to whatever's happening in front of me.

"I'm going to go back to work," I feign.

"It's Monday night, Sean. You're done for the day."

"MacMillan wants more guards on the wall tonight."

"Why?"

"I didn't ask."

"Why are you avoiding me?" Dad asks, puzzled.

I don't answer. I take a deep breath and exhale.

Face to face, we stand in silence.

Monday. October. 2191. Sam separated already. I can't piece together the timeframe. I don't know why he's here, or how, for that matter. None of this makes sense.

I turn around and start to walk away.

"Don't regret this," mutters Dad. "Don't regret this chance to see us. You never know when we'll be gone."

I don't stop. I don't cave to this trickery Caroline's thrown at me no matter how much I want it to be real. If I'm going to survive Cirque de Chance, I have to keep walking.

"Very good, Sean," echoes the familiar voice of Caroline.

A blue beam lights up in the darkness around me. Then, another light turns on, and sitting in the arena are Sam and Miles. There's no one else in sight.

He's alive, I think, but don't emote. I've come this far; it's in my best interest to keep pretending that I'm some emotionally-resistant robot—the kind of monster Caroline wants us all to be.

It doesn't matter how difficult what I saw was, I can't think about it. I need to erase it, to become a monster—one that I can control, for the time being.

I start to walk toward Sam and Miles. Yet, the closer I get, the more evident it becomes that they're behind some sort of enclosure, like the glass contraption we all had to wait in during our first task.

Sam's leaning against the glass. His eyes are red, the tip of his nose is red, even his cheeks are rosy. It's clear what my test did to him. Just seeing it was probably more than enough after completing his task, regardless of what it was.

A door opens at the end of the contraption.

Sam moves toward the door, but Miles doesn't budge. Unlike Sam, whose pigmentation is apparent as to what distress the task caused him, Miles's face is completely devoid of color. His pupils are enlarged, and his normally light brown skin has become almost fawn in comparison. Whatever he saw, it terrified him.

I finally make it to the door where a follower I've never seen grabs onto my wrist and tries to throw me in, but I leave my weight in my legs so I barely budge. After what I just saw, I may be faking my emotions, but that still doesn't mean I'll be pushed around like I'm worthless. I know my value here even if no one else does.

I eventually step in, and the moment I do, the man pushes my shoulders making it seem like he's the one who got me in there.

"Really?" I gripe.

He doesn't give me a response; instead, he heads across the way to allow whoever's next to enter.

"Sean?" murmurs Sam from behind me.

"Yea?"

"How did you do that?"

"Do what?"

"Hold back?"

I press my lips together and fold them back before taking a quick glance at Miles. "Caroline wants us to fail, Sam, so we can't show her we're vulnerable."

"But it's not that easy," he quietly spits out.

"I know it's not, but in that task, I knew it wasn't real. Our house, Dad, the words he said. None of that was real. It doesn't matter how great it was to see his face, or how great it was to hear him speak; that doesn't change the fact it wasn't real."

"But in mine, it almost was. . ."

"How so?"

"Abby was there. She recreated an event that only Abby and I knew," he says, his voice getting louder as he progresses. "I don't know how she could have done that!" he finally shouts.

"We can't worry about that, Sam. We have to focus on working our way through whatever's next, not the past." And even as painful as it is for me to say that, it's true. It sucks, but it's true. We can't dwell on the suffering Caroline's already thrust at us in a series that supposedly has four events.

"You make everything sound so easy," he says indignantly.

If only he knew that our pain was the same. No matter what we spoke about in our room the night I was falling apart, it seems Sam's forgotten that he was the one who told me to fake it, to keep my head on my shoulders and keep progressing. It's one thing to tell someone else to do it, and another to try it yourself. Everything sounds easier when the burden doesn't hang over your own head.

I walk to the end of the enclosure. Sam remains still, as does Miles. I want to say something that will help both of them, but I don't know what that is. Like Sam told me to do, I'm faking it, and the second I let up, I'll crumble. And it's best if I don't let that happen, no matter how much it kills me.

After all, maybe I'll see Elise sooner than anticipated.

Elise

Nothing about what I just watched was enjoyable. I had to see Abby again. I watched Sean speak to his father, who I never got to meet. Rosie spoke to Collin in the library; Ella to Malcolm in the forest; Miles to his twin brother who was killed two days after Miles found him during his Separation; and Marcus. . .Marcus saw Kyle, and it became apparent that he loved him.

Caroline didn't just recreate an environment that was familiar to everyone, she remade a situation that was personal to all of them for different reasons. She found a way to rebuild worlds lost, moments past, and worst of all: souls of the deceased. I don't know how she did it, and I don't know if I want to know. It's too unbelievable to fathom. It hurt just watching it from above; my chest ached watching these people I've come to love suffer for no reason other than Caroline's selfish belief that love is a worthless emotion.

The whole situation was seemingly set up to make them confront a *weakness* they've been trying to move on from. It was horrible. I don't think Miles will recover. After seeing his twin, Isaac, Miles broke down. I've never seen such sorrow, such overwrought, pure suffering. It was horrible.

And sadly, that's why he was the only one who *failed* in any sense, but at least failure in this task didn't yield the same consequences as the last one. Caroline tells me failure here will show itself in the next task—though I still don't know what it is.

Like Sean, Sam, and the others, I will be in the dark until it's time.

I just hope the next task isn't an emotional rollercoaster like that one. I can't imagine watching someone's mentality break into pieces even more than what I just saw. If Miles has to endure another moment like that, it might kill him. Even if the task itself doesn't do it, the sheer agony of the breakdown might.

"Elise," echoes Katrina from behind me. "It's time to go back in. Caroline wants to speak to you."

"That's all she ever wants to do with me," I chide.

Katrina bites her lip and turns to face me.

"Yes?"

Her eyes angrily fold inward; she releases her lip and irritably speaks. "You were given an opportunity better than the rest of us, so shut up and deal with it."

"What's your problem, Katrina?" I retort, uncertain if she's going to turn this rage into another incident.

"You're my problem. Now get inside."

I could fight back; I could give some smart remark, but I don't. Katrina's bigger and stronger than me and I'm already on her bad side, so it's in my best interest to avoid ticking her off again. The last thing I need right now is another dislocated shoulder.

I head toward the door at the back, but before I have a chance to step through it, Caroline steps out. She puts her hand on my chest and lightly pushes me backward. "Elise," she mutters apathetically.

"Yes?"

"What did you think of that task? And don't give me some sad story about how what you saw impacted your state of mind."

"I-I. . ." I bite back. I need to stop being honest. I need to start lying. "I thought it was. . .quite the challenge."

"Just quite the challenge? Nothing else? You didn't think it was heartless, cruel, demeaning, crude, or just plain evil? Knowing you, I expected you to shout at me." Mocking my past expressions, Caroline leans toward me. Face to face, she whispers, "Did it make you weep?"

I lean closer to her. "I felt nothing."

"Good," she smirks. "That's how it's supposed to be."

I don't respond. Caroline doesn't deserve it. *She never does.*

Caroline snaps her fingers. "Katrina."

"Yes?" she answers.

"Could you go and fetch the weak one?"

"Yes," she firmly replies before stepping away.

"What do you mean, 'the weak one?'" I ask, my focus directed toward the door, almost certain who I'll be seeing shortly.

202

Caroline glides toward the large window overlooking the arena. "Wasn't it obvious?"

I don't say anything because, sadly, in the eyes of Caroline, Miles *failed*. When he saw Isaac in the forest, he broke down. He wept to the point that his words were inaudible, or at least blubbered to the point of incoherency. His brother tried to console him, but since he was just an illusion, there wasn't much his words could do. Miles knew it wasn't real, but that didn't stop his emotions.

Based on the context, Isaac was born before midnight and Miles was born after, so, by law, they were separated on different days despite being twins. I've heard of this happening only one other time, but that was way before I was sent out, so I don't know exactly how that ended. I just know this time, it was awful. Everyone's lost family members through the course of Nimbus's ritualistic game of Separation, but I can't imagine anything more difficult than losing the one person you were born within minutes of simply because rules prevented you from exiting on the same day. And, of course, the fact that if you're within eyesight of Nimbus after being separated, you'll be shot at; thus, why Isaac was shunned into the woods awaiting Miles's Separation the following day.

Unfortunately, by the time Miles got to Isaac, Isaac was in bad company. He owed the Shadow Lurkers food one day in. If he didn't have any by sunset the following day, they were going to kill him. Isaac mentioned that running away wouldn't work, that they would be found and killed together, but that didn't stop Miles from doing everything in his power to escape his brother's fate. He ran, and he dragged Isaac with him.

Though, if there's one thing I know about the Lurkers, it's that you can't escape. They're everywhere.

Miles and Isaac spoke about surviving together for eleven years even though they knew they couldn't forage the amount the Lurkers wanted, and then the recreation stopped. The whole time Isaac was speaking about his fate, Miles wept. He tried to speak, but he couldn't. Eventually Caroline concluded his task without a word, and a follower dragged him to the exit area outside the active arena.

Outside of Miles, everyone else at least attempted to speak to the individual in his or her task, and everyone had a sense that no matter how real it felt, it wasn't real. Miles was the only one who seemed to be without a grip on the situation.

"I'll take your silence as a yes," speaks Caroline, her gaze still on the empty stage in front of her.

The door flies open. The handle slams into the wall.

"Here he is," hisses Katrina, as she pushes Miles onto the floor in front of me.

He doesn't move. He doesn't fight back. He just remains there on his knees, his face toward the ground.

"Miles, Miles, Miles," repeats Caroline.

Katrina closes the door, and remains in the room.

"Do you know why you're here?" continues Caroline.

Miles doesn't speak.

His silence almost insults Caroline. "Well, are you going to say something? Or shall I show you why you're here?"

He stays quiet.

Katrina steps toward him. Caroline does the same. I remain near the door, unwilling to participate in whatever they're about to do to him.

"All you have to do is say something, anything," says Caroline caustically.

Miles buries is head into his palms. Yet, he doesn't weep aloud. He just lies there, hunched over and quiet.

"Katrina. . ." mutters Caroline. "What do we do to failures of this task?"

"Invade the mind."

I step into the conversation. "What are you going to do?"

"Just watch."

Caroline rolls up her sleeves.

Shit.

I want to warn Miles, but my words can only do so much. There's nothing I can do to stop Caroline from using his chip against him no matter how much I want to. If she's ever going to believe that I'm not a failure, I have to let her work without intervention—even if that means allowing her to hurt someone I care for.

Miles stays on his knees with his head down as Caroline steps toward him.

"Miles," she mumbles.

He doesn't budge.

"This won't hurt—" she cuts off as she jams her index finger into the back of his head, "—a bit."

Miles falls limp onto his chest as the walls around us create a picture. No longer can we see the arena around us, but instead we're elsewhere. It looks like Nimbus, but disfigured. Rather than a steel wall surrounding the town, there are long, shaven spears—and every few spears has a head on it. Miles is in the middle, near the platform where Nimbus's orator sends kids out for Separation. And just as he is here, he's still on his knees.

Caroline pushes harder. I can see the blood sliding down her wrist. Miles jolts up—not here—but in this moving image plastered on the windows of this room.

"Where am I?" he says, his voice coming through the walls rather than from his immobile physical self.

Caroline speaks out loud, her hand still buried in Miles's scalp. "You're exactly where you don't want to be."

"It looks like Nimbus," mutters Miles as he stands up. "But where is the wall?"

I step closer to the wall to my right. Everything is happening in first person; I, too, am in Miles's shoes. I can see what he sees, but my emotions differ.

"Where's the wall?" he says again.

His arm encompasses the screen as he wipes his eyes, blurring what we see for a quick second. Then, he falls back onto his knees. . .and screams.

And that's when it becomes apparent to me. The heads on the spikes are all the same. They're all Isaac.

"What are you doing to him?" I say vehemently.

"Indulging his fear."

"Why? Why does he have to see what he already saw, but in a worse manner?"

"Because he failed," she spits back, furthering her nail into his skull. Blood no longer lightly pours out, but it spills out to the point that any more pressure and she might kill Miles right here, right now.

"Stop it!" I yell. "Let him go!" I rush toward her, but before I can push her away, Katrina shoulders me onto the floor.

"Let her work, bitch," curses Katrina.

Miles's scream reverberates off the walls. The image disappears. But Caroline hasn't stopped pressing.

"What happened?" I ask, motioning my head side-to-side, waiting for the movie-like images to reappear.

"He's passed out," mutters Caroline. "Katrina, get Marisa."

I quickly stand up. "What did you do to him? Why did you take him there? Why did you press on his chip until you almost killed him?" The questions spew out like a waterfall in a flood, unable to stop falling.

"He failed. This was his second chance to prove me wrong and he failed again."

"That doesn't mean you had to do that!"

So much for holding back my emotions.

"Have you learned nothing?" Caroline hollers as she stands up. The blood drips from her hand onto the floor; each drop explodes on the surface, painting it red.

"How am I supposed to learn from torture?"

"How are you not? You survived ten damn years outside of Nimbus. Did you learn nothing from your Separation?" She continues to shout as she steps closer to me. "What did you think those eleven years were for? To be happy and free? Bullshit!"

"They were hell!" I yell back, unable to be calm in any sense.

She gets closer. "Exactly, Elise. They were there to make you loathe existence. They were set in front of you to make you stronger, to make you see why this world is imperfect."

"Every world is imperfect," I mutter.

"Except Halcyon." She comes within an inch of me, again. "Halcyon harbors those feelings that nearly killed you outside of Nimbus and turns them into power. It turns them into fuel to ignite the raging fire set forth by Separation."

"That fire made me want to end Nimbus. It didn't make me want to kill everyone."

Caroline takes a step back. . .and slaps me.

I don't fight back. I don't let the stinging sensation in my cheek make me pounce. I do nothing.

"Wake up, Elise. You could be dead because of your devotion to someone else." She pauses, and walks back to the end of the room. "Look at Miles."

I refuse.

"His attachment to his brother could lead to his death. It almost did. If he didn't pass out, I'm sure I would have created enough torment that his mind would have become putty in my hands."

"But why? Why hate everyone when instead you could use everyone to build something great?"

"I don't know how many times I have to reiterate this to you: Not everyone is strong; not everyone is smart; not everyone has the willpower to survive. A society where everyone is equal is the most idiotic thing I've ever heard." She turns back to face me. "As I said before, why you were chosen to create our next circle is beyond me. You clearly lack every quality of a leader."

Katrina and Marisa enter the room.

"At least I don't rely on hatred to survive."

Caroline scoffs. "And that, my dear, is why you will fail."

My palms start to sweat. I can see myself charging Caroline through the window; watching as she falls to her demise. Yet, I can't get myself to do it. I can't make her suffer because the second I retaliate, that's when her followers will make Sean and Sam languish in an unbearable reality—one in which we all lose.

I grind my teeth.

Marisa tends to Miles. She's stopped the bleeding, but he hasn't awoken.

The ends of my jaw pulse against my cheeks. "Caroline. . ." I mutter.

"Yes?" she answers softly, almost casually like she didn't just call me a failure.

"How does pressing into someone's chip cause those hallucinations?"

"There's a small device on the tip of my finger. Marisa has it as well."

Now you tell me.

"Why does she have it, too?" I shoot a look her way. She makes sure to avoid it.

"She had to make sure you two didn't die on your way here. Wasn't it obvious? Or are all of you really that easily fooled?"

I close my eyes and tightly dig my eyelids into my upper cheekbones. "She was our nurse. Why would we think she was doing anything but tending to us?"

Caroline laughs. "You should never trust anyone you don't truly know, Elise."

"Then why am I to trust you?"

"I never said you had to trust me. You just need to learn from me, or perhaps the DZ will change their mind."

I sigh. "It's more likely that you'll just kill me instead," I whisper away from Caroline's ears. She doesn't say anything to me.

"He's waking up," effuses Marisa.

"Take him away," instantly responds Caroline, much to my chagrin.

"What are you going to do with him?"

"Take him back to his room. He has less than twenty-four hours to recover before tomorrow's test."

"The next test is tomorrow?" I snap back.

"Yes."

"Why so soon?"

Caroline laughs. "You'll see." She waves her arm. Katrina grabs my elbow and starts guiding me toward the door. Marisa puts her arm around Miles and leads him to the exit, as well.

The door shuts on its own behind us. A sepia-themed series of lights illuminate overhead, leading us down a hallway overlaid with gold and cerulean fleur de lis wallpaper, and disjointed floorboards that creak with every few steps. Once we reach the end, Katrina twists and pushes open a door that steers us back into the main lodging—where, of course, the lush greens and ugly browns make up the entirety of the surrounding colors.

"Katrina, you can go. I'll take them both to their rooms," softly announces Marisa.

"Are you sure?" responds Katrina, almost baffled.

"Yes, I would like to check Elise's wounds and I need to make sure Miles is okay."

"Whatever."

Katrina walks in the opposite direction.

"Don't bother with my injuries," I sneer. "I don't need your help."

Marisa grabs onto my arm. "Just walk," she quietly says.

I try to shake her off, but she doesn't break.

"Just walk," she repeats.

"What's going on. . .on?" stutters Miles.

"Listen," whispers Marisa. "Is Katrina out of sight?"

I turn back. I nod.

"You're getting out of here tonight."

I stop in my tracks. Miles keeps moving, his head still seeping a bit. "What did you say?"

"Hush. I can't do this anymore. You're getting out of here tonight."

"Why? Since when do you care about us?"

"Since Miles could have died. If she had gone a centimeter deeper, he'd be hemorrhaging right now. I can't watch her do that anymore."

Her words seem pure, but she lied to us. It's tough to believe her even if her silence and her demeanor seem sincere.

"How do I know this isn't a gimmick?"

"You don't."

"So, why should I trust you?"

We near my room. Marisa pulls out a small plastic bag. "You can't, but in here you'll find everything you need to know." She hands it to me, opens the door of my room, and steps toward me. She motions for me to lend an ear. I do, and that's when her words become haunting, her tone becomes honest. "Get out, Elise. Get all of them out, or you will all die."

She reaches for the handle and disappears from my sight into the eerily calm hallway of this hell.

Sam

I still don't know why I had to see her. None of it will probably ever make sense. Caroline's ability to create what she created seems unreal, almost fake. But that doesn't change the fact that it happened, that I saw Abby, that I spoke to her.

All the emotions were raw; they were real. Just like the air around my now-missing pinky, the whole incident poked at my pain, it dug itself into my psychological wounds and planted itself there, waiting to see if I burst, if I bled.

But I didn't.

I'm still standing.

I don't know how, but I am.

I ache to the core; my body feels like an invisible hand keeps trying to push me down, like it keeps attempting to flatten me. I don't know what it is, or how to stop it. I just know I can't let it win; I can't let this game kill me. Not after I've already made it this far.

My fingers, all nine, lie entwined upon my chest. Sean sits in the chair across from me with his neck arched back, his eyelids blindly staring at the ceiling. Caroline keeps throwing us back into this room after each event with our only exits being meal times and tasks. There's a bathroom in here, but it's more of a stall than its own room.

I start to tap my index finger on the back of the opposite hand. Not a rhythmic beat by any means, but just a tap—a gentle poke to let my body know it's still here.

I muster my brother's name, softly. "Sean. . ."

He doesn't look at me. He barely moves, but he answers, "Yes?"

"We have to get out of here."

He remains still, unyielding to his posture. "I know."

"So. . .how do we do it?" I keep tapping.

"I need to find a way to talk to Elise."

"How are you going to manage that? Caroline doesn't let any of us speak to her."

He sits up. "She might let you. After all, she keeps saying the DZ has plans for you. . .whatever that means."

"But that's not Halcyon. That's another place we know nothing about."

Sean's voice becomes even more hushed. "Doesn't matter. Your fate seems to be life in some capacity. Mine," he grimaces, "Mine seems to be death."

His words don't faze me. They glide over me like the air in this room—they're there, but that doesn't mean I need to spend every second thinking about them. Sean's scared. We all are.

"Maybe I can ask Noah to let me talk to Elise," I say.

"You need to get to Caroline. Noah won't care."

I exhale. "It's not that easy."

"It's not supposed to be." Sean stands up. "If it were, we wouldn't be here. The decision to avoid Halcyon altogether would have been unanimous."

I can't help but feel that was a jab at me, but I hold back my bitterness. I'll never know why I listened to Caroline. "I'll find a way."

"You need to." He walks to the end of the bed and sits down. "This may sound cliché, or like the worst line in one of those old movies you used to watch with Dad, but we're counting on you, Sam. Every last one of us."

My eyelids fall. I take a slow breath and repeat myself, "I'll find a way."

Elise

Marisa gave me a map and a key.

It feels like I'm supposed to find a chest, like this is some sort of joke. Even the map has sporadic holes in it like it's an antiquated treasure map, and the key, the key's not modern: It's gold with two small downward protrusions upon the end and a circle on the opposite side. It's ancient. It looks like it should open the door to a castle.

None of it makes sense.

But it has to. *It has to.* When we left Nimbus, Marisa didn't appear even slightly against us. There were moments where she was silent, or indifferent, but she never showed any outward disdain toward any of us. Then again, if I were in her shoes, I wouldn't attempt to blow my cover either. And that's why all of this is so difficult to sort out. One minute she's with us, the next she's not, and then she flip flops back? *Or was she never with us?* My forehead starts to ache.

I take off my shoe and shove the key underneath the arch of my foot. Then, I spread the map out upon the bed.

It doesn't look anything like the world outside of Halcyon, nor does it look like Halcyon itself. The curvature of some of the shapes makes it look like this building, but if it's that, it seems we haven't even seen a third of this place. Caroline's shown me around to a few rooms, but if this is the layout of her home, I haven't seen anything.

I lean closer.

Certain lines have thicker, darker scribbles in half-inch diameters across them. *Doors?* Some areas have 'EX' while other lines are simply marked with 'C-AV.' I don't know what any of it means— what's what, or who's who. None of this makes sense. I don't get how Marisa thought I could sort this out without any clues, without any guidance as to what I'm looking at.

My best bet is to hope 'EX' means exit and 'C-AV' means avoid in some form. I doubt it means audio-visual. I haven't seen a camera in this entire place, but I'm still not going to knock out the possibility that Caroline has this whole place bugged. She's been a step ahead as long as she's been around.

With that, I take a final glance at the map and fold it up before tucking it into my back pocket.

As is the story of our existence, the almost fictional world we live in, the second I push the worn, yellow sheet into my pocket, a knock thumps against the bulky wood of my door. In steps Katrina.

However, she's not clad in the cloak the followers typically wear. She's wearing an outfit similar to the black silk get-up Caroline gave me, but hers is an off-white cream color. It looks like she's in her pajamas.

I push my bangs out of my eyes, but I make no attempt to comment on Katrina's attire.

She fakes a grin and crosses her arms. "Caroline wants to see you."

"When doesn't she?"

Katrina huffs and rolls her eyes.

I walk toward the door, trying not to show any sort of limp as the key presses against the bend of my foot.

The second I get a step ahead of Katrina, it starts to feel like her eyes are glued to what's behind me, like she knows what I possess. A slight trickle of doubt slides through my cheekbones, causing me to grit my teeth, but I don't look back. I keep in stride and try not to add any more doubt to her constantly disapproving view of me.

"Elise," she mutters.

I stop with one foot in the hallway, but I don't look back.

"I hope you know that everyone will die."

My tongue pushes past my teeth and settles itself behind my upper lip. "You underestimate us."

"You have that backwards," she quips. "We're always one. . .step," she steps behind me, ". . .ahead," she steps in front of me. Craning her neck back to look at me, she smirks the unfriendliest of smirks I've ever seen. "You may escape to make another world for the DZ, but even you will die a cold. . .lonely. . .death." Then, she smiles like we're the best of friends and everything she just said was as cordial as a thank-you card.

"Can't wait," I sneer.

"This way," she says sharply.

Down the hall we go with only one turn to get in front of the door that exits onto the floor of the arena.

"What are we doing here?" I ask.

"After Caroline spoke to you last she realized that she couldn't end today's events the way she did, so she's set up something for you and one other."

"It's only been about an hour, or less."

"Doesn't matter. Caroline's a genius. She knows what she's doing."

I smirk—the same unfriendly, cruel smirk Katrina showed me seconds ago—unabashedly poking fun at her. "Caroline's a psychopath."

Our gibes continue, our clear hatred for each other blossoming with each and every situation we're forced into together, until that door opens.

Nobody but Caroline stands on the arena floor. All the lights in the entire area are on. I can finally see where the audience sits, and just like their shantytown, their seats look horrifically uncomfortable. They're stone. Almost as if this is supposed to be some sort of coliseum, their seats circle the entirety of this place going dozens of rows deep. Considering the fact that everything else in Halcyon is modeled after a select period of time, it's odd that where we go to prove our strength is as ancient as it gets. Then again, it's not.

"Another will be joining us," Caroline says aloud, seemingly to herself, as her focus isn't on me.

"Who?"

"You will see."

"Who is joining us, Katrina?" I ask.

But Katrina doesn't respond.

"Hello," I say sarcastically.

Nothing.

I look back and she's gone. The only person who stands in eyesight is Sam. Distraught and teary-eyed, he lunges toward me.

"Sam!" I cry.

"Elise!"

"What are you doing here?"

Wrapping his arms around me, he winces before quickly pulling away. "Sorry. . . .it's my finger. I-I can't do much with it. It's too sensitive."

"It's okay," I smile. "But why are you here, Sam?"

"Noah told me I was to come out here, that there was something special planned for me."

"There is," echoes Caroline's voice.

I turn around. "And what is that exactly?"

"Follow me."

I grab onto Sam's hand, and he onto mine. "Where do you think we're going?" he asks, his questioning heightened by his wandering gaze.

My mouth feels dry. I'm not sure why Caroline would allow Sam to see me, why all of the sudden I'm not completely alone or stuck with Katrina. "I really don't know."

"Do you think we'll be okay?"

"I hope so."

"Nobody's getting hurt tonight," resounds Caroline's voice as if she's been listening to every word we say. Then again, we're the only three here, making it nearly impossible not to hear at least a tidbit of any conversation that were to happen.

"Then where are you leading us?" I ask. She pushes open a door. Sam and I remain a short distance behind her. Surprisingly, Caroline remains still, holding the door open. Again, I ask, "Where are you taking us?"

Sam moves through the door ahead of me. I follow. Caroline regains her place in front of us.

The room is dimly lit. The walls are grey, maybe made of stone; it's hard to tell when I can barely see, and I have no desire to touch them to figure out just what they are. We take a few strides before veering right. Muted yellow bulbs cling to the ceiling above us, leading us who knows where.

We take another right.

Then, a left.

We walk for a few paces before a stairwell presents itself in front of us. It can't be more than five feet wide, but it has to be at least forty steps. Caroline starts walking up it—still directly in front of us with no one else around.

I look down at Sam. His eyes are wide, searching for clues that refuse to present themselves.

"Caroline," I stammer. "Where are you taking us?"

She keeps walking, still unresponsive to anything I say.

"Caroline!" I shout, my nerves taking over.

"Just keep walking," she softly replies.

I don't want to keep walking. I want to take this key out of my shoe, jam it into her back, and twist. I want to turn her into a toy as I keep spinning, and spinning, and spinning the key until she falls down the steps and lands headfirst on the floor below.

I can see it, too. I can see her falling. I can see her getting what she deserves, but no matter how many times it replays in my head, I can't get myself to do it. I don't know why, either. *Why shouldn't I kill her when I have the chance?*

We reach the top of the stairs. Caroline pushes open another door, this time into a room with such intense light that I'm forced to close my eyes the second I step into it. I keep moving, but without my sense of sight.

Sam squeezes my hand.

I stop.

Slowly, like a newborn baby, I open my eyes. We're in what looks like a diner, or a café of some sort. There are booths lining the walls with small tables placed in the middle. Each table has two to four chairs, a white tablecloth, and a small burning candle. The booths are a dark red, almost maroon color while the walls are wood-paneled and completely barren in terms of art. There are unique moldings at the intersection of the walls and the ceiling, but outside of that, there's nothing interesting. It's just another place for Caroline to schmooze us, another part of Halcyon that she can gloat about even though it means nothing to us.

"What is this place?" asks Sam.

A man steps into the room. I don't recognize him. He's about the same height as me and he's wearing white pants, a buttoned white jacket, and an equally unappealing, rounded white hat. There's a pin on his jacket, but I can't make out what it says.

"This is only the finest establishment in town," he laughs, his belly shaking with each breath.

Caroline grins. "This is Sal's. It's a restaurant with an eclectic menu of old-fashioned favorites."

"Why are we here?" I ask while I look around.

"I have a lot I need to talk to both of you about, and I figured this was the best place to do it. None of my followers are present. Nobody in town is here, either. The only other person is our chef, Sal."

"Why bring us alone?"

"Should I not have?"

"I don't know, Caroline," I groan.

"Why don't we grab a seat," motions Caroline. "Where would you two like to sit?"

"Anywhere. It doesn't matter."

"Sam, where would you like to sit?"

"I don't care," he answers.

"Sal, we'll take my favorite booth," announces Caroline as if it matters in some capacity.

"Nothin' but the best for you!" widely smiles Sal as he leads us to a booth, literally, two steps to our right. He quickly hands us each a menu and disappears through a door behind the bar.

I open the menu.

Sandwiches *Served with your choice of chips, deviled eggs, potato salad, pickle, or coleslaw*

- *Liver (cooked liver, red onions, spinach, tomatoes, and mayo on white or wheat)*
- *Baked Bean (baked beans, bacon, and mayo on white or wheat)*
- *Hot Beef Steak (steak, caramelized onions, and cheese on white or wheat)*
- *Egg Salad (egg salad on rye)*
- *Tutti Frutti (dates, raisins, dry figs, walnuts mixed w/ orange juice, whip cream, and sugar on buttered white bread)*

I shut the menu without so much as looking at the rest of it.

"That was fast, Elise. Find something you like?" politely asks Caroline like she's genuinely interested in what I say or do.

"I'm not hungry."

"You should eat. Sal has lots of good things on the menu!"

I swallow in disgust in an attempt to forget what ingredients I saw in the last sandwich on the menu. "I'll pass."

"Sal," Caroline says loudly, but not loud enough that if there were other patrons here, they could hear it.

Sal immediately comes back into the room.

"We'll all have a plate of your famous Chicken a la King."

"Any sides or appetizers?" asks Sal.

Caroline doesn't so much as glance at Sam or I. "House salad for each of us as an appetizer."

"What about a drink?"

"Waters for everyone. Also, a chocolate soda for Sam and a bottle of the 2180 House Red for Elise and I."

"I don't want any wine," I retort.

"Don't be so naïve, Elise." She then turns her attention back to Sal. "That will be all, Sal, and don't rush. We have time."

Sal nods and returns to the kitchen without so much as a blink.

Biting at the inside of his cheek, Sam looks at me then at Caroline. ". . .what's a chocolate soda?"

Caroline smiles. "Just wait, you'll love it."

What's that supposed to mean? Why is she acting so happy, so joyful, so full of ecstasy in a situation like this? I hate it. I want to leap across the table and smash her head into the wall. I want to pounce; I want to end her. But I can't.

She shifts her attention to me. "So, let's get down to the real reason why we're here, shall we?"

I look at her, wide-eyed, and blink. No reason to speak. She knows this is all we care about—not this restaurant or the food—the fact that we're alone with *just* her.

Caroline folds in her bottom lip before looking over at Sam. "You both play a part in the future of our world. Each of you has a role chosen by a higher power: the DZ."

Sam quickly interrupts. "What does DZ mean?"

That's the question you chose to ask? I think to myself.

"Dead Zone."

"Why do they call themselves that?"

Caroline laughs. "They don't call themselves that. That's just where they exist; that's where they thrive."

"And where is that?" I ask.

"I cannot answer that, Elise."

"Why not? Do you not know where it is?"

"I know, and through what you've seen in the past, I'm surprised you don't already know. But, that's okay, you'll learn it in due time, but not from me."

Sal brings out our beverages.

I grab the water and take a drink.

Sam stares at his unique soda. "This looks like dessert," he mutters to himself.

"It sort of is in a way," smiles Caroline. "Try it. You'll love it."

I throw myself into the conversation. "Why are you being like this?"

"Like what?"

"This. Nice. Polite. Everything that you're not."

She scoffs in the most sarcastic of ways. "Oh, Elise. I'm always this nice." She pours herself a large glass of wine before filling another glass halfway and setting it in front of me. I don't touch it.

"You're not, though."

She takes a drink—an excessively large one—before trying to refocus our discussion. "Anyways, like I was saying before, you each have a role in the future of this world. Elise, you know yours, but Sam," she turns to face him, "you don't know yours."

"What's Elise's?" he asks while maneuvering his spoon around the ice cream floating atop a bed of chocolate syrup and carbonated water.

"Why don't you answer that for him, Elise?"

Why? Why am I here when she can tell these things to Sam herself?

I take another drink of my water. The chilled liquid slides down my throat; I can feel it cooling my chest as it disappears further into my body. I grab the glass again. But, I don't drink anything. I just hold it. I let the condensation cool my palms.

Sam softly says my name. "Elise?"

I keep fidgeting with the glass, but my eyes shift toward Sam. Just my eyes. I keep my head still, my body rigid. "I-I'm to create a new circle. . ."

"What do you mean?"

"Nimbus was a circle. Halcyon is a circle. There's a third circle we're yet to see, and I'm in charge of the fourth."

He looks at me with puzzled eyes. "I'm not sure exactly what you mean. Why does there have to be another circle? Why are they circles?"

I finally manage to take another swig. "You remember that marking we saw on the tree and the bodies of those from the library?"

He nods, his spoon still going around the slowly melting ice cream.

"Each of the circles in that marking represents one of the three zones. The bottom one was blacked out, indicating that Nimbus failed. The other two are still clear because they're still functioning."

"But why do you have to make a fourth one? Why are you in charge of creating something from scratch?" He releases his spoon. It sinks into the glass. "I don't get any of this."

"Neither do I, Sam. I'm still confused by everything that's going on."

Caroline reaches for the wine bottle since she somehow managed to finish her glass while Sam and I were talking. As she pours, she doesn't look up, but she speaks. "None of this is supposed to make sense to you guys, but I was informed I needed to tell you."

"Why? Why do they want us to know anything? And why, of all people, do they want me to know?" bickers Sam.

"Because you're the key, Sam."

Sam's face goes white. Ghostly white. "Wha-what did you say?"

"You're the key. Your survival helps the DZ find the perfect world. Your failure to, well, fail, is what keeps them creating. It's what keeps them wanting to make the perfect society that will live forever."

"So, that's not here?" I laugh, amused.

"Halcyon is perfect," angrily retorts Caroline. "Just because the DZ sees Sam as this invincible deity doesn't mean my tests won't kill him." She sips her wine. "There are three circles, each with different theories on perfection. Nimbus's clearly was dreadful and that's why it failed. Mine has already killed four from your group and one is nearing his demise. In the long run, the DZ will see that my circle is perfect, and there will be no need for you, Elise. And, of course, they'll realize they chose the wrong child to believe in."

Sam digs his nails into the edges of the table. "Why did they choose me? Why am I some sort of key to creating this perfect circle?"

"Because of your past. Your genealogy."

He digs deeper. "What do you mean? And if it's my genes, aren't they Sean's, too?"

"In a way, yes. But he's already survived his eleven years. You're young. You're new to everything and that's what makes you the perfect guinea pig."

"But what do my genes have to do with any of this? There are plenty of families in Nimbus who have all survived Separation."

"But none who did what you did. None who fought back. Plus, it's not like you were chosen before you killed MacMillan. You weren't chosen until the DZ saw how ruthless you could truly be, until they saw you fire nearly a dozen arrows into a man and refuse to yield to the fact that he was dead after the second one." She takes another drink. "They realized your resilience was key to determining which of our current three circles is the strongest. So far, with one down, you only have to prove they made the right choice two more times."

"How was I not chosen until after I killed him? There was someone in my head the entire time I was outside of Nimbus, so wouldn't that mean I was chosen before then?"

Caroline softly cracks her neck. "There were discussions beforehand that you could be the key."

"What does that mean?" asks Sam, his fingers clawing at the wood.

"That they tested you early."

"By getting in my head and forcing those horrific nightmares? By scarring my mind, my body, and everything about me? Just to test my resilience?"

"Yes."

"Why couldn't they wait? They knew how horrible it was outside those walls."

"Our future won't wait."

"Why not?" I ask, sliding slightly closer to the end of the table.

Caroline heavily exhales.

Sal sneakily places salads in front of each of us.

"Because the DZ is never satisfied."

I flinch my jaw. "Why?"

"There's a reason they want you to create another zone rather than being satisfied with three. There's a reason I was sent out to create Halcyon; why I sent Vincent to make a third. There are reasons for everything even if I'm not privy to them." She finishes her second glass and quickly pours another.

Sam's eyes droop. His fingers fall off the end of the table; he moves them toward his eyes. Rubbing the end of his thumb and index finger against his eyelids, he sighs. "And what happens if I survive your tests, Caroline?"

"You won't," she laughs.

"But what if I do?"

"Then the DZ will end Halcyon."

"Just like that?" I say.

"Just like that. Halcyon would disappear just like Nimbus."

"Nimbus is still functioning," I add.

Caroline smirks. "Okay, sure."

"What do you mean, Caroline? We lived in Nimbus for three more months after MacMillan's death. Nimbus never disappeared. It's still there."

"Then why is it blacked out on the map?"

"To show that its leader is dead," mutters Sam.

"Nope. To show that it failed. Nimbus has been wiped off the map," divulges Caroline.

"What do you mean?"

"After you left to come here, the DZ destroyed it and everyone in it."

Zeke. . .

"You're kidding, right?" I say. "You're joking with us, Caroline, aren't you?"

"No. The DZ has always had a plan for a failed circle. When one is overcome by revolt, it is culled." She moves her fork around the greens upon her plate. "However, after Nimbus failed, the rule changed to accommodate you guys."

"What is it now?"

"Failure to kill the kids who brought down a circle means the dissolving of the one that couldn't succeed. A revolt or uprising no longer needs to cause it. Only you guys can cause it."

"And what if we succeed here and then we succeed in the next place? What if I create a world and it somehow fails?"

"It can't. If you can clear three societies, you've found perfection."

All of this is coming at me so fast. Caroline's told me bits and pieces about my role in this world, but never like this. I finish my water. Sal appears out of nowhere to refill it before disappearing back into the void that seems to be the rest of this place.

And to think that she's telling the truth about Nimbus, that it's been wiped off the map. . .I just can't believe it. I can't believe that my brother could be dead, that those who chose not to join us were killed for nothing. It doesn't make sense. None of it makes sense. *Why would the DZ kill off the foundation it needs to stay afloat? Why would it kill those who have proven they're strong just to find their ideal society?*

Sam finally digs his spoon into the melting ice cream in front of him. He smiles when it touches his lips. But only after swallowing it does his jaw tighten, and his lips furl. "Why do we need perfection?" he asks aloud while keeping his head down. His eyes remain focused on the beverage, but he doesn't touch it again. He just sort of stares at it. His eyes appear to be searching without movement, as if he desires only one response. Which, we both know, he won't get.

"Why wouldn't we need it?" answers Caroline. Plucking a piece of spinach from her plate before digging her fork into a radish, she takes a bite.

"I asked you."

She chews. She rolls her eyes. She seems to be falling back into the version of herself I've been around this entire time. "If a world isn't perfect, it shouldn't exist. We need perfection to guarantee a society that lives forever. Not one that falls into the misery of the past. Didn't you ever learn how Nimbus came to be? How the DZ sent Aldous to create a world devoid of the inadequacies of its predecessor?"

"We didn't. We were told it was war that caused the city to fall."

Caroline guffaws. "Oh goodness. They really changed the curriculum in school once I left." She takes a sip of her water. "What exactly did they tell you?"

"War. That's the gist of it. That the politics of the past weren't working out, and a war broke out. People fled, blood was shed, the world fell apart. That's all we know."

"They really did start to fill your heads with rot. That's MacMillan for you. That old fart was getting worse and worse as the years went on. He became more and more careless, so it only makes sense that he started filling your heads with lies over time. He must have really wanted everyone to fail."

"He did," mutters Sam.

"So what really happened?" I ask.

"The city was culled just like Nimbus was after it failed."

"How did the city fail?"

"Its methods were futile. Its handling of conflict was horrendous. Society doesn't need light pleasantries to survive; it doesn't need a system built upon greed, lust, and gluttony. A world needs strength. The only competition should be to determine who's the strongest mentally, physically, and emotionally. Nothing else is needed."

"So, essentially the world needed to be a little more like this place?"

She smiles.

"But that doesn't answer my question. How did it fall? What caused it to crumble?"

"The gas."

"What gas?"

"Yea, what gas?" repeats Sam.

"Can't we just eat and stop talking about how everything began? Can't we just enjoy this time together before Sam takes his third test tomorrow and fails? Wouldn't you rather remember this time with him, Elise?" She takes a small bite. "You need to stop focusing on how everything came to be, and instead focus on your future."

I laugh. "Says the person who has a society built to be a replica of the past."

"I just like the aesthetic," smirks Caroline before prodding her fork into the leafy greens upon her plate once more. "Now, why don't you two start eating and drinking, and we'll have a lovely evening?"

"Everything you've told us is the exact reason why none of that is possible," counters Sam. "It's impossible to be happy when every meal could be the last."

"Even more, we can't be happy around you," I sneer.

"Well, I guess it'll just be Sal and I dining tonight then." Caroline snaps her fingers.

Noah and Katrina step through the door Sal's been coming in and out of.

"So much for being alone with you," I laugh.

"You knew they were here, Elise. Don't pretend you didn't."

I exhale loudly—like a bull preparing to chase the matador.

Caroline grins and softly says, "I always know what you're thinking."

"Not always."

"Oh yes, always."

Katrina and Noah step behind us. We stand up.

The key digs into the arch of my foot but I don't cringe, I don't show any signs of discomfort.

Caroline's right. She has access to my thoughts, but there's no way she can know everything I'm thinking, there's no way she's always active in my mind. She told me once that the chip is only still in my head so she can ensure I'm paying attention—and I am. Whether or not I agree isn't up to her.

"Now, run along, you two, and don't tell the others what I told you tonight."

"Why not?" responds Sam as he scratches the back of his head.

"They don't need to know that you two are better than them."

"They have just as much of a right to know what's going on as we do."

"They do," whispers Caroline, "but telling them will only make matters worse. . .and we can't have you guys trying to escape, now can we?" She drifts her stare toward me; the key presses deeper into my foot. I grit my teeth.

"How would we escape when we don't know a way out?" I cringe internally, thinking that Caroline might know what Marisa gave me.

"Don't play the fool, Elise. You're too smart to play that character."

I look away. If she's going to be deceitful in an attempt to pry out what I know about this place, it won't work. I won't show her any weakness. I won't hand her the key to our deaths. "I've never played any character, Caroline. You should know that by now."

"I like to think I know you, but the chips have their limitations."

I tilt my head back.

She looks directly at me. "Alas, if they were put in in Halcyon I'd know, but Nimbus was always technologically behind. So, I guess I'll have to trust what I know." Yet, as the words come out of her mouth, her eyes slant toward her nose; her eyebrows arch. She then, ever so lightly, tilts her head upward. Immediately, Katrina grabs my arm—Noah grabs Sam's—and we're whisked away.

Sean

Sam's been gone for over an hour now.

Where he's at is beyond me. I just hope he's okay. I like to believe he's strong enough to hold his own, but I can't read Caroline; I can't tell what her end game is. Then again, I don't know what mine is.

I'm trying to resist my emotions so I can better focus on the task at hand, but that's easier said than done. Attempting to feign contentment has led to my mind being even more hyperactive than normal, as if it's analyzing every second more thoroughly. Like it's trying to plan out my reaction, or lack thereof. It's frustrating, but I have to do this. I have to be strong.

I have to survive.

A knock comes at my door.

Nobody knocks here. Usually Noah just barges right in.

"Yes?" I answer.

The door creaks slightly ajar. Marisa slides through the crack and into the room.

"What are you—"

She cuts me off. "Noah and Sam will be back shortly, so you need to listen carefully." She steps closer to me, her pupils enlarging the nearer she gets. "You are getting out of here tonight. I gave Elise a map and a key to the elevator up."

"When? How?"

"The vent in Marcus's room connects to the one in Elise's. He will be paying her a visit at midnight tonight. From there, they will come get the rest of you."

"Does he know?"

"Yes."

"Aren't the doors locked from the outside?"

"Yes."

"Then how do you expect this to work?"

227

"Marcus has a key. It works for every door, I believe."

"What do you mean, 'you believe?' What if it doesn't work for someone? We can't leave anyone behind," I quickly stammer. "I'm not escaping without any of them."

"Hush!" she mutters. "It should work for every door. I'm quite sure. Trust me."

"Why should I? And how can anyone get out of their room if the key only works from the outside?"

"Because I can't watch Caroline kill any more innocent people, and Elise's room is different. There are locks on both sides because Caroline feels Elise should be able to move more freely."

"How do I know this isn't a trap? How do I know you're not just lying to me to put us into even more danger?"

"You don't," she whispers before taking a few steps back. She looks left then right, even though there's no one else in this room, before twisting the doorknob behind her.

I stand up and rush toward her. "If this is a trap, I will kill you," I say, the words effortlessly sliding off my tongue.

Her lips tighten, but she doesn't speak. She slowly pulls the door toward her back, and slithers out like a lizard escaping the ominous glare of its predator.

What the hell was that?

I remain by the door. The muscles in my neck become tense.

One second I'm stuck in the silence of this room contemplating what's next in Halcyon, then I'm thrown into an escape plan. I know life can switch directions at the drop of a hat—as it frequently has in this world—but to be changed this drastically by someone whose trust has evaporated is absurd. Marisa hasn't done enough to warrant any belief in what she says. The only thing I would trust her with is bandaging my wounds. . .*with saving my life.*

She's kept Sam alive. She's kept Elise alive.

But others died and she did nothing.

I begin to rub the back of my neck. I don't know what to think. I don't know what to do.

I need to stop thinking about what this means.

I just need to believe it's real.

It's crazy. It's absolutely against how I would normally think about life and death situations, but I shouldn't think anymore. Overthinking is what kills you. If I keep spending my time thinking about every possible outcome, the hesitation on what's right will be the end of me.

I just have to trust the one person who might be even less trustworthy than Caroline.

I'm going to die. We're going to die.

Oddly, I laugh. I'm not sure why. But I laugh.

And just when I become more uncomfortable, Sam enters the room.

"Are you okay?" he asks. "I thought I heard laughing in the hallway."

"I have no idea."

He looks at me weirdly before continuing. "Oh, okay," he stutters. "What just happened was weird."

"What happened?" I ask before walking toward the sink at the back of the room.

Sam paces around behind me.

I turn on the faucet and splash water into my face. The lukewarm moisture relaxes me, but it doesn't push away the mental strain I've put on myself.

"Caroline is grooming Elise. . .to be. . .like her," he slowly spits out.

"What do you mean?"

I wipe my face off on my shirt.

"She's supposed to create a new world, or zone, or circle, or whatever. Something like Nimbus, or Halcyon, but with a different philosophy." Sam's cheeks quiver. I can almost hear his teeth rattle.

"Why?"

"The DZ chose her."

"Why?"

"I don't know!" he shouts, throwing both of his hands onto the top of his head. "None of what she told us made a whole lot of sense. And besides that, she told us not to tell anyone."

"Like what she says matters. Is that all she told you?"

He looks down, away from me.

"Is that all she told you?" I repeat.

"Yea," he murmurs.

"She just told you about Elise? She didn't tell you anything about yourself?" I move toward him. "She took you for a reason, Sam. What else did she tell you?"

"That I'm some sort of key. I'm a guinea pig. I'm the one who's supposedly capable of surviving everything."

"How so? How would they know that?"

"I don't know!" he shouts. "I don't get any of it, but that's what she told me."

I walk toward him. I want to wrap my arm around him, but I also want to be sure he's telling me everything, that he's not holding something back because it's something I wouldn't want to hear. "Did she say anything about the rest of us?"

He doesn't answer. He slides his hands down to his sides.

"Sam. . ."

"No," he answers bitterly.

I stop. I don't need to hear anything else. Hell, I don't care to hear anything else. They're using Sam as a lab rat, and Elise as the scientist. The last thing I need to hear is that the cheese doesn't exist, that the maze is unending, and there's no prize for finding a way out. And I don't want to hear that the scientist can't even solve the puzzle thrown in front of the animal.

But there is one thing I want to know. "Did she say anything about the next test?"

"No."

"Nothing?"

"Nothing."

"Okay, good. Well, then, there's something I need to tell you, too."

He gazes around the room, never settling his focus on me.

So, I continue. "We're getting out of here tonight."

He laughs—the same uncomfortable laugh I fell prey to the moment before he walked in.

We're going to die, I think again. *This isn't going to work.*

I shake my head. Not two shakes from side to side, but many. I need to clear the roadblock stopping me from being who I said I'd be.

"A plan is in place, Sam," I say.

"And what's that? To just walk out of here without a single person seeing us?"

"Marisa told me the plan. Elise and Marcus know, too."

"Marisa?" he exclaims, loud enough that I'm forced to rush toward him and put my hand over his mouth.

"Yes, her. She gave Elise a key. She gave Marcus a key. They each work for separate things, but they're our way out." I remove my hand.

"And you trust her?" he asks, an air of ambivalence about him.

"She's kept us alive this far, hasn't she?"

"But she betrayed us. She led us here! She brought us to this misery, and she's just as guilty as Caroline for the deaths of our friends!"

I wrap my arm around his head, silencing him again as I hold my hand over his mouth. "You need to be quiet, Sam. We can't trust a single person here. Who cares if it's a trap? This is our only chance. We have no other plan in place, so we need to just hope that she means well."

"Do you hear yourself?" he mumbles beneath my palm.

"What do you mean?"

"'We just need to hope that she means well?' What is that about?"

"I don't see what you mean."

"She could be setting us up to die faster."

"But what if she's not?" I loosen my grip. "Do you really think she would go through all of this just to kill us before we even complete the next two tasks?"

"What if this is one of the tasks?"

I throw my hands onto my cheeks and massage my jaw. The tension. The aching. All of it makes a difficult situation even more strenuous. "And so what if it is?"

"Then maybe we shouldn't listen to Marisa. . ."

"Do you hear yourself now?"

"Yea, I do, loud and clear. Even if she's somehow telling you the truth—which I'm certain she isn't—there are no guarantees we can get past the followers to get out of here. And if we do, we don't even know where the exit is."

"Elise has a map, too, so I'm sure we can find it," I softly reply, my forehead pulsing with indecision the more we debate about how to handle this.

"You seem rather certain." He walks toward the end of the bed.

"I am."

"But you know how many times we've been certain and ended up on the wrong side of things, right?" He falls onto the comforter and throws his head back onto the pillow. "The only way out of here is by winning, Sean. That's it. There's no other way." He rolls over.

"Do you really believe that?"

He remains facedown, silent.

I move toward the bed. "Sam?"

Nothing but a deep inhale and exhale covered by the weight of the blankets emits from him.

I sit down on the end. "There has to be another way out of here. Even if Marisa is lying, there's a way. They get in here somehow, so there's a way out. I know there is."

The sheets unravel behind me. "I'm not saying there isn't a way out. I'm just saying there's no way we can get to it right now. Caroline's always watching. Plus. . ." he trails off.

"Plus what?"

"It seems we still have our chips, so Caroline knows where we are at all times."

"They didn't take those out in Nimbus? Isn't that what Dr. Tierney did?"

"I thought so, but Marisa was there, too." Sam sits up. "We've been played since we were in Nimbus, Sean. That's why we can't escape."

"But I still don't have my chip," I mutter. "Shouldn't that matter in some capacity? I mean, it mattered when we took down Nimbus."

"Good things don't happen twice," grimaces Sam.

"Unless we make them happen."

He rolls back over.

"Sam, this is happening," I say faintly. "We're getting out of here tonight."

With his face pressed into the bed, he reaches up for the pillow. Once it's gripped in his forefingers, he pulls it down over his head. And, just as muffled as before, he speaks. "Like I said, good things don't happen twice. If they did, we wouldn't be here." He pushes the pillow up a bit. "Nimbus was the first bad thing. Halcyon is the second. There's no good left."

"But just like we did in Nimbus, we'll determine our survival," I respond. "Evil can't always win."

"It might not always win, but it certainly doesn't fall for the same tricks twice."

15 May 2192

Elise

The clock strikes midnight.

I can't sleep.

And it doesn't help that the grandfather clock in the hallway rings louder than anything else in this godforsaken place. It doesn't go off every hour, but at midnight and noon it rings like it's about to explode. It's annoying.

I roll onto my side. Faded fragments of light shine through the neatly designed transom window above my door. Splitting into smaller beams against the wall, the lights form into miniature honeycombs upon the painted plaster.

Bit by bit, my mind draws a line between the gaps shining in front of me; subconsciously trying to connect them all into one.

A slight rattle comes from the vent at the end of the room.

I look up, but see nothing.

My focus falls back to the wall; my thoughts continue to trace nothing. I roll to the other side. *If I'm going to sleep, I can't stare at the light.*

I roll onto my stomach. Now, facedown, I see nothing but the darkness behind my eyelids. If I can't fall asleep this way, I'll never fall asleep.

The vent rattles again.

That's it. I'm up.

The rattles grow louder. They seem to be getting closer to my room, as if something is about to be pushed out of the vent—but I don't know what.

I sit up and push my back against the wall.

The sound becomes more apparent. The thuds echo louder and louder then, almost abruptly, they return to the silence in which they came from.

I take a deep breath, my attention still on the vent at the end of the room.

The silence remains until, almost out of nowhere, the grate near the ceiling falls to the floor and clatters against the tile below the sink.

"What the hell?" I spit out, unable to see what may have caused the grate's demise.

"Shhh," answers the invisible nuisance.

"Who's there?"

"It's me. Marcus."

"What are you doing in here?" I quickly fire back. "How did you get in that vent?"

"We're leaving tonight. Didn't Marisa tell you?"

"She said to get you all out, but she didn't tell me when or how."

Marcus steps into the light—the honeycomb beams illuminate the dust upon his shirt—and toward the end of my bed. "She gave me a universal key that unlocks these doors, so we can get everyone out. She told me you have a map and another key. That's all I know."

"And you trusted her so willingly?"

He exhales heavily. "What other choice did I have?"

I nod. "True."

"We should get going. Someone may have heard that grate hit the floor."

I swing my legs over the edge of the bed. "Let's hope not," I mutter before heading to the closet at the end and taking off these ridiculous silk pajamas. Quickly throwing on some jeans and a hoodie, I slip back out toward Marcus.

"Do you have the map?" he asks.

"Yea, but I don't understand it completely."

"Let me take a look."

I hand him the map before heading to grab my shoes near the door. As I hurriedly slide them on, the key jams into my foot. "Ouch!" I shout—almost too loudly.

"We both gotta be quiet," laughs Marcus.

He laughed. He didn't throw anger at me. He didn't solemnly say that all this noise could kill us. He's different than when I last saw him—he's eager. I wonder what changed.

I move toward him. Looking over the map using the limited light in this room, I mumble his name. "Marcus."

"Yea?"

"Why the sudden uptick in attitude?"

"It's not real, Elise. Nobody's happy right now, so sometimes we have to fake it to stay alive." He drags his finger across the map, seemingly trying to strategize an exit. "Sean's been doing it for a long time."

"How do you know that?"

"I can read him. He's different."

"How so?"

"It doesn't matter," he retorts. "We need to get out of here."

"Does the key she gave you work from in here?"

"I hope so."

"And what if it doesn't?"

"Then I'm climbing back in that vent. I think I saw a turn back there."

I fold my lips together and look toward the door.

Marcus heads toward it. He pulls a key out of his pocket— one entirely different in appearance than the one Marisa gave me. Pressing it into the lock, he turns it left. It clicks. He turns back and looks at me. "It's time. . .also, your room is a lot nicer than mine."

"What can I say, Caroline. . ."

"Is a bitch?"

I grin. "Yea, that."

Slowly pulling the door toward him, Marcus surreptitiously sticks his head out into the hall. I maneuver myself behind him, but don't crane my neck outward—mainly because I fear I'm not stealthy enough. For some reason, when it comes to sneaking around, I always feel like a klutz. In the city when I was searching for Sam, I fell into a puddle in the middle of an empty street. If I could trip in the open in the past, I can do it again in the present.

"It's clear," he whispers before skulking into the hallway.

I lightly step behind him.

He takes a few steps to our right and quickly unlocks the first door beside my room. "Miles is in here. He's awake, but he's still pretty defeated from what happened. Can you help him while I get the others?"

I nod.

Hovering toward Miles's room, I slightly open the door and slide in. The light's on and Miles is sitting upright in a chair parallel to the door. His eyes are open, but he doesn't seem to be staring at anything. "Miles?" I whisper.

He turns his head to look at me, but he doesn't answer.

"Are you okay? Can you walk?"

He blinks.

"I'll take that as a yes. Let's go."

He stands up. As a precaution, I step next to him and wrap my arm around his. He moves slowly next to me, almost like his feet are glued to the floor.

What Caroline did to him was unnatural. It wasn't just cruel; it was abhorrent. She invaded his mind and attacked the one wound he'd been trying to conceal for years. She pried and pried at it until there was nothing left for Miles to do, until there was no longer anything covering the scar. Now, it's open and bleeding—and none of us know if it will ever stop.

"We need to move faster, Miles," I mutter.

His feet move a little quicker, but not much. His eyes are still wide, basically unblinking. He's like a robot.

We get into the hallway. Marcus already has the others outside. Sean, Sam, Rosie, and Ella, they're all there, and they're all we have left. We came with twelve. Now, we have seven. The group's dwindling but it's not gone; everyone who's still alive is alive for a reason. *Even Miles.* He survived Caroline's nightmare. *He's still here.*

"Is Miles okay?" asks Rosie instantly as she tries to understand what's happening.

"He doesn't look right," adds Ella.

"Caroline did a number on him," I say. "She made him endure that second test another time, but in a worse fashion."

"Do we even want to know how bad?" replies Rosie.

"You don't. I was there and I haven't forgotten it. And it doesn't help that she dug into his head toward his chip."

"Why would she do that?" fumes Ella.

"To further his suffering because he didn't succeed on the last task the way she would have liked."

"That's absurd," murmurs Rosie. "But as bad as it is, we have to get moving. We can't just stand here and risk getting caught."

"Agreed."

"Now where do we go?" asks Sean.

"I have a map."

"Can I see it?"

I release my grip on Miles to hand back the map. Ella grabs onto his elbow. "Keep it. I have somewhat of an idea where these hallways go."

"Why don't we just scrap the map and go through the arena like we did earlier today?" asks Sam.

"Where does that lead?" questions Ella.

"Caroline took Sam and I to a restaurant through a door at the end of the arena. I think the restaurant was up on the main road, too. . .so. . .it would exit into the open," I softly answer.

"Do we want to go into the open, though?" states Marcus. "Wouldn't it be best for us to follow the map to an exit rather than risk being confronted in the arena?"

"Do you really think anyone's in there right now, though?" wonders Rosie.

"There's no way we can know until we take a route," stammers Sean. "We just need to get moving before someone finds that we're out here."

"Let's split up then," mutters Sam.

"NO." I angrily assert. "We are getting out of here together, not in groups."

"Sh-she's right," stammers Miles. "We-we have to get out-out togeth-together."

The fact that he's stuttering makes my mind ache; it makes me even more furious with Caroline that she subjected him to such torment and now he can barely focus. He can barely speak, walk, or do anything. I don't know if he's simply broken, or if she legitimately did damage to his brain by pressing so far into his skull. No matter the case, Miles's state is completely Caroline's fault. And the longer removed he is from what happened, the worse he seems to be getting. He didn't stammer right when he came to; he seemed like he was going to recover, but now, I'm not sure.

Caroline will have to pay for this.

"Let's move forward now, then," chides Sean as he steps ahead of me. "The map says we turn right here rather than going straight toward the arena."

We all instantly follow.

"Marcus or Elise, do either of you know what 'C-AV' stands for?"

"No, but I feel like we should avoid those areas," I answer.

"Why's that?"

"Maybe it means something like, 'Caroline-Avoid.' We can't be too sure, but it can't hurt to avoid it."

"Okay, we'll bypass those areas. That means we have to turn left here."

Once again, we follow. None of us knows which way is right to begin with, so at this point we just have to believe the map Marisa gave us is right—which is still semi-troubling for me.

Can we trust her?

I want to ask the others, but I don't want to stall any longer. I can't be starting a public forum to determine if we'll actually escape; that would just ensure we don't make any progress.

A dull light flickers on ahead. Though its color is limited by seashell glass wrapped around a sconce, it produces just enough light to show us two hallways. I look over at Sean.

He looks down at the map. Tracing his finger around a certain portion of it, he glances forward. "Going forward there's an 'EX.' Left has a 'C-AV' and right has nothing, but it does show that there's a hallway."

"Let's go right."

"Why not forward?"

"I think that will take us to the arena."

"Are you sure?"

"Enough."

"Okay, we'll go right."

The light behind us flickers off, but those in the hallway to our right remain dim, but on. No flickering, no inconsistencies. The bulbs don't emit enough light to make us as visible as the sun would, but they do shine enough that if someone were to step out of a room, they would see us.

We continue down this hallway. There are no doors on our left and only a few on the right. The wooden frames are the same color as the ones where we've slept, but that's where the similarities end. There aren't any tables with different imaginative vases upon them, the walls aren't a mixture of green and brown; everything is cream and black. The sconces are silver with black trim.

"Why would Caroline change the color scheme midway down a hallway?" quietly laughs Rosie.

Marcus responds, "She doesn't make any sense."

"Or does she?" mumbles Sean. "Right where the walls changed color, there's a marking on the map. It's not an 'EX' or a 'C-AV,' but there's a small arrow pointing toward the wall at this very spot."

"Are you sure it's right here?"

"It has to be. Based on where the next intersection is, this has to be the spot."

I step closer to the wall. Just like the arrow in the farmhouse pointed to a phrase upon the wall that I've been trying, but unable, to forget—*you will not find solace in the hollows of night*—this one seemingly points to a crease in the wallpaper where the two separate colors meet. I bend down.

"But what's here?" questions Marcus.

"I don't know," answers Sean.

I slide my fingers across the trim. Nothing jumps out. I slide them upward where the two wallpapers meet. Nothing. "There's nothing here," I sigh.

"There has to be. Why else would that arrow be there?"

"Maybe it's a mistake."

"The map can't be wrong," mumbles Sam. "It just can't be."

"Why can't it be?" laughs Marcus. "You know who we got it from."

"Who?" mouths Ella.

I look over at her. Her pupils are slowly enlarging. Sam sneaks across my line of sight, but I keep my focus on Ella.

"Who gave us the map?" she asks again.

I tuck my chin into my upper chest. "Marisa."

"And we trust her?" she says cynically.

This is just what I wanted to avoid. "We have no other choice."

Ella huffs.

"She's right, Ella. We have no other choice. We have to hope this is our way out. After all, Marisa was never actually mean to any of us."

"She didn't have to show the knife before she stabbed it in our backs," Ella angrily responds as she grinds her teeth.

The space around us tightens. The tension in the air is nearly palpable, but before any of us can spend too much time debating the rationality of our situation, something clicks.

"Found it," smiles Sam.

"Found what?" questions Sean.

"What the arrow means." As Sam firmly presses his shoulder into the cream side of the wall, it opens inward.

"Are you sure we should go in there?" asks Ella uncertainly.

"I think we have to," mutters Sam.

"Why?"

"We need to get out of Halcyon."

Ella holds back. I can see that she wants to speak, but she's afraid someone will just contradict her. Instead, she lightly exhales and nods.

I step closer to her, as Sam enters the room.

"It's going to be okay, Ella."

"You can't be sure. None of us can."

"Would you rather stay in that room waiting for another task—a task that could claim your life?"

She sticks out her chin while simultaneously gnawing at the insides of her cheeks. "No."

I extend my arm. She enters into the room just behind Sean.

Marcus guides Miles in. Rosie follows, but before she gets completely in, she looks back at me and smiles. I smile back.

We're almost there. We have to be.

I look left then right. No one's around. I move my left foot forward, but the second I try to take a step with my right, it doesn't move. It's like it's been locked in place. It's unwilling to listen to what I want.

I try to move my left leg back, but it won't budge either. *What the hell is happening?*

Poking his head back out of the room, Sean looks awkwardly at me. "C'mon, Elise," he whispers.

I can't.

"Elise?"

I didn't say that out loud?

"Are you going to say something? Come on, we need to keep moving."

I'm speaking!

But apparently I'm not.

He reaches for my arm, but just before he can grab onto it, the door begins to close. Sean steps back and puts his shoulder into it, but it continues to move. "What the heck is going on?" he loudly exhales. "It's like it's being pushed from the other side."

"Sean!" shouts Sam from the opposite side of the door. "What's going on? The door's shutting, you need to get in here!"

"Elise is still on the other side!"

They keep yelling. These cries have to be heard by the followers—if not by Caroline.

I try to move again, but my limbs don't react. I'm stuck.

The door keeps sliding. Sam reaches for Sean's arm.

Marcus's hand appears. He reaches for Sean's arm, too.

My eyes widen. Sean's do the same.

What's happening?

His jaw drops. His pupils dilate. His cheeks stiffen; a tear falls. Sean's visibly distraught, but before he can fall back into the hallway, before he can try and save me from whatever's happening, Marcus and Sam yank him into the room.

The door slams.

"No, no, no!" I shout. Shout. Aloud. I just yelled. I try and move my legs. They move. My arms. They're functioning. Everything works, but when it mattered I couldn't move. Unlike the past when I was too scared to move, this time was different. I couldn't move. Something else was blocking my extremities from receiving my brain's signals to move; something was preventing my words from being audible.

The chip.

Caroline can enter our minds, but at no point has she been able to limit our movements. The DZ was capable of doing that with Marie in the fields—they're why she carved the symbol into her neck, but Caroline doesn't have that power. At least, to our knowledge she doesn't.

"Why didn't you go with them?" echoes Caroline's voice in the hallway. "I figured you wanted to escape."

"I do."

"Then why didn't you follow?"

Rather than say what she thinks I'm going to say, I bite my tongue and instead respond, "Because that's not the way to escape. If they're to leave, they have to prove their worth."

She smiles. "Do you really believe that, Elise?"

"After running through the hallways looking for an escape, I figured that wasn't the way to go. There are better solutions."

"Exactly. Anyways, that entrance leads nowhere. The room they're in is just a trap."

"What sort of trap?"

"They're not going to be hurt, but they'll spend some of the night in there before tomorrow's early task." She steps closer to me, and still there remains no visible sign of any followers in this hallway. "You see, every person who works for me was given a map. I understand how difficult it can be to walk around here without knowing where each hallway leads. Yet, each map is different. Each map has a different arrow drawn onto it that leads to a different room like the one your friends are in."

"What do you mean?"

"I set traps like these to ensure none of my followers are stupid enough to help someone who wants to give up on the Circus—who wants to flee instead of finishing their tasks."

"So, you know who gave me the map?"

"Of course I do. Based on where we're at, it was Marisa."

"What will you do to her?"

"Her punishment will fit the crime."

"What's the punishment for this?"

"Follow me and you'll see."

"I don't want to see. Why can't you just tell me?"

Caroline smirks. "You need to see, Elise. You need to understand the importance of the Circus; the importance of the life you were given, of the path the DZ has chosen for you. If you don't learn how to deal with enemies in your midst, your world will fail just like Nimbus."

I bite back my disdain and nod for Caroline to proceed.

She gives me that bogus grin she always does before turning around and walking down the hallway.

"Can you at least tell me where we're going?"

"The same place we always go."

"The arena?"

"Yes."

It only takes a few strides and two rights for us to find ourselves in the dark of the arena. There isn't a light shining above, nor is there the unmistakable blue line wrapping itself around the area. It's completely black.

Caroline claps.

A beam of light shines down from the center of the roof. Yet, it illuminates nothing. The only thing it showcases is the ground.

"What was that for?" I ask.

"You'll see."

She claps again.

To our left, Noah, Katrina, and two followers enter. Slowly behind them another man is pushing Marisa forward with her hands tied behind her back. They keep walking until they're in the center of the arena, until they're the subjects the light has cast itself upon.

"What are you going to do to her?"

"That's up to you, Elise."

I dig the tips of my fingers into the lacerations on my palms. I can feel my nerves' desire to pick at the scabs until I bleed.

"How would you like to execute her?" asks Caroline maliciously.

"Execute her?" I reply, baffled. My fingers start to dig into my hands.

"Yes, you get to choose her fate."

"Why does she have to die?"

"Because she committed treason."

"Did she, though?"

"She sought to escape. She tried to help others escape. That's unforgiveable, Elise."

"But she didn't try and escape herself. If she wanted to do that, she could have done that at any point. She didn't have to lead us here if she truly didn't want to be here!" I say, nearly raising my voice to the point of a scream.

"She never led you here, Elise. I did that. She was merely the go-between." Caroline gives me one of her infamous smirks before continuing her speech. "I was the one who guided you and Sam here."

"It doesn't matter how we got here. What matters is that she didn't commit treason just by giving me a map."

"She tried to help contestants escape their fates, Elise. That's horrendous. I don't know why anyone would ever try to do that in Halcyon. The law states that if you enter the Circus, you either survive or you die. Nowhere in any decree does it state that if you're simply too tired or have no desire to compete, you should be allowed to leave. That's not logical!"

"How isn't it?"

"Your questioning of this upsets me, Elise. You didn't escape with your friends because you saw that it was flawed, so you should understand. The fact that you're trying to fight against the outcome of this gathering is ridiculous. Now, choose how you will kill Marisa."

I give up. "I won't kill her, but I won't stop you."

"You have to do it. Just remember what I showed you. Remember the fate those who commit treason deserve. . .remember my mother."

Your mother who wanted a better life? Yea, I remember her.

"Do you have a gun?" I softly ask.

"Of course."

She snaps her fingers. The man who was pushing Marisa forward walks toward us.

He holds out a handgun. "There's only one bullet in it, so it's best if you get closer to your target," he says.

"He's right, Elise. And if you turn and point the gun at me, the four others will have you dead in a split second."

I take the gun. One of my cuts bleeds onto the end of the weapon. "What if I turn and shoot one of them?"

Caroline tilts her head. "That wouldn't be very nice."

"But what would you do to me?"

"Why don't you go ahead and try it to find out?"

I can't tell if she's being sarcastic or not, and a part of me wants to see if she is. I need to test her nerve; I need to know how committed she is to keeping me alive, so I point the gun at the follower beside me.

He doesn't balk. Nor does Caroline. They both just look at me. In fact, the man leans his head into the barrel.

"I'll shoot him," I warn.

"You won't, though," replies Caroline.

I pull the trigger.

He falls dead onto the ground. Nobody storms at me. Nobody pulls a gun on me. Nothing happens.

"I told you I would pull the trigger. I'm not killing Marisa."

"I never really liked him anyways, so that's not a big problem."

"What?" I say baffled.

"He just seemed a little odd to me," she replies. "Plus, I have plenty of other good men."

I don't respond. I bite back my frustration, my confusion. Everyone within Halcyon is odd; if Caroline felt the strange ones needed to be eliminated, she'd start by burning this whole place to the ground. Alas, she'd never see that. She's too blind to notice the delusion, to see that everyone else is just as insane as she is. Really, she revels in it. And the longer we're here, the more apparent the insanity becomes.

"Noah, would you please come here," calls Caroline.

Noah lightly jogs over to us.

"Would you please give Elise your knife?"

He doesn't hesitate. He quickly reaches into his robe and pulls out a knife. The blade has to be at least six inches long; it glints in the limited scope of light we have.

I take it. "Now what?"

"Well, you won't be able to take a swing at Noah. He's my best fighter, so even if you tried, he'd have that knife turned on you faster than you can blink. So, you're to go up to Marisa and kill her with it."

I drop the blade.

"I won't do it."

Visibly angry, Caroline steps toward me. Chest to chest; eye to eye, we look at each other. I can smell the wine she had at dinner. It's masked any other potential scent to the point that I want to vomit.

"If you don't kill her right now, I will ensure the DZ chooses another to take your place. Someone like Noah or Katrina who have the know-how and wherewithal to create a new circle." She leans forward and presses her forehead into mine. "Now, pick up that knife, and slit her throat."

"I won't do it. You don't have the power to overrule the DZ, Caroline. You and I both know it."

"I don't have to overrule them, Elise. I just have to tell them what you're doing right now. About your fear to kill."

"I'm not afraid. I just killed someone, didn't I? And they obviously chose me despite my inability to kill MacMillan, so I doubt whatever you have to say about this incident will change their tune."

Caroline scoffs. "Oh, they'll listen, and you'll regret this decision."

"I doubt it."

Caroline steps back and snaps her fingers. "Katrina, kill Marisa."

But before Katrina has a chance, I shout, "Wait!"

"Why?" says Caroline bitterly. "Why should we wait any longer?"

"She's your only doctor."

"Looks like I'll just have to find a new one."

"How will you do that?"

"I just have to ask the DZ. They'll give me what I want."

"Then why didn't you ask them long ago to give you someone else instead of me?"

Caroline grits her teeth. She looks away and doesn't respond.

"Why won't you answer me?" I ask angrily, my head starting to ache.

She turns around and steps toward me. Arching her neck, she looks in the direction of Katrina. Without so much as a word, she snaps her fingers.

I hear a thud.

Unknown

I had to prevent Elise from moving. I had to stop her. If I didn't, someone else would be dead.

If they all ended up in that room together, Caroline would have opened it up and killed everyone but Elise and Sam. I just know it. She doesn't care for any of them; she only cares that they partake in her circus.

And it's not even a damn circus.

I just wish I could tell Elise what I did, why I did it, and who I am. I wish I could escape this prison and get to them. The longer I watch them suffer, the longer I aid Caroline in her quest to prove Halcyon's worth, the more I hate myself. I can't keep feeding her. I can't keep promising the people here that I'm just like the rest of them.

As much as they think I'm the same as they are, I'm not. And the longer I pretend that none of this bothers me, the more I'll hurt myself. My mind is weakening. My heart is aching. The conscience this world tells you to rid yourself of, is coming back. Being coldhearted and ruthless is easy for some, but even Separation couldn't make me what the DZ wants me to be.

I only have to play along for so much longer before I can finally run, before I can leave this ruthless zone behind.

Just a few more days, I think to myself. A few more days to plan my escape, a few more days to ensure everyone's survival. If I bolt without a plan, what I did for Elise will have been pointless. And even though I don't know her, I can't do that to her. I can't just keep her from her friends without ever being able to tell her why.

Soon enough, I will see them. Before I know it, I'll meet Elise, and I'll save her. I'll protect her from these monsters that hide here; I'll protect all of them.

Halcyon won't be where they die.

Sam

Something echoes in the hallway.

I don't say anything. I know everyone else heard it.

We're trapped in this dingy, little room. There's light, but that doesn't make it any better. The floor is hardwood and there's a mattress in the corner. That's about it. There aren't any tables, vases, artwork, cupboards, windows, doors, anything. This room is essentially a prison, but it was put here for a reason. Why though, is something none of us can figure out.

While Miles rests on the mattress, the rest of us—minus Sean—have been switching seated positions on the floor every few minutes. Sean, unlike everyone else, has been alone in a corner of the room with his knees huddled against his chest.

My stomach twists every time I look at him. This is *my* fault. I kept him away from Elise, away from the love of his life, the one time he finally got a chance to be with her in Halcyon. She's not in this room because of me. If I didn't insist he make it in here before the door closed, he would still be with her. . .wherever she is.

She should be here.

Even if 'here' is trapped in a small room with barely any light, at least we would be together; at least Sean would be happy.

Another sound echoes in the hallway, but this one is different. It sounds closer.

"What was that?" murmurs Rosie.

"I don't know, but it sounded like it came from the hallway," answers Marcus.

"Do you think someone's out there?"

"Someone has to come get us at some point, don't they?" questions Ella.

"You would think," responds Marcus.

I peel the drying skin off my upper lip with my forefingers. "What if nobody ever comes?" I add while wiping the blood from my lip on my sleeves. "What if we die in here?"

"We won't."

"How can you know that, Marcus?"

"Because even if no one comes, we can find a way out."

"Why haven't we found one yet, then? We've searched the walls for a hollow point. We've searched every nook and cranny, and we've found nothing. The only thing in this room is dust and spiders." I look away and wipe my lip again. "So, don't act like there's an exit when it's nonexistent."

"We got in here, didn't we? We can get out," Marcus snaps back.

"Did you not feel the force of that door? We can't get out that way!" I shout, the blood sliding onto my teeth.

"I felt it, Sam. But that doesn't mean we have to keep believing that every damn corner we turn is the last one."

"You're one to talk," I gripe.

"I know. . .that's why you should listen to me." He looks at the wall to his left. His eyes remain firm on it as he speaks again. "We need these delusions of grandeur. We need these crazy ideas that life goes on beyond these walls—just like we did in Nimbus. It doesn't matter if you don't believe them, you need them. We need them, or we'll all die."

"That seemed to be the route you were taking before," I quip.

"Sadly, it was. In a way, it still is. I'm just trying to find my footing like the rest of you." He looks back toward the center of the circle before shifting his eyes to Sean. "I'm sorry that we forced you into this room with us, Sean. I know we couldn't have known what was going to happen, but we could have realized that it would be better for Elise to have you rather than Caroline. If we left you out there, maybe we wouldn't be trapped in here. I'm sorry."

Sean doesn't even glance at Marcus. He keeps his head atop his knees.

"You don't have to respond because I know that if anyone is capable of surviving, it's you. The gloom and doom of Halcyon can't kill you."

I'm bitter, but he's right. "What changed in you, Marcus?"

"Nothing. I'm still angry, but I'm fighting it."

For the first time in what feels like forever, Marcus isn't spewing nonsense about how death is our only exit. He seems somewhat like his former self. Sadly, I'm sure Miles's status has made him reflect. He knows death is an easy exit, an escape from this torment, and although it's better than being broken, it's still not the direction anyone needs to go.

Another noise rings closer. This one has to be outside the door.

"Someone knows we're here," whispers Sean ominously. "And I don't think that's a good thing."

"What do you think is going to happen to us?" asks Rosie.

"Something painful."

"Why do you say that?"

"We tried to escape." He puts his head back atop his knees.

The wall starts to shake.

The area where we came in starts to move.

"What's going to happen to us?" moans Ella. "Is this room the end?"

Marcus stands up and moves toward the opening. "It can't be. We've made it too far to die here."

"That's right," answers Caroline, her voice bouncing through the slight opening and into the room. "You won't die in there, but death is coming. It's coming for all of you."

"Wh-when. . .?" mumbles Ella.

"In fifteen minutes," answers Caroline.

"Where?"

"The same place it has claimed the others."

"The arena?"

"Of course, my dear," Caroline says dryly.

The break in the wall is now completely open. Caroline, Noah, and Katrina stand in the hallway. There are a few others behind them—others I've never seen. They're wearing the same blue cloak the followers wear, meaning we probably shouldn't try to make another run for it—especially not right here.

"Now, get out," she barks at us. "Get out of the room."

I look back at Marcus. He nods for me to go forward. I look over at Sean. He's standing, but not moving, nor is he looking at any one of us directly.

"Come on now, get out, or maybe you will die in there."

I step out. Rosie follows behind me. Marcus and Ella help Miles out. Sean joins at the rear.

"How did you know we were in there?" I ask.

"Nobody knows my home like me, Sam. I designed it specifically to weed out cowards like you."

"We're not cowards," I softly respond.

"What was that?"

"We're not cowards," I say, barely louder.

"Uh huh. Sure."

Caroline snaps her fingers.

Noah grabs my arm. The other followers grab hold of everyone else.

"Where are you taking us?"

"You really should pay more attention, Sam," answers Caroline bitterly, with an almost fierce disapproval of even having to answer me.

"We're going to do the next task," utters Marcus.

And as always, we have no idea what it is.

The first test was the only physical one. The second felt like she was trying to destroy our mentality, like she was trying to break us in a way that the outside of Nimbus couldn't. Since both of those failed, I don't know where she could go next. Unless she pins us gladiator-style against each other, I can't see the circus winning.

We take a few turns through the maze before we're all back on the arena floor. All of us. This is weird. Only during the first task were we able to watch the others compete, so I wonder if this one is similar in stature.

"What's the next event?" inquires Rosie.

"The next one is the only one I have a name for," answers Caroline. Turning around to face us, she pulls her ivory cane from her robe. Alluding to that same showmanship she presented at the start of Cirque de Chance, she starts to walk toward the center of the arena. Yet, unlike the past, with each tap of her cane on the ground a light blue spark emits from it. The farther she walks, the larger the sparks become, until she stops.

What's going on?

Raising her cane into the air, Caroline points it upward. Almost immediately, a strike—like a bolt of lightning—from above pierces the tip of the cane; Caroline then swings the stick down into the earth.

Everything goes dark.

The stomping begins. Two stomps. Pause. Two stomps. Pause.

A light returns, and suddenly the arena is filled with an audience.

I turn to Rosie. "Isn't it pretty late?"

She just stares at me and doesn't provide a response. Almost as if she can't hear me—that or she's too entranced in Caroline's act.

"Tonight. . ." echoes Caroline's voice overhead. "Tonight, our warriors from Nimbus will take on the third task, my favorite one. . .what is it called?"

The audience stops stomping.

"I asked, what is it called?" rings Caroline's voice louder than before.

And that's when it becomes clear. The entire audience shouts, in perfect unison, "The Breakdown!"

"The Breakdown!" echoes Caroline overhead. "That's right!"

What's the Breakdown? Is she going to make us see something tougher than the last task? Is she going to make us choose between our life and another's?

Caroline takes a deep breath—one that's audible enough to echo through her microphone. "We're all, well, except me, afraid of something. Whether it's a decision we made in the past, or one we'll have to make in the future, something lingers in the minds of the weak." She pauses and directs her attention toward all of us. "This task will test the limits of your mind. It will prove the strength of regret and the impact of hesitation. The Breakdown will show us who you really are."

I turn to Rosie again. "What does any of that mean?"

Rosie's head is shaking, almost convulsing.

"Rosie. . ."

"I don't want to die, Sam. I don't want to die."

I don't know what to say. Rosie's been tougher than me thus far. She's been the only one who's really kept me grounded. I cough. "We've made it this far. She's just trying to scare us," I murmur. "We're going to be okay."

She grabs my hand.

Her palm is sweaty. I can feel her nerves, and it hurts. I think these tasks are finally taking a toll on her; I think Caroline's mind games are actually working.

Caroline continues. "Now, our first competitor will be the ringleader who tried to stage an escape from Halcyon for our competitors: Marcus. Marcus, would you please step forward."

He does.

A spotlight shines on him.

"Would you come to the center of the arena?"

He begins to walk toward Caroline.

"Very good. I figured you'd hesitate, but you haven't. So far, you seem ready to take the challenge head on. I admire that."

Marcus keeps walking, his head held high.

He eventually makes it to Caroline, whereupon she puts her hand on his shoulder. "Marcus, do you remember what you saw in the last task? Do you remember your conversation with Kyle?"

Marcus nods.

"Good. Well, the last test was about your emotional strength and how one deals with grief. You passed that test easily. Not many people can handle seeing a loved one reincarnated in a form that doesn't last." Caroline sarcastically claps. "This next test is similar in nature, but it's only about you."

"What do you mean?" asks Marcus.

"The Breakdown is how you confront the pain of your biggest regret."

"So, what, you're going to put me in a chair and be my therapist?"

The audience laughs.

"That would be even more fun," chides Caroline. "But no. You will see."

The entire arena goes dark again.

After a few seconds, a light illuminates center stage where Marcus is standing alone in a forest.

A few feet in front of him lies another man, but he doesn't look familiar. He has a muddied backpack, a hole in his jeans, and what looks like blood on his shirt. I can't really make out his face from here, but from what I can tell, he's dead.

Marcus walks toward him, then speaks aloud. "I know what you're trying to do, Caroline. I know why you put Alfie here."

Caroline doesn't answer. The arena remains silent.

Marcus kneels next to the man. "This isn't my biggest regret, Caroline. I remember killing Alfie for being my equal. I remember stabbing him in the stomach after I promised him refuge at the library. All of that eats at me, but it's not my biggest regret."

His equal? What happened there?

The area goes dark again.

Marcus doesn't seem like the type to hurt someone else unless that person hurt him first. Whoever Alfie was, he had to have done something to Marcus. He had to have gone after someone or something Marcus loved.

I squeeze Rosie's hand and lean toward her. "Did you know about that?"

"No," she whispers. "Marcus went on one scavenging trip by himself after becoming our leader. I had no idea this happened during that."

The lights come back on. Marcus is standing atop the library. It's night. Another man is next to him.

Marcus turns to face the man. "Shane. . ." he whispers.

The man, whose physical features I can barely see in the darkness, steps closer to the ledge of the building.

Marcus watches. I can see his shoulders falling forward, but he doesn't move, he just watches.

"I'm sorry," cries the man.

Still, Marcus doesn't move.

Shane takes another step toward the ledge. He reaches his arm toward Marcus, as his back faces the street below. "I'm sorry," he weeps.

Marcus doesn't reach forward. He doesn't do anything.

Then, the man falls.

"This isn't it either," says Marcus aloud, a noticeable break in his voice. "I know I could have saved Shane. I know I lied that he was killed by the Lurkers, but this isn't my biggest regret."

Everything goes completely dark, but only for a split second. Now, Marcus is in the forest once more. Recreations of all of us are behind him, along with many others from the library. Malcolm is ahead of us. *I remember this.* He's chasing Thomas. He's running toward his death—his death unintentionally created by Marcus.

Marcus steps toward Malcolm.

Malcolm keeps moving after Thomas. The visions of ourselves remain still behind them.

Marcus takes another step forward. "M-Malcolm," he stutters. "M-Malcolm stop moving."

Malcolm doesn't respond. He keeps going after Thomas until he's facedown in the mud with a bullet between his eyes.

Marcus falls to his knees.

The arena goes dark another time.

What is happening? I think to myself. *This is supposed to be his biggest regret, yet Caroline keeps forcing him to relive many of them. Why?*

She said we would all die here. She's said many times that the circus would claim us. At first I didn't believe her, but now I think it might be true. You can only fake your way through so much before the mask falls off.

The light shines back on Marcus. Now, he's in the glass contraption we all stood in before our first task. Kyle stands beside him.

Marcus looks up.

Noah motions at the end of the glass for Kyle. Marcus attempts to embrace the fake version of his friend. Although, they're not actually touching, it's clear that Kyle's whispering something in Marcus's ear.

I take a step forward. *I need to see what's happening. I remember this.*

Marcus falls to his knees—his head goes through the hologram.

Then, Kyle disappears, and Marcus hobbles back to his feet.

"Had enough?" remarks Caroline.

Marcus doesn't answer.

I turn back to Rosie. "What did Kyle whisper in his ear then?"

"I-I'm not sure."

"Does Ella know?"

Rosie relays the question to Ella.

Ella shakes her head.

For what feels like the fiftieth time, everything goes dark.

But unlike the past few times, it remains dark for at least a minute, if not more. And when the lights come back on, Marcus is nowhere in sight.

"The first contestant has completed the task, but I will not answer if it was a success or failure. The other contestants will learn that once their turn is complete. With that said, next to compete is Sam Martin."

Rosie's hand sweats more against mine. Mine returns the anxiety.

"Would you please step forward, Sam?"

I let go, but I don't step forward.

"I don't like repeating myself," says Caroline almost sourly.

I have a bad taste in my mouth, but if I keep standing here, it will probably only get worse. I fight against the hesitations holding me back and step forward.

"Keep coming."

My feet go forward, but my mind remains behind with the others.

I don't want to endure what Marcus just dealt with; I have no desire to see the moments I regret because, unfortunately, I regret too much. There have been too many times where I've failed to succeed, where I've faltered under pressure.

"Hurry along now," says Caroline. "We don't have all night." Then, she laughs. . .to herself. The audience slowly laughs behind her, but it's so uncomfortable that I almost cringe.

I eventually make it to her.

"Do you know what you'll see, Sam?" she asks.

I shake my head. I don't want to answer because maybe she doesn't know my biggest regret. She has to know that Abby's death bothers me, but outside of that, *how can she know what eats at me every day?* I laugh internally. *Did you not just watch what happened to Marcus?*

The lights start to dim.

"No answer, huh? Well, enjoy your test," smirks Caroline before disappearing into the darkness outside the small circle of light I'm standing in.

The light keeps dimming. Eventually, it disappears, and I'm standing alone in complete darkness.

But unlike Marcus's task, a beam of light quickly finds itself cast upon on me. Yet, the beam is shaking back and forth, and everything around me is still relatively dark.

I take a step forward. The light stops shaking.

"Where am I?" I say aloud.

The air around me thickens. I take another step, and another. With each step I take, the light follows; it almost guides me toward the pain I'm supposed to feel. But the farther I walk, nothing changes. I don't know what I'm supposed to see because based on everything I can see around me, this isn't Nimbus—this isn't where Abby died.

That means Caroline truly knows that Abby's death isn't my biggest regret. She knows there's nothing I could have done to save her despite my cries stating otherwise. *But how?*

I keep walking; a door pops up on my left. Another one shows itself on my right. The more steps I take, the more doors that pop up. Yet, somehow, none of this looks truly familiar. It feels like somewhere I've been, but it's not set up like anywhere I've actually walked through or seen.

"Where am I?" I ask again.

But just like the prior task, she doesn't answer. *I don't know why I keep asking.*

Eventually, a door several steps ahead to my right opens up.

And as much as I don't want to go into it, as much as I don't want to see what Caroline's trying to show me, I have to. I have no choice. If I don't face my regret head on, she might kill me.

My steps become slow, almost like I'm walking through glue. The light stays ahead of me, guiding me toward this opening.

The second I make it to the door, the light disappears and a new one shines inside the room. At first glance from the hallway, the room appears empty.

I take a step in.

And I regret it. I regret the step almost as much as what I see.

My skin starts to crawl. My bones start to ache. My head feels like it's about to explode because there. . .chained against the wall. . .is Ann. The one woman whose death I feel completely responsible for. I'm the reason she was taken into this room and beaten to death. I'm the reason the Lurkers killed her. I can see it in her eyes; her dark blue pupils look upon me like she knows. The cuts, the bruises, the blood around her, it's all my fault—and I can't look away.

No matter how much I want to turn around and prove to Caroline that this moment hasn't defined me, I can't. Ann's death eats at me in a way no other could, not even Abby's because unlike

Abby's death, my mouth is what killed Ann. My lack of courage killed Abby. My words killed Ann.

I couldn't have stepped in front of a gun to save Ann. I couldn't have told the Lurkers to take me instead. No. The only thing I could have done was not let my mind get the best of me and force me to bicker with Arthur. But it did. And she died because of it. She died because I acted like I didn't care what happened to everyone around me, because I felt that my death in that dungeon was certain.

And here I am. Alive.

I try not to let myself kneel beside her bloodied corpse, but the weight upon the entirety of my upper body is heavier than I imagined. Every part of me aches, and my stomach feels like it's about to explode.

No matter how much I want to stay strong, I can't. I can feel my eyes watering; my stomach only worsens the more I stare at her.

So, stop staring.

My mind's right, but I can't. I can't move. It's like that moment has manifested itself inside me again, and I'm stuck. Elise isn't here to rescue me from the depths my psyche has fallen to, and Caroline sure as hell wants to see me break. She wants my knees to buckle.

And they might.

I close my eyes because for whatever reason, I can't turn around. My body won't allow it, so the least I can do is try to force the memory away. I squeeze my eyelids tightly against each other, just hoping that Ann will disappear, that this whole memory will fade away and I'll be standing in the center of the arena as a survivor of another round.

I take a deep breath, and while doing so, my right eye forces itself slightly open. Open enough that I can still see her, that I can still feel the torment coursing through every inch of me.

I fall.

Everything around me goes dark.

A hand grabs onto the back of my arm. Another hand does the same. They lift me onto my feet and start to drag me away. Everything's still dark. I can't see who's taking me, or where I'm going. I'm just hoping I didn't fail.

Sean

Sometimes we don't allow ourselves to feel pain because we know how much it will hurt. Instead, we move forward pretending the past didn't happen, almost as if we're in a trance—a trance that protects us from our emotions, our reality. It's odd. It's like we would rather deal with the pain when more is piled on top of it, as if we'd prefer to let everything out at once.

I know not everyone is like me, but in times like this, sometimes the best thing I can do to carry on is to shelve my pain. Then, wait until I escape whatever hell I'm in before opening it back up—even if that means I suffer more.

For Marcus and for Sam, they faced the agony head on. Marcus tried to keep faking his way through the motions, but eventually he couldn't. Sam, on the other hand, knew he didn't stand a chance when he saw that girl. I could see it in his mannerisms. He was shaky. He looked on the verge of convulsing. I hated it.

I hate every second of this, but I can't let my guard down any more than I already have. I have to keep up this façade that everything is alright, that I'm as tough as nails. It doesn't matter that I'm not; it doesn't matter that I'm just going to add more fuel to the fire burning inside of me; none of it matters. The only thing that matters is getting the hell out of here. . .alive.

The lights go off.

Miles is being taken away. Where, though, I don't know.

Unlike Marcus, Sam, and Rosie before him, Miles remained on his knees the entire time. Occasionally he would place a hand on the back of his head, but that was it. Yet, Caroline kept showing him the last task. She kept repeating what he had already seen because, for some reason, that must have been his biggest regret. I mean, it makes sense. It almost killed him. And it seems that death in some nature is a part of all of our regrets. Even Rosie saw people from the library she failed to save.

Death is as natural as breathing, but that doesn't mean we want to focus on it—that doesn't mean we want to see it every waking moment of our lives. But, that doesn't matter to Caroline. As long as she gets to make us suffer in any capacity, she can scratch it off as a win in her book. After all, she's already killed some of our friends, and I have a feeling Miles won't last much longer.

The lights turn back on.

Either Ella or I is next.

I grab her hand.

She squeezes mine.

"Whatever happens, we'll be okay," I softly speak.

Her head bobs.

I squeeze her hand back.

"We'll be okay," she whispers. "We'll be okay. We'll be okay."

"Just remember that you've made it this far with the knowledge of what you may see because you lived it. You can't let it eat you just because you'll be seeing it again."

"I'll try not to," she mutters. "I'll try not to."

A loud echo rattles across the entirety of the arena. "Up next, we have Ella. Get up here, Ella!" shouts Caroline.

I turn to face her.

Her cheeks are flushed.

I wrap my arms around her. She wraps hers around me. "You got this, Ella. You'll be okay."

She forces a smile and lets go. Her breathing increases.

"Step forward, my dear," says Caroline.

"Go. You got this," I say.

She takes two steps forward, shrugs her shoulders, and lets out a large exhale. Then, she walks toward Caroline with an air of confidence that completely overrules the vibe I just got from her.

Once she reaches Caroline, Caroline looks into the audience and not at Ella. "After that last performance, do you guys think Ella will give us more of a show?"

The audience lightly claps.

"Come on. Really? Nothing more than that? I know what you're going to see, and I think you're going to like it. Now, let me ask you again. . .are you ready for Ella's show?"

The crowd erupts in sheer pandemonium. It's entirely unbefitting to everything that's happened prior, but that's Halcyon: Nothing makes sense.

Caroline taps her cane on the surface. Two streaks of cerulean encircle Ella. Then, everything goes dark once more.

A few seconds later, the lights come on. We're back in Nimbus.

At least a dozen kids stand in front of Ella. Behind her is a transparent recreation of the wall along with a few guards and a foreman who reads the Separation Decree.

The foreman starts to read the names of the kids in front of him. Ella remains firm in the middle of it all.

For some reason, this whole situation seems familiar, and I can't figure out why. I've never seen a Separation with more than five kids. Including Ella, there are twelve in front of me. *This can't be real.*

The man keeps reading the document, but as he reads Ella's name off the list he slows down, almost intentionally—as if in doing so he's making her relive the moment more than before, as if saying her name along with eleven other kids will make her suffer even more than she did on her Separation Day. When he finishes saying her name, Ella steps toward the kids in front of her. Their glazed-over, expressionless faces look right through her.

She takes a few more steps toward the group before stepping in line with them. She now looks like she was never out of place.

The foreman then reads the last paragraph of the decree:

"By decree of Eldridge MacMillan, you are now excluded from re-entry into Nimbus until you pass the Earliest Nimbus Trial for Returning Youth or E.N.T.R.Y. Said test will take place if the individual is alive and if the individual is in a functioning mental state in exactly eleven years."

The doors ahead of everyone start to slowly open.

The foreman rolls up the document.

Guards step toward the sliding steel.

Ella turns to her right, looks at the boy next to her, and starts to cry. He looks back as if he's listening rather than understanding what she's doing.

Then, the moment comes.

Rather than heading toward the gates to go outside, half the group makes a dead sprint back into Nimbus, but not Ella. She stands still, but she's visibly shaken.

Why does this sound familiar? When did this happen? Whenever it was, I must have been outside already, but it feels like something Sam told me. If not him, then Abby.

With guards chasing the six or seven kids who tried to sprint back home, Ella and the others don't move. None head outside to start their eleven years of isolation. No. They all wait. It's almost as if they're awaiting a punishment.

Minutes pass before all the kids are caught and brought back to the front of Nimbus. At that point, Eldridge MacMillan makes an appearance.

He lines the six kids up in front of the others.

He pulls out his gun. Two guards beside him do the same. And without a moment's hesitation, they begin to shoot the kids in the knees one by one. Only one knee each, but enough to ruin any chance of survival outside the walls.

The kids scream, cry, shriek, everything. The sheer horror of what just happened even has those who stood their ground shaking.

The cries don't fade. We can all hear them. Caroline must want us, or at least Ella, to hear them. They only get louder. Parents try to intervene, but the guards block them off. It doesn't appear that anyone has a chance of getting to those kids; it's just evident that they're going outside in that state and as rough as it is, it's of their own doing.

Ella is still standing, though. Her cheeks are red, they're quivering from what I can see, but she's still standing. She hasn't fallen to her knees like all those before her. She's fighting the agony; she's holding on.

For how much longer, though, I don't know. The sounds coming from these kids are making my skin crawl.

As the endless screams continue, MacMillan shoots his pistol into the sky. That doesn't stop the cries, but it quiets the families.

MacMillan speaks, "How dare you cowards try to flee! How dare you defile the laws of Separation! Each of you deserves a punishment far worse than what I've given you; you all deserve to die. So, consider yourselves lucky. You've been given a second chance."

The weeping only intensifies after MacMillan's speech.

He fires his gun again. "Now get outside the wall! All of you!"

The lights above start to fade, and from what I can see Ella hasn't fallen.

The arena becomes pitch black, as it has every time so far, which means one thing: It's almost my turn.

I have a slight idea about what I'll see, but I'm not going to think about it. I'll just wait until I see it and pretend that I don't. Or, at least show that I'm paying enough attention to give Caroline a sense that her methods are working.

Light is restored to the arena. Caroline calls my name. "Sean Martin, would you please come up here."

I immediately begin the short trek toward her and the stage.

"Do you know why I saved you for last?" she asks.

"No," I say as I reach her.

"Do you know the old expression, 'Save the best for last?'"

I nod.

"Well, that's why you're last, Sean. Yours is going to be the most enjoyable to watch."

I tilt my head down and scratch the back of my neck.

"Do you have any ideas about what you may see?" she asks.

"No," I lie.

"Excellent," she smirks. "Well, enjoy the show."

I roll my eyes. The lights fade, but are quickly relit.

And just like Ella, I'm in Nimbus.

I'm atop the wall.

There are trees all around me. A few guards walk past, but nothing substantial happens. It almost feels like Caroline put me atop the wall to jumpstart the potential of showing me multiple regrets like she did for Marcus—and if any place would get my blood pumping, it would be here. I killed too many kids while atop this wall just to save my own skin, to keep a job I didn't even like.

It didn't matter what they were doing, I still killed them; I wounded them; I hurt them, all because MacMillan told me to.

Despite having a plan in place outside the wall with Elise, it took until Sam's Separation for me to truly realize that I needed to fight back. Almost as if when I got home, everything I had done and planned outside the wall meant nothing, like being back in Nimbus restarted my entire life—but it didn't. Being back home just meant the struggle was tougher. It just meant that my brain was clay for MacMillan to shape. And I let him do it. For a few weeks, I let him push me around. I let him kill with my hands.

I turn around. I don't want to see the trees. I don't want to see a kid wander past. I have no desire to see the harm I caused.

I've tried to forget it. I've tried to move past it, but apparently I can't. I watched everyone else complete this task, and while a few of them were in Nimbus, it didn't faze me—but I guess you can't truly feel regret until you're back in your old shoes. Now that I'm standing here, everything's coming back full force. . .and the worst part is: I can't fake it. I'm trying. I'm trying to force it out, but it keeps coming.

I hear a shot. I can't tell if it's real or in my head.

Then another, and another, and another. They keep coming. The wall turns red. The lights go out.

My chest hurts. I can feel the pain I've been trying to bury creeping to the surface—and Caroline didn't have to lift a damn finger to make it happen.

Now, she's going to make me suffer through everything I've repressed, which means nearly everyone I killed or failed to save will make an appearance. It'll be a get-together of people I would have rather stayed home to avoid—one for which I would have faked an illness to get out of. But, now, I'm here, and I can't leave.

So, it begins.

The memories flood in one by one, making me relive them for less than a minute, just enough to remember them. After a few incidents I don't care to think about again, Caroline starts to replay my most vivid memories. First, I see the twins Elise and I killed, but unlike the day when we ended their lives from a distance, Caroline has placed them directly in front of me. Their red, sullen eyes soaked with tears from their struggles; their cheeks stiff, rigid from a lack of food to the point that the bones are nearly visible; the girl's hair is a mess, hanging over one of her eyes like it's covering a scar. There they stand, practically already dead.

Next, I'm atop the wall again. I'm alone, but there are voices coming from beneath me. I look down. Sam, Elise, Marcus, Miles, Ella, Rosie, and. . .Abby are standing, shaking in front of MacMillan as he walks across the stage mocking the hanging corpses behind him. *Not this. Not this again.* I hear a faint scream, a gunshot, more screaming. Abby's dead. MacMillan's dead. The lights go off in the arena, and I'm quickly relocated to the surface—to the center of Nimbus—with them. I'm right next to her dead body; I'm standing above Elise almost as if I'm a spirit. Nobody notices me. Nobody talks to me. I'm just there, hovering over Abby's body, knowing that I could have saved her; knowing that if I fired one shot after killing Jaxon—despite the fact that I was wounded—I could have killed MacMillan and saved her life.

Again, before I have a chance to completely soak in the woe, I'm thrown elsewhere. I'm bouncing back and forth like a ball that refuses to yield to gravity. I haven't been given any time to process what I'm feeling, and it's to the point that I feel a physical pain from it all, but emotionally I'm lost. I almost want to feel it, but at the same time, I can't imagine just how awful it will truly be when it hits me.

And then Caroline does it. She gives me no chance of pushing any more pain atop my collection of nightmares because now, of all places, I'm in the city. And I know what I'm going to see, but no one else here does besides Caroline. Elise has never heard this story, nor has Sam. What they're going to see, and what I'm going to visibly remember for a second time, is going to break me.

When I first made it to the city after running for days in search of something outside the walls of Nimbus, I met a girl. It wasn't Elise. Her name was Evelyn. She had been separated about a week before me, and when we first met in the city, she was on the verge of ending it all.

And just like her, I was defeated. I was afraid. I was uncertain what the future held for me, but at the same time, I was too afraid to do anything rash. Evelyn wasn't.

The images in front of me start to become clearer. The city's deserted except for us. Evelyn stands in the middle of an empty street, her red hair blowing in the wind. The rest of her is as grey as the sky.

With her back facing me, she seems oblivious to my presence.

Even though I only had two days with Evelyn, she spoke to me like she knew more about this world than anyone. She wanted to survive her eleven years, but a part of her felt that she wasn't strong enough, that she would be better off quitting before it truly started.

I told her many times that we could stay together, that we could make it eleven years with each other, but it didn't matter. When your mind's made up, it doesn't matter how much someone tries to fix it; a broken key can't fix a jammed lock.

I tried. I tried so hard to tell her what we could have, what we could be together, but I couldn't penetrate the barrier between us. I couldn't get to her; I couldn't save her.

Yet, here she is once again.

I don't want to walk to her. I don't want to relive this moment, but I have to. *You don't.* But, I do. I feel obligated. I feel I need to make up for what I did, for how I couldn't save her then, even though now I know I can't. I can't go back in time and help her; I can't fix the past.

I take a step.

Evelyn turns around. Her cheeks are emaciated; the sheer loss of color makes her freckles more visible. She takes a step toward me. I reach out my hand. She, hers. We're still dozens of feet apart.

The arena goes dark again.

We're brought back into the light inside the tower where I hid. Evelyn's with me. She's standing by the window.

Evelyn, I think. *Why won't you talk to me? Why won't you eat?*

I take a step toward her. She steps closer to the window.

"Evelyn," I say aloud.

"Sean," she whispers faintly.

She can hear me?

No one else was able to communicate in this event. *Why can I?*

"Why are you standing so close to the window?" I ask.

"Look out there, Sean. Do you not see what we're forced into? Do you not see the torture, the strain, the bloodshed upon this city?"

"I see it, Evelyn, but that won't be us."

"It already is, Sean. Can't you see? We're already dead."

"But we're not, Evelyn. We can make it. You know we can."

She places her hand upon the glass. "Our stories are different, Sean. Our paths go different ways."

I take a few strides toward her.

The glass shatters and the environment fades to black.

My legs collapse under me. My body tenses up and starts to spasm.

I could have saved you. I could have saved you. I could have. . .

267

16 May 2192

Elise

What the hell happened yesterday?

I thought Cirque de Chance was bad after the first two tasks, but to watch everyone relive their worst regrets was brutal. I tried to look away, but each time I did, Katrina made sure I turned back around and kept my eyes on the arena. No matter how much I didn't want to see my friends' suffering, I had to. I had to learn why Caroline chose these tasks, why her world is built upon mental strain.

And as much as I hate to admit it, she has a point.

You can't survive in this world—in any world—if regrets easily bog down your mind. Then again, I'm one to talk. Every day I think about the past; every day I become weaker and more vulnerable to slipping into a world of regret. Maybe I need to appreciate what Caroline's created; maybe I need to accept that her model is good.

Stop it! I think. *Stop thinking this maniac is right.*

I stand up and pace across my room.

Step by step, I can see what *they saw.* I can see the suffering. I can feel it. In a fit of anger, I pound my fists into the wall. My shoulder stings with the motion.

What has Caroline done? Who was Evelyn? Who was the kid Marcus killed? What did Ella whisper to that boy before her Separation? Every little thing I want to ask, I can't. My questions can't get answers until we escape.

A knock comes at my door.

I don't respond. It wouldn't matter if I did.

Caroline pushes it open. "Mind if I come in, Elise?"

"Would it matter if I said 'yes?'"

Caroline laughs. "Not really."

Her cloak glides across the floor as she walks toward the sofa parallel to the door. Lifting the ends of it up, she drapes it to her left before taking a seat and crossing her legs.

"Why are you here?" I ask, itching my ankle.

"To ask your thoughts on the last task."

"Do you really want to know what I think?" My skin becomes red.

"Of course. I always do."

I keep digging and digging into my leg. I don't know why, but my ankle itches beyond belief, and the more I scratch, the worse it becomes. The further I dig, the sooner I'll draw blood.

"Why are you so itchy?" asks Caroline.

"I-I'm not sure," I stutter.

"Nothing gets better if you keep prodding at it. Come, sit down next to me."

I lift my hand away. The area's irritated and stinging, but I try to avoid it—just as I plan to avoid sitting beside Caroline.

With my back against the wall, I glance away from her. "So, what do you want to know?"

"Anything. I figured you'd ask how I did that, or why; really, anything."

I peer down at the red. It's growing. It's almost as if I stepped in poison ivy, but I know I didn't.

"Stop thinking about it. It's probably from stress," laughs Caroline. "You really need to calm down and just enjoy everything."

Enjoy you torturing my friends?

"Come, sit down," Caroline says again.

I oblige. The arch of my foot aches as I walk toward the couch. Taking a seat at the opposite end from Caroline, I lean farther away from her.

"Now will you tell me your thoughts?"

"It was interesting," I reply.

"Just interesting?"

"What more do you want me to say? That I enjoy watching you torture my friends?"

"Maybe not in those exact words," smirks Caroline. "I just figured you might be curious as to how I was able to obtain those memories."

"I know the DZ helped you. They always help you." I look away from her; my voice becomes hushed. "Seems you can't do anything without them."

Caroline laughs as though she heard me.

"What was that about?"

"Oh, nothing, Elise. I just love how you think I'm completely reliant on someone else rather than being capable of controlling what I've created myself."

"Then tell me how you got those memories. Tell me how you created those settings. Tell me how you were able to break them."

"There we go! That's what I wanted to hear." She rests her arm on the back of the couch. "Now, where should I begin?"

Begin wherever you want. Whatever you're going to say is just a part of one big lie anyways, I think to myself. Nothing Caroline does is by herself. She may have come up with this circus, but she hasn't done anything within it without the help of the omnipotent overlords whom none of us truly know anything about. We just know they're the ones who are in charge; they're the ones who've been tormenting us since Day One.

I finally muster up a light, "I don't care."

Caroline pretends she didn't hear me. "Well, I won't divulge all of my secrets because when you create your own world, you need to learn how to do things your way. You can't be copying another. You'll see when you visit Vincent's circle that none of them are the same."

My interest piques more with the mention of his zone. "What's his world called? What do they do there?"

"He's changed it so many times since he started it, but right now I think it's called 'Umbra.' However, I'm not allowed to tell you what they do there."

"Why not?"

"All of these circles need to be veiled in mystery, Elise. That's what keeps them interesting."

"Who are you hiding from? It's just me, Caroline. You can tell me."

"Nope. You'll just have to wait and see."

"Why? Who's it hurting by telling me? Especially if I'm going to see it eventually."

"DZ's orders. You can't know until you go."

"That's ridiculous. They chose me for a reason, and they won't even let you give me a heads-up about my future?"

"I don't make the rules outside of Halcyon," replies Caroline.

"Why not? Why do you take orders from some people nobody knows a damn thing about?"

"Because they're everywhere."

"That's it? That's the only reason? That's pathetic," I chide. "There's no reason one group of people should govern three separate areas. You've created this place, so you should have complete control of everything that happens around you."

"I do," smiles Caroline. "I'm glad you're so full of vigor right now, but questioning the DZ's methods is almost like questioning a deity and telling them they're wrong."

I can't help but laugh. This whole conversation is pathetic.

"Laugh all you want, Elise, but you'll learn when your time comes that there's a reason we don't rule everything."

I stand up. "But you rule your own space like you rule everything. MacMillan was the same, so why not stretch that beyond one secluded area? Why not make the whole world the way you want it?"

"I don't have time for this." Caroline stands up. She looks directly at me and exhales. "There are some things in this world that you have to—and will—see for yourself, but there are also others that you never want to see. Everyone has a secret, Elise, and some are more valuable than others."

She's acting like she knows something, but I feel that if I try to get it out of her, she'll just storm out. Then again, I don't really care.

"What secret are you talking about?" I ask.

"Nothing. I don't know everything the DZ knows, but I do know there's always a reason."

"What are you saying, Caroline? I feel like you're trying to tell me something."

"I'm not, my dear. I'm not."

My dear? What was that about?

"Okay. Can I at least ask you one thing that's bothered me since we got here?"

"Does it have anything to deal with the other circles?"

"No."

"Okay, go ahead."

I take a few steps back and start to pace around the room again. "Before we left Nimbus, there was this girl named Melanie who told Sam not to listen to 'her.' It sounded like she was talking about you because she also mentioned Halcyon." I turn back to face Caroline. "And awhile back when we had dinner for the first time as a group, Sam asked about how you knew her, but you told him to ask another question. So, what I want to know is: How do you know about Melanie, and how does she know about you? She still had her chip. She couldn't have made it this far."

Caroline sits back down. "Do you think I always stay down here? Do you think I never leave?"

I don't answer.

"Well, sometimes I venture away from this chasm. Sometimes I need to see what the world is like above ground."

She begins to fidget with her cloak; her nails pick at a hanging thread.

I still don't speak. I just watch, hoping she'll at least tell me how this encounter happened and why Melanie was unable to speak for weeks.

"When I do this, I go back."

"To Nimbus?"

She nods.

"Why? I thought you hated that place."

"I do, but when you're in charge of something as great as Halcyon, you need to remember your roots; you need to know why change was needed."

I go silent again. I don't want to coax out any unnecessary information. I just want Caroline to tell me what happened.

She keeps digging at the fabric. "On one of these trips, I ran into a girl just past the barrier. She was quite confused by my garb, my age, everything. She just stared at me like she had seen a ghost. . .and, the thing is, the DZ doesn't like that I go on these walks. They don't like that I leave Halcyon."

She rips the thread off.

"So, when I do one of these and someone sees me, I have to take action. I have to hurt them. I have to show them that it was all in their head and that I never existed, because all they know is of Nimbus and nothing else."

"What did you do to her?"

"It's what I didn't do."

I open my eyes wide.

"I didn't take action. I just spoke to her. I don't know what came over me, but I just started speaking to her." Caroline quickly stands back up. "It's not like me to do that. I had never done that before!"

"Was there something about her that made you want to talk to her?"

"I'm not sure, but we spoke. I told her my name and where I was from. Those were my mistakes."

"So, you never hurt her yourself?"

"No. I told her to turn around and go away."

"Did she?"

"No. She was too in awe of everything."

"What happened after that?"

"The DZ sent someone."

"Who? To do what?"

"I don't know who, but to hurt her, to make her remember me as nothing but trouble. . . as nothing more than a painful nightmare."

Caroline looks away.

There's more to this. There has to be. She seems vulnerable about the subject; she seems more willing to open up and tell me about her past than she ever really has. I don't get it.

"So that's how I met her. Does that answer your silly question?"

"Almost."

"What else do you want t—" Caroline briefly stops talking. She inhales quietly, in a manner similar to a sniffle. "—to know?"

"Why does the incident bother you?"

"It doesn't," she bites back.

"Then why can't you look at me?"

"Because."

I walk over to her. "Why, Caroline?"

She angrily turns toward me and stands up. "Because she's my damn niece."

"And why do you care about that? You don't care about anyone else, so don't act like that bothers you."

"I didn't hate my sister. I never did."

"Did? As in you do now?"

"As in she's dead now just like everyone else from Nimbus. Her death is on your hands," mutters Caroline. She speeds toward the door. Upon reaching it, she places her hand on the frame and turns back to look at me. "You missed your chance to learn more about the tasks, Elise. You pried when you shouldn't have. Now, goodnight."

17 May 2192

Unknown

I had to get out of there. I had to run; if I didn't, they would
have eventually found out my motives—just like they'll eventually
find out what I've done.

I couldn't stand to watch the DZ torture these innocent kids
just to create an unattainable society. I couldn't sit by and allow
myself to become a puppet to their evil ways because the longer I
participated, the more Caroline asked for. And I certainly couldn't
allow myself to feed her any more, especially after the last task. *I still
can't believe I gave her those memories. I can't believe how much I supplied her
with.* These kids are from my home, and I tortured them by proxy.
It still hurts. It doesn't matter that I'm away from the DZ; what I did
will haunt me forever.

It doesn't matter what the DZ promised me. It doesn't matter
that I was secure, that I was guaranteed a role in their society for life.
None of it mattered; none of it matters now, either. I'll never go back
and do those heinous things; I'll never return to their ways. They can
promise what they want, but I'm not going back. I'm never going
back.

Every day it was the same thing. Every minute was the same
painful task of supplying Caroline, of observing Halcyon's torment.
No matter what I wanted, I wouldn't get it. I had to believe
everything they said; I had to listen because of what they told me
when they first added me to their taskforce: They *had* Wesley. They
had my brother.

But that was a lie. It had to have been. I worked for the DZ for
a few years and not once did I see him, nor did I hear about him.
They probably just assumed I'd forget what they told me, and instead
give my heart and soul to their cause.

Well, I didn't forget. And I never will because if they didn't have Wesley, he could still be alive. *I hope he is.*

And if he's not, at least he's in a better place. At least he's free from this nightmare.

But the group Caroline has isn't. Now that I'm free, I'm going to save them. I'm going to stop Caroline. I'm going to kill her.

I itch the back of my neck. I can feel the scars from the carved outline of the DZ against my fingertips. *At least they didn't update the marking*, I think. *At least they didn't black out Nimbus like they did on the map.*

The sky becomes grey.

I'm in an opening, surrounded by nothing but blighted grass. While the DZ is underground, the area around it is filled with trees to mimic a forest, so all I've seen for the past few years have been those trees and the inside of that madhouse. Not to mention a live feed of Halcyon at all times, and worst of all: the inner-workings of those Caroline has tortured. I felt Miles's pain. I actually felt it. And I'm the one who supplied Caroline with the memories to hurt him. Every second of pain they relived was my fault. I hate it. I absolutely hate it.

But I had to do it, or I thought I did. Wesley was my reason, but the lack of his presence finally made it clear to me that I needed to get out. I went years without him. I can go the rest of my life with his memory.

Now, I have to use what they did to me as fuel to save those I almost killed.

I just have a feeling if I tell them everything, they won't listen. If I tell them their suffering was my fault, they might kill me, too. Sadly, it's something I have to do. I have to make right the errors of my ways, and that's why I have to find Elise first. I have to tell her that I shut off Caroline's access, that they're offline in Halcyon—and the only way to do that before the DZ finds out is to run.

Sam

We've been in this horrible room since the last task. All of us. It's been silent for a day or two now. We've been fed, but nothing else has happened. It feels like Caroline is trying to make us absorb what we last experienced for longer than a day, like she wants it to sink deep inside of us until we're weighted to the floor, unable to move.

I know some of us truly feel stuck. Miles does. Marcus does. Sean does. Rosie does. I do. Ella's been tough, but she's still shaken. Though, out of all of us she's the only one who's been able to stomach her regret. She moved on in the past, and she moved on again when she saw it once more.

I wish I could do that. I still see Ann when I sleep.

Whenever I've seen death, torture, or the horrors of the circles, I've been able to move on, but when it comes to Ann or Abby, I stand still. There's just something about them that I feel completely responsible for. Like they could still be alive if I had done something, and there's no worse feeling than failing to stand up when it truly matters. I know that there was nothing I could do once Ann was taken, but I could have prevented her demise by just shutting up, by just controlling the dark thoughts.

But, in reality, I couldn't. And I still can't. The darkness has overcome me yet again. It's revisiting me when I didn't invite it and it seems prepared to stay.

I look around the room. A dim bulb flickers in the corner above Miles as he lies facedown in the mattress. He hasn't eaten more than a few crumbs recently. It's sad, but I don't know what to do. Whatever happened to the back of his head has made it harder for him to stomach the re-imaginings. A few feet away from him sits Marcus. He's been silently mouthing phrases all morning as if he's trying to debate himself. It's like he's trying to argue why he should overcome, why he should be who he said he would be. Next to him is Rosie. Lying on her side, she aimlessly stares at the wall across from her, only blinking when her eyes dry out. In the corner beside her is my brother. Sean has his knees tucked against his chest in a manner that makes him look unapproachable, which stinks. I want to talk to him, but I'm afraid. I'm afraid my darkness will mesh with his and we'll both fall apart even more, and really, I don't want to make him think about that girl anymore. I don't want his mind to succumb to the cruelties that overtook hers.

Ella sits to my left. She's just twiddling her thumbs. I look over at her.

She stares out of her peripherals back.

"Ella," I mutter.

"Yea?"

"How are you holding up?"

"Okay," she answers, still twiddling her thumbs.

I cross my arms across my chest and bury my hands underneath my armpits. "H-how?" I stutter.

"How what?"

"How are you handling what you saw?"

"The key is to realize that you're still here and your past can't define you." She stops twiddling and looks over at me. "Sean told me that I've made it this far knowing what I may see, so I shouldn't let it eat me just because I'd be seeing it again."

"And that's helped?"

"Yep. It was tough in the moment, but being away from it makes it all the more true that it doesn't matter anymore."

I tilt my head down. "Can I ask you something about your memory, then?"

She starts rotating her thumbs around one another again. "Y-yea, sure."

"What did you tell the kid next to you?"

Her fingers pick up speed. "I. . .I told him to run."

"So why didn't you run, too?"

"My legs locked up. It's like my mind knew it would be a bad idea."

A brief silence finds its way between us.

I pull my hands out from underneath my arms. A light scent of sweat comes with the motion. As I do so, the aching in my chest and arms returns, almost as if the end of our conversation indicates that I'm going to fall back into the hole I've been digging since the last task.

I take a deep breath.

Ann's bruised cheeks. The dried blood atop the lacerations on her body. Her bloody lips.

I exhale.

The images fade.

I turn back to Ella.

"Ella," I say again.

"Yea?" she answers.

"Do you think I should talk to Sean?"

"Probably. Mind if I join?"

"Not at all."

I stand up. Ella follows. We both slowly move over toward Sean.

Still sitting with his knees against his chest, he doesn't move at the sight of us.

"Sean," I whisper, leaning toward him.

No response.

"Sean, are you okay?" asks Ella softly beside me.

No answer.

I sit down to his right. Ella to his left. "Sean, you have to talk at some point. The longer we all sit here in silence, the quicker we'll all die."

"We're already dead," he says unemotionally.

"But we don't have to be. We can keep living in Evelyn's na—," but before I can finish my sentence, Sean turns toward me and immediately, without hesitation, slaps me.

My cheek stings. It's even worse than when Abby threw a mixture of ice and snow at me back at the farmhouse. "What the hell was that for?" I gripe a few seconds too late.

"Don't say her name."

"Why not? She's dead!" I angrily shout. I can feel the eyes of the room turn to me.

"Don't say her name," he says again.

"Evelyn!" I shout.

He slaps me even harder.

It aches, but I'm not stopping. I'm miserable. He's miserable. We're all in some sort of hell, but if the only way I can get my brother out of it is to get hit, I'll do it. We need Sean to survive, and even if he's a little lost right now, I know we can find him.

"Are you going to keep slapping me?" I ask while adjusting my jaw.

"Only if you don't listen."

"Why does her name offend you?"

Sean doesn't answer.

"Why does it bother you?" asks Ella.

Still, nothing.

I stand up and lean over Sean. Then, with one swift movement, I kick his shin as hard as I can.

He quickly stands up and pins me against the wall. My back crashes into the wood with the force of what feels like a thousand pounds. I wouldn't be surprised if he fractured my vertebrae, but I don't care.

"Why are you letting Caroline's mind games consume you?" I exhaustedly mutter.

He just holds me tighter against the wall.

"You can keep hurting me, Sean, but I won't stop trying to wake you up!"

He digs his palms further into my shoulders.

I can't move my arms. My legs are practically dangling. There's nothing I can do.

I shoot a glance at Ella.

"Sean," she says. "Remember what you told me before it was my turn to compete?"

He stays silent.

"You basically told me the past couldn't control me. You told me I would be fine, and look!" she yells. "Turn around and look, Sean. I'm fine. You're fine. Marcus is fine. Sam is fine. Rosie is fine. We're all fine, but we're all choosing to suffer." Ella puts her hand on Sean's shoulder and tries to pull him back a bit. My feet hit the ground. "Look at everyone, Sean. We're all still alive, so who gives a shit about what you didn't do? Who cares? You're here. They're not. And as much as this may suck to hear. . ." she takes a breath, "get over it."

Get over it? Really? That's your speech?

Sean lets go of me. "You can't just get over mental anguish."

"No, you can't. You can't just get over anything, but you can fight it. You can ignore it. You can move on. You can do what we've all been doing since we got here: You can fake it."

"So I can let all the pain pile on top of me when we get out?"

"Yep, then you can cry. But right now, you need to wake up and help us get out of here."

With my feet firmly on the ground, I move in front of Sean. "She's right," I quietly say while trying to stretch out my back.

Sean presses his lips together. He tilts his head to the side and looks at Ella. "Do you not know how many times I've done that? Do you not know how many times I've faked it to get through this hell?"

Nobody answers.

"Every damn day," Sean complains. "Every day I've held back my pain to see tomorrow, and. . .eventually, it becomes impossible."

"But it doesn't have to be that way," I mutter. "You've pushed past it before; why is it so hard to do it again?"

Sean doesn't answer.

Ella looks over at me before turning back toward Sean. "He's right, Sean. You've hid away this memory for over eleven years. Just seeing it again shouldn't create a strain bigger than what you first experienced."

"I was naïve then!" he shouts. "I didn't understand death. I still don't. But I knew she could have been saved. I knew she wasn't meant to die then."

"And just like her, none of us are meant to die now," I say.

Sean punches the wall. "You guys don't understand. You didn't survive for eleven years. None of you did!" He removes his fists; a slight indent stays behind. "You can't fathom the depths your mind will go to rid the emotion of regret. No matter how much you think you've forgotten something, no matter how much you think you've buried it, you haven't. It will always come back."

A silence overcomes the room. Marcus steps closer to me. "Just because it comes back, doesn't mean you have to let it stay," he murmurs. Rubbing the back of his neck, he looks directly at Sean. "For too long I've let the memories of my dead friends haunt me; I've let them torment me. I've let them take up a residence in my mind that I can't deny. But death. . .death doesn't have to be the end for everyone. Death can mean the beginning for someone else." He releases his hand off his neck and steps next to Sean. "I know the pain Evelyn has put on you. I know what it feels like to feel responsible for someone else's suicide, but that's not your fault. She chose her end just like Shane chose his." Marcus sniffles. "We can't let their endings be our endings."

Sean puts his hand on Marcus's shoulder.

Marcus turns to hug him.

"Okay," says Sean, muffled. "I'll keep fighting for her."

I smile.

Sean lets go of Marcus and walks over to Rosie. "Rosie, it wasn't your fault." He turns back to face Marcus. "Kyle loved you, and I know you loved him. Cherish that. Don't let it consume you. Use it just like I'll use Evelyn's memory to fight."

"I'll try, Sean," says Marcus.

"I know it wasn't," mutters Rosie. "I know."

"So, why don't we finally try to find a way out of this place rather than furthering our descent into madness?" smirks Ella.

I smile. "That sounds like a great idea."

Sean turns to face Ella, but instead of speaking, he hugs her.

I move toward them. Marcus and Rosie follow.

Regrets exist for a reason. Like grief, they always hang above me, but at this exact moment, there's no such thing as regret. The only thing that exists right now is this. Us. And our determination to truly escape.

Sean steps back from the group hug. "We need to find a hollow point. I know we've searched before, but we need to search again. High, low, middle, the ceiling, the floor, no matter where, we need to look. I'm sure something exists. Caroline likes to make us suffer, but she also revels in the possibility of our escape because. . ." he pauses, ". . .if we're to escape and we're caught again, she gets to double the pain." He steps into the middle of the room. "But, if we escape and we're not caught, we're free. And to me, that's worth the risk."

Marcus steps beside Sean. "He's right. Ella and Rosie take two walls. I'll take the floor. Sam, hop on Sean's shoulders and check the ceiling for an exit." He doesn't mention Miles, nor does anyone look in his direction.

We know his fate, and as awful as it is to accept, we all know the reality of his situation.

Sean bends down. "Climb on," he mutters.

I do.

He lifts me up. I place my palms on the ceiling and start to feel around. Every few inches, I knock in hopes I'll find an opening.

Ella does the same on a wall to my left. Rosie copies on one to my right. Marcus lies flat on the floor and crawls around in search of the same sound, in search of the hollow barrier that gets us out of here.

We all knock several times over, but nobody announces that he or she found the exit. Sean carries me all around the room, but everywhere I touch feels the same as the area before it. *Maybe there isn't an exit. Maybe this truly is an inescapable hell.* We're in the right corner of the room now, and I still can't find a way out. I'm sure I could find a way to damage the ceiling and dig upward, but even then I doubt we'd find a real escape within the next 24 hours.

I look left. Ella's moved to the wall to her right. She has her ear and her fist placed against the plaster. She knocks and moves a few inches over before repeating the process. Rosie does the same on the wall behind us.

"Sean," I mutter.

"Yea?" he answers.

"We need to try the tops of the walls above where Rosie and Ella can reach."

"Good thinking."

We immediately move over to where Ella last tapped. I place my ear against the wall and knock once. Nothing.

We move a few inches and repeat. Still nothing. After clearing the entirety of the wall, there's been nothing to indicate a way out. We repeat the same steps on the next two walls, and still, nothing. There's one wall left and I'm quite certain it'll yield the same results as the other three.

"Has anyone found anything?" asks Marcus as he slides over to the corner by Miles.

"Nothing," I answer.

"Nope," respond Ella and Rosie in unison.

"Maybe there isn't an escape then," he softly replies, clearly upset.

Sean moves me toward the last wall. I knock. Nothing.

We move a few inches to the right. Nothing.

"I don't think there's an exit," I quietly whisper.

Sean keeps moving. I keep knocking. My attempts continue to fail to yield results.

I tap Sean's shoulder. He bends down and lets me climb off. "I don't think there is either," I say.

"It seems we have to wait," sighs Rosie. "I guess Caroline really made this room inescapable."

"But there's one place we haven't looked," adds Ella.

"Where?" I question.

She takes a few long strides toward Miles. Pushing her feet into the wall, she leans her weight into the mattress and slides it into the center of the room. "Under here."

Marcus quickly slides toward her—almost immediately falling into a prone position the second he realizes he missed a spot. He starts knocking right away.

"Ella's right," he exclaims. "I've found the spot!"

"Where?" asks Sean.

Marcus knocks twice before moving his hands around the area. Eventually, he finds a crease. Sticking his nails into the opening, he pries open a part of the floor. "Here."

"What are we waiting for?" smiles Ella. "Let's get the hell out of here."

Elise

It's been two days since the last task. I'm surprised Caroline's taken more time between the third and fourth than she did between any others. She must truly want to make everyone think about the past; she must want them to fall deeper into the murky waters of their own personal hell.

Shit, I know I'm already sinking and I'm not even participating.

At least unlike the other days when Caroline made me spend a majority of my time in my room, today she has me in the office with the vase with the birds on it. Though, she's not here. I've been pacing for about twenty minutes and there have been no signs pointing to her arrival. Everything around me is quiet.

I walk over to the glass enclosure surrounding the vase of Halcyon—at least, I assume that's what Caroline calls it. Whatever it is, it still holds no meaning to me. Two birds that get to be with each other forever, but don't get to reap the rewards of their love mean nothing to me. As long as I get to be with Sean, I don't care what happens. We could be stuck in a well flooding with water, our fate awaiting us, but I wouldn't care. I'd die with him. I'd drown in his love. It's sad, but it's honest. I've lived through enough hell that if I were to die beside him, it would be okay. It would be better than creating my own world and dying alone leading it.

I don't want to live like Caroline. I don't want to trudge through a world of unhappiness just because I get to be in charge. That's insane, not to mention stupid.

I place my hands atop the glass. *I wonder if there's an opening.* Searching around the top and down the sides of the case, I feel for something to grab onto. After a few seconds, my fingers catch on a small slit near the center of the glass. I dig my finger into it and slide it to the left. It opens.

I grab the vase. It's light. And smooth. None of the artwork is chipped, nor does any of it look even slightly better up close.

I should break it.

I glide my fingers across the image; I stop upon the sea. Vast and endless, the blue painted upon this piece seems to cover a majority of the vase, and it's not appealing. Everything about this so-called art bothers me. I lift it above my head.

"I wouldn't do that if I were you," rings an unfamiliar voice.

"Why not?" I answer.

"Because if we're to escape, we have to be quiet."

"Who are you? Show yourself."

Suddenly, a woman dressed in the same light blue cloak as the followers steps into my line of sight. Her dark blonde hair hangs just past her shoulders; her vibrant blue eyes shine perfectly against the robe. She has her hands tucked into the pockets.

"Who-who are you?" I stutter.

"My name is Ava Pearson."

"Why does that name sound familiar?"

I lower the vase.

"I believe your group has talked about me before, or at least my brother, Wesley."

"H-how do you know that?"

"I know more than I would like to, Elise, and that's why I've come to help you."

"How did you get in here?"

"Just like I said, I know more than I'd like to." Removing her hands from her pockets, Ava steps toward me.

I take a step back.

"Don't be frightened, Elise. I have much to tell you, but we have to act fast."

"Why should I trust you?"

"Because I know how to get out of here. I know how to put an end to everything."

She takes another step.

I take another back.

"Prove it," I mutter.

"Prove what?"

"Prove what you know."

She takes a breath. "If you insist." Moving over toward the chair, she takes a seat and looks off to the right. "Your full name is Elise Eleanor Watson. You don't like to tell people your middle name because you think it's an ugly name. You had an older brother named Zeke, and your parents were John and Isla Watson. I say 'had' because, unfortunately, Nimbus has been destroyed." She then looks back at me. "Your favorite author is F. Scott Fitzgerald, you love chicken and noodles, and twice you've frozen in the face of fear for reasons you can't explain. Well, Elise, those reasons were me. I stopped you from getting yourself killed. I stopped you from moving on MacMillan and I stopped you from entering that prison with Sam, Sean, and the others."

My jaw drops.

"Is there anything else you'd like to know?"

"How were you able to stop me from moving?"

"I worked for the DZ."

The second she says that, I drop the vase. It shatters.

"Now, we have to move. If you don't trust what I know then keep being Caroline's guinea pig; keep watching those you love suffer—but if you want to escape, take my hand and follow me."

I've never been one for split-second decisions, but in the moment between despair and complete misery, you'll do anything to avoid slipping further into hell—even if the outcome is unknowable.

I take two steps forward. Ava grabs my palm.

She guides me into the hallway. Then, she whisks me away into the madness of this building all while turning corners like she understands the maze. It frightens me. It excites me. It messes with every instinct I've ever had.

I don't know this woman, nor am I sure I want to, but *who else knows all that about me?* Only Sean, or my family. Nobody else. I don't know how anyone could obtain that much information about me; really, I don't know why anyone would care that I'm a fan of classic literature—or that my middle name is. . .ugh. . .Eleanor. I may love old books, but that doesn't mean I love antiquated names.

Ava turns a few more corners before pulling me into a room I've never seen. It's not very large, but it has a few paintings, a minibar, and two leather chairs.

"Where are we?" I ask.

"Just a quick hiding place," replies Ava. "Caroline's probably in that other room by now, confused as to where you've gone."

"What will she do once she realizes I'm not there?"

"She'll try to find you."

"Does she have cameras to see where I might be?"

"Yes, but I've blocked them. I've shut off access to your chips and I've blinded her in this house."

"H-how?"

"I broke the control panel in the DZ. I've shut down access to all of your chips; yes, all of them. Everyone but Sean still has theirs. Even Caroline has hers."

I reach for the nearest chair. I fall into it. "Why does she have hers?"

"The DZ likes to keep track of everyone who left Nimbus."

"Do you still have yours?"

"No."

"Why not?"

"Like Sean, I was separated twice, but MacMillan didn't know my fate, so my chip was removed when I returned from my Separation." She moves over to the chair across from me. "Sean and I have been immune to the DZ's mind games, but everyone else was subject to them. Now, it'll be months before the DZ is able to fix and reconfigure what I broke."

No more nightmares, I think. *No more horrible visions.*

Ava pushes her bangs to the side. "Now, we have time to escape. We have a window."

"What about the others?"

"They've found the hatch."

"What hatch? How do you know?"

"You sure do have a lot of questions," grins Ava.

"You say a lot of things that need answers."

"Fair enough. I went into the room where they were imprisoned and it was empty. The mattress was out of place from where I last saw it through my lens in the DZ, so they must have found the escape hatch."

I itch the back of my head. "But why would there be an escape route in there? Why would Caroline want to allow them the possibility to get out?"

Ava leans forward. "Because Caroline knows where the door goes. She knows if she gets to the exit before they do, she'll be able to make them suffer even more."

"So, she built an exit just for the potential of doubling their torture?"

Ava nods. "Yea."

"I guess I shouldn't expect anything less."

Everything Ava's told me is insane, but I believe it. I believe all of it. We all knew Wesley had an older sister. We knew someone was separated twice before Sean. It all lines up. But, still, one thing bothers me.

"Ava," I mutter.

"Yea?"

"How exactly were you able to stop me from moving? How were you able to see and do everything at the DZ?"

Ava drags her hand up and down her face, her fingers massaging her temple down to her cheekbones in the process. She sighs, and lowers her hand. "Those chips have complete control of anyone who has one. In the DZ we're able to do anything we want just by accessing someone's chip. We. . ." she stops.

We?

"We can make someone hurt themselves; we can make someone see something they never want to see; we can freeze a person in place. Anything you can think of, the DZ has the power to do."

"Why do they feel they need to control us? We're not robots. We should be in charge of our own bodies."

"That doesn't matter to them. Their idea of a perfect world hasn't been discovered yet, so they'll do whatever they can to obtain it. . .even if that means torturing those trying to find it."

I bite my bottom lip. "So, why did you stop me twice?"

"I didn't want you to die. Your place in this world is too great to be lost by foolish moves."

"Why do you say that?"

"Because there's just something different about you. If you had charged MacMillan, he would have shot you on the spot. If you had followed your friends into that room, Caroline would have killed them all right in front of you. But by avoiding entrance and telling Caroline you didn't want to follow them in, she started to sense that you were succumbing to her methods—even though, we both know, you weren't and still aren't."

"How do you know that she would do that?"

"Because the DZ doesn't truly care what she does, and she knows that."

I grind my molars. "So, she really could kill me and it wouldn't matter?"

"Yes. The DZ has backups in place for everything. They're always prepared."

"Does that mean they have backup access to the chips?"

"They did," smiles Ava.

I can't help but smile back.

A noise echoes in the hallway.

"We should probably get out of this room," she whispers.

"Where will we go?"

She grabs my hand and pulls me out of my seat.

Slowly peeking out into the hallway, Ava looks both ways before hurrying me back through the corridors. We go straight for a few seconds before hooking right then left, straight, right, right, left, and left again. It's to the point that if I had two minutes to escape this place or die, I would just sit down, cross my legs, and accept my fate. *I am absolutely lost.*

We jump into another room. Unfortunately, this one is a bathroom.

Ava shuts the door behind us and locks it.

"Ava," I softly say.

She looks over at me, but doesn't say anything.

"H-how did the DZ get those memories? Do they save every little moment of our lives into some sort of backup?"

She nods.

"Every. . .thing?"

"Yes. They have every detail of everyone's life—even their own."

"I have to ask then, who was that girl Sean saw? Who was Evelyn?"

Ava leans her head against the door. "I don't hear anything," she whispers.

"Ava, who was that girl?"

She looks back at me. "Evelyn was what they call in the DZ an 'Apathetic Meanderer.'"

"A what?"

"Apathetic Meanderer, or an 'AM.'"

"What are those?"

"They're kids who grew up in the DZ who were intentionally beaten most of their lives, so that when they were sent into the outside, all the emotionless and painful responses they fed to others would make them break easier." Ava leans her back against the door. "They were orphaned kids that the DZ fostered into being depressed, senseless, indirect killers."

"Why the hell would they do that?"

"I don't know, Elise. That's one of the reasons why I left. They don't just torture you guys out here. They torture anyone and everyone who doesn't work for them."

"How did you manage to work for them, then?"

"Ignatius took a liking to me when I was separated for the second time."

"Who's that?"

"The leader of everything."

"Why did he take a liking to you when they don't seem to like anyone?"

"He must have seen something in me I didn't see in myself."

My head starts to hurt. There's too much to process. I move the back of my hand up to my forehead.

"Are you okay?" asks Ava.

"Yea. . .I'll be fine."

"Let's just not focus on everything I know right now. Let's focus on getting everyone out of here alive."

But how? We don't know where they are. We don't know how many people are looking for me—or for us. We don't know enough about anything. And as much as I'm beginning to trust Ava, I still don't believe it's that easy; I don't think we can all just get out of here without some sort of repercussion.

I almost feel like she should help everyone else flee and leave me here. Maybe if Caroline has me, she won't chase after them; maybe if I'm still here, they'll survive.

Stop it, Elise!

After all, it's not like I'd be sacrificing myself. Even if Caroline has free will to kill me, she doesn't seem like she would.

"Where's the way out?" I softly ask.

"The same way I came in."

"Which is. . .?"

"Just down a few more hallways, but I don't think we're going to take that route."

"Why not?"

"Because I want to make sure everyone else is safe."

My heart skips a beat. I can't reiterate enough how little I know about Ava, but everything she has said has been the right thing. It truly seems like she's here to help us, that she wants to make up for her past. Either that or she works for Caroline and this is just another test.

It can't be.

Ava grabs onto my hand once more. "Follow me," she quietly says.

Pushing open the bathroom door, we stride into the hallway.

Ava squeezes tightly. My palm starts to sweat. "It's going to be okay," she reassures me.

Yet, I can't help but feel that it won't be. Nothing is ever as easy as she makes it seem. We've tried to run; we've tried to flee, but everything we've ever done has led us down an unyielding path of suffering. Even if we can get out of Halcyon, *who's to say we're not quickly pulled into the third circle?* We know nothing about Umbra other than that it's run by a man named Vincent. I mean, Caroline's not even sure that's what it's called.

Though, if anyone were to know something about it, it'd be Ava.

She pulls me down another hallway.

I want to ask her, but not yet. Not while we're in the open.

We twist and turn down several hallways before Ava finds the spot where the wall opened and the others disappeared. The same spot where the hideous green and brown aesthetic becomes a cream and black one; the spot where it seems Caroline had a great idea about repainting, but then decided halfway through that she'd be better off doing something else—whatever that may be.

Ava lets go of my hand before launching her shoulder at the wall. It opens.

"Why does it open from out here so easily?" I ask.

"No clue, but I'll take it," she answers.

Once the door is completely open, we step inside. The room is barren. The only thing in here is that mattress Ava mentioned beforehand. *I can't believe Caroline made them stay in here for days.*

"What the hell is this place?" I exhale. "This is a dungeon."

"Pretty much."

The more I look around the room, the more intrigued I become about what's next. In the city outside Nimbus, I was trapped in a dungeon. In Halcyon, my friends were essentially placed in one. It almost seems that every society we walk into believes that the best way to get into someone's head isn't through some game, but by placing them in a room with limited light and letting their minds destroy themselves.

"Hey Ava. . ."

"Yea, Elise?"

"Do you know anything about Umbra?"

"Unfortunately, I don't know much. I was assigned to watch over Halcyon. Someone else is watching over that place."

"So, you know nothing of that world?"

"I know that a man named Vincent is in charge and that it has something to do with cleansing and purifying, but I don't know what."

I look down. "I wonder what that means."

"It doesn't matter. We won't be going there anyways."

"I hope not."

"I know so," smiles Ava. Reaching back for my hand, she pulls me out of my trance. "We need to get down through the hatch to see if we can catch up with them before it's too late."

I shift my jaw. "I think one of us has to distract Caroline if they're to get out safely."

"But we should still have time right now if we just hurry. Caroline's offline. She probably doesn't know they're down there yet."

"But what if we don't have time? What if she just found out through some other method? I can't risk Caroline killing all of them when there's a chance they could escape while she's preoccupied."

"What are you saying, Elise?"

"That I should stay here." The second I say it, my shoulders tense up and my throat becomes dry.

She lets go of my palm. "We can all escape." She looks back at the mattress before falling onto her knees beside it. Feeling around for an opening, she looks back at me. "We can all get out of here alive."

"There will always be a 'what if,' though," I say in a hushed tone. "There's always a chance something bad happens. . .and I just feel that. . .maybe I could prevent it."

"So what are you suggesting we do?"

My stomach twists. It feels like someone is wringing out a damp towel. "That I stay and you find the others."

Looking back at the floor, Ava stops moving her hands. "Found it," she says enthusiastically. Quickly prying open the hatch, she sticks her head through the opening. "I'm not seeing anyone," echoes her voice.

"Ava, I'm staying," I say, my stomach tightening further the more I think about it.

She turns her head back around to face me. "As much as it pains me to say it, you're right, Elise." She stands up and walks over to me. "Before we do this, we need to come up with a quick plan to ensure that everyone gets out of here safely."

"Okay," I nod.

"What do you want me to do once—or if—I find the others?" she asks.

"Use what you know of this place to get them out. I assume this path leads to an actual exit since it seems Caroline likes to spread the idea of hope before stomping on it."

"I can do that. What will you do?"

"I'll go back into the hallway and start making noise until Caroline finds me. When she does, I'll just tell her I got lost wandering around the corridor. I'm sure she'll believe me."

"Why are you so sure?"

"I just have this gut feeling that Caroline sees something in me that reminds her of herself, but just like you were uncertain what Ignatius saw in you, I'm not completely sure either. I just have this feeling." The stiffness in my shoulders lessens.

"Sometimes that feeling is enough."

"Yea."

"But how will you get out?"

"I still have the key Marisa gave me."

"Do you know what it's for?"

"Unfortunately not."

"Can I see it?"

I move toward the wall behind me. Letting my back fall, I slide off my shoe. My sock has small red splotches on it. *Great.* I slide the key out and hand it to Ava.

"This is quite a key," she grins. "Is it for a treasure chest?"

I laugh. "That's what I thought!"

"With the way this world is set up, I bet it's for something clever. I bet it's your escape."

"That's what I'm hoping."

She hands me back the key. I stretch out the arch of my foot before placing the key back on the insole.

Ava tucks her bangs behind her ears and turns to face the open hatch. "We need a contingency plan if the key is worthless, though."

"What do you think?"

She turns back toward me. "A time frame."

"What do you mean?"

"If we escape and we don't see you in, say, two days, we need to know what to do."

"If you don't see me in the fake city above Halcyon at sunset two days from now, get them away from here. Don't come back for me. Get them away. I will find you."

Her expression shifts. "What if they don't believe me?"

"Make them."

"How?"

"Tell them everything you've told me. Your knowledge of this world will be enough. I wish I had something to give you, something for them to know that we met, but I don't. . . . I-I trust that your words will be enough."

"I hope so."

"Me too."

Ava moves toward the hatch once more. "Two days, Elise. We can do two days."

"I know we can, but I have just one more question."

"Yea?"

"Was it you who spoke to me before we first met Noah and the others?"

"It was."

"How come you only did that once? Why didn't you try it multiple times to show me who you are?"

"I couldn't."

"Why not?"

"I almost got caught the one time I tried it." She exhales. "While I had access to your chips and I could do almost anything to you, talking to you was forbidden by Ignatius."

"I guess that makes sense." I force a slight smile. "Well, I'm glad I finally got to meet you, Ava."

"Same goes for you, Elise. Now, we have to get moving."

"One more thing," I say.

"Yea?"

"Do you know how I can get out of here to meet up with you guys later?"

"Come into this room, jump down the hatch, and follow it to the end. Your way out will be there."

"Thank you."

Ava grabs my hand. "We'll get out of here, Elise. I know we will."

I nod.

With one swift movement, Ava closes the hatch, and disappears.

I quickly step out of the room and try to pull the door shut. It slides slowly, but surely. Though, I can't get it completely shut. I leave a few inches of space and start to wander away from this area.

Now, I just have to find Caroline, and hope that Ava finds the others. And as much as it pains me that they could all escape while I rot or die in Halcyon, I feel better knowing that more could survive than would die within the next two days.

Sean

This tunnel seems unending. The hallway looks like it goes on forever—even the lights, which hang on both sides, show no sign of stopping in the distance. There are little hatches above that are similar in appearance to the one we came through, but they're sporadic. It sort of feels like we're just heading even deeper into the maze that is Caroline's world.

"We've been walking forever," says Sam, his voice bouncing off the cement walls surrounding us.

"It can't have been that long," responds Marcus. With one arm over Miles, he trails slightly behind the group. "It's probably only been thirty minutes."

"Thirty minutes is more time than I expected to spend even further underground," gibes Sam.

"At least we're not in that room anymore," I add.

Sam doesn't say anything.

"He has a point," mutters Ella. "Even if we have to walk ten miles, at least that puts us farther away from that bitch of a woman."

I chuckle. "Tell us how you really feel, Ella."

She steps up beside me and grins. "Don't act like I'm wrong."

"I'm not."

"That's the most true thing you've ever said," says Rosie from ahead. "I could walk forever if it meant I'd never see her face again."

I look around. Everyone's smiling. Even Miles. Despite the ache in the back of his skull, he's improving. With Marcus's help, he's been able to keep up with the rest of us. He's still not speaking much, but his mannerisms are returning. It doesn't matter that it's not much; it's enough for us. It shows that he might make it after all.

I'll never forget this moment. It's the first time in months that I've seen so many smiles. Elise may not be here right now, but I know she'll find us. I know she'll make it out, too, and we'll create more memories like this. We'll create moments of bliss—moments that can't be stolen from us by psychopaths like MacMillan or Caroline, or whoever else is out there.

"Where do you think all these hatches lead?" asks Sam from ahead.

"Probably to more rooms like the one we were in," answers Rosie.

"Why do you think that?"

"I don't know, just a feeling. Caroline seems like the type to have more dungeons than bathrooms."

Beside me, Ella glides her fingers against the wall but keeps her focus forward. "Do you think we should open one?"

"That's probably not a good idea," I quickly answer.

"Why not?"

"What if Caroline's behind the one we open?"

Ella looks at me and half-smiles, "Good point."

"Can you imagine if that happened?" laughs Sam from ahead. "What if we chose one at random and she was just staring back at us? That would suck."

I grin.

The only echo in the hallway becomes that of our footsteps.

Yet, the farther we walk, the louder our steps sound. The more it starts to sound like there are more people walking than just us.

"Do you guys hear that?" I softly ask.

"Hear what?" replies Sam.

"I hear it, too," says Marcus in a hushed manner.

"I still don't hear it," says Sam.

"Everybody stop moving," I whisper.

Everyone halts.

The noise gets louder, and louder, and louder. But I don't turn around. I just keep my eyes forward. "Nobody look. Everyone run," I mutter.

Yet, nobody does it. Nobody listens.

I don't hold back. "RUN!" I shout.

Everyone begins to sprint down the hall.

My legs are trying to move faster than my body will allow them to. I haven't truly run in weeks, and my body's not prepared for the sudden athleticism. But if there's one thing that erases all limitations, it's fear.

The lights become a blur beside me as I run away from the noise. I keep my distance behind Sam, Rosie, and Ella, but my legs never stop churning. I have no idea what I'm running from, but if it's Caroline or her followers, I can't afford to stop. None of us can.

"Sean!" shouts a voice from behind me. "Sean!"

"Stop!" yells another.

But I don't. I can't.

"Stop running!" echoes behind me. "Stop!"

Finally, I yell back, "Why?" but I keep moving forward.

"Just stop!" comes the voice—one I can't discern. My ears are flooded with the same fear that's overcome my legs, making it so everything is a blur. Not just the path in front of me, but the sounds around me.

"Should we stop?" asks Rosie, out of breath, as she slows down ahead of me.

Sam stops. "It sounds like Marcus." He, then, turns around and looks at me. His pupils dilate. "There's someone else with him and Miles."

"Who?"

"It looks like a woman."

"Elise. . ." I whisper.

Rosie turns around. I follow suit.

"Who is that?" asks Sam, perplexed. "That's not Elise, and. . .it doesn't look like Caroline."

"I-I have no idea." Her hair is shorter than Elise and Caroline's. It's just past her shoulders, and it's a dark blonde color. I can't see the entirety of her face, but everything I see from here is unfamiliar. Nothing about this woman is recognizable. I really have no idea who she is.

"Guys, come here," shouts Marcus.

We move forward in unison—almost like a march; our steps are in sync.

The closer we get, the clearer her face becomes. Her eyes are a different color than any I've ever seen. They're blue, but not bright or dark. They're steel. Steel blue. Her lips are slightly chapped; there's a small scar beside her nose on her left cheek; and, of all things, she's smiling.

"Who are you?" I ask.

"I'm Ava Pearson. Elise sent me."

"Ava Pearson," mumbles Sam. "Are you. . .Wesley's sister?"

She nods. "I am. Have you seen him?"

Sam shakes his head.

Ava doesn't say anything. She simply looks at the rest of us, almost perplexed, but intrigued.

"How did you get here?" I ask.

She doesn't hesitate. "I broke in."

"Why would you do that?" questions Ella.

"To help you guys."

"How did you know we were here?"

She pushes her hair out of her eyes. "I used to work for the DZ."

"Then why the hell are you here now?" I angrily ask.

"Like I said: I'm here to help you guys. I saw what you went through, and I. . .I just couldn't take it anymore, so I shut down the DZ and Caroline's access to you. You're completely invisible in their eyes right now."

"Why didn't you come before the tasks even began?"

"Because I didn't know what they would be. . ." she trails off. Taking a light breath, Ava turns toward me. "I just got control of the room to view Halcyon's doings; I had no idea what I would see, and it's not like I could just watch one and leave. The DZ would suspect something."

"And they don't suspect something now?" questions Marcus.

"By now, they know what I've done, but it'll take weeks for them to regain access and months to get it running to the level it was at before, or to the extent where they have control. But I still think it's best if we move quickly."

"What kind of access did they have?" asks Sam.

"Everything, Sam. They can see and do what they please."

Sam looks at the nub where his pinky used to be.

I can feel my teeth grinding, clattering against one another with uncertainty. *Why should we trust this woman? Why should I believe that Elise sent her?* Yet, before I let my mind run rampant with questions that could slow our escape, I look to Ava. "Where's Elise?"

"She stayed. She figured she could distract Caroline while you guys escaped. She didn't want anyone else to get hurt."

My eyelids start to become heavy. My blinking becomes rapid as they rise and fall over my pupils without my control. I brush my palm against my forehead. "Di-did she have a plan for herself to escape?" I stutter.

"Yes, she has a key we assume is for the elevator out. Marisa gave it to her before she was killed."

"Marisa was killed?"

"Yes. That's how Caroline knew you were in that room. There are several rooms like that throughout this place; each one corresponds to a different follower."

"What do you mean?"

"You guys had a map, right?"

I nod.

"All the followers have maps. Each has a different spot that leads to a secret room like that. Based on the room you were in, Caroline knew Marisa had given you the map. Therefore, she had Marisa executed." Ava steps toward me. "There's a lot I need to tell you guys, but we have to get out of here first."

"Why should we trust you, though?" Sam asks, hushed. "Just because you know so much isn't a reason to trust you. You worked for the enemy. How do we know you don't still work for them?"

Ava bunches her hair into her hand behind her head. Slowly lifting it higher, the three circles mark becomes noticeable on her neck. It's smaller than what we've seen before, but it's there. It's red; it's irritated; it's complete. No circles are dark.

"When Nimbus was destroyed, the marking had to be updated. Every member of the DZ had a scheduled time to get their scar 'fixed' as they called it. All that means is, they were going to hurt me even more. They were going to burn out the ring that represents Nimbus." She drops her hair. "Today I was supposed to have mine 'fixed,' but I couldn't do that. Nimbus was my home. I didn't agree with MacMillan, but it was my home."

She rubs her hand against the back of her neck, and looks away.

Nobody speaks.

She then turns to face me. "And Sean, I have something for you."

I look at her, confused.

"I believe this is yours," she says as she pulls something out from underneath her cloak. "I took your hook before I was taken in by the DZ. I hope my theft didn't harm you guys, and the firewood and food treated you well."

I take it from her. I don't know what to say. I just know I trust her. I know we need her. We need her knowledge of this world if we're going to survive it.

Ava turns to look at everyone else. She opens her mouth. "You don't have to trust me right now, but I will prove my worth to you. I will prove that we can survive this world without abiding by the ideals of the DZ—the Dead Zone. That's what they are, and that's what they'll eventually, truly be."

"I believe you," exhales Marcus. "I believe you can help us."

"Thank you," smiles Ava.

"I believe you, too," says Rosie.

Ella nods beside her.

"I feel the same as the others," I nod. "You helped Elise and I when we were hungry. Although I wasn't awake for the barter, I appreciate what you did for us."

Sam acquiesces, albeit almost unnoticeably.

"But Ava. . ." says Marcus.

"Yea?" she answers.

"Do you know what exactly happened to Miles? We know what the tasks did to him, but the back of his head has been lightly swollen, and it occasionally bleeds. It seems Caroline, or someone, hurt him, but we don't know how because he won't speak about it."

"The DZ gave Caroline access to your chips—yes, the DZ can still access all of your chips—" but she's cut off before she can continue.

"I thought our chips were taken out when we returned to Nimbus," states Ella.

"Unfortunately not. Everyone but Sean and I still have theirs."

The collective emotions of the hall get darker. Everyone's visibly shaken—except Sam. And, sadly, I understand why. Someone's always been in his head, so to hear this just seems like icing on top of the devil's cake.

"What the hell? Why weren't they taken out?" furiously fires Rosie. "They were supposed to be taken out!"

"Marisa was given orders to ensure they weren't," says Ava. "I'm sorry, but there was nothing I could do."

Rosie storms away down the hall. Ella follows her.

"How did we get past the barrier if they're still in?" asks Sam.

"The chips were adjusted to allow free roam, but the DZ could still follow you, and. . .control you." Ava looks down the hall. Rosie and Ella have stopped and are pacing back and forth. "Anyways, Caroline was able to make Miles relive painful memories all while adjusting the reality of them by simply using this small, almost invisible, microchip on her finger that she would press into his scar where the chip is. They would connect and she would be able to control what he saw. However, she kept pressing and pressing with his. Eventually, he passed out and almost hemorrhaged."

"Do you know if he'll be okay?"

"I'm not sure, but I like to think he will be because, well, he passed out on my account. I wasn't in the room when Caroline started to torture him, but the second I walked in, I ensured her access was cut off. So, when Miles's chip was blocked, Caroline wasn't able to worsen the memory, but she was still able to press into the wound. Thankfully, she let go and he survived."

Miles looks over at Ava. He doesn't speak, but he smiles. His eyes start to well up.

Ava walks over to him and wraps her arms around his shoulders. She whispers something inaudible in his ear.

He weeps.

Rosie and Ella come back—their expressions of discontent slightly lifted.

"Thank you for saving him," mutters Marcus.

"It's not a problem. I couldn't stand to see any more of your group fail—especially after Kyle." Ava lets go of Miles and moves over to Marcus. "I know what he meant to you, Marcus. He was more than just a mentor. He was the love of your life, and for him, we'll all get out of here. I promise."

Marcus smiles. "Thank you, Ava." Without allowing himself to succumb to the teary-eyed sadness I know he feels coming, Marcus looks over at me. "We should probably keep moving. Who knows if Caroline knows we escaped yet."

"He's right. Let's keep moving," agrees Ava.

"Before we go, what do you think the DZ will do once they regain access to our minds?" asks Rosie.

"Hopefully they don't."

"But what if they do?"

"I don't think they'll torture you because I'm the one who broke their systems. If anything, they'll come after me."

"And you're okay with that?"

"It's not ideal," grins Ava. "But I know what I did was treason in their eyes, and I don't care. If they come for me, I'll fight back. I'm never going back there." Her eyes shift to the ground. "Never," she whispers under her breath.

Veering the subject back to the present, Sam looks over at Ava. "Do you know how far we have to go?"

"Sadly, I don't," she answers. "I never actually saw this part of Halcyon."

I look over at Sam. "Well then, I guess we better just keep walking."

"Or we could run again?" chides Ella.

"Act-actually. . ." mumbles Sam, "we should."

"Why?"

"Turn around."

I pivot to the left.

The distance is darkening. One by one, the lights are going out.

"Someone knows we're here," mutters Ava anxiously. "We should run."

I take a step back and wrap my right arm around Miles. Marcus keeps a hold on his other side. "Let's go," I nod at him.

Marcus nods back.

The others start to run ahead of us. Marcus and I put our weight into Miles's back, essentially lifting him into the air, as we carry him forward.

Our strides grow longer, but we're still considerably behind everyone else, and the lights aren't yielding to our fears. They're bound to catch up to us. I fear we'll be buried in the darkness before any semblance of an exit presents itself.

I try to push our pace, but it's difficult carrying another body, no matter who it is. And we can't just leave Miles behind. He can move, but if he were to run on his own right now, he would probably still be near where we started.

The lights are catching up.

Sam, Rosie, Ella, and Ava still haven't indicated they've found an exit.

"Do you see anything?" shouts Marcus.

"Nothing yet!" answers Ava.

And then, the worst thing that could happen, docs. The lights begin to go out ahead of us. One by one, like the others, they're fading to black in front of us.

Marcus and I stop. I release my grip on Miles.

"What the hell do we do?" I pant.

The others stop. Ava turns back toward us.

"I have two matchboxes," she responds. "I was saving them for the nights above Halcyon, but they'll have to do right now."

She tosses one to me and keeps the other for herself.

"Everyone get in close."

"I'll take the front," I declare.

"I'll cover the back," adds Ava.

The darkness is closing in. Only a few bulbs remain before we're completely covered.

"You can't be afraid of the shadows," murmurs Sam. "We can't be afraid again."

I grab his hand. He grabs Rosie's. Rosie grabs Marcus's. Marcus grabs Ava's while Miles holds onto the back of Ava's shirt. Ella grabs Miles's other hand before latching onto the back of my shirt. It's not a perfect circle, but it'll do for now.

And just like that, the lights go out. We've officially entered the dark underground.

I light a match.

Ava lights one, too.

The warmth of the flame keeps me more on edge than the black. It falls toward my fingers like a fog seeking the earth. But before it can reach my skin, I blow it out.

Ava's match is still burning. It barely illuminates the path in front of me, but I'm pretending it does. I can't afford to waste light when we're not sure how far we have to go.

Her match burns out.

I light another. "How many matches do you have?" I ask.

"About a dozen," answers Ava.

"My pack only has five or six more, so don't light yours until mine dies out. Just keep a weapon ready in case something comes from the back."

"Okay. I have a knife."

We quietly creep forward.

Sam's hand sweats in mine.

My match dies. "Light, Ava."

She does.

I stick my hand out. Blindly using it as a guide, I pick up the pace.

"I hate this," murmurs Rosie.

"We all do," adds Marcus. "We just have to believe an exit is coming."

"One is near," mutters Sam. "I can feel it."

I don't say anything.

Ava's light fades.

I swipe a match, but the stick breaks. I grab another. The same thing happens. I try one more. It works. Holding it outward, I see that it showcases the cracks in the cement, even illuminating a few scurrying insects in the process. But before we can get too far, the match dies. Almost as if water was poured onto it, it failed at nearly the same rate as those that didn't ignite.

"Ava, I'm down to two matches," I mutter.

"Take a few of mine," she replies. Quickly lighting one of her own, she pulls a few extras from the cardboard. I let go of Sam's hand to grab them, but the second I do, Ava's match burns out.

Complete darkness consumes the circle.

"Just light another," I utter.

"Okay," answers Ava.

I can hear her feet move as she turns back away from the center of the group, but the sound of a match swiping never comes.

"Ava?" I murmur.

"Sean, light one of yours," says Marcus.

I oblige.

Ella shrieks.

I turn around. The flame illuminates two followers, one man and one woman. Standing directly in front of Ava, they each have a grim look.

"How the hell did you get here?" I angrily quip.

"We know this place a lot better than you guys," answers the man. "You really think you could escape that easily?"

"We still will," says Ava.

"I don't think so," adds the woman. "You're only about a hundred yards from the door to the elevator, but it's too late." She pulls out a knife.

The man reaches toward the waistband of his cloak.

Ava tilts her head to the side, her right eye open wide.

Without thinking, I blow out my match.

Shifting feet echo against the cement. A quick yelp emerges. Steel clatters on the ground. A gun fires. Yet, no screams come. No cries. Nothing.

I reach for my last match.

I light it.

There stands Ava with the two followers bleeding out behind her. The man's eyes are wide open as blood gushes from the center of his forehead. The woman writhes on the ground beside him, a dark red pouring from her throat as she tries to stop the blood from spilling.

"Holy shit," says Sam, amazed.

"I survived my eleven years just like some of you guys," smirks Ava. "Now, let's get the hell out of here."

Elise

I've made it back to the room with the vase of Halcyon. Its pieces lie untouched, scattered upon the wood. I take a seat.

"Took you long enough to get back," creepily speaks Caroline as she slides into the room like she was walking directly behind me the whole time.

"What are you talking about? I've been here the whole time."

"Don't play dumb with me, Elise. I'm not sure where you were, but you weren't here. I came immediately after I heard the vase shatter."

"How did you hear it shatter? I didn't think you were near me, room-wise, when it broke."

"That's not important," she quickly bites back.

Ava really did blind Caroline.

"If you say so," I sarcastically reply.

"Don't be smart with me, Elise. How did the vase break?"

"I picked it up and it slipped out of my hands."

"Why did you feel you needed to pick it up?"

"I just wanted to see it up close."

"It was in the case for a reason," she angrily says. "You don't need to go destroying things that aren't yours to begin with."

I glare at her. "You're one to talk."

"What do you mean?"

"All you've been doing since we got here is destroying my friends' lives. You're not allowed to tell me not to break things. If anything, I earned that one."

She huffs before moving to the back of the room near the shattered remnants of the vase. "Elise," she quietly says.

"What?"

"Something feels off here."

"I only broke the vase," I say.

"No, no, it's not that. Something about Halcyon feels different."

"What do you mean?"

She picks up a shard of the vase, and slowly walks back toward me. "I'm not sure. Do you feel it, too?"

I stiffen my back against the leather of the chair. "I don't know what you're talking about, Caroline."

She looks at me. Her widened eyes scream suspicion; her incessant biting of her lips shows she desires what I know. She's starting to frighten me with the way she looks.

I inch to the side of the chair.

She steps closer to me.

"I don't know anything, Caroline. Why the hell are you acting so strangely?"

Swiftly, she lunges toward me. The shard brushes against my cheek. Her eyes probe mine for an answer to her delusion. "Something's different about Halcyon, Elise, and I feel you know why."

"What's different? Why can't you just tell me?"

"I'm disconnected," she murmurs. "I can't see."

"Can't see what?"

She presses the piece into my cheek. I try to squirm more to the side, but I'm as far as I can go. "Everything."

I wiggle my way out of the chair and glide across the room. "What the hell is going on, Caroline? Why are you acting like this?"

"You know damn well what's going on, Elise! Just tell me how you did it. Just tell me and I won't hurt you."

"Did what? I don't know what you're talking about."

"Blinded me from the DZ! How did you do it?"

"I didn't do anything!" I shout back.

"Yes you did!" yells Caroline as she stomps toward me. "I know it was you! You're the only one who could have figured it out. You were chosen for a reason, and now you feel you can come here and take down Halcyon, too?" She holds the sharp edge outward at me again. "I can't let you do that, Elise. I can't let you win."

The air between us tightens. I need to hold my ground even if it means blood will be shed. I lean toward her. "I didn't do," I pause and lean closer, "a damn thing."

"Then how did this happen?" She steps closer. The fragment is an inch from my neck.

"It could have been anyone, or anything."

"It had to be someone," she says. "The DZ doesn't fail."

"Just because they hadn't failed you before doesn't mean they can't fail you now."

"You don't understand, Elise! The DZ is omnipotent. They can never fail."

"Anything can fail, so what if they do?"

"Then we all die."

"Why do you say that?"

"If there's no DZ, there's no world."

"Or is there finally a perfect world?"

She drops the shard, and instead, slaps me. "Don't be so foolish."

I want to hit her back. I want to kill her, but something inside stops me. Something buried deep down that I thought I once lost trumps every fiber of me wanting to hurt Caroline. I'm not sure what it is, but it's almost like I feel for her.

It's just the previous vulnerability talking.

It has to be.

I finally spit out, "The DZ doesn't control you, Caroline."

"They don't control me. I created this, but they do guide me. Without their knowledge, Halcyon is nothing. Without their archives, this place would be nothing more than that. . .just a place."

"And what's wrong with that?"

"Everything!" she shouts. "Haven't you learned anything yet? In order to survive, rules must be set, order must be maintained, and people must die to ensure society outlasts its surroundings."

"We'll never live that long," I gibe.

"We won't, but a circle can. . . and Halcyon is supposed to be that circle."

"Who says it still can't be?"

"Someone clearly says it can't be," retorts Caroline. "And I think that someone is you."

"I don't know why you keep accusing me. I didn't do anything."

"You keep saying that, Elise, but I'll never believe you."

I don't respond.

At this point, I don't know what I can say. Maybe I should just tell her I did it. Maybe I should put my neck on the chopping block.

"Just tell me, Elise. Did you or didn't you cut off my access?"

I don't hesitate. "I didn't do it, Caroline. I swear. I may not like you or Halcyon, but I didn't blind you. I wouldn't even know where to begin to manage that."

She picks the shard up once again. "You know, Elise, you never were a very good liar."

I take a step back; I can feel the wall approaching behind me. "Caroline, don't do anything stupid. I promise you, I'm telling the truth!"

"It wouldn't be stupid to kill you. Maybe it would be the smartest move I ever made," she says wryly, holding the piece toward me.

I take a small breath. The anxiety coursing through my veins slows. "If you swing that at me, I'll kill you," I say firmly, knowing good and well that I don't have a weapon to defend myself with.

She laughs. "Oh, Elise. You're funny."

Finally, I step toward the shard. It presses against my chest. "Go ahead, Caroline. Kill me. It won't save you."

Her upper lip flares; her devious eyes glare menacingly.

"I'll do it," she mutters.

"Go ahead."

"Hold on," broadcasts Noah's voice through the open door.

"You better have some good news, Noah," snarls Caroline.

"I wouldn't say it's good news. The contestants escaped. . .and do you want to know why?" he says angrily, gritting his teeth as he steps farther into the room.

Caroline doesn't answer.

"They escaped through that damn hatch I told you not to include in those rooms!"

Caroline inches toward Noah. "When a hatch opens, two followers are dispatched into the tunnel. You know that."

The veins pulsing in his neck, Noah tilts his head upward and to the side. "We're cut off from the DZ, Caroline. The cameras are dead everywhere. We didn't know they opened it."

Caroline's hands tremble. The shard falls back onto the floor. "But you know they opened it now, don't you? It's not too late!"

"It's too late. I checked. The two that made it down there are dead. Someone killed them."

"How?! They didn't have any weapons!"

"I don't know."

"What do you mean you don't know? You should know, or you'll end up just like them!"

"How am I supposed to know when I can't see a damn thing, Caroline?"

"Did you go to the top? Did you try to stop them once you realized they were gone?

"No, I came to tell you!" Noah glares.

The longer they argue, the stiffer each of their jaws has become. I remain still behind them.

Pulling out her cane, Caroline uses it to step nearer to Noah.

"So, you're telling me you didn't find them, two of my followers are dead, and you didn't even bother to go to the top to see if you could still catch them?"

"Yea, that's what I'm saying. You shouldn't have built the hatch to begin with. If anything, this is your own fault."

Those words don't sit with Caroline. She lifts her cane toward Noah and swiftly, almost effortlessly, jams it into his chest just below his sternum. He falls back, blood seeping through his shirt and onto his cloak.

"Wh-what the heck?" he stammers, his hands groping at the cane.

Caroline pushes further and further.

Noah falls to the ground.

I pick up a shard.

She rips out the cane. "You should have found them," she says vilely before turning back to face me.

"Caroline," I murmur. "Why did you kill him?

She doesn't answer my question. She points the cane at me; blood drips from its end, quietly splashing upon the wood. "I'm going to show you the real power of Halcyon, Elise."

"What do you mean?"

Yet before she says anything, her cane's crashing against the side of my head.

Sam

The elevator doors slide open. In front of us sits a small stairway to the surface.

I quickly hop out and run up the steps.

"I never thought we'd make it up here again," I mutter.

"But we did," smiles Ella. "We made it."

And, now, here we stand a dozen feet or so from the edge just outside the fake Halcyon we originally thought was our new home. A gust of wind pushes through the illusion, blowing dirt toward us and ultimately into the depths of the real Halcyon—into the nightmare that still possesses Elise. She's still down there, and none of us know when, or if, she'll make it up here.

I turn back to see if the others have all made it to the top. Sean steps up and kicks a rock into this ghost town. With his eyes on his feet, he kicks a few more into the distance.

Marcus and Miles step up behind him and slowly venture down the street and into one of the buildings.

Rosie and Ella walk up behind them.

Ava's the last one to the surface.

The second she gets to the top, I step next to her. "Ava," I mutter.

"Yea?"

"What's Elise's plan?"

"She has a key. Marisa gave her a key that we think leads out of Halcyon through another way."

"Does she know where to go?"

"She knows about the route the hatch leads to, but for now, she told me she was going to go back to Caroline because she knows Caroline won't hurt her—thus, giving us more time to escape."

Ella chimes in. "But what if Caroline changes her mind?"

"If that happens, Elise will kill her," answers Ava.

"Is that what she told you?" I ask.

Ava shakes her head. "No, but I just believe she'll do what she needs to do to meet up with the rest of us. She told me if she's not up here in two days, we're to leave, and she'll find us."

I bite at my bottom lip. "It sounds like neither of you had a real plan."

"Sadly, we didn't." Ava looks over at Sean; Rosie is walking toward him. "We didn't have much time. She just told me to get you guys out of here."

"Well, what do we do now? Where do we hide for two days?" I ask. "Once Caroline or her followers learn we're gone, won't they come for us?"

"We wait around this area. Caroline can't see what we're doing up here or anywhere, so we can hide in this town. . .assuming these buildings are legitimate in some capacity."

"But what if someone comes up here looking for us? We don't have any weapons."

"I have the gun and blade from the two followers I killed. Those will suffice for now."

I shrug my shoulders.

"What was that for?"

"When we first got here, Caroline had dozens of followers basically push us into Halcyon. I just don't know if two weapons in the hands of one person can save us."

Ava grins. "Those other followers won't be coming. They're not the same as the five Caroline has at her beck and call. Plus, I can give the gun to Sean. I've heard he's a good shot."

I look away. Marcus exits the building him and Miles were in. Miles isn't with him.

"What do you mean the other followers aren't the same?" asks Ella.

I turn back to the conversation.

"They're for show. They're there to scare you. Only a couple of them can actually fight. The rest were sent by the DZ at Caroline's behest to build this grand illusion that being a follower of her methods would grant you life in Halcyon." Ava huffs. "It's ridiculous."

"But one of them killed Derrick," I say under my breath.

"I guess he crossed one of the bad ones."

"I guess," I utter. "Anyways, shouldn't we be getting out of the open?"

Marcus moves toward us. "Guys," he says nervously.

"What's wrong, Marcus?" inquires Ava.

"There's someone in that place. . ." hc trails off.

"Who?"

"He said his name was Ignatius and that I was to tell the rest of you to follow me back into the building."

"Shit. . ." mutters Ava.

"Where's Miles?" I ask.

"He's in there with the man."

"Is there anyone else?"

"N-no," he stutters. "I just saw him." Marcus turns to Ava. "Ava, who is he?"

"He's the leader of the DZ."

Marcus's jaw drops.

What the hell is he doing here alone? I think to myself. *Is he here for Ava? Is he here for me? Is he here for all of us?* I wish I could answer myself, but I'll never be able to until I come face to face with him, and I don't think I want to do that.

"I think we should run," I say softly.

"And leave Miles behind?" asks Marcus angrily.

I don't answer.

"Everyone stay here. I'll go to him alone," says Ava apprehensively.

"He'll kill you," Marcus chides.

"Not if I kill him first."

I look in the direction of Sean. He and Rosie are on the opposite side of the street from where Ignatius allegedly is. Rosie seems to be talking, but Sean's head is still aimed at his feet.

I wish I could go over to him and say something, but I can't. Brotherly love just isn't the same. Nothing will fix that hole in his chest until Elise appears.

Moving my head back toward Ava, Marcus, and Ella, I close my eyes and sigh. "We all have to go together. We can't risk losing you, Ava. We need what you know if we're going to survive anything."

"Ignatius wants me, Sam. He doesn't care about you guys."

"That's a lie!" I shout. "The DZ has been following us the entire time. They put our friends from the library on the path to Halcyon. We watched Marie essentially kill herself because the DZ had control of her, so don't you ever say they just want you. . .they want all of us."

"Okay, Sam."

I grab Ava's hand. She grabs onto Marcus's. Marcus grabs Ella's.

Rosie turns back and looks at us. She says something to Sean in the process.

He finally lifts his head.

We stride toward him.

"Sean," I say softly with an ounce of fear in my voice.

"What's going on?" he replies.

"The leader of the DZ is in that building across the way. Marcus says we have to go see him."

"Why?" he responds angrily. "Why is he here?"

"He knows what I did, Sean. He know that I cut off their access to the chips and that I came to rescue you guys," answers Ava.

I add, "Plus, he has Miles and we won't just run and let him die."

"Is it just him?" asks Sean.

"He's all I saw," replies Marcus, his voice still a bit shaky.

"Then let's kill him."

Ava tosses Sean the pistol.

I grab onto Sean's hand. He holds the gun in the other.

Ella reaches for Rosie's palm.

I take a breath. I can't believe what's happening. One second we're free, the next we could be dead.

And now, we stride toward the ruler of everything we know, toward the man who could have us erased from history.

But we won't let that happen. Our story isn't over yet.

20 May 2192

Elise

My head still aches. It's been pulsing for a couple of days. I think Caroline cracked my skull.

She hasn't said anything to me since she killed Noah. She's kept me locked away in my room with only occasional visits by Katrina for food. The vent's been repaired and the key has been taken, leaving me without an escape.

I'm not sure what her end game is, and I don't think I want to know. I just hope the others made it out. I just hope Ava found them and freed them. And if it's been more than two days, so be it. Their survival is more important.

I roll over onto the aching side of my head; the bruise hates the instant movement, but ultimately likes the comfort of the pillow.

I sigh.

My body hasn't been bothered by what's likely coming, and my mind has seemingly accepted that I'm going to die here. After all, there's nothing I can do. Caroline's planning something that will kill me; she's planning to show the DZ that her circle is the strongest, and by ending me, she'll win them over. Or, so she thinks.

But even if I die, Ava will save everyone else.

And if she doesn't, at least we died trying.

. . .even if that's the dumbest thing ever said.

The End

Made in the USA
Columbia, SC
20 June 2019